MOTHERTRUCKER

Driving On

Wendy 'Mothertrucker' Priestley

Copyright © 2004 Wendy Priestley

Wendy Priestley has asserted her right under the Copyright, Designs and Patents act of 1988 to be identified as the author of this work.

All characters in this publication are fictitious. Any resemblance to any real persons, living or dead are entirely coincidental.

ISBN 978-1-4710-2390-3

Published by
Lulu
For
for Mothertrucker Books

First edition printed in 2004 by Wendy Glindon Publishing

This book is dedicated to all the British truckers who have been imprisoned abroad through no fault of their own.

I would like to say a big thank you to trucker, John Mills. His experiences in a Bulgarian prison were the inspiration for this story.

Thanks also to Nick Garlick for his help and advice.

CHAPTER ONE

"Damn!" Carol could hear the telephone ringing as she struggled to get her key into the lock. Her fingers were freezing in the icy air and refused to work properly. The wind blowing her mass of auburn curls across her face.

At last the key turned and she pushed open the heavy oak door, stepping inside onto bare wooden floorboards, taking care not to knock Bruno over as he followed her through. Kicking the door closed to keep out the biting winter cold, she dropped the big Alsatian's lead and grabbed the receiver.

"Transcon Haulage!" she tried to sound unruffled and businesslike as she answered.

"Carol? Hi! It's me." Tony's voice was music to her ears.

"Tony! I'm so glad to hear your voice!" Carol slipped off her thickly padded winter coat as she spoke, lying it next to the phone on the big round table in the hallway.

"Everything all right?"

"No, not really. I've just this minute come in from the Vet's. Bruno is far from well."

"Poor old Bruno! What's the trouble?" Tony sounded genuinely concerned.

"Luckily, not as bad as I thought," said Carol. "They think he has a kidney infection. They gave him a couple of injections and prescribed a cocktail of tablets, but he looks awful, the Darling, all thin and wobbly!"

The 'Darling' had flopped by her feet, big brown eyes staring listlessly at her as she spoke.

"They say he may have the 'trots' for a couple of days but should pick up soon. He's young and strong." Carol continued. "Apparently it's one of those things German Shepherds are prone to."

"Well let's hope he will be okay. Lucky you haven't finished restoring the house and put expensive carpet down if he is going to have accidents all over the place!"

"Thanks for that!" Carol replied wryly. "But you are right, of course, and it's too cold for him to sleep outside, not being well and everything, so I suppose bare floors are easier to clean up."

She mentally crossed her fingers that it would not come to that.

"It's absolutely freezing here!" She went on, changing the subject. "The wind is bitter and it feels like it may snow. That's ALL I need, not having the central heating in as yet. Bit like living in a barn at the moment!"

"It's quite cool here too," replied Tony. "Being so close to the mountains we do get a little chilly in the winter to say the least!"

Carol could picture Tony, the morning sun shining down on his Italian farmhouse, La Casaccia, the snow-capped mountain peaks gleaming in the distance. "Do you ever get snow?" Carol could only imagine the baking heat of the summer.

"Oh yes! Any time now, but even then the sun can be hot. The ski people love it!"

Carol could never work that out. How people went skiing in the thick snow but still managed to get sun-tanned at the same time.

"Hey, the reason I called was to tell you that it'll be at least two weeks before I am in England again. We have the Frankfurt and Munich runs to do next."

"Yes, I know." Carol sighed. "I do miss you though." Two weeks sounded like an eternity right now. But business had to come first and the German orders had come at a good time.

"I miss you too, Cara Mia!" Tony's voice lowered as he spoke, giving Carol a warm glow. "It will soon be Christmas and we must decide what we want to do. I want to be with you if I can."

"And I with you, but what with families and all……. and I have no idea what Katy is planning as yet. University finishes in the next few weeks for the winter break, so no doubt she will land on me soon!"

Carol's high spirited daughter usually acted impulsively and rarely announced her arrival. Carol had learned from experience to expect Katy when she arrived!

"I'm sure we can work something out about Christmas, we still have some weeks left."

"It will soon come round." Tony answered. "But as you say, we will work something out."

"Yes, I'm sure we will." said Carol. "Oh, by the way. Jeff shipped out late Wednesday night. He should get to you some time tomorrow all being well. He has a trailer load of waste paper to unload at the factory outside Florence on Monday morning."

"It was good you managed to get the waste paper contract." Tony replied. "No point in driving all the way out here with an empty truck."

"Yes, absolutely!" Carol agreed. "It has certainly helped us out. We need all the luck we can get starting a new haulage company."

"You are doing fine!" Tony reassured her. "We are all happy with the arrangement this end and it will be good to have Jeff here for a couple of nights. We can have a good talk about how things are going, run some more ideas off each other."

They chatted on for a while then said their goodbyes. Carol dropped the receiver and looked down at Bruno. His big, soulful eyes gazed back at her. He was obviously feeling very sorry for himself.

"Come on you!" Carol reached down and helped her beloved pet to his feet. He wobbled slightly. "Let's get you settled somewhere comfy while I get on with things."

She led the way into the kitchen where she had laid an old duvet in a corner for Bruno to lie on. As she settled the ailing dog onto his makeshift bed she thought of Tony.

Was it really only six months since they first met? She found it hard to believe. She felt as though she had known him forever. She threw the kitchen window open, disregarding the rush of cold air and took a deep breath, dispelling the smell of damp plaster and brick dust from her lungs.

Her mind wandered back to the summer when they had first met. It had been her first trip abroad as a truck driver, with her closest friend, Gina, riding along to keep her company. They had set off with enthusiasm, making their way across France and over the mountains into Italy with surprisingly little trouble, only to break down on a dusty back road in the hills, barely a few kilometres from their destination.

Frustrated, hot and tired, they had climbed down from the oppressive heat of the cab to sit in the shade of a group of peach trees. To add to their troubles they had found a small stray dog, cowering in the bushes, pathetic and starving and heavy with pup.

That's when Tony had found them, coming to their rescue with his battered pick-up truck like a knight in shining armour. Not in the least ruffled by the sight of two ladies, a broken down truck and a pregnant dog in the middle of nowhere, he had calmly taken the situation in hand, escorting them back to his home in the hills, offering them the warm hospitality of his family. He had even gone so far as to repair their stricken truck, making sure that they could continue on their way in the morning.

It had been a fortuitous meeting in many ways. Tony's 'Poppa' had been looking for a haulage contractor to deliver regular loads of the fat green olives that grew in abundance in his fields behind the house, and his fine olive oil, fresh from the presses.

It had been that meeting that had encouraged Carol to take the big step of striking out in business and starting a haulage partnership with Gina's husband Jeff. A step that right now seemed to hold good promise for the future.

And Carol had lost her heart almost at once to the handsome young man with the mass of dark curls and the diamond-grey eyes. His calm gentle manner was unlike any man she had met before. At first she hesitated at the thought of falling in love, especially with a man seven years her junior. But as Gina had been quick to point out, age was simply a matter of numbers and true love had never learned to count. Carol took a deep breath of air and closed the window, picturing the lovely rustic farmhouse in the Tuscan hills, nestling amongst Poppa's olive groves and sheltered from the heat of the day by peach trees and the grape vines, clambering over the veranda.

Mamma would be busy right now, getting the family meal prepared, with help from her eldest daughters, Tony's beautiful sisters. Tony would be busying himself, helping Poppa with his work about the olive groves and the oil presses. He would also be cleaning the truck, Carol's own Ford Transcontinental. Her pride and joy, proudly displaying the company logo, Transcon Haulage, emblazoned on the doors and its own personal name, 'The Fighting Spirit', airbrushed on the front. The old truck held fond memories for both of them.

Tony would probably be doing some running repairs on the old truck as well. Carol thought ruefully. Although Tony had not mentioned it, she doubted that there would not have been at least one minor repair that had needed to be done. But usually they were only minor problems and Tony kept the old truck up and running and fit to do the runs… so far!

The runs from Italy to England with both trucks loaded to capacity with Poppa's fine olives and freshly pressed olive oil were becoming more frequent, with both Tony and Jeff doing regular runs.

Although she and Jeff had started the whole business venture on the grounds of collecting the loads of olives and oil from La Casaccia and

hauling them to England, they had jumped at the opportunity of the German delivery runs. The order from the German buyers was a good thing for Tony's family business.

His younger brother, Marco, had negotiated the deal on one of his many trips to the city. Marco dealt with most of the family business on the administrative side and had contacts in many places. Carol was happy with the order as it meant more work for Transcon Haulage. A new company needed all the business it could get.

In her wildest dreams, Carol had never expected things to get under way so quickly or run so smoothly. A tiny voice in the back of her mind kept telling her that something had to go wrong sooner or later, but so far things were looking good.

Of course, having Jeff as a partner and Tony driving her own truck was an ideal situation for Carol. It gave her financial security, something she had never known before. In fact, up until today and the worry of Bruno, she had few problems apart from getting the old house in order after years of neglect had allowed it to go so badly downhill.

Carol made herself a coffee, staring through the window at the overgrown woodland garden and beyond to the empty haulage yard, partly hidden from view by the ivy clad brick wall and tall trees, stark against the dull grey sky.

This last six months had been amazing. In fact the last eighteen months had been amazing. Carol sometimes had to pinch herself to believe it was real. She often expected that she would suddenly wake up and find it was all a dream. And find herself back at home, in her old house, in the tiny Derbyshire village where she had grown up, going out to work each day behind the bar of the local pub to make enough money to keep herself and Katy clothed and fed.

But it was no dream. She had moved to the outskirts of London, become a truck driver, and was now co-owner of her own haulage company.

And this was certainly no dream! More like a nightmare! Carol looked around her. The rambling Victorian house, standing grandly atop the run of stone steps and overlooking the haulage yard, was certainly nowhere near the end of its renovation. Time was the greatest enemy. What with doing her share in the running of the company and working full time as a Driving Instructor in the Heavy Goods Driving school where she herself had learned to be a trucker, painting and decorating had to take a back seat most of the time.

After buying the old house off old Bill Winters at the end of the summer she had began with enthusiasm, stripping every room of the faded, grimy wallpaper, and employing a local plasterer to make good the powdery walls beneath.

She had torn up the worn, dirt-trodden carpets, taken them to the tip and discarded the faded curtains that had hung limply at the grimy windows. At least she now had a blank canvas to work with. That was a start.

But now Bruno was sick! She had taken time off work to take her adored pet to the Vet. A visit that had eaten into the better part of a day.

Not that Carol resented it for one moment. Bruno had been with her through good times and bad and deserved only the best. But as if that wasn't enough, to top it all off, the Mini was playing up. It had hiccuped and coughed its way to the Vets and limped back, a strange smell emitting from under the bonnet.

Carol sighed and picked up her coffee, sipping the strong liquid as she looked about the room, trying to plan beyond the newly plastered walls and bare wooden floors. The kitchen had originally been a gloomy, narrow scullery with two small pantry rooms leading from it. She had called in a local builder to knock down the unwanted walls making a large, airy kitchen with room for the old, scrubbed pine, table and chairs. It was a great improvement, but the job had taken longer than Carol had first imagined. She was itching to get the room completed. In fact she was itching to get the whole house finished, but she knew she had to be patient. Not something she had in abundance, but she wanted it done properly and knew that meant taking her time, planning ahead and not cutting corners.

She had high hopes for the place and could see exactly how she wanted it in the future. But right now she was tied. The main thing was to get the heating installed in the cold, uninviting house. Only when that was in place could she begin the redecoration that she had planned.

Feeling frustrated, she decided to leave it all behind for the day and take herself off to the gym. Exercise would make her feel better and help her think straight. Usually a brisk walk with Bruno twice a day kept her mind alert and her enthusiasm fresh, but Bruno was in no state for a walk, brisk or otherwise. She decided to take the bus. The mini would surely die before she got there.

*****

Carol shivered at the bus stop. The woodland lane, though lined with trees, gave little shelter from the icy wind. As she waited, her mobile rang its cheerful electronic tune. For once she had remembered to slip it into her pocket.

"Hi, Derek." Carol recognised the number.

"Hi, yourself. How's Bruno?"

Carol explained about the popular canine's condition then went on to tell the saga of the mini.

"Well, no problem there really." Derek said cheerfully. "Just get into work on Monday and when you finish, take the truck home. You've got plenty of room there to park it, haven't you?"

"Of course! Why didn't I think of that? I had been thinking of borrowing Jeff's car while he was away in his truck. Never occurred to me just to bring one of the training vehicles home."

"Nobody would think you were a flaming readhead," Derek chuckled. "That was definitely a 'blonde' moment!"

Carol laughed with him. Derek had been her instructor and mentor during her heavy goods training days. Now she worked with him in the heavy goods driving school and he had become a firm and trusted friend.

"Anyway," Derek continued. "Think about how much money you will save in not running a car. You can spend it on wallpaper and stuff!"

"Very true. You are right yet again! I just don't know how I managed to get so far through life without your help!" Carol joked.

"Just sheer luck girl!" Derek laughed. "Anyway, see you Monday lunchtime. You only have one student on training next week, so you won't have a hard week. Just as well, with Bruno under the weather and your heating engineers coming in."

"Yes, and thanks for the late start Monday, I will be able to see the workmen get under way before leaving for work." Carol could see the bus making it's way round the bend in the lane towards the stop.

"Gotta go, Honey, the bus is here. See you Monday."

Well that was one problem solved, thought Carol as she boarded the bus and settled in her seat for the ride to the High Street. Just use the Driving School's training truck for a runabout. She decided not to think about going grocery shopping, but amused herself with a picture in her mind of the heavy truck parked up in the Supermarket car park.

The bus dropped Carol at the end of the High Street, a short walk to the gym. She strolled along amongst the busy throng of shoppers, pausing by the window of the 'Michelle's' exclusive corner boutique and peering inside through the beautifully dressed, mullion window.

Gina, immaculately turned out as ever, was busy helping a customer choose a dress. Carol caught her eye. "I'll pop round later!" she mouthed, gesturing through the glass.

"Come for dinner!" Gina mouthed back while her customer was distracted by studying the attention to detail on the proffered gown.

Carol gave the thumbs up sign and continued on her way. She glanced up above the shop front of the Pizza Restaurant to the windows of the flat where she had once lived on her arrival to the town.

It seemed like only yesterday that she had moved in there to be with Nick, her unreliable, womanising, truck driver boyfriend. It also seemed like a lifetime away. Nick was well out of her life now, and Carol was glad of that, could never regret meeting him and impulsively moving away from her country home to be with him. Had she not done that, then her life would not be as full as it was right now. And, of course, she would not have met Tony. *'Everything in life is for a reason.'* Her dear old Pop used to say. Carol knew he was right and dearly wished he had lived to see how well her life was turning out.

Carol made a mental note to call up to the flats on her way home for a flying visit with Gill, her old neighbour. She had always got on well with Gill and her two small boys. It always amazed Carol how Gill took everything in her stride and managed to juggle living in such a small flat with her husband and two little boys and still manage to keep sane! She would pop in and keep Gill up to speed on what had been happening in her life. Gill loved a good natter, and Carol always believed in never losing touch with friends.

Rounding the corner she walked down the alleyway which led to the rough gravel parking area used by the gym members. There were a number of cars, parked at a slight angle in the narrow area. Carol was just about to make her way up the heavy iron staircase to the entrance when one car in particular caught her attention. She walked towards it, curious to see what make it was, and what was written on the piece of paper in the side window.

The car was bigger than Carol could ever remember seeing, other than in American movies. Long and low, the metallic blue paintwork was slightly dull but the black vinyl roof was immaculate as was the gleaming chrome bumper and trim.

Chrome lettering announced 'Chevrolet' across the front of the bonnet and 'Impala' on the rear wing. She read the notice in the window.

'For Sale. 1964 Chevy Impala. Good Price to Good Home!'

Carol stood back and admired the car. It was beautiful, or at least Carol thought so. There was a telephone number on the notice. She did not have a pen with her, or anything to write on.

Typical! She would ask in the gym, they may know whose car it was, or she could borrow their pen and paper.

All thoughts of exercise had gone from her mind as she bounded up the iron staircase and went inside. Ignoring the sweating activity, she approached the reception desk and enquired about the car.

"The big blue Yank you mean?" The man in the muscle vest at the reception desk seemed to know exactly which car Carol was asking about. "Oh that belongs to Spyder over there." He pointed in the direction of a young stocky man, straining on the leg press ."Sorry to interrupt your workout." Carol apologised as 'Spyder' climbed off the machine, wiping sweat from his face with the end of his T-shirt.

"That's okay." he smiled cheerfully. "I needed an excuse to stop. I'm well out of condition."

"Well you look okay to me!" Carol said politely, not being able to take her eyes off his hair, fascinated by the carefully rolled 'quif' and wondering how it stayed in place. "I believe the American car outside is yours."

"The Chevy? Oh yes, that's my baby! Why do you ask? Interested in buying her?"

"Well yes, actually." Carol replied. "My own car has just bitten the dust and I had planned on doing without for a while but when I saw your one...... well, I think it's just a beautiful car!"

"Yes, she is!" Spyder agreed with enthusiasm, delighted to meet someone who obviously thought the car was as beautiful as he did. He gestured towards the door, lifting his jacket from the wall hook and slipping it on against the cold, outside air.

"I wouldn't think of selling her under normal circumstances, but I have been out of work for a while and now my other half is expecting again and what with Christmas coming up... well you know how it is."

Carol nodded. She knew only too well how it was. She had been there herself many times in the past. They walked down the iron staircase and went over to the car. Spyder produced a set of keys from his pocket and unlocked the door.

"Pretty much original she is," he said proudly. "Bench seats and column change. Runs lovely she does. Passed her MOT without a problem last week and road tax exempt too. Nothing to pay in a car this age. Classic you see."

Carol raised an eyebrow. That was interesting – and another good reason for liking the big car. Spyder turned the key and the big engine immediately leapt into life.

"Listen to that!" Spyder instructed enthusiastically. "There is nothing to beat that big block Chevy sound is there? Real meaty."

The engine did indeed have a distinctive sound. A low, vibrant throbbing, not unlike her truck, Carol thought. Spyder heaved the big bonnet open and stuck his head inside. "Just look at that! V8 with a four-barrel carb. Clean as a whistle too!"

"Sounds good." Carol was bound to agree, Spyder's enthusiasm was infectious.

"Chromed cylinder head, chromed air filter, rocker box cover and water pump, new leads...."

"Well, I am no expert when it comes to engines." Carol interrupted, getting lost on all the technicalities. "But I know what I like when I see it, and I do like this car. Very much!"

"It's left-hand drive you know." Spyder pointed out. "Will you be okay with that?"

Carol nodded. She hadn't noticed at first. "Yes, I'm sure I'll get used to it. The question is how much are you asking?"

"Twelve hundred." Spyder replied almost wincing as he spoke. "But I'll take an offer!" He added quickly. Too quickly! He could have kicked himself. He hoped he did not sound desperate, but only he knew how much he needed the money.

Carol had never paid more than a couple of hundred pounds for a car in her life! She had owned a succession of old bangers and had planned, now the business was starting to do well, to get herself a fairly new car in the not too distant future. This sounded like a lot of money for such an old car, but on the other hand this was a lot of car!

She wanted it and the more she stood there admiring it the more she wanted it. She glanced at her watch. "The bank closes in half an hour." She said, trying to sound businesslike. "If you will take a straight grand I can go and get the cash and take the car off you this afternoon."

Spyder was speechless. He had not expected anything like this. He would have taken half that amount, he was that desperate.

"Well er....well, yes, okay!" He gathered his wits. "I will have to go back home and get the paperwork and clear my gear out first."

"That's fine." Carol said happily. "I will skip the gym, go and get the money and if you don't mind, you could bring it round to my house later. I will give you a lift home again!"

Spyder was happy to agree and grubbed around in the spacious glove compartment for a pen and paper.

Carol wrote down her address and telephone number and handed the paper back to him.

"Oh! You live at Winters old place! The big old house next to the haulage yard!" Spyder looked shocked.

"Yes, do you know it." Spyder gave her a strange look. "Hmm, sort of." He obviously did not want to clarify the matter any further.

Carol decided not to ask any questions. She had to catch the bank before closing.

*****

"Hello you! You're looking brighter!" Bruno waved his tail in greeting as Carol closed the door behind her. Still a little quiet, he had certainly improved since the mornings rush to the vet. "Those jabs and tabs must be doing the trick, hey Boy." That was one thing less to worry about, Carol thought as she busied herself, switching on the oven and leaving the door ajar to take the chill off the cheerless kitchen. She walked through to the living room at the rear of the house, switching on the dated gas fire, which stood incongruously on the hearth of an old Victorian fireplace. The furniture was covered in dust sheets and packing cases lined the far wall. Although the room smelt musty and uninviting, Carol loved it. She loved the aspect of the room, on one side looking through the big double doors into the Victorian conservatory and beyond, into the garden, and the opposite wall, housing an elegant pair of sliding doors leading into the spacious drawing room at the front of the house. Bruno padded behind her, waiting to see if she would sit so that he could settle at her feet.

Had she done the right thing, she wondered. Buying a car that was older than herself, and not a conventional one at that. She had always acted on impulse but this time she doubted her own sanity. Not to mention the fact that she had a whole house to put to rights, and hopefully be in some sort of order before Christmas. She had always enjoyed Christmas. The festive feel about the streets, the ceremonious decorating of the house and, of course, the tree. This year she hoped to be with both Tony and her lovely daughter Katy at Christmas dinner.

She plonked down on one of the big easy chairs, disregarding the dust sheet. Bruno immediately snuggled up as Carol absently fondled his ears as she stared about the room, dreaming her plans of renovation.

She relished the thought of restoring each room to its former glory. Replacing the broken glass panels in the conservatory, filling it with tall plants and cane furniture. A place to relax and enjoy the tranquillity of the rambling garden in the balmy summer evenings to come.

Old man Winters had sold her the house fully furnished. That had been a bonus. Most of the furniture, although old and neglected, were good pieces including some lovely antique cabinets amongst other, rather shabby fifties and sixties pieces.

Carol had piled all the unwanted junk into the old workshop in the yard and carefully cleaned and polished the items she intended keeping. She had brought her sofa and chairs from her High Street flat and other sentimental pieces she had collected over the years were stored in boxes in one of the upstairs rooms. But mainly she was starting afresh. A fresh start for her new life.

*****

The unmistakable sound of the V8 engine drew closer. Carol glanced out of the window to see the big blue Chevrolet cruise through the wide gates into the haulage yard, crunching slowly across the gravel and coming to a halt beside the large, ivy clad, workshop leaning against the yard wall.

"Hello, we meet again!" Carol called in greeting, walking round the side of the house from the kitchen door as Spyder climbed out of the car, carefully locking it behind him and checking the doors were secure. He waved at Carol with a grin and made his way down the side of the workshop, through the small wrought iron gate and along the pathway towards the house.

The 'Teddy Boy' hairdo that had so fascinated Carol no longer looked out of place as Spyder was now in full dress mode of crepe-soled shoes, drainpipe trousers and long black overcoat. Carol smiled. She loved a character and had already taken to the eccentric young man.

"Come in the back way." said Carol. "I'm just sorting out Bruno's dinner then I'll put the kettle on."

"That's what I like to hear." Spyder said cheerfully. "Could do with a cuppa after all the running about I've been doing this afternoon." He followed Carol into the kitchen, looking around him and patting Bruno who had found the energy to rise from his bed and investigate the stranger. "Blimey! Didn't realise how big this place was! Nice house though!"

"I thought you knew the place." Carol remarked, mixing a tin of meat into handfuls of crunchy dog biscuits and placing them in front of Bruno. "You seemed to know it when I told you where I lived."

Spyder sighed, settling himself on one of the high-backed wooden chairs at the scrubbed pine table. "Well, it's a bit of a story actually. You know I said I was out of work?"

"Yes, you did say." Carol filled the kettle and clicked it on to boil.

"Well this place is partly the reason."

"Really ! How so?"

"Well the company I was working for put in a bid for the yard earlier this year. Wanted to flatten it out and build another factory. They make frozen food packaging, so there is always plenty of demand what with fast food being all the go now. Anyway, they had taken me on thinking the deal was in the bag and they were definitely going to expand, but when we heard they had been gazumped, they took the factory to the midlands. No good to me all that way away so I had to jack in the job. Been trying to get back in to a decent job ever since."

Carol was amazed. "Gazumped! I didn't GAZUMP!" She handed Spyder a steaming mug of tea. "The deal was that old man Winters preferred to sell the house and yard in one lump rather than separately. A tax dodge or something. He would have actually made more money by selling separately, but then the tax man would have taken more. Oh, I am not exactly sure how it worked but I made my offer and he took it."

"Just like that! You bought the whole place? Business and all? I'm impressed!"

Carol pulled a wry face. "Not exactly 'just like that' really." For some reason she felt the need to explain things to this straightforward young man.

"I did have a house of my own in Derbyshire which I'd rented out to my two best friends. It just happened that at the right time they asked if they could buy it from me, and as this place had just gone on the market, I took the opportunity. The business, though, is new. The old one that Mr Winters had run for ages was defunct." Carol explained. "My friends husband, Jeff, has all the official papers, the C.P.C Licence, or Certificate of Professional Competence, to give it its full title, to be allowed to run a haulage company, so we went in to business together. I'm sorry it affected you though."

"Hey, no worries! You weren't to know were you?" Spyder shone Carol a good-natured grin. "Still, you came to my rescue today, buying the car off me like that."

Carol laughed. "Was that a reminder? Yes, I have got the money!"

"Hey, no!" Spyder looked embarrassed. "It wasn't a hint or anything! Just saying that's all." He took a swig of tea. "You have got a lot of work on here haven't you? Who's doing it, your husband?"

"Husband!! Good God no! I haven't got one of those!" Carol pulled a face. "No, I've got the lot to do myself. When I find the time that is!" Carol sat down at the table with Spyder and opened a packet of crunchy chocolate chip biscuits, pushing the packet towards him.

"What sort of work do you do?" She asked, crunching a biscuit and catching the stray crumbs in her hand.

"Well I have been looking for a job as a mechanic, but I am actually a painter and decorator by trade."

"What! Really!" Carol's mind started to work overtime.

"Yes really, and a bit of building work whenever necessary."

"And you're out of work! And you want a job! Look no further!" Carol waved her arm expansively around the room.

"Oh!" Spyder beamed. "You want your kitchen finishing off!"

"I want the whole HOUSE finishing off!" Carol stated. "Apart from this kitchen, I have the hall landing and stairs, a bathroom, five

bedrooms and three other rooms down here to 'finish off' as you call it."

"Wow!" Spyder helped himself to another biscuit. "This has been my lucky day!"

"Your lucky day? It's not exactly been bad for me either." Carol laughed. "This morning I had no car and no hope of getting any wallpaper on the walls and now I have a great car and a decorator who's not booked up 'til next Michaelmas!"

"When can I start?" Spyder asked. Carol laughed again. She loved his enthusiasm.

"Well not right this minute. I am off out for dinner tonight but as soon as possible from my point of view." She got to her feet. "I'll show you around, let you get an idea of what's needed. It's a big job!"

*****

"Can I make a suggestion?" Spyder had listened politely while Carol had shown him from room to room, telling him what she had in mind.

"Of course." Carol replied, sitting down on the bottom tread of the wide winding staircase. "I am always up for a second opinion."

"These old houses." Spyder said thoughtfully, leaning over the banister rail. "They usually speak for themselves if you know what I mean. Class like. Don't need overdoing, if you don't mind my saying."

"No, not at all, do go on!"

"Well you've had the main alterations done, the kitchen walls taken out and made good and all the walls skimmed nice and smooth."

"Yes, well after I stripped off the old paper I could see that they needed it."

"Exactly! But they don't need much more. Look at these ceilings."

Carol looked. The ceilings in every room were works of art. Panels of plasterwork broke the plain flat expanse above, the cornice-work elegantly carved and in good condition.

"What I would do is concentrate on the ceilings." Spyder went on. "Take a basic colour, magnolia is good, and two other colours, say white and lemon.

Do the main body of the ceiling in magnolia, pick out the fancy panels in lemon then the main sweep of cornices in white. Do the walls in magnolia to compliment the ceiling and that's all it will need. Classy, subtle and understated. You can then change the mood of each room with different colours and textures in your furniture, curtains and cushions and things. Light and bright in summer and rich and exotic in winter! The effect would be stunning."

Carol was taken aback. He was absolutely right, of course. It was the most simple route and she could see that it would indeed be a stunning effect.

"You have hidden depth Mr Spyder!" She said. "I am totally amazed. Where did you learn all this?"

Spyder looked sheepish. "Always fancied going in for designing and stuff but sort of got waylaid. Too busy fiddling with cars. Always in the garage taking an engine apart or re-spraying bodywork. There is

not enough hours in the day sometimes." He grinned. "But I always give my Suzie a hand when we redecorate at home though!"

Carol clasped her hands together in mock prayer. "Say you will take the job. Please!!"

"Can I start tomorrow? The DIY places are all open all weekend. No need to wait until the heating's in place to tackle ceilings."

"YES! Absolutely, it's a deal!" She raised her hand.

"Deal!" Spyder grinned as he slapped Carol's hand with a loud high five.

*****

"Michaelmas? When's that then?" Spyder turned his collar up against the biting wind.

Carol laughed. "A few weeks ago!"

"Oh, Right!" Spyder climbed into the passenger seat next to Carol.

"By the way." Carol started up the Chevy to run Spyder back home. "What is your real name? I can't believe you were christened Spyder!"

There was a short silence. "Hector."

"Oh!"

"But don't tell anybody!"

"My lips are sealed!"

*****

CHAPTER TWO

"Carol! You make me die, you really do!" Gina leaned over the back of the pale cream sofa to peer through the leaded windows panes and view the pale blue Chevrolet standing in her driveway.

"Yes I know, I know, but you must admit it is a lovely car." Carol joined her friend at the window. "Even in the dark you can see the chrome shining."

Gina straightened up, carefully brushing an imaginary piece of fluff from her silver-grey cashmere top.

"That's the glow from the street lamp!" she pointed out, dropping the pale gold curtain that she had moved slightly aside, back into place and carefully smoothing the folds so that they were in perfect alignment.

"Wet blanket!" Carol screwed up her nose and turned from the window, flopping onto the sofa, quickly followed by Phoebe, Gina's spoilt tortoiseshell cat who could spot an empty lap at fifty paces.

Gina drew down an elegantly scalloped, parchment blind, obscuring the window and the view of the driveway. "Well first you decide that you will save money by not having a car at all then within moments you've bought yourself a tank!"

"And found a workman to go with it." Carol said quickly in defence.

Gina giggled. "That's what I love about you Kiddo, life is never dull with you around! But won't it cost the earth in fuel?" Gina was always practical.

"Hmm. Obviously take more than the mini, but on the other hand I never go far. Just to work and back mainly so it won't matter will it?"

Carol convinced herself. "Anyway, it was a great feeling to be able to see something I wanted and buy it without having to worry about the money first."

"Yes, the business is ticking over nicely." said Gina. "Jeff and I went through the accounts while he was home. It's looking good and I can never remember seeing Jeff so happy."

"I'm happy as well." Carol replied with feeling. "Although I often have to pinch myself to make sure it is all really happening."

Gina's high heeled slippers clicked on the tiled floor as she headed into the kitchen, her well cut charcoal skirt swishing about her slim ankles. "Yes, me too." she called back. "I believe it is the best thing that has happened in a long time. With you and Jeff being equal partners I don't feel left out of anything."

"Left out! Why on earth would you feel left out? Jeff is your husband and I am your best friend so of course you are as involved as we are!"

"Yes, I know." said Gina, returning with a tray holding a pot of filter coffee, two mugs and a jug of cream. "That's why I volunteered to do the books. Make sure you two don't think you are millionaires before your time!"

"Fat chance of that!" Carol laughed, taking the mug of coffee that Gina handed her. "But we are doing surprisingly well for beginners."

"With a bit of help from Tony and family of course." said Gina. "And how is the delicious Tony?"

"Still as delicious as ever." Carol replied, smoothing Phoebe's silken coat. "He called today, reminded me about the German jobs. He is doing one and Jeff the other but I forgot to ask which was which."

"Oh, Jeff 'phoned just before you arrived." Gina informed her.

"Oh, right, where was he calling from?"

"Not too sure exactly where, though he said he had gone through the Mont Blanc tunnel and was heading down towards Milan. He'd just parked up for the night. He's had no hold ups so he's taking his time."

Jeff always allowed plenty of time for the long haul across the continent.

"That's good." Carol replied, pleased that so far there had been no major hiccups in their joint business venture.

"Jeff's doing Frankfurt I think." Gina told her. "Or at least that was the plan when he left, but you know how things get changed, and he didn't mention anything about it on the 'phone. Probably know more when he has spoken to Tony."

"As long as it works well." Carol replied. "At first I thought Jeff and I should be doing all the trucking, being business partners and owning one truck each, but it makes life a lot easier if Tony works my truck and I keep my job on and do my bit for the business this end. Makes sense for now."

"And you see as much of him as I see of Jeff the way things work." Gina pointed out.

"Yes, you're right. Jeff runs from here to Italy and Tony runs from Italy to here so there is no difference really."

"True." Gina agreed. "Although if things get really busy I reckon we must think of getting another truck and another driver."

"Sounds good." Carol replied. "At first I thought that the olive run would just get us started but I am amazed how many outlets there are for olives and olive oil. Actually I have had another idea as well."

"Go on." Gina refilled their coffee mugs.

"Water!"

"Water? What about water?"

"Well remember when we were at La Casaccia in the summer? Well, perhaps you didn't notice as you were busy getting involved with Mamma Gina in the kitchen, but behind the farmhouse is a lovely natural spring. Crystal clear, ice cold water straight from the mountains."

"I think I am getting your drift." Gina was quick to pick up the idea. "Italian spring water, still or sparkling, in beautifully designed bottles with an elegant label."

"You took the words right out of my mouth!"

"Have you spoken to Tony about it yet."

"No, it only occurred to me this afternoon but I will mention it next time we speak. It will be a good little line for the family business and of course another outlet for deliveries for us."

"Well I think it's worth looking into, and I'm sure Jeff will too." Gina had faith in her husband's forward thinking.

"The other thing I wanted to speak to Jeff about was Spyder."

"Why? He doesn't have another car to sell does he?" Gina giggled.

"Another car! Gina, you just wouldn't believe what he has!" Carol set down her cup. "He's got three or four cars, or should I say 'Hot Rods' or 'Customs' scattered in various garages by all accounts, and when I ran him home this afternoon, he invited me in to meet his wife. Honestly, it's like a time warp in there!"

"Really! How so!" Gina was intrigued.

"The whole place is done in 1950s style. Even his wife, Suzie, is in with the mood and dresses the part: All the time it seems."

"Really." Gina repeated. "How old is she?"

"All of twenty five or six I reckon. But she's a real rockabilly chick. All turned up jeans, flat shoes and ponytail."

"I know who you mean!" Gina's memory clicked. "I've seen her shopping in the High Street with her little ones, two boys I think. Not my style, of course, but I must admit she looks good like that."

Carol smiled. She could not for the life of her imagine the immaculate Gina in anything resembling turned up jeans!

"Yes, that's her." she agreed. "Two little boys, Shane and Ashley, and yes, she does look good, in fact the whole house is the same. Marilyn Monroe and James Dean memorabilia about the place and old American street scene pictures on the walls. Pride of place in the living room is a genuine, full size, Wurlitzer juke box!"

"Wow! I would love to see this. Where do they live?"

"That estate, you know, the old one over the river. Used to be council, but most people have bought now. Spyder and Suzie bought theirs a couple of years ago. And you will just HAVE to see the dining room. The seating arrangement is made up of half of an old American car! Oh, I just can't describe it properly I will have to take you for a visit."

"I would love to, but would they mind?"

"No, they are a lovely couple."

"They sound it." Gina smiled. "Wonder if they would be interested in some of that old stuff that Winters left behind in your house. You know what they say, one man's rubbish is another's treasure, or something like that."

"Hmm, good idea. I'll mention the stuff to Spyder and let him have a good ferret round. I certainly don't want any of it."

"Anyway, so where does Jeff come in?" Gina remembered.

"Well, Spyder is going to be doing the work in the house for me and reckons it will take three or four weeks to complete."

"Gosh, he's fast. Is it going to cost the earth?"

"That's the point. We had a chat and agreed that I would employ him on a weekly basis 'til the job is done. After that I thought if he was a good worker that we may keep him on as a handyman type. He is pretty good at almost everything I think, mechanics included. He could keep the yard tidy and take care of the trucks and do any odd jobs that need doing."

"Has he got a Heavy Goods licence?" Gina asked, immediately thinking ahead.

"No, but we can cross that bridge if and when needed." said Carol. "After all, If we need him to have a licence I could train him up myself."

"Of course!" Gina laughed. "But it doesn't seem five minutes ago that you sat here panicking that you'd never be able to drive a truck yourself, never mind teaching other people to do it!"

Carol pulled a face. "I know. Amazing how life turns out isn't it?"

"It certainly is! Just see how well Spyder works with your renovations and take it from there. You have got a few weeks work for him so there's plenty of time, and no doubt Jeff will have met him by then."

Gina gathered up the tray of coffee things. "Come into the kitchen while I dish up. I've made 'Pollo con Salsa de Florentine' from Mamma Gina's own special recipe!"

Gina had been in heaven helping her Italian namesake in the wonderful country kitchen in the Tuscan farmhouse where she and Carol had met Tony's family for the first time.

"I hope you didn't catch your own chicken!" Carol remarked, remembering seeing Mamma Gina with a chopper in her hand!

"Er... no! It's from the High Street Butcher. Free range though!" Gina announced.

"I'm sure it will be delicious." Carol assured her. She had remembered how hungry she was and Gina's cooking was second to none.

*****

A damp, grey mist swirled around the truck stop as Jeff pulled the big Volvo Globetrotter off the Autostrada and dropped into a low gear to creep through the rows of parked trucks, looking for a suitable place to pull up.

His eyes were tired after hours of staring into the distance and his body was stiff. He knew from experience when to call it a day and park up for the night. No point in risking life and limb to get another few miles down the road. A few more kilometres would take him to Milan, after that it was straight down to Florence.

Not much time left on his 'tacho' anyway by now he decided. This place was as good as any.

Seeing an empty space between two parked trucks, Jeff eased the 'Silver Lady' over to a slight angle before swinging the wheel then gently coaxing the long, heavily laden trailer into the narrow slot between the two high sided trailers.

Satisfied that he was neatly tucked out of the way, he clicked the handbrake on and switched off the engine. He revelled in the quietness in the cab as the big diesel engine closed down and slipped into silence.

He eased himself from behind the wheel, standing in the centre of the cab between the seats and stretching the stiffness from his body. He loved this cab. There were not many trucks that a man of Jeff's stature could stand up straight in, never mind stretch and move around. The 'Silver Lady' was his second home and he had everything he wanted to hand. Except Gina of course.

He pictured his lovely wife, dressed in the cream satin wrap he had bought for her last birthday. Her long, pale blonde hair shimmering about her shoulders as she checked that he had clean underwear and toiletries packed in his travelling bag, and insisting in making him a light breakfast of coffee and scrambled eggs before he left for his trip.

He always missed his beloved Gina, even after being married so long. To Jeff there was no-one to compare with his beautiful wife, his real life fairy princess. Tiny and delicate with porcelain skin, spun silk hair and graceful demeanour, it never ceased to amaze him that someone with such an air of fragility could be so strong and capable with a razor sharp mind. He reached for his warm jacket and wash-bag. He would phone Gina, take a shower then get something to eat. After that a good nights sleep would do him nicely.

The lorry park was crowded. The convenient pull in and good restaurant was a popular stopping point for many drivers travelling toward the busy industrial areas of Italy or driving home to England, Belgium or France, laden with return loads of goods.

Jeff looked around to see if he recognised any of the drivers, standing around, chatting or checking their loads. Nobody looked familiar, so Jeff set off towards the big glass doors of the restaurant, bowing his head against the dull, damp air. Not actually raining, just 'coming down damp' as his old housemaster in the children's home used to say. A good description, Jeff had always thought, of the damp drops of air gently falling on his shoulders.

"That you 'Jock'?" Walking through the restaurant door, Jeff caught sight of a tall, strongly built man with bright ginger hair and beard to match.

"Och! Jeff man, long time no see!" Jamie McGregor put down the magazine he was studying, sitting up at the bar and slid off his seat, hand held out in welcome.

"Oh I'm still around Jock." Jeff grinned, clasping the Scotsman's hand. "What the hell else would us dyed-in-the-wool truckers be doing?"

"Well it's sure good to see you. I heard a rumour that Winters had gone bust. Thought you must be either standing in the dole queue or taken a change of career!"

"Change of career! Not after all these years mate!" Jeff laughed as he joined the big Scotsman at the bar. "And as for the dole queue.... well, never done it in my life and if I have anything to do with it, never will!" Jeff called the barman to bring them a couple of beers.

"So who you running for now?" asked Jamie, with typical truckers curiosity at the movements of his fellow drivers.

"Owner driver now!" Jeff announced proudly.

"G'way! Never! Going it alone? Good luck to ye' Laddie."

"Not exactly alone." Jeff took a swig of the cold beer, relaxing onto the high wooden stool and leaning his elbow on the bar. "Old man Winters went broke earlier this year. Decided to cut his losses and run while there was still something left to take. Put the old house and the yard on the market."

"You bought up Winters Haulage then!"

"Hell no!" Jeff told him. "Nothing left of the business to buy. The whole thing was finished, and I would have been in a bit of a mess too had things not turned out the way they did."

"Go on laddie." Jamie was keen to hear what had happened. Changes in the haulage world could sometimes have a knock-on effect on them all.

"Well a good friend of my Gina's bought up the property. Bought the house and the yard along with it. Had also just heard of a regular contract that needed filling so as I hold a CPC licence we got together and bought one truck each off Bill Winters and set up between us in a completely new company."

"A friend of your lady wife you say!" Jamie grinned mischievously, wagging a finger at Jeff in mock warning. "Would watch out there laddie if I were you. She's a right fine bonnie lassie your missus!"

Gina had often travelled abroad with Jeff, her delicate beauty and sparkling personality making him the envy of his fellow truckers.

Jeff laughed. "Nothing to watch out for Jock! Gina's friend, my partner, is a lady! A very attractive lady truck driver as it happens!"

"Och! blow me!"

Jeff laughed at the surprised expression on Jamie Mcgregor's bearded face. "These women are taking over Laddie, I tell you, taking over!"

As he spoke a slim, olive skinned girl with waist length raven hair, appeared from the washroom area. Dressed in stylish combat trousers and leather boots she swung a sheepskin coat over her shoulders as she strode towards the exit.

"Ola, Maria!" Jamie called as the girl reached the door. "Ola, Scotsman!" The girl called back, flashing a dark eyed smile at the two men as she pulled the door open and headed towards a big Renault Magnum in the truck park.

"Maria from Valencia," said Jamie by way of explanation. "Delivers engine blocks for the car plant there. What did I tell you Laddie? taking over they are!"

"Well I was certainly grateful for this one taking over the Winters property." Jeff stated firmly. "Sure suited me the way things have worked out."

"Och! don't get me wrong now!" Jamie went on. "Not knocking the lassies, och no! In the main they do just as good a job as any of us. It's not like in the old days when you needed brute strength and ignorance to do this job." Jamie took a swig of beer. "Aye lad, in the old days when I were a wee bairn, my father used to take me with him for the ride and I used to watch the way he drove. Crash gearbox, no power steering." He grinned. "Had to have muscles like Sylveste to get the thing round corners and about twenty two stone of weight behind you to push the clutch down! Those were the days eh?"

"Yeah! Right! Those were the days true enough." Jeff said wryly. "And don't forget no sleeper cabs. The best you got was a blanket roll to lie over the seats. No cab heaters in the winter and nine out of ten, if the heater did work then it was stuck on all through the summer, cooking you to death! Yep, those were the days!" Jeff was not quite forty but had been doing the job so long he could well remember the rough old ways.

Jamie Cameron roared with laughter. He could remember it all too well.

"These modern trucks drive like cars." Jeff went on. "But I have to say, Carol's got Winters old Ford Transcon and if she can handle that then I'm sure she can drive anything."

Jamie raised a bushy eyebrow. "The old Transcon eh! That still on the road? Amazing!"

"Only just, but so far it's kept on running, even though bits do fall off the old girl on a regular basis!"

"Och! Anyway, tell me what happened to that other Winters driver? The one that got nicked in Dover for trying to smuggle in a lorry load of dope!"

Jeff pulled a face. He was never surprised at the way things got exaggerated in trucking circles.

"It wasn't dope, it was cocaine and not a lorry load, it was a few pounds. Not that it makes any difference to me, drug dealing is drug dealing whatever the amount." Jeff spoke adamantly. "He was a bloody idiot and no mistake. But you knew Nick. He always was a flash bastard and didn't do any favours for anybody. He ended up getting six years inside. Got sentenced last month and serves him right too!" Jeff had no time for drugs or those who dealt in them.

"True!" Jamie agreed. "Filthy stuff these drugs. Can't abide the blokes who profit out of 'em!" He called the attention of the barman to bring them another bottle of beer each. "May as well enjoy a drink Laddie, not driving any more this day!"

"I'm with you there." Jeff agreed. "I'm well in front of myself so that's me 'til morning."

"Getting back to what's-his-name … Nick." Jamie was curious. "Six years you say! What a stupid fool, and he had that bonnie looking lassie didn't he? Flaming red hair and those lovely emerald green eyes, everything in the right place too! Wouldn't catch me risking six years inside with a lassie like that to go home to each night!"

Jeff laughed. "That's Carol!"

"Carol?"

"Yes, Carol! My business partner, my Gina's friend!"

"Och! Bloody Blimey! How come you have all this luck." Jamie was genuinely taken aback. "No man should have ALL the best looking lassie to himself, you lucky dog you!"

"Very lucky!" Jeff agreed with a grin. "Came as a bit of a surprise at first. Carol had only held her licence a couple of weeks and gone to old man Winters for a job. Shunting, she thought it was, but you know the old man. Shoved her straight in at the deep end and sent her to the waste paper plant outside Florence with a reload out of San Guistino!"

"Did she get there?" The run was not an easy one and no green driver should have been expected to do it.

"Get there? Not only did she get there, with my Gina riding shotgun all the way I may add, she got there, broke down, got the truck repaired and only ended up securing a regular run from San Guistino to Britain for anyone who could handle it. So on the strength of that, she went straight back home and bought Winters old house and yard!" Jeff inclined his head to quantify his tale. He had great admiration for Carol's strength and tenacity.

"Och! You don't say! Now there's a gutsy lassie if ever there was one!" Jock raised his glass to the absent Carol.

"You can say that again!" Jeff agreed, looking round to see if there were any places left at the tables behind them. His stomach was reminding him that it needed attention. "Why don't you get us a table Jock." he said sliding off the high bar stool. I'll grab a quick shower and phone home then we can have a good meal and put the world to rights."

"Aye Laddie, put the world to rights over a good dinner, now that would be a great thing to achieve!"

Jeff grinned. "Maybe not all in one day, eh Jock? But we can have a good try!" He clapped the tall Scot on the shoulder and headed towards the driver's washrooms and the small public telephone booth. He needed to hear Gina's voice before he could settle for the evening.

*****

Carol opened the kitchen door. Bruno immediately bustled through and scampered to the end of the large, wild garden, disappearing amongst the frost covered trees to relieve himself in the cold morning air. No 'accidents' had taken place in the night, much to her relief. She was pleased to see him looking so much better. Not exactly leaping around, but better none the less.

Carol had dressed quickly in jeans and jumper, slipping on a fleece body warmer and tying her mass of flaming auburn tresses into a band to keep them in some semblance of control and pulling on sturdy trainers over her warm socks.

She walked outside inhaling the sharp air, and heard the sound of a car, crunching across the gravel in the haulage yard. Spyder had arrived. Or at least it was bound to be Spyder. The lime green pick up truck with loud orange flames emblazoned down the sides could have belonged to no one else!

"Not too early for you am I?" Spyder called cheerfully, seeing Carol as she walked from the side of the house to meet him. He was hauling a piece of machinery from the back of the pick up that Carol vaguely thought was an upright vacuum cleaner.

"No, not at all." Carol replied. "I am up and dressed and ready for anything!"

"Good-o! Look what I borrowed from my mate last night!"

"Terrific! Er.. what is it?"

"A floor sander o' course!"

"Oh! What's that for then?"

"Sanding floors!" Spyder gave her an odd look.

Carol gave up and helped Spyder heave the machine round the side of the house and into the kitchen. "Okay." She said. "No doubt you have a plan in mind, so I'll make a pot of tea while you tell me all about it!" By now Carol was resigned to Spyder's enthusiasm and more than willing to listen to his ideas.

Spyder sat down at the table. "Well, I was thinking about this place last night. Talking to Suzie about it, and thought what a waste it would be to cover all this lovely wood with boring fitted carpet."

"Go on." Carol was doubtful. The floors were hard and uninviting and she had been looking forward to covering them in luxurious pile to wriggle her toes in.

Spyder was visibly pleased that his ideas were open to consideration. "If I were you, I would go for sanding down all of the downstairs floors, getting them really clean and straight then giving them a couple of coats of clear sealer. All you need then is a really nice rug in each room, easy to roll up and have cleaned if it gets mucky, or shift out if you fancy a party!"

Carol poured the tea.

"I knew my mate had one of these lying around so nipped out and picked it up." Spyder went on. "Thought if you liked the idea I could get stuck in today. May as well get all the dirty jobs out of the way before starting on the painting!"

Carol was thinking. "Toast?" she asked, dropping a couple of slices of bread into the pop up toaster.

"Won't say no." Spyder replied, waiting for Carol's reaction to his ideas.

"What about the floors upstairs, in the bedrooms?" Her mind's eye beginning to picture the finished effect.

"Carpet definitely!" Spyder was getting into his artistic stride. "I think soft aqua green right through, all bedrooms, hall, landing and stairs. Go lovely with the magnolia walls and the lovely natural wood. The whole house would have a gentle, calm feel to it. Green is always good. You can put any colour with it. If you think about it nothing clashes with grass!""Why on earth have you not been snapped up by one of these television programmes that improve peoples houses?" Carol laughed, lifting the hot toast from the toaster and spreading the slices liberally with butter.

Spyder grinned. "Too busy with the motors. Had to turn down all those celebrity designers how ever hard they begged!"

"Glad you made an exception to your rule for me then!" Carol said, joining him at the wooden table and biting into a piece of toast.

"Good way of keeping an eye on the old girl out there!" Spyder glanced through the window to where the Chevrolet was parked, next to his pick up in the yard. "Make sure you look after her right and keep her up and running."

"I knew it wasn't my womanly charm that got you, or the offer of a job!"

"Well, that did have something to do with it! So what do you think? Do we sand or do we not?"

"We sand!" Carol had made up her mind. It sounded lovely and Spyder's ideas would save her months of work and probably look as good, if not better than what she had originally planned."

"Great!" Spyder rubbed his hands together. "Can't tell you how good it will be to be working again!"

"Great to meet someone who isn't afraid of a bit of work." Carol replied. She had met many who were.

"Never have been." Spyder drained his tea cup, got to his feet and reached for the sander.

"How far has he got with all this sanding then?" Gina enquired, stroking Bruno's ears as she and Carol sat talking at the kitchen table. Bruno repaid her by slobbering on her chocolate brown, tailored trousers.

"Not sure." Carol replied, passing Gina a piece of kitchen roll to wipe the damp patch. "He's been at it since first thing this morning, finished the room at the front and started on the back. I've just kept on supplying him with mugs of tea and coffee. Must be dry work."

"Bound to be. He is certainly keen isn't he?"

"Says he's glad to be working again." Carol answered. "I've told him he has to stop to eat though. I got some lovely fresh bread rolls, and made a huge casserole for us all."

"Smells yummy!" Gina smiled. "Is there anything we can do to help do you think?"

"Well not really." Carol replied. "I feel quite frustrated not being able to get stuck in, but there is nothing we can do at the moment except keep Spyder filled up with drinks to keep the dust of his throat, though it's not as bad as I imagined. His sanding contraption sort of vacuums up the dust as it takes it off."

"Clever! And it certainly does a good job." Gina had peeked at the first completed floor and was suitably impressed. In fact she had wholeheartedly agreed with all of Spyder's décor suggestions. "I reckon you could just stand back and leave him to it. Let him have a free hand and finish the lot!"

"I was thinking that myself." Carol agreed. "Would sure take the pressure off, and I think he would enjoy the responsibility."

Gina nodded. "When I was chatting to him earlier, he was thinking of stripping the old paint off the doors and skirtings and giving them a coat of clear varnish too. Said it would all tone in better."

Carol laughed. "He's right, of course. I think I have found a treasure, don't you?"

"I am sure you have. Don't let him go. I'm sure Jeff will like him too, and he would be far too good to lose."

"I am beginning to think that myself!" Carol agreed, peering into the oven to see how the casserole was coming along.

"Have you heard from Katy?" Gina asked, changing the subject.

"Not this week." Carol replied. "Last time we spoke, she was off to stay the weekend with some friend or other in the Lake district. They are planning on a few good walks and a climb or two. I honestly can't keep track of which friend is which sometimes but as long as she's happy. She didn't mention what her plans were for Christmas, but I'm pretty sure she will be coming home."

"Probably bring half of the University with her if I know Katy!" Gina laughed.

Carol raised her eyebrows. "Yes, you're probably right. She does have a habit of collecting any waifs and strays that are around. She also said she just might go to Derbyshire to visit Andy and Anna after the Lakes, but you know how things change with Katy. Actually she did mention that she would ring this weekend."

"Oh, good! I hope she rings while I am here, I could say hello." Gina adored Katy. "And how are Andy and Anna. The baby must be due any time now."

"Yes, it is. Christmas week if it arrives on time. I have promised to try and find the time to visit but what with moving in here and trying to get some semblance of order..... well you know how it is!"

"Only too well!" Gina replied. But it's all too easy to lose touch with good friends. One has to MAKE the time, and you know how much you love to visit your old house."

"You are right of course. Not to forget that I will be Godmother to the baby, so that must be something to make time for. Can't be a proper Godmother without regular visits."

Gina smiled. "You will make a wonderful Godmother." She said firmly. "And it will be nice for you to see another little one growing up in the same house that Katy grew up in. Playing on the same swing in the garden I shouldn't wonder." Gina looked a little wistful.

Carol decided to change the subject, well away from babies. Gina and Jeff had been hoping for a baby for some time now but so far nothing had happened. But sometimes these things took time and with Jeff being away for most of the week, maybe timing was an important factor.

"Casserole's nearly ready. You hungry?"

"Starving!"

"Me too. I'll yell for Spyder, see if he can hear me over the noise. He's certainly earned a break!"

"Let's get this table clear and wiped down." said Gina, her fastidious nature was never to be curbed. "We can put a nice clean cloth on and eat in style!" She reached into the bag she had brought with her, pulling out a piece of startling white damask material.

Carol smiled at her. Even in the midst of a building site, Gina would have calmly produced a tablecloth and polished cutlery, whereas Carol would be happy to wolf down fish and chips straight from the paper.

Both women, entirely different, almost opposites, but with a friendship that made them closer than sisters. It was something to be valued.

*****

CHAPTER THREE

Jeff clicked the splitter switch on the gear lever and blipped the accelerator. The powerful Volvo engine in the 'Silver Lady' immediately responded and picked up speed.

Without the trailer attached to hold it back, the big 'Globetrotter' unit drove like a car as Jeff steered it up the steep incline on the narrow, unmade road into the hills towards the tiny Tuscan village of San Guistino.

Jeff hummed along to the music on his cab stereo. Lionel Richie, good old blues and soul as always. None of this up to date, tuneless so-called music for Jeff. He liked a tune he could remember and words that he could understand and sing along with.

Lionel Richie had been played at his wedding to his lovely Gina and he treasured the memory and held it dear.

The light was fading as the winter sun slipped down behind the far off mountains, lighting up their snow capped peaks with a glorious rosy glow, and flickering through the tall pine trees lining the steep, potholed road.

He had made good time, arriving at the waste paper plant outside Florence in the late afternoon and hauling the 'Silver Lady' with the trailer, loaded to the legal limit with used paper, into the loading area. The factory was closed and locked up for the weekend. The workers at home, enjoying their day of rest with their families.

The smell from the plant was revolting. Even in the evening air the nauseating, rancid smell wafted from the closed doors, filling Jeff's nostrils. He shuddered at the thought of having to work in such a place.

He had done his time as a factory worker in his youth, straight from the children's home. There had been little choice at the time. An 'honest job' for all of the boys being sent out to make their way in the world had been allocated to each of them and accepted without question. But after taking charge of his own future and securing the job at Winters Haulage he had never looked back. Being a trucker was all he knew and all he wanted to know. Life on the road was good for Jeff. No one looking over his shoulder, telling him what to do or when to do it. And now he was his own boss in his own truck. Life was perfect.

He had been sickened by the thought of losing his job when Old Man Winters had decided to sell up and retire. The firm had been struggling for some time so nobody would take it on as a going concern. There would have been no work for Jeff.

It had been a gift from the Gods when Carol had bought the old house and yard and not only that, had secured the olive run contract.

After finding a convenient spot to unhook the trailer, checking that the brake was secure and that the landing legs were placed on firm solid ground, he had climbed back into the cab and driven away. No point in spending the night alone in an empty lorry park when a couple of hours easy driving would take him to San Guistino. He was looking forward to spending a pleasant evening with Tony's family, having a shower and a comfortable bed to sleep in. He could be back at the factory first thing Monday morning with no trouble after a pleasant stay at the La Casaccia.

Jeff eased the big cab round a tight bend in the narrow road. Up ahead he could see the tall, wrought iron gates enclosing the long gravel drive leading to the farmhouse and glimpsed two young boys chasing about amongst the trees that shaded the track to the house. Jeff pulled the lever at his side, giving a loud blast on the twin air horns.

The two small figures appeared from the trees and ran towards him shouting excitedly.

"Hello Paulo, hello Georgio!" Jeff called down from his high cab seat, slowing down to snails pace as the boys, shouting exited greetings, clambered onto the steps of the cab, hanging on to the open windows and swinging on his wing mirrors.

"Hey, careful, you two!" Jeff warned. "Trucks are dangerous you know, I don't want you getting hurt! Scram! Go and get your Poppa, and where is Tony eh? Tell him Jeff is here."

Laughing and shouting, the two boys scampered off in search of Poppa. Jeff smiled, as he pulled the big Globetrotter forward, through the gates and up towards the house.

Maybe one day he and Gina would have lively boys running around the place, climbing onto his truck and demanding rides. The thought warmed his heart. Not that Gina was more than enough to fill his heart. He adored her and she was constantly in his thoughts. Life without his beautiful wife was an unbearable thought, but one that was not worth consideration. Jeff had complete faith in Gina and knew that she loved him and would always be there for him on his return to England after his many trips abroad. She always had been there. Loyal, loving and beautiful she was the one thing in Jeff's life that was constant. He would telephone her this evening as always and tell her where he was.

Drawing near to the house, Jeff eased the big truck to a crawl and glanced towards the barn. The old Transcon, Carol's 'Fighting Spirit', complete with trailer stood forlornly, its cab tilted downwards, the curtain sides of the empty trailer pulled back. More trouble with the old girl, thought Jeff as he swung the 'Silver Lady' alongside and switched the engine off. The silence was bliss after the constant dull roar of the powerful engine.

"Hello there, Jeff Boy!" Jeff turned to see a short, stocky man with an ample paunch, ruddy cheeks and a shock of silver grey hair, striding his way.

"Poppa! How the Devil are you?" Jeff beamed, dropping down from the high cab and holding out his hand.

Startling grey eyes twinkled as Poppa clasped Jeff's hand in a firm grip. "Can't grumble lad." Years of living in the Tuscany hills had done little to take the edge off Richard Copeland's broad, Stoke on Trent accent. "Keep smiling, that's what I say!"

'Poppa' was always smiling. In fact the whole family seemed to be constantly happy as far as Jeff could see on his numerous visits, collecting the fresh olives that grew in abundance on the surrounding land.

"Good advice Pops." Jeff replied with a grin. "Long faces only look good on horses!"

Poppa laughed and clapped Jeff on the shoulder. "Wasn't expecting you 'til tomorrow, Lad"

"Yeah, I know, but I made good time. Dropped the trailer at the paper plant and came on up here. Didn't think you'd mind putting me up for a couple of nights. Could do with a good old chat about the business and things. Make some plans and the like."

"Course not Lad, course not! Tony will be here soon, we can have a good old natter. We've already had dinner I'm afraid, but I'm sure Mamma will find something for her visitor."

"Don't want to put you to any bother." Jeff was hungry but polite as always.

"No bother Lad! Mamma will force feed anybody that comes through her door, you should know that by now." Poppa chortled.

The two men walked together towards the long, low farmhouse. Even with the cool of the night air the door was open wide and Jeff could see, beyond the veranda, into the kitchen and the hive of activity taking place.

Mamma Gina was in her domain, the kitchen, along with her daughters, busily attending to washing up and storing the various pots and pans that had been used to feed her large family.

"Jeff! Santa Maria, you come already!" Mamma flocked forward, her ample frame filling the doorway as she bustled through to crush Jeff in a breath expelling embrace.

"Mamma, please! You will make Poppa jealous!" Jeff laughed as Mamma patted his face affectionately.

"Poppa, jealous! Poof! Never so! Maybe do him some good, think Mamma have handsome young man to kiss!"

Poppa raised his eyes to the ceiling in mock despair. Jeff laughed. "They could not handle you Mamma!" He grinned. "You are too much woman for simple young men!"

Mamma beamed happily and returned to her cooking pots. "Claudia." She spoke to her eldest daughter, who was collecting the debris from the vegetables and piling them into a bowl. "Make-a the table clear and put out dishes for Jeff. Carlotta, getta bread, Sophia getta fork, knife, spoons, the vino!"

Mamma's daughters happily went about their allotted tasks. Jeff smiled. He loved to watch Mamma Gina running her kitchen with military precision and all the girls, happy to fit in and do their parts.

Jeff decided to keep out of their way for a moment and strolled onto the veranda. The cool evening air was sharp and fresh, the smell of the olive groves drifting across the slightly damp atmosphere. The first of the stars were beginning to appear in the rapidly darkening sky as Jeff leaned over the rail, staring over to the big barn and the trucks parked at its side.

Poppa followed him out, wisely leaving Mamma plenty of room to direct manoeuvres in the big farmhouse kitchen. "Come on now you two!" He called over to Paulo and Georgio who were playing with a scampering group of puppies in the doorway of the barn. "Have you fed the donkey?"

"Yes, Poppa. Amico has his hay and we have put food down for the dogs." Paulo replied, rolling a fat brown puppy onto its back and tickling its tummy.

"Good lads." Poppa nodded his approval. "But it's time you boys were off to bed now. The two little ones have been asleep for hours!"

"But Poppa, they are babies!" Called Georgio, or at least Jeff thought it was Georgio. "We are big now, nearly nine!" The twins were like peas in a pod and Jeff often had trouble telling which was which.

"Big enough to get yourselves to bed then." Poppa stated firmly. "No need to get one of the girls to help you is there?"

Grudgingly the two dark haired boys did as their father bade them and headed for the house.

One of the pups, bolder than the rest, began to follow, then deciding there was more fun to be had with his litter mates, cocked his leg against the wheel of the 'Silver Lady' before scampering back to the others.

Jeff pulled out a packet of tobacco and some papers and rolled a cigarette offering the packet to Poppa.

"Real baccy!" said Poppa with relish. "That's good. Can't stand these foreign tailor made's."

Poppa had lived in San Guistino for over fifteen years but had valiantly resisted being localised. He spoke little or no Italian and still considered Italy to be 'foreign' and England to be 'home' but at the same time, extolling the virtues of living in such a wonderful place, declaring he would never leave and sympathising with everyone who had the misfortune to live elsewhere!

The corners of Jeff's mouth crinkled with amusement that was lost on the older man.

"More trouble with the old girl then?" Jeff exhaled a stream of pale grey smoke into the cool evening air. The Transcon tilting sadly alongside the barn, looked like the poor relation against the gleaming 'Silver Lady'.

"Gear linkage gone." said Poppa. "Tony's off now getting the bits. Not that big a job, just a nuisance really."

Jeff nodded. It was amazing that the old truck had made so many trips from England to Italy without collapsing completely. "Wouldn't dare mention to Carol about getting rid of her though." Jeff continued. "She's desperately fond of the old 'Fighting Spirit'"

"Yes, she is that." Poppa agreed. "My Tony's just as bad. Every time something goes wrong, off he goes, getting the parts, sorting it out and gluing it all back together. I think it's a romantic thing me-self!" He added, conspiratorially.

"Well if it wasn't for the old girl breaking down in the first place," Jeff added. "Those two would never have met. In fact probably none of us would have met and we would not be all working together like we are now, so I reckon we do owe the old work bus a favour."

"Aye, Lad there is that!" Poppa agreed, puffing on his roughly made cigarette.

"Mind you, if it had broken down somewhere else, then the girls would not have found the pregnant dog and landed you with another six mouths to feed!" Jeff added with a grin, watching the antics of the pups.

Poppa shrugged good naturedly. "When you've had nine kids like Mamma and me, little Toby and her bunch of pups don't make much difference!" He leaned over the veranda rail. "Strange how things work out though. Fate,

Mama always says, her being religious and all that. I just believe in good timing. Life is made up of timing, good or bad. It just depends which path you take and when you take it."

Jeff nodded. "Who knows what's round the next corner in life, eh?"

"Or why it's there?" added Poppa. "When I were a lad living in Stoke, if somebody had told me I'd one day be an olive grower, living in Italy with a family of nine kids I'd have never believed 'em. But here I am, happy as larry and wouldn't change a thing!"

"Things certainly worked well for you." Jeff remarked.

"I don't believe in fighting fate." said Poppa. "Reckon it was written in the stars right from the off. Come to think of it, even when the eldest five were little and Mamma and me were still in Stoke, I had this feeling something was missing. Always felt like we were just waiting for something to happen."

"And it did."

"It did that. Our little Gino dying, sudden like, made the difference. Shifted us out here that did. Mamma needed to be near her own family."

Jeff nodded. He had forgotten, for a moment, that the family had lost a child and felt a pang of guilt for having done so.

"It was a dreadful time and no mistake." Poppa went on quietly. "Tiny little mite he was, just learning to sit up then suddenly…gone. No one ever gave us a real explanation. These things happen they said. A terrible blow, nearly killed Mamma. She could hardly cope with the other kids. Tony was only thirteen and Marco and the three girls, they all felt it too, of course. I had to get Mamma back here as soon as possible, she needed her own mamma."

"But the family are all happy now." Jeff tried to lighten the conversation.

"Would never have believed we could be again, but yes, we are now." Poppa nodded thoughtfully. "So there you are." He went on. "I always believe things happen for a reason and now here we are with four more kids running around. I believe you have to wait for the right time, can't rush fate Jeff lad!"

"Very philosophical." Jeff stated. "But true. Who knows what any of us would be doing now or how our lives may be different had we taken a different route, at a different time, a different day."

"Or the Transcon had done Carol's first run without breaking down!" added Poppa, flicking the end of his cigarette into the gathering gloom. Its dying spark glowing on the ground for a moment before fading from sight.

The men's philosophising was abruptly ended by the arrival of Mamma Gina, bustling purposefully from her kitchen. "The food! You come Jeff, you eat, you go thin and get sick you not eat!" Mamma swooped through the door onto the veranda, waving her hands and ushering Jeff back inside to the table as though he may die from hunger. No chance of that here. Had Jeff not known Mamma's ways in her kitchen he would have thought they were expecting another dozen guests.

"Sit! Sit! Take food!" Mamma swept her arm grandly towards the table, laden with a whole cold ham, a board of cheese, and dishes of boiled eggs, finely chopped salad, a jug of red wine, chunks of bread and of course olives.

"Hell's Bells Mamma!" Jeff laughed. "Don't tell me I have to eat ALL of this! It's a feast!"

Mamma glowed with pride. "Nobody leave Mamma's table wanting the more!" she announced, feeling satisfied that her visitor had been offered enough hospitality.

"That, Mamma, is certainly a true statement!" Jeff agreed as he picked up a knife and started to help himself.

*****

Gina kicked off her shoes as she stepped through door, scooping them up in her hand and walking immediately up the stairs and placing them neatly in the rack that ran the length of the long row of wardrobes in her bedroom. Phoebe dashed up the stairs alongside her, purring her greeting and leapt onto the bed, watching with interest as Gina slipped off her cream woollen coat and carefully brushed off any traces of dust before hanging it neatly alongside the varied selection of winter coats in the tall robe. "Off there pest!" Gina lifted Phoebe gently but firmly from the neatly smoothed bed and selected a fresh satin night-gown and wrap from a deep drawer in the fitment. She noticed the small red light flashing briskly on her answer-phone at the side of her bed and clicked the switch as she undressed.

"Gina! Good heavens, where ARE you!" Her mother's irritated, clipped tones filled the room.

Gina raised a resigned eyebrow and folded her tailored trousers, hanging them in the wardrobe before taking off her soft cream jumper and dropping it onto the bed.

"I have called twice now and you were out!" her mother continued accusingly. "This just will NOT do Gina, we have to make arrangements for Christmas. I MUST know if you are coming here or are Daddy and I coming to you. Although of course here would be better!"

Of course it would, thought Gina. Mother could take complete charge and make a whole social production out of the occasion. How many people this time?

"I've pencilled in Councillor Graham to have lunch should we dine here...." Oh! What a surprise! "...and possibly that charming couple that have moved into The Grange, that quite well known poetry writer chappie and his French wife, you know who I mean. But you really MUST get in touch about it Dear!" Her mother's voice trilled on. "We MUST make firm arrangements, you KNOW Daddy can't stand to be left wondering, he'll get himself in one of his states and end up besides himself! Now DO call me as soon as you get this message. Good evening Dear!"

Who else, Gina wondered, had a mother who ended her message with 'Good evening!'....and as for Daddy being besides himself..... The only thing that stressed Gina's father was Gina's mother!

The answer phone bleeped to herald a second message. "Hi-ya Darling." Jeff's voice. "Just called to say good night. I've arrived at San Guistino. Mamma Gina has fed me to capacity as usual and I'm off to bed now. Miss you lots. Love you loads!" The sound of kisses then, "Sleep tight Darling."

Gina smiled, staring at the phone for a moment before resetting the answer mode. Bless him! He made her feel so safe, secure.

Wearing only delicate lace, coffee coloured bra and panties she walked over to the full length mirror and studied her image. At thirty two years of age she still had the figure of a teenager. Tiny in stature, her small waist and well toned body had changed little over the years, her skin unblemished. She turned sideways, sliding her hand over the gentle curve of her stomach. What sort of a mother would she make, she wondered, although there were no signs so far to say that it may ever happen. How would she know how to behave with a baby?

She certainly had learned no maternal skills from her own mother. If she had ever been upset or ill it was always her father that Gina had turned to. She could remember him coming into her room in the night and cooling her brow with cold cloths when she had a fever and swinging her high in the air when she was happy and laughing.

Her father had stood by her when she had met Jeff and told her parents that they were to be married. Her mother had been appalled. Her daughter to marry a truck driver! It was something she had never accepted and Gina got the distinct impression that she was simply waiting for her daughter to see sense, leave this unsuitable match and allow her mother to arrange a far more acceptable union.

Gina flicked off her bra and stepped out of her panties, walking across to her en suite bathroom and standing under the shower, closing her eyes as the stream of hot water washed over her.

She had avoided the whole family-Christmas-dinner issue the year before, flying off with Jeff to spend Christmas in the Canaries, but now they had the business to run they had decided to spend Christmas at home. Her mother would be difficult to avoid.

She sighed, remembering the lovely time she had spent in Italy at the end of the summer, with Jeff and Carol and Katy as guests at Marco's wedding. They had danced late into the night on the dry baked ground outside the La Casaccia. The music from the small band of musicians, drifting gently across the evening air, tiny lanterns flickering through the trees, lighting the tables laden with food and wine.

Carol and Tony had been lost in each others company, dancing together or holding hands as they strolled through the cool of the balmy summers night. The whole family had been laughing and happy, eating the feast that Mamma Gina had prepared and drinking many jars of the fruity local wine with Marco, and his lovely bride Guliana, the centre of attention.

Gina felt slightly envious of such a close family life. What a contrast to a family occasion spent with her mother.

She decided to forget about it until tomorrow. She would call her mother then, no point in doing it now and spoiling her otherwise pleasant evening.

Jeff would go along with any decision that she made. He was easy going and as long as Gina was happy, then so was he.

As her body relaxed under the rush of warm water, her mind wandered back to the early summer, to the brief affair she had allowed herself to become involved in. Mark Cameron, the young, up and coming solicitor, so charming and exciting, sweeping Gina off her feet. Jeff had taken second place in her heart for some time until she had seen Mark for what he was. A charming womaniser, married with two small children and, to Gina's horror, also having an affair with his leggy young secretary.

She had been hurt and shaken at the time, not sure of her own feelings, wrestling with inner turmoil. She had been glad, that right at that moment, Carol, who had stood by her solidly without question, had been offered the job of driving to Italy. Gina had jumped at the chance to ride along with her, supporting her friend on her first nervous steps into the trucking world and clearing her own mind in the fresh mountain air. She had laid her ghosts and was now clear about her future. Jeff was her rock, her strength and she wondered why on earth she had ever risked losing him or the warm security he gave her.

Jeff would never know, never find out that his adored wife had betrayed him. Gina did not believe that confession was at all good for the soul. Just the opposite in fact and was strongly of the opinion that a still tongue was the best way to avoid hurt and pain. Despite her fragile appearance, Gina was a strong minded woman and would take her secret to the grave.

She sighed and switched off the shower, wrapping her hair in a soft white towel and another about her body, she padded barefoot across the thick carpet to her dressing table.

Phoebe leapt onto the bed again to take a keen interest in the proceedings as Gina set about drying her hair and preparing for bed. She had enjoyed a pleasant day with Carol, but now her mother had called. That always put a damper on her spirits. The hum of the dryer, swirling her long blond hair about her shoulders soothed Gina's annoyance. She loved her father and felt that she did not see enough of him, but she knew he would understand when she came up with a suitable excuse for not spending Christmas in the company of her mother

*****

"You sure don't do things by halves do you?" said Derek, spooning sugar into his mug of tea. He leaned back on his old swivel chair to see out of the office window to where the Chevy was standing, tucked in amongst the 'L' plated training trucks, all neatly parked up for the night.

Carol knew that Derek always called into the office for a couple of hours on Sundays. It was a good time to catch up with paperwork without the distractions of trainees and check that the lorries were all in good running order for the start of the new week ahead. It was a good time to catch him for a private chat and proudly show off her new purchase.

"Never did!" Carol replied sitting down with her own tea on the other side of the desk. "You know me, I don't stop to think. Eyes closed, both feet straight in!"

Derek laughed. "Well I don't think you have made a mistake with the Chevy. It's in great nick and a real collector's piece."

"I just love it!" Carol replied. "Even though some may think it's a bit of a bus!"

"Speaking of which," Derek turned back towards her. "I have got something I would like to run by you."

"Really!" What's that then?"

"Well we are pretty busy here as you know, but there is an opening for expansion."

"That's good isn't it?" Carol remarked. Since her own training days at the Heavy Goods Driving School she had seen how many more applicants for training were turning up every week. The school had a good name and was building on its reputation.

"Oh, yes!" Derek replied quickly. "Trouble is we can only take so much work and the backlog is piling up. I have bookings for well into next year." He put down his cup and picked up a sheaf of paper from the desk, handing it to Carol.

"I've been approached to train some coach drivers for this company." He pointed to the name on the headed papers. "Snag is we don't have a coach or anywhere to park it. We are tight for space as it is."

Carol looked through the papers. "They are offering quite a lot of work aren't they?"

"Yes, they are. That's why I wanted a word. If I buy a coach, or even two and hire a couple of coach instructors, would you consider renting me some parking space in your yard. You seem to have more than enough space for your two trucks."

"Of course!" Carol did not hesitate. "I would be more than glad to help out. You don't have to pay rent!"

"Oh, yes I do!" Derek insisted. "I run this business properly and I pay rent for my parking. No arguments on that!"

"Okay." Carol held her hands up. "If that makes you feel better."

"That's a deal then." Derek looked pleased. "What I'll do, is go and have a look at the coaches I have in mind then when I get them, the trucks can go in your yard and the coaches in here. I will make sure they are parked up neatly and don't interfere with your own trucks."

Carol knew Derek would be as good as his word. "When old man Winters had his business up and running and was doing well he had six or seven trucks parked in that yard, trailers and all, so I'm sure we won't be running out of space just yet." she laughed.

"You never know what the future may bring though." Derek remarked. "You may expand to the point where you will need an even bigger place!"

Carol raised her eyes. "Hey slow down! We have only just got started. I've never even considered getting any bigger than we are now. Take it steady and enjoy what we have right now, that's what I think. Bigger company, bigger worries!"

"You could be right." Derek agreed. "But the way the old Transcon keeps playing up it might be a good idea to think about another for replacement."

"Yes, I know!" Carol grudgingly agreed. "I am terribly fond of the old girl though, after all, she got me out and back in one piece on my very first trip and I'm a bit sentimental about her. What's more, so is Tony."

Derek looked doubtful. "Sentiment is all very well. But business, as they say, is business, so you have to be sensible sometimes."

He reached for a magazine that had been lying open on his desk. "Saw this and thought of you," he said, pointing to an advert, ringed round in felt tip pen. "Sounds like just the sort of thing you could be doing with, and the price isn't bad either."

Carol looked at the photograph of a truck and written details, 'Volvo Globetrotter Tractor unit for sale'. There were more details of mileage and maintenance.

"Doesn't sound bad, but what do I know about buying trucks?"

Derek laughed. "What did you know about running a haulage business, but that didn't stop you starting one!" He chuckled again, shaking his head. "Take that home anyway and give it some thought. We can always check it out together if you fancy the idea."

"Thanks, I will certainly give it some thought, and I'll definitely take you up on the offer of looking at it with me if I decide to go ahead."

Derek nodded. "How are the home improvements coming along?"

"Very well, or so I believe." Carol replied. "Spyder even turned up this morning to get some more done, there is no stopping him, and reckons he will have the sanding finished by the end of the week. I had to insist he went home early this afternoon to spend some time with his family, but tomorrow I'm leaving him in sole charge of keeping an eye on the heating engineers and giving Bruno his tablets on time when I come in to work."

"Sounds like you trust him." Derek remarked.

"Yes, I do actually." Carol replied. "He comes across as genuine and honest and I had no worries about him being there while I came to work."

"That's good." Derek remarked thoughtfully. "Good workers can be hard to find. Seems most people like a free ride these days."

"Not him." Carol laughed. "Can't seem to stop him when he gets started. In fact I am seriously considering taking him on full time to help out with the trucks. He is a good mechanic too."

"That's handy." said Derek, getting up from his chair and walking over to the small sink to rinse the cups. "Maybe he can do some bits for me as well. I could do with a good maintenance man on the team."

"Well if the trucks are in my yard he can just do the lot."

"Well that's another problem solved. You certainly met him at the right time."

"Yes, it was a good bit of timing to say the least." Carol followed Derek out of the portacabin office, zipping up her thick jacket against the biting wind as she waited for him to lock up for the night. "I'll have a word with him and see how he feels about it. But I can't say for definite until I have run it by Jeff. After all, when he has finished my personal work, his wages will be coming out of the company account if we agree to keep him."

"True," said Derek. "No mad rush. Any time yesterday will do!"

Carol laughed. "Jeff will 'phone tonight most probably, I'll mention it then."

"Fine." Derek held the Chevy door open as Carol climbed in, sliding across the big leather bench seat to take her position behind the steering wheel. "And remember, the rent I am paying for the parking will be for you personally. It is your land you know, not the property of Transcon Haulage!"

"Yes, I know." Carol looked serious. "I just find it so hard to believe that I have got so much now, whereas it wasn't that long ago that I had little or nothing."

"That's life!" Derek grinned. "Full of surprises, but you've worked hard for it, so good luck to you girl!"

Carol waved as she drove off. Yes, things were going well. So well it was almost too good to be true. With everything falling into place at the right time, she nearly asked herself what on earth could go wrong.

Then she remembered that she would be leaving her house full of workmen in the morning so thought better of it.

*****

CHAPTER FOUR

As usual, Monday had been hectic in the driving school. New trainees, nervous and excited about the proposition of learning the skills required to drive the heavy trucks, arrived in the yard, keen to start out on a new career as truckers.

Carol had tried hard to concentrate on the job in hand but always on the back of her mind was the thought that her house had been invaded by workmen! She desperately hoped that all was running smoothly, with no problems or hitches and that she would not be faced with any major disasters on her return home.

Carol locked the Chevy and folded her coat around her before running the short distance through the haulage yard and up the wide stone steps leading to her front door. The temperature was dropping rapidly as the light faded into dusk, the sharp winter wind lashing her hair about her face. It had been a tiring day and she was glad that there was no sign of Spyder's car in the yard. Not that she disliked the company of her new found helper, but tonight she needed to relax, alone and in peace.

As she swung the solid oak door open she was met with a warm glow. Heat at last! Warmth! Luxury!

Carol leaned on the closed door, glancing around and enjoying the unexpected warmth enveloping her as Bruno, looking more like his old self, padded out of the kitchen, his paws scuffling on the bare wooden floor.

"Hey, this is more like it isn't it Boy!" She hunched down to fondle Bruno's ears as she looked around. The big square hall, still with a fine layer of dust from Spyder's sanding, proudly displayed its new radiators, glowing their heat from under the tall windows either side of the door and another along the side wall, warming the way to the kitchen. Carol realised how ancient man must have felt upon discovering fire!

She slipped off her thick coat and walked across to open the door into the big drawing room. Spyder had finished sanding the floor and had stripped the old flaking paint from the skirting boards and doorframe.

Carol sat on the window seat beneath the huge bay window, trying to form a picture in her mind of the room completed and restored. The panelled ceiling, subtly painted to accentuate its detail and the marble fireplace, now bereft of

48

the unsightly gas fire, cleaned and polished and of course a huge square rug, oriental perhaps, in the centre. She sat for a moment, the bare bones of the finished scene in her mind. But right now a cup of tea and a soak in the tub took priority over her reverie. No doubt Jeff would call this evening, keeping her up to speed on his progress and the latest information on the German orders.

Passing through the hall on her way back to the kitchen she caught sight of a note beside the telephone on the circular rosewood table in the hallway.

'Checked that all was working well and signed for the heating. Finished the skirtings and doors and started on the banisters and spindles on the staircase. Gave Bruno his mid morning tablet. Hope it's all okay. See you in the morning.' He had signed off with an 'S' and a tiny spider sketch.

Carol smiled, flicking the switch on the kettle. He certainly was a treasure and she was glad to have found him.

*****

Carol slid down the length of the deep bath, luxuriating in the scented water. Disregarding the bare plaster walls and the flaking ceiling, she felt content to enjoy the warmth permeating around the big old house at last and relaxed her aching muscles, letting her mind wander.

She had come a long way in a surprisingly short time. The business was building up nicely and she had met a wonderful man. She had a job she enjoyed and very soon she would have a comfortable home to relax in. Life was good, and for the first time felt that she no longer had to worry about every penny spent as she had in the past. What more could she ask for, life was perfect!

Her only slight tinge of sadness was that dear old dad had not lived to see his daughter's success. He had supported and encouraged her so well over the years that she had struggled to bring Katy up alone. Always on hand with a kind word and a few pounds to help out. He, himself, only too aware of the problems of bringing up a child alone after losing Carol's mother when she was hardly more than a baby.

It had been a heartbreaking time for Carol when he had died so suddenly just after Katy's tenth birthday. How proud he would have been to see his only daughter running her own business and to see how well Katy had turned out.

Carol herself was fervently proud of her vivacious, nineteen year old daughter, studying hard at University and looking forward to graduating and making her way in the world. Pops would have been proud of both his girls! He would have liked Tony as well. Carol was sure of that.

She would speak to Tony this evening, call him when she had bathed. Had the Transcon made its trip without mishap this time she wondered, although Tony had mentioned nothing of it during his call on Saturday. The big old truck was showing its age badly and Carol knew that it would not run forever. It seemed like every trip called for a quick running repair to keep it on the road, but she knew Tony was desperately fond of the old truck and wondered how on earth she was going to broach the subject of selling her on for scrap and buying a newer, more reliable vehicle.

Well there was no need to mention it just yet. She might have a look at the truck that Derek suggested first. Maybe it would not be what she needed. But if it were, then she would choose her words carefully so as not to upset Tony too much.

Carol slid her head under the water, her mass of auburn curls floating about her face as she reached for the shampoo and lathered off the dust of the day.

She rinsed her hair, stepped from the bath, and pulled the plug. Wrapping herself in a big fluffy towel and piling her hair in another, she walked across the wide landing into her bedroom.

Another huge room with wooden boards beneath her feet, bare plaster walls and a beautifully ornate cast iron fireplace, discovered boarded up and hidden behind a sheet of plywood.

Carol sat at the delicate rosewood dressing table by the big sash window. Left in the house by old man Winters, she had carefully cleaned and re-polished it to reveal fine gold inlay edging the beauty of the grain, topped with finely turned triple mirrors. She had done the same with the matching rosewood chaise lounge, cleaning years of grime from the wood and re-covering the worn velvet upholstery. She had chosen a deep crushed crimson velvet. A bold choice for a bedroom but Carol was not afraid of bold choices. She felt it reflected her personality and loved the brilliant flash of colour amidst the unfinished, bare rooms.

She ran the hairdryer quickly over her thick mass of shoulder length curls, leaving it slightly damp and pulled on a pair of jogging pants and a fleece top. She had no plans to cook this evening and decided to settle for a sandwich and a mug of tea before curling up in her favourite chair and trawling through the pages of the Truck Trade magazine. She really had to consider a replacement for her old truck sooner or later.

*****

Carol finished her sandwich, sitting comfortably in the big armchair, gloriously close to the radiator in the cluttered back room. She had thrown off the dustsheet and pulled up one of the packing cases to act as a side table for her tea tray and had relaxed to her favourite Elton John ballads as she dined. She reached for the telephone, curling her legs underneath her as she sank back into the cushions and dialled Tony's number. After a few moments the line connected.

"Pronto!"

"Ciao, Claudia!" Carol recognised the husky voice of Tony's sister.

"Carol! How are you?" Without waiting for a reply Claudia chattered on. "We are all well and I am right now helping Christo and Maria to get ready for bed. You will want Tony, yes? and Jeff? They are both here. I call them for you. Ciao, Carol!"

Giving Carol no time to reply Claudia set down the receiver and could be heard calling for Tony and Jeff, and shouting for the children, partly in Italian, partly in English. Typical Claudia! Carol smiled, picturing the usual evening chaos that added to the charm of the unique Anglo-Italian family. After a moment, Tony was there. "Ciao, Cara mia"

"Hello, Darling." Carol curled up tighter, sinking further into the cushions as she cradled the phone. "How are things? Jeff is with you I hear."

"Yes, he has been here since Saturday evening, went to unload this morning and is back with us again. Nice to have him here as we can have a good talk about business. He is talking to Marco at the moment. Marco has more business for you."

"Really!" Carol was surprised. "Marco certainly puts some business our way. Apart from your business he has found the German orders and now you say there is more?"

"We keep things within the family." Tony stated simply. "And the new business is good for us too."

"Really," said Carol. "What is it?"

"Well it's a big one. Jeff and Marco are discussing it now. Bigger than the German orders and wanted right away. Two truck loads of best oil to Bulgaria as soon as possible."

"Bulgaria!" Carol was amazed. "I never thought of anybody in Bulgaria wanting olives or olive oil."

"Well obviously they do!" Tony replied his voice sounding amused at Carol's words. "Obviously the quality of our oil is renowned, and the best part is that there are two complete reloads to be picked up directly after dropping the load. Very convenient."

"Well yes, that is good." Carol agreed. "We hadn't arranged the re-loads from Germany as yet. I was going to ring the agent when you were ready to tip the loads."

"No need with the Bulgarian job, Marco will arrange everything."

"What is the reload?" Carol asked.

"Two whole loads of children's toys." Tony replied. "Plenty of those required so close to Christmas. Good quality, but made a lot cheaper in Bulgaria apparently. The factory is in Sofia, I believe. Not got all the details yet, I've been busy outside."

"Are they in a rush for this delivery then?"

"Well the buyers want the oil as soon as they can get it, but of course getting the toys loaded and delivered in time for the Christmas shoppers is the hurry bit as you can understand, and it's a well paid job too due to that fact."

"What about the German order?" Carol asked. She did not want to lose what may be a regular run for a one off job.

"Not sure yet." Tony replied. "You called as we were trying to sort it out. Work out how best to fit in both jobs. Jeff was going to run it by you as soon as we had the timings and routes in front of us, make sure it would work first."

"I see." Said Carol. "All right then, as soon as it's worked out on paper ask Jeff to ring me back and we can agree it."

Carol was determined that as an equal partner nothing should be done without both her's and Jeff's agreement.

"Of course." Tony understood Carol's fierce determination run her business properly. It meant a lot to her and he understood that. "By the way, the Transcon lost some gear linkage on the way back here." Tony informed her.

"Oh hell! Whatever next. The old girl's falling to bits."

"Don't worry." Tony was quick to reassure her. "I got some replacement parts and fixed her up again. She will be fine now, or at least for a while."

Carol glanced guiltily at the open page of the Truck Trade magazine at her side.

"Well thanks for that, once again you are my Knight in Shining Armour! You sure know how to get the best out of the old 'Fighting Spirit'."

"Oh, she will be fine for a while I'm sure Cara Mia! Don't worry. I have your best interests at heart!"

Carol loved to hear him re-assure her that all would be well, both with the truck and between themselves, but she knew the Transcon was on borrowed time. She just didn't have the heart to say this out loud to Tony. Not after he had just told her he had fixed it up ….. again.

They said their goodbyes and Carol picked up her magazine. Somehow she could not concentrate. She wondered how long it would be before Jeff rang with details of the Bulgarian run but knew that she should give some serious thought about obtaining a better truck for her side of the business. But when she did find one, how would she break it to Tony? He loved the Transcon and would surely be disappointed, possibly feel she was ungrateful after all the time and effort he had spent keeping it on the road.

It was a dilemma but she knew the only way forward was a new truck. It had to be done she decided, but she would pick her words carefully when explaining to Tony.

*****

The sound of the telephone ringing woke Carol with a start. She had dozed off in the big armchair in the unaccustomed warmth of the room.

"Transcon Haulage" she tried to shake the sleep from her eyes.

"Hi, Carol. Sorry to ring so late but there's been a lot to sort out." Jeff was apologetic.

"That's okay." Carol replied glancing at her watch. "I had dropped off in the chair actually. Had the central heating installed today and it's now far too cosy!"

"Hey that's good! Should imagine it's made a world of difference."

"You could say!" Carol replied with feeling. "It's absolute luxury!"

"Great." Jeff laughed. "Anyway, to business. Marco has negotiated a deal for two truck loads of olive oil to be delivered to a distributor in Bulgaria."

"Yes, Tony outlined it earlier." Carol was wide awake now and paying attention.

"Right, well apparently this order has to go straight away. Not so much the delivery being a rush job, but the reloads are kiddies' toys, so of course, they must be back to England in time for the Christmas shoppers so it has to be done right away to get the full benefit."

"Yes, I can see that." Carol replied. "But what about the German orders?"

"That's the good thing. There is no immediate panic for those. They want the stuff on a pretty regular run, every month, but the contract hasn't started yet. More or less up to us, within reason of course, when we start the deliveries. The Bulgarian job is maybe a one off, but it is for two whole trailer loads to the same place and re-loads from the same area, well that in itself is a bonus. Not having to trek another five hours to pick up the reload is great, and saves a lot of time and money. Speaking of which, the rate is excellent."

Jeff ran through a few figures, clarifying the rate for the job.

"Sounds good." Carol agreed. "As long as it doesn't damage a regular contract. We can't afford to grab a fast buck at the expense of a more regular run."

"Sure, I know that." Jeff agreed. "But I have talked it over in detail with Tony and Marco and I can't see a problem with it."

"Okay, I will bow to your judgement on this one then." Carol conceded. Although she intended to be involved with every transaction, she trusted Jeff's judgement. If he reckoned the deal was good she would go with it. "What's the plan of attack then?"

"Right, Marco is booking us onto a ferry for Tuesday evening. So we load up Tuesday morning and drive down to Bari, that's the port town on the heel bit of Italy. Should do that easily within the day. We get the overnight ferry there to Durres in Albania then drive through into Macedonia and then straight on into Bulgaria."

"You make it sound easy." said Carol. She realised that she was not at all sure where exactly Bulgaria was and made a mental note to look it up on the map.

"Well, we hope it will be." Jeff went on. "After getting off the boat first thing we should be able to make Sofia by the end of the day, if everything goes according to plan of course. I personally have my doubts about the route but Marco thinks it will be the quickest way to go. It will be handy if we can get tipped before bedtime and reload first thing the next day, then head back to England overland via what used to be Yugoslavia, through Austria and straight on up to the boat at Calais."

"Sounds like you've been doing your homework." Carol was impressed.

"Yes, we've been working out the timings most of this evening. That's why I was so late in ringing. Wanted to get it all down just so, to run by you." Jeff always played fair. Everything was equal between them.

"Well if you're happy with it, then we go with it." said Carol. "But if you see any problems then get back to me."

"I will." Jeff promised. "But so far it seems pretty idiot proof!"

Carol laughed. "Depends which idiots we are dealing with."

"Well we're muddling through so far aren't we girl." Jeff laughed.

"So far so good!" Carol agreed. "As long as the old Transcon hangs on in one piece. Actually," she lowered her voice almost conspiratorially, "I'm seriously considering replacing her, but dread mentioning that to Tony, he's so fond of the old thing and I think he's proud of the way he keeps her going." Jeff smiled at the telephone. "I reckon you will have to do something sooner or later." He sounded amused.

Carol decided not to ask what was so funny and changed the subject. "Oh, by the way, I have a guy doing some work in the house for me. So far he has been brilliant and also does mechanics. I wanted to have a word with you about taking him on to do odd jobs and running repairs etc. I was going to wait 'til you got home and introduce you but seeing as you will be away a while...."

"I take it this is the famous Spyder we are talking about." Jeff cut in. "I spoke to Gina just now and she was singing his praises most highly."

"She was? Well he is a nice guy and a good worker too."

"We could do with another hand on board. Do some of the donkey-work so to speak, so why not? I trust your judgement too, so take him on for a trial period. Can't do any harm that way, what do you think."

"Good idea. I will let him know tomorrow. I think it will work out well."

"Fingers crossed eh!" Jeff replied. "By the way, when I was chatting to Gina I mentioned that we really should consider getting computers installed. Business's these days are all computer compatible, so I reckon we should start to think about getting a bit more up to date, what do you say?"

Carol laughed again. "Computers! This idea from a man who, up until a month or two ago, refused point blank to carry a mobile phone!"

"Yeah, yeah, I know, rub it in. Gina always accuses me of being a dinosaur so perhaps it's time I got 'with it'!"

"I agree. Computers could be a bonus. But don't forget neither you nor I can handle one!"

"Gina has it covered. She, of course, decided to go to evening classes and learn what to do. You know Gina. Something needs doing so she just goes out and finds out how!"

"Good old Gina!" said Carol. "She always knows the right thing to do. She is so infuriatingly capable, if she wasn't my best friend I'd hate her!"

"Tell me about it!" Jeff laughed. "For a tiny little china doll she sure is one tough lady!"

"Thank goodness we have got her!" Carol agreed. "Aren't we the lucky ones! I will ring her tomorrow and have a chat about it."

"Any excuse for a chat with you two isn't it!" Jeff teased.

"Absolutely!" Carol agreed. "We can always find something to talk about, but computers will make a change!"

Jeff laughed. "Okay 'Ginger Nut', gotta go now and get some sleep. Early start in the morning now the Bulgaria thing is on. Will keep you up on proceedings as we go."

"Bye for now then Jeff, sleep well."

"And you, 'night kid."

Carol put down the receiver and stretched. Bruno shuffled to his feet expectantly.

"Sorry mate." Carol ruffled his ears. "I meant to take you for a short trot out tonight but you will have to make do with a run round the garden before your bedtime tablet."

She got to her feet and walked through to the kitchen, opening the door and letting Bruno through to disappear into the darkness of the garden.

Blast! She had forgotten to mention the spring water idea. Never mind, no rush, the water would be there whenever she remembered to speak about it. Carol yawned, she was too tired to think straight.

She leaned through the half open door and gave a low whistle. Bruno appeared out of the gloom, hesitating, then going back to sniff with great interest, under the half rotten door of the small brick building backing onto the house, a disused outside 'privy' that Carol had every intention of knocking down at some stage.

"Come on you!" She called sharply. "Nothing there of interest, you silly hound!"

Bruno gave one last sniff then grudgingly padded back into the kitchen.

Carol gave him his last tablet, cunningly wrapped in a cube of cheese, then made herself a cup of hot chocolate and switched off the lights. A warm bed with a hot drink. What a luxurious life she led!

*****

Jeff was smiling as he walked back into the cosy room where Tony, Marco and Poppa were sitting, each with a glass of wine.

"What's amusing you lad?" Poppa queried.

Jeff laughed. "Nothing much." He answered, stretching his long legs in front of him as he sat comfortably on the overstuffed leather sofa.

Tony and Marco, so alike in appearance except for Tony's startling grey eyes and Marco's dark liquid brown ones, were looking through papers at the big oak desk by the window. Marco, every inch the businessman, immaculately dressed, seated in the black leather swivel chair and Tony, dressed in jeans and an open neck, rough woollen shirt, perched on the corner of the desk, swinging his long legs.

Tony looked up from the papers detailing their journey. "Did you manage to bring up the subject of the Transcon and suggest that it may not live forever?" he asked hopefully.

Jeff tried to look grave. "Tricky one that, Tony! Maybe you should mention it first." He was trying hard to keep from smiling.

"I suppose I should." Tony replied. "Just don't want to upset her."

"I can't for the life of me see anyone getting sentimental over a truck!" Marco put in with a puzzled look.

"Well no, Mr Big Business." Tony gave his brother a dig in the ribs. "YOU wouldn't."

Marco shrugged. It was beyond him. "I buy my Guliana beautiful jewellery and good china, but if it breaks, it breaks!"

"But you, my little brother, are not a sentimental, romantic fool!" Tony grinned.

"I am romantic!" Marco looked affronted. "Remember the secret honeymoon I planned for my Guliana. A beautiful villa on the Isle of Capri, just for the two of us. That was romantic!"

"Yes, of course son." Poppa broke in. "You two just have different ideas, that's all."

"That's a point." Jeff remarked. "Where is the lovely Gulianna? I haven't seen her?"

Marco raised his eyes. "Her sister has given birth to her first baby, so of course my Guliana has rushed to her side. No doubt will spend as many days as possible fussing over the newborn, while her new husband is neglected!"

"Ha! Marco is secretly delighted to be an uncle." Tony laughed, digging his younger brother in the ribs. "Especially when they are naming the baby after him." His diamond grey eyes twinkled with mirth.

Marco grinned disarmingly. "Not exactly after me. His third name, apparently, will be Marco so I am in line only after his father and grandfather have been honoured. I will see him myself when I go to Pisa to collect Guliana."

"Marco has a soft spot for bambinos." Tony winked at Jeff. "He was always the first to rush to help Mamma when the little ones were new born. In fact he was a dab hand with nappies by the time he was ten!"

"Thank you brother!" Marco stretched back in his chair. "My masculinity and businesslike demeanour has just been completely shattered!" He gave his elder brother a shove, dislodging him from the corner of the desk.

"If you think this is bad you should have seen them when they were little!" Poppa remarked, refilling Jeff's glass from a large carafe. "Always goading each other, but best of friends all the same."

"Doesn't solve my problem though," said Tony. "I still have to find a way to talk to Carol about the truck."

"I think that is best left up to you Tony," Jeff said seriously. "Not the sort of subject any of us would want to interfere in."

Poppa gave Jeff a sidelong glance, and received a wink in return. This was going to be fun!

*****

It's just along here I think." Derek glanced at the address on the piece of paper in his hand as Carol drove through the gathering gloom of the late afternoon. She steered the Chevy carefully along the winding country lanes, passing farm gates and expensive houses on the way. Woodland lay on both sides of the road, broken only by driveways and smaller side turnings leading into the sea of trees.

"Epping Forest." said Derek. "A bit upper crust round here girl, very Ferrari's-in-the-driveway kinda place. Used to be a favourite haunt of Henry the eighth. He was always knocking about in the forest around here. Taking pot shots at wild boar and waiting 'til his wives had been beheaded so that he could look for another one!"

"Typical man!" Carol replied. "There was a sign back there saying 'Queen Elizabeth's Hunting Lodge.' Nice to know the daughter took over and beat the old boy at his own game!"

Derek laughed. "Trust you to get that one in!"

"Nice area though." Carol remarked, slowing for a particularly tight bend. The Chevy had never been built to negotiate English country lanes.

"Hmm! Footballers and stockbrokers can afford it round here. Or the farmers that have been here for years." Derek replied. "Slow down, I think this is the place."

Carol pulled in through a wide gate and into a large haulage yard. A dozen trucks were standing in a line, parked against the wall heralding J.S.M. Logistics. "That's the one we want to see I think." Derek pointed to a Volvo Globetrotter at the end of the row of vehicles. "Let's give it the once over."

The two walked over to the truck. It was locked, but as far as they could see, in good condition and well kept.

"Afternoon! Mr Landers?" A smartly dressed man walked across from the building, striding past Carol and holding his hand out in greeting to Derek. "Phil Manning at your service, nice to meet you. I see you've found the truck." He handed Derek a set of keys.

Derek glanced at Carol who was walking round the truck, studying the bodywork and leaf springs for signs of rust or damage and giving the vehicle a general visual check-over.

Derek shook the man's hand. "Seems clean enough." He nodded towards the truck. "Had her from new I believe."

"Yes, Phil Manning replied. "Always like 'em new and under warranty. We are just about to get a new fleet so these will all go under the hammer pretty soon."

Overhearing, Carol felt slightly envious and wondered if she would ever be able to afford one new truck, never mind a whole fleet.

"Can we take her for a test run?" Derek enquired.

"No problem." Phil Manning replied cheerfully. Then, turning to Carol. "If you would like to wait inside, Darlin' my secretary will make you a coffee while we do the bizz with the truck."

Derek tossed the keys to Carol. "Let me introduce Mrs Landers. Carol will be doing the driving." He announced, straight faced. "She is the buyer, not me!"

Phil Manning looked a little taken aback. "Oh! er….. sorry, just thought, well obviously presumed….." he ran out of steam.

Carol smiled sweetly and held out her hand. "Landers, Carol Landers." She announced, James Bond style. "I own Transcon Haulage."

"Oh, sorry. You must think I'm a bit of a dinosaur, or a male chauvinist pig, .. or both!"

Carol laughed. "You're forgiven! Can we take the truck out for a run then? You can come with us if you wish."

Phil Manning smiled sheepishly. "No thanks. I trust you to bring her back, after all I don't think you will want to leave without that will you?" He inclined his head over towards the Chevy.

"I don't think anything would make Carol leave her Yank behind." said Derek climbing into the passenger seat and settling back as Carol slammed the door and started the engine.

The big truck pulled gracefully out of the yard and swung effortlessly down the forest lined lane. Carol was impressed. "Nice drive." she said, slowing down and experimenting with the unfamiliar gear box.

"These usually do drive nice," Derek replied "I think this will do the job for you, no problems." He twisted round to inspect the inside of the spacious cab as Carol swung round at a big roundabout, the signs heralding the entrance to the motorway, and headed the truck back towards J.S.M Logistics yard.

"Yes I think so too." Carol was impressed by how easily the truck handled. "It's pure luxury after struggling with the old Transcon."

"Hey! Don't tell me you're converted!" Derek laughed.

"I do believe I am." Carol admitted. "Yes, this is the one. You were right, I have to admit. This will certainly do the job and no mistake."

She pressed the brake. The big truck responded immediately, slowing smoothly almost to a crawl as Carol dropped the gears, swung into the yard, and reversed back into position. "Could do with a new trailer to go with it though." she pointed out, switching off the engine. Wonder if this guy has a trailer for sale. Reckon we could do a deal for the whole rig."

"Yes, that's a shrewd move. The Transcon can keep its own trailer then and be handy for a bit of shunting. May as well keep the old girl on for a while, you never know when you will need it. Don't burn your boats too soon." Derek advised.

Phil Manning appeared from the office door, glancing expectantly at Carol as she climbed down from the high cab.

"Here we go." Derek said in a low voice. "Let's get this deal sorted."

Carol smiled. Yes things were getting under way. A new truck was just what Transcon Haulage needed. She just had to find the best way to explain to Tony.

*****

CHAPTER FIVE

"That was really tasty." said Gina, placing her knife and fork neatly on the empty plate and sitting back on the plush padded seat, brushing imaginary crumbs from her fine woollen skirt.

Carol finished her last mouthful and pushed the plate away. "Yes," she agreed settling back comfortably. "The salmon was lovely, we are never disappointed here, they always do a nice meal."

The pub restaurant was busy but not too crowded. The girls had managed to commandeer their favourite table for a midweek treat, close to the big open fire, which crackled comfortingly as they ate, casting a warm glow onto the copper pots and fire irons in the hearth. The rough wooden mantelpiece decked with boughs of greenery, berries and pinecones for a seasonal atmosphere.

Gina drained the last drops from the bottle of house wine into their glasses and raised her glass. "Here's to the new truck." she announced as the glasses chinked together.

"And to the progress of Transcon Haulage." Carol added.

"Speaking of which…." Gina pulled a folder from her soft leather shoulder bag and handed it to Carol. "Some details of the computer courses on offer," she said happily. "Jeff thinks it would make us far more efficient, and I reckon he is not far wrong. Everyone else seems to be using computers now. I intend to take the course then I can show you as we go along."

Carol glanced through the papers, holding back her stubborn curls from falling across her face as she leaned forward to read. "It makes sense of course. Tony says that Marco is installing one at the La Casaccia. He already has one in his office, of course".

"Thought we could go to this place." Gina pulled an advertising leaflet from the pile. "When you buy the computer from them, they send a man round to install it and give you a quick course on how to work it. Just the basics of course, then the complicated stuff can come later!"

Carol took the leaflet. "Reckon we could go and get it sorted out this weekend. We could put it in the small room at my place. The one leading off the hallway that we pinched a slice of for extending the kitchen. I intend to use that as an office of sorts, so sooner than later is best don't you agree? I suppose I will get the hang of it eventually. Can't be THAT hard. Just something else to understand I suppose."

"Hmm! Kids don't seem to have any difficulty." Gina remarked. "But then, they have been brought up with them haven't they? We were taught everything using pencils and paper!"

"Good grief! That makes us sound old!" Carol pulled a face, looking round for the waiter. "Shall we order coffee?"

"Yes please, but make mine an Irish one. I fancy a night-cap."

"Me too. Great not to be driving for a change. I am almost teetotal now what with driving most evenings and teaching in the mornings. Can't afford to lose my licence," said Carol. "Glad I decided to get a taxi tonight though. Makes a nice change."

"You deserve it. We all need a treat once in a while." Gina told her. "Anyway, I am considering getting a car now. I've not needed one for so long, with the boutique being only a short walk from home it didn't seem worth it, but now you live a bit further away I think a car would be handy."

"Not one of Spyder's surely." Carol giggled. The idea of the glamorous Gina in a 'hot rod' was not a picture that easily sprang to mind!

"I was thinking of a nice little BMW myself." Gina replied, ignoring Carol's ribbing. "I have some savings so I could buy it myself, but of course, I will mention it to Jeff first and see what he says. He may want to get me one for Christmas, you know how he likes to buy me things and I don't like to undermine him by showing TOO much independence!"

Carol laughed. Gina was the most independent woman she knew but they both understood how much Jeff liked to buy gifts for his wife.

"Why not? Sounds like a good idea to me. You could nip over to me more often without the bother of cabs."

"Or pestering you to take me shopping or pick me up." Gina answered.

"Don't be silly! It's never a bother, you know that." Carol stated quickly.

"Yes Kiddo, I know you don't mind, but I still think it's only fair, and anyway, I rather fancy the idea of a nice classy little car just for myself."

"Good for you." Carol smiled. "Can't have the partner's wife seen on buses or riding a bike! Make the company look poor!"

Gina laughed. "Hadn't thought of it that way, but now you come to mention it....." she brushed back a lock of golden hair that had fallen over her shoulder. "Wish you hadn't mentioned Christmas." She said flatly, her expression changing. "My mother is on the warpath about the dreaded 'family dinner'!"

"Hmm, you did mention it." Carol gave her friend a sympathetic look.

"Trouble is." Gina continued. "I have to be honest, I really don't LIKE my mother! I love Daddy but I just can't love her! Is that a dreadful thing to say?"

"Not if it's true." Carol answered frankly. "I'm not in a position to discuss feelings for mothers. Mine died when I was four so I only have a very foggy memory of her. I just remember a safe sort of feeling and I think I can vaguely remember her face but not sure if it's through really remembering or looking at old photos."

"Oh, I am sorry!" Gina had forgotten. "I don't mean to sound selfish but Mother and I have never really liked each other I believe. Do you know, I can never remember her hugging me, even when I was tiny. Never kissing me or telling me that she loved me."

"That is sad." Carol could never imagine not hugging Katy or telling her many times how much she was loved. "But there is no need for you to feel guilty. People only get out of a relationship, what they have put in you know. Maybe if your Mum had put in a little more, then you would have had more to give back in return."

"I think you're right. Daddy was always the one I turned to. He always praised me and showed affection, showed how much he loved me all the time and I adore him!"

"Well there you are then! There are no laws that say you HAVE to like your mother. You have to be honest with yourself, and if you don't want to spend Christmas with her then be straightforward and just tell her!" Carol leaned over the table and grasped her friend's hand. "Blame me if you like." she said helpfully. "Tell them I invited you to my new home for the first Christmas or something. It's true anyway. I would love to have you and Jeff there!"

"Thanks Kiddo! I'm not sure Mother will go for that but I will give it some thought."

"Whatever you do," said Carol firmly. "Do what you feel is right for *you* – right for you and Jeff of course."

"Yes, you're right again I know." Gina sighed. "I think I will. Jeff tolerates Mother through a cloud of best scotch along with Daddy!"

Carol laughed. "Well there you are then. And speaking of drink, where is that waiter?"

The waiter was still not in evidence so Carol went in search of his hiding place, returning a couple of moments later.

"Guess who I've just spotted?" she announced, sliding back into her seat.

"Who?"

"Mark Cameron! Over there in the next bar!"

"Really!" Gina craned her neck to try and see. "Who is he with this time. The wife, the secretary or somebody completely different."

"Not the secretary." Carol shook her head. "Never seen the wife so don't know."

"Should we say hello do you think." Gina said devilishly. "Would LOVE to see his face if he IS with the wife."

"Gina! You're terrible." Carol giggled. "And to think, you were so keen on him at one time!"

"My one hiccup in life." Gina pulled a face. "To think I actually considered leaving Jeff for him. Can't believe it now. Not to mention the small fortune I spent on sexy lingerie! Hmmph!"

Carol laughed "These things happen." she said supportively. "None of us lead totally blameless lives. That's what makes us human I suppose, and he did come in very handy when I was buying the house. Helped me make a much lower offer than I thought I would have to." The waiter arrived with their coffees steaming in tall mugs. Gina clasped her hands around her mug relishing the warmth seeping through her fingers. "Yes, that was strange. Fancy him being the solicitor that old man Winters was using to sell the property."

"Fate!" Carol stated simply. "Must have been. Anyway, it all worked out for the best so that's all right then."

"Hmm, true, although it doesn't stop me from feeling like a complete idiot for falling for all the smarm and charm!"

"Well I am in no position to speak." Carol replied. "After all I was the one who lived with the dreadful Nick for a year before seeing him for what he really was. And look where he is now. Serving time for drug running! Not to mention catching him with a girl young enough to be his daughter! What a great judge of character I am!"

"Hello, I thought that was you over at the bar." Mark Cameron had walked across and was standing next to them, an elegant brunette at his side.

"Oh, Mr Cameron, er Mark, I didn't see you." Carol lied, extending her hand and glancing at his companion.

"My wife and I were just over in the corner." Mark explained coolly. "A quiet drink before heading off home." Caroline Cameron eyed the women suspiciously. It was clear she knew her husband's failings.

Carol smiled at her. "Your husband was most helpful when I was buying my property."

"I'm sure!" Caroline Cameron said flintily.

"Good solicitors are so hard to find." Carol went on smoothly. "This is my friend, Gina Meredith. Her husband and I have started up in business together. We have our own haulage company now."

"Really! That's a positive move." Mark sounded impressed. "I trust all is going well?" He fished a card from his breast pocket. "If I can be of any assistance in the future…."

He handed the card to Carol although his eyes were on Gina. "My office is different, I've changed companies. I'm with Barrington-Green and Partners and now specialise in Criminal Law. Not that I expect either of you two ladies to need my services on that score." He smiled disarmingly. "But I do diversify!" Again, his eyes on Gina, who smiled politely but showed no other reaction.

"Thank you." Carol smiled sweetly, slipping the card into her bag. "I hope we won't be needing that sort of help but there may be others matters that arise in the future that may require the services of a solicitor."

"Every business needs a good solicitor at times." Mark replied, his charming manner not missing a beat. "It was nice to see you again." He took his wife's elbow and turned to leave. The women nodded politely to each other.

"Have a safe journey home." said Gina graciously, speaking for the first time.

"Thank you." Mark guided his wife from the table and headed for the exit. The girls sat in silence until the Camerons had swept elegantly through the pub doors.

"Well! What about that then." Carol looked at Gina as both women relaxed into their seats. "How do you feel?"

"Fine! Nothing at all. It's the wife I feel sorry for. Did you see the look on her face. She must know what he's like. Anything in knickers is up for grabs as far as he's concerned and if her expression is anything to go by she knows it only too well."

"Don't put yourself down." Carol replied. "I'm sure he only goes for upper class ladies! The wife looked straight out of the pages of Vogue magazine."

"Don't forget the secretary." Gina reminded.

"Well, okay then," Carol conceded. "With one or two exceptions maybe!"

"Glad I saw him though." Gina went on. "Prove to myself that I felt nothing."

"That's good." Carol replied warmly. She had seen the turmoil that her friend had gone through during her brief affair with the smooth talking solicitor. "You're over him and I'm over Nick. We have both been through the wringer and come out all the better for it, stronger too!"

Gina raised her Irish coffee. "To us!" she announced. "What a pair we are!"

"But a pair of winners just the same!" Carol clinked her glass onto Gina's. "I have Tony and you have Jeff. The business is going great guns and all is well with the world."

"United we stand!" Gina laughed.

"Absolutely! Isn't it wonderful to feel on top of the situation?"

"Wonderful!" Gina agreed fervently.

They were both strong women who had got their lives together. Nothing could hold any fears for either of them any more.

*****

The throb of engines vibrated through the bowels of the boat as Jeff sat in the cab of the 'Silver Lady' waiting for the ferry to dock. He and Tony had breakfasted early after a nights sleep in the tiny cramped cabin, tucked away in the bowels of the ship, ignoring the temptation to join the holiday people enjoying the hospitality of the small ferry.

He glanced into his wing mirror to see Tony, sitting in the cab of the Transcon parked directly behind him. The younger man eager to venture out on this new journey, expanding both his families own business and pushing Transcon Haulage forward towards expansion.

The smell of diesel was hanging in the air. Although the rules stated that no engines should be started before the boat had docked and the ferry doors were opened, there was always one who could not wait and insisted on starting the engine in the confines of the lorry deck and filling the place with fumes.

There was a slight bump as the ferry touched the side of the docks and was hauled into place. The clatter of doors opening and the ramp being lowered followed almost at once and daylight flooded in to the gloom of the lorry deck.

Jeff turned the key and the 'Silver Lady' leapt into life. All the other drivers did the same almost simultaneously and the noise of a hundred engines filled the deck.

One by one the trucks moved forward, following the instructions of the landing crew and making their way across the iron ramp and lurching onto land.

Jeff and Tony, in tight convoy, followed the stream of trucks across the ramp and into the lanes, weaving their way through the busy Durres harbour and through to the customs check point.

Harbour check points had always been notorious hold up areas in the past but what with the changing laws some were now only a formality. Jeff was fervently hoping that this would be the case this morning and waved his passport at the control point, hoping to drive straight through. Not so. An expressionless Albanian official stepped in front of him holding his hand out and signalling Jeff to park up in the narrow slip road alongside the control hut.

"Passaporte! Papers!" The uniformed guard held out his hand. Jeff passed him the running sheets for the truck and handed his passport out of the cab window as Tony drove the Transcon past and slowed to pull into the side, a little further along, to wait for Jeff.

The guard scrutinised every inch of paperwork with great care then signalled Jeff to get out and follow him. "Cargo!" The guard demanded, pointing at the trailer. Jeff sighed and started to untie the clips that held the heavy curtain in place across the side of the trailer, heaving it open and sliding it halfway along the length of the trailer, exposing the load.

The guard peered inside then climbed up and studied the load of palettes, solid with drums of olive oil. Jeff prayed that the guard would not want to exercise his authority and puncture the drums to check the contents.

Luckily the guard seemed satisfied and climbed down, then walked carefully around the truck, scrutinising it for any hidden nooks and crannies that may hold contraband goods.

Satisfied, he abruptly waved Jeff away. "Forward!" he ordered, his face expressionless as he looked Jeff in the eye. "You go!" Jeff nodded politely and drove the Volvo away from the customs point and over to the siding where Tony was parked.

"You must have a guilty face!" Tony's grey eyes twinkled with mirth as he wound down the Transcon window. "They just waved me right through!"

"Story of my life." Jeff grumbled, hauling the curtain back into place and painstakingly refastening the clips, making sure they were tight and safe. "There could be twenty trucks all smuggling gold bullion that would drive straight through, but me!....." he waved his arm expansively, "I would be the one they stop and find twenty fags over the top and fine me!"

Tony laughed. "Well they seemed happy enough with you this time." he remarked. "As soon as you're done here we'll get off and make some headway. It's only about an hour's drive across Albania to the border at Macedonia. We can stop there for a break then about four hours driving, straight on into Bulgaria after that. No problems that I can see. If the map is to believed, there should be another good rest stop just after the Bulgarian border. We can check the maps there for the delivery place."

"Right," said Jeff, snapping the last fastening into place and stepping back to check all was well. "Let's crack on then." He jumped back into the truck and swung back onto the narrow lane leading from the docks. He was on strange ground here and hoped that the maps were accurate. He and Tony had spent hours planning the route, but a route was only as good as the map you were going by, as Jeff well knew from experience, so was determined to keep alert for discrepancies in the journey.

Tony kept tight to Jeff's tail lights. He was new to this part of the world so set his trust completely in the older man's experience and was happy to follow Jeff's lead.

Although Jeff had never ventured to this part of the world, experience had taught him confidence. He had studied the map carefully and knew pretty much where he was going.

He swung the big truck confidently through the bustling town of Durres. The ruins of the Roman amphitheatre rising majestically into view, high on the hillside, sitting proudly aloof above the more modern buildings. Jeff had read a little about the country and was always interested in seeing what was around him. He remembered that they would bypass the historic town of Tirane, famous for its fifteenth century national hero, Iskander who's statue stood in Skendenberg Square, named in his honour.

Jeff would have loved to have had the time to park up and explore the city and the surrounding villages but knew this was not an option. This job was vital to Transcon Haulage and if the customers were satisfied, who knows how many trips they would be asked to make. He glanced in his mirrors to make sure Tony was still close behind.

He could see direction signs ahead and wanted the younger man safely tucked into his tail lights.

Following in Jeff's wake, the old Transcon coughed a little then pulled bravely as the two trucks hauled out of the town and onto the 'A' road heading towards their destination. Once on the straight long road, Tony felt they would have little trouble in keeping together on the short run across Albania and into Macedonia. The maps were a little vague but Jeff had said he felt sure they would find a good road taking them to the borders of Bulgaria. Tony's main worry was finding their way across the centre of Sofia. All cities were clearly signposted so even the worst navigator could find their way to the city itself. Finding the actual small street or factory was in itself a major task.

His mind wandered to Carol and the problem of gently explaining to her that another truck would indeed be a good investment. He was staring ahead, watching the Silver Lady accelerating into the wide carriageway and trying to find enough power to catch up. He vaguely wondered if another Volvo Globetrotter would be a good purchase. There were a lot of units on the road still running well despite being a good few years old, but a well looked after unit would certainly be good enough to last a few years and not cost the earth either. He decided to ask Jeff to allow him to drive the Silver Lady for a little way to see how he felt about the Volvo. It may be best to try one before advising Carol that it would be a good buy, he considered. Yes, he would do that. When they stopped for a break he would ask Jeff if he could have a few miles in the Silver Lady. If Jeff could be persuaded to part with his precious truck for a few hours that is!

******

Watery sunshine was trying its best to break through the pale grey sky as Carol drove the Chevy out of the driving school yard. According to the weatherman there was some unseasonably warm weather on the way, although Carol had seen little sign of it up until now.

Still, the faint golden glow lifted Carol's spirits and she hummed along to the radio as she drove through the town and turned into the quiet forest lane leading to her home. She had been pleased at the early finish. That would give her a whole afternoon to help Spyder and catch up with some washing and more unpacking hopefully.

She would collect the new Globetrotter tomorrow. She had paid with bankers draft so there would be no hold up with the transaction. Carol had felt dubious at first, buying a new truck and sinking more money into Transcon Haulage but now she felt elated. Even a certain kind of freedom, making a decision like that all by herself and not having to worry about the opinion of anyone else or the disapproval, more to the point. She did wonder if Tony would be pleased about it but pushed any negative thought immediately out of her mind. She was happy and confident and would not allow anything to dampen her spirits.

She steered the big car round a sharp curve and accelerated along the winding lane towards her house. She loved the sound of the big block V8 engine as it pulled effortlessly round the bends and swayed gently over the slight bumps in the lane, finally pulling strongly up the steep incline towards the yard gates. Carol pulled into the yard and parked next to Spyder's loudly flamed pick up truck. The day had gone well but she was always glad to get home, make herself a welcome cup of tea and relax.

Bruno, ever eager and very much his old exuberant self, bounded to meet her as she opened the door, leaping over a bulging backpack thrown unceremoniously in the middle of the hallway.

Katy had arrived!

Carol could hear voices, drifting from the kitchen. Katy had always made friends easily and was probably chatting to Spyder as if she had known him for years.

"Hello!" Carol called, divesting herself of her thickly padded coat and walking towards the kitchen.

"Mum! Hi!" Katy shot through the kitchen door and flung her arms around her mother, hugging her tight. "Oh, it's good to see you!" Katy's dark eyes shone with pleasure, almost matching her glossy dark chestnut hair, well cut into a short bob, framing her face.

"It's good to see you too." Carol replied, holding Katy at arms length so as to get a good look at her vivacious daughter, casually dressed in cream combat trousers and khaki shirt. "A surprise as usual!"

"Oh, Mum, you know me. Last minute decision and all that. I got a lift from some of the guys who were off down to Dover for a booze run to France. They dropped me off in the town on the way."

"Well I'm certainly glad they did. It's lovely to have you home."

"Shall I put the kettle on?" Spyder stuck his head round the kitchen door. His dark hair covered in dust. "I know I could do with one. All this chattering makes me thirsty!"

"Yes, of course." Carol slipped her arm around Katy's shoulder as they walked together back into the kitchen. "You know I never say no to a cup of tea. I take it you two are old buddies by now."

"Of course we are." Katy laughed. "Hey, you struck lucky finding this one Mum. He has worked miracles on the old place already, and he tells me he has only been here a week."

"Seems like longer." Carol answered. "I feel like I have known him forever."

"Is that a compliment?" Spyder queried, plopping tea bags into mugs.

"Sure is!" Carol replied. "You're pretty much part of the family already."

Spyder beamed happily and reached into the fridge for the milk. "I certainly know my way round the kitchen and what time Bruno has his tablets anyway." he remarked.

Katy dropped to her knees to cuddle Bruno. "He seems okay to me, don't you boy?" she observed. "Let's hope it's nothing that will re occur. You probably caught it in time, which is just as well as I have GREAT news and don't want anything to spoil it!"

"What's this then?" Carol reached three mugs from the cupboard and passed them to Spyder.

"I've passed my driving test!"

"Katy! Congratulations, Darling, well done! I didn't even know you were learning to drive!"

"Didn't want to tell you." Katy laughed. "You would have inundated me with advice and warnings so I just did it on the quiet."

Before Carol could reply Bruno shot to his feet and woofed at the sound of the doorbell.

"That may be Gill." said Katy following Bruno towards the front door. "I saw her as I was walking to the bus stop and said she should pop round with the kids straight from play-school. I haven't seen them for so long and I knew you wouldn't mind Mum!"

"Better make sure there's plenty of water in that kettle!" Carol laughed, still reeling from Katy's surprise news. All plans for the afternoon now set aside as the sound of voices and children's chatter approached the kitchen.

"Well, hello stranger!" Carol gave Gill a hug then bent to cuddle the two small boys, eagerly looking around them, hoping for biscuits. Carol produced a packet of chocolate chip cookies and tipped them onto a large plate for the boys to help themselves.

"You have certainly got on with this place, girl." Gill remarked, peering around to admire the improvements.

"I said to Frank the other day, maybe we should think about getting a bigger place. Something with a garden for the boys to play in. Frank Junior loves his football but kicking a ball about on the balcony isn't really on is it?"

"Absolutely!" Carol agreed, a little surprised that Gill wanted to move. Maybe she had underestimated her friend's private dreams.

Gill had been a good neighbour and friend but had always seemed perfectly happy to stay in the small flat above the Pizza Restaurant in the high street and never expressed any wish to Carol to move up in the world. Carol felt slightly guilty for making the presumption that Gill had no hopes and dreams of a better life and a better home. "You really need a garden for children to play in." Carol went on encouragingly. "Katy was never indoors when she was little."

"Mum used to lock me out!" Katy announced wickedly, aiming a wink at Gill.

"Oh! Yes! Absolutely! Of course I did." Carol retorted, pulling a face at her. "On a regular basis rain or shine but ESPECIALLY in the snow!"

Katy laughed. "I was such an abused and underprivileged child!"

Carol stuck out her tongue. "Well, if you were abused and underprivileged, then it has certainly done you no harm. Perhaps more parents should try it, little Miss I-can-drive-a-car-now!"

Spyder was busy pouring out mugs of tea and listening with amusement at the good-natured banter between his new found employer and her daughter.

"Can we play in the garden Auntie Carol?" Little David, almost four years old, leaned hopefully on the back door. Bruno backed him up with an eager expression, tongue lolling ears pricked towards the closed door.

"It's a bit chilly out there." Carol was doubtful. "It's starting to get dark and it might rain."

"Oh they'll be fine!" Gill had no such worries about her offspring. "Wrapped up well they are, and a drop of water never hurt anyone!"

"Tell that to the passengers of the Titanic!" Spyder remarked wryly as he opened the door and stood back as Bruno and the two children shot through into the garden wilderness.

Katy giggled. "Oh that was wicked!" she said slipping on her thick fleece jacket. "I'll go out with them anyway. We can play hide and seek, wear them out before bedtime."

Gill gratefully gave her the thumbs up sign as Katy followed the excited boys outside and closed the door. "Phew! Peace at last." she sighed, settling down on one of the kitchen chairs and helping herself to a biscuit. "Katy certainly seems to be happy with her life. How is university going?"

"Oh, she loves it." Carol replied. "Leeds, apparently, is 'the' place to be for students according to Katy. Don't ask me when she finds time to study, she always seems to be out on some activity or other, or off for a night on the town! She does have to get some study done though."

"That's why she's here, apparently." Spyder remarked, tidying his tools into a large canvas bag. "Wants to get some revision time in peace. She reckons she will stay a week or ten days and break the back of what she needs to get done."

Spyder appeared to be one step ahead of Carol with knowledge of Katy's plans.

"Good luck to her." Gill was delighted that Katy was happy. "She was telling me about the work she is training for, caring for disadvantaged kids or something. That's worthwhile."

"She has always had a rapport with the little ones." Carol replied warmly. Her pride in her daughter was apparent. "Mind you, she seems to get on with everyone, adults and children alike."

"Bless her! By the way, I saw Gina on my way here." Gill informed, tucking into biscuits, dunking happily. "Told her Katy was here and that I was coming over. She said she would be here too, straight from work." The urban grapevine was working well.

"Is it always open house?" Spyder enquired, squeezing in next to Gill's rather tubby frame and helping himself to a biscuit.

"Usually," Carol replied fishing around in the cupboard and bringing out a second pack of biscuits. "Every place I have lived has been the same, but I like to make people welcome, make them feel at home."

"She does that." Gill informed Spyder. "Nicest neighbour I've had in years. Not like this new one!" She added with a grimace.

"Oh really." Carol was naturally curious about who had moved in to the flat that had been her home for over a year. "I heard someone had moved in to my old place but no idea who they are."

"Single mother I think." Gill raised her eyes and dunked another biscuit. "Seen a chap, or maybe more than one, come and go but nobody permanent. One kiddie, little girl about two years old, always scruffy. I think..." Gill lowered her voice conspiratorially. "I think she sleeps most of the day and leaves the poor little mite to fend for itself. Always up playing music until the early hours though. Definitely on State handouts!" She finished with a snort.

Carol shook her head. She herself had been dependent for a short time on state handouts after her husband had walked out when Katy was a baby, leaving her to manage alone. But Carol was not the type to let fate kick her down and keep her there. She had got a job and a childminder and made life for herself and Katy as good as she possibly could. After being a single mother herself for so long, she had little patience with others who presumed life owed them a living.

The back door flew open. "Bruno's found rats!" David's little face was flushed with excitement. "Hundreds of 'em!" He held his arms wide to quantify his statement.

"Rats! Where?" Carol set down her cup and followed the small boy into the gathering gloom of the garden.

"What's this about rats?" She enquired to Katy who was standing with Frank Junior peering through a crack in the old 'privy' door. Bruno sniffing with great interest, pushing his nose into a broken corner of the tightly jammed door.

"Not sure." Katy replied. "Bruno just won't leave this spot alone and when we came over to find out what was so interesting we heard a scuffle and saw something shoot out and disappear into the bushes."

"Yes he's been taking great interest in this for some time." Carol remarked. "Was it a rat then?"

"Dunno, could have been anything in this light. The boys just presumed it to be rats. We had better have a look though, don't you think? You don't want them nibbling their way into the house!"

"Hells Bells! Whatever next." Carol tugged at the partly rotten door which had obviously not been opened in years.

"Hang on, I've got a torch." Spyder arrived, wielding a large flashlight as Carol managed, at last to yank the door part way open.

Gill, still in the safety of the house, slammed the kitchen door shut behind him. She preferred to watch the proceedings through the kitchen window. No rat was going to run up her skirts!

Spyder peered inside. "I can't see anything can you?" Carol took the torch from Spyder and squeezed herself a little closer inside the door. Old paint tins and rags were heaped in one corner along with a broken bucket and various other bits of discarded items. Spyder managed to pull the door wider.

A sound made Carol look more closely at the pile of rags tucked behind the old broken toilet. Three pairs of eyes blinked back at her. "Oh good grief! It's not rats it's cats! Well kittens to be precise." She backed out of the tiny building to announce her find. Bruno immediately pushed his way in to investigate. The children tried to follow. "Hey keep out you lot!" Carol ordered. "They are probably frightened to death and we don't want their mother scaring off for good. Bruno! Leave them! Come out of there!" Bruno slapped his tongue across the hapless trio of kittens then grudgingly obeyed. "Come on now, everyone inside. Give the mother a chance to come back."

Everybody trooped back into the kitchen. "Auntie Carol's got kitties." Announced Frank Junior. Gill still looked uneasy.

"It's not rats." Carol reassured her, handing the torch back to Spyder. "Some stray cat has had kittens in the old outside loo. That's what has been interesting Bruno this last week or two." She opened a cupboard and peered inside. "Poor thing must be starving, I'm just wondering what we can put down for her."

"I want a kitty! Can we have one?" David looked pleadingly at his mother.

"No, Darlin' we can't have cats in a flat. Hardly enough room there for us lot never mind anything else!" Gill replied firmly, feeling greatly relieved that no rats were in evidence.

David looked crestfallen. Katy bent immediately to the small boy and cupped his face in her hands. "Never mind sweetie. Why not ask Auntie Carol if you can keep a kitten here and come and see it when you want to." She glanced up at Carol as she spoke.

Carol raised her eyes to the ceiling. "Oh why not! I can't say I am short of room here. What's another mouth to feed anyway!" David's face broke into a smile as Carol opened a small tin of salmon and tipped it in to a dish. Oily fish was good for nursing mothers. She poured milk into another dish. "Here, you and Katy take this outside and place it inside the door so that mother cat can find it when she comes back."

"Can I have a dog and keep him here?" Frank junior decided not to be left out.

"You can share Bruno!" Carol and Gill chorused together. Katy giggled and led the way outside with David, carefully carrying the dish of food following behind.

"That girl's a natural with kids." Gill announced. "She would make a great teacher or nanny or something."

"Well, I think teaching is the way she will go." Carol replied, peering through the kitchen window to watch as Katy showed the small boy how to place the dish carefully under the gap in the broken door. "But maybe Social Services in one of the child sectors. Whatever she feels is right at the time I suppose. As long as she is happy."

Carol glanced at her watch. "Gina will just be leaving the boutique I think. I could call her and ask her to pick up a tin of cat food on her way here."

"It's okay, I'll bring some in tomorrow." Spyder put in. "Our cat's a bit fussy and there's always a tin or two knocking about that she won't touch."

"Thanks Spyder that's a help."

"Well I'll be getting off home now." Spyder announced, reaching for his jacket off the back of the kitchen chair. "Can I give you and the boys a lift Gill? I have to pass the high road on the way."

"Ooh! Lovely. Better than hanging about waiting for buses!" Gill drained her mug of tea and got to her feet, calling the boys to hurry and get ready to leave.

Carol smiled gratefully at Spyder. As much as she loved to see Gill and the boys she wanted a little peace and to spend time with Katy. Gina was expected soon but that was different.

*****

CHAPTER SIX

A fine mist of snow was falling gently, clouding the late evening sky with a ghostly light as Jeff pulled the 'Silver Lady' into the crowded truck stop, the only one they had seen in hours of driving along miles of barely maintained roads and tiny villages. The wheels of the 'Silver Lady' crunching on the snow as they pulled in amongst the motley throng of vehicles.

Tony had kept up well, despite the narrow roads which had been little more than dirt tracks in places. The failing light giving them more problems as they hauled the two big trucks through heavily wooded areas and tiny huddled villages, keeping a constant watch for any pinprick of lantern light that may be hung on the back of a horse drawn cart.

Tony pulled the Transcon in behind Jeff as the two trucks slowed to a crawl, looking for a parking space.

There seemed to be no firm arrangement between cars and trucks in the busy service stop. It looked like every man for himself as cars darted between huge trailers and parked in a space big enough to take either the 'Silver Lady' or the Transcon. Jeff saw a large battered truck ease out of a bay over at the back of the parking area and headed towards it with almost indecent haste. He hauled the big Volvo into an arc, clicked the gearstick into reverse and swung into the space almost as the departing truck vacated the spot. Tony trailed after him in the hope of another parking area presenting itself.

An untidy pick-up truck with two goats tethered in the open back was in the bay next to Jeff. The driver, a swarthy weather-beaten man of indiscernible age, and a young lad that appeared to be his son, sitting happily in their seats eating rough bread and chunks of cheese.

Jeff climbed down from the 'Silver Lady' and leaned into the cab, pointing towards the Transcon. "You let my friend park?" he asked with a gesture and held out a packet of English cigarettes.

The older man looked over his shoulder at the Transcon then looked back at Jeff and the proffered packet of cigarettes. He shrugged his shoulders. "OK." The universal acknowledgement muttered through a mouthful of food, large crumbs of bread falling from his mouth as he spoke and clinging to the ragged beard around his chin. Without uttering another word he snatched the packet from Jeff's hand and turned the ignition key. The pick-up lurched backwards, the hapless goats almost losing their footing as the driver, still pushing food into his mouth, steered the vehicle roughly out of the bay and across the front of another parked truck where he nonchalantly switched off the engine and continued his meal.

Jeff immediately leapt into the vacated spot and stood his ground as Tony hauled forward, swinging the trailer into position to reverse into the narrow bay next to the 'Silver Lady', honking of horns ignored as smaller vehicles spotted the space and tried to encroach.

"Well done lad!" Jeff clapped Tony on the shoulder as the younger man dropped down from the cab. "That was a tight one but you got in there okay."

"Wasn't sure it would fit at first." Tony admitted, his eyes sparkling with the achievement. "But there was no other choice so in she went!"

Jeff laughed. "Surprising what you can do if you have to! We'll get our break here and something to eat and make sure we fill the tanks before we leave. I was getting worried that there was nowhere in this bloody country that sold diesel! No chance we will make it over the border tonight though, even make it TO the border in fact. Our timings have certainly gone out of the window. We're running out of driving time, it's dark and we're not sure exactly where we are just now."

"Can't believe we made such a huge mistake with the maps!" Tony observed. "I didn't think for one moment that there would be no autoroute through Macedonia! Surely there must be one somewhere!"

It had been a hard drive on the potholed roads across country. The snow had been falling heavily in some parts and Jeff had hauled to a stop in what was the only place to pull in at the side of the road and fitted snow chains on his wheels.

The Transcon, however, carried no such refinements so Tony had to keep tight behind Jeff, steering his wheels into the tracks left by the 'Silver Lady' and trusting in fate that the hills got no steeper than they could handle.

The mountain ranges at times had looked worryingly close, rising threateningly on both sides as both men had silently prayed that the route they were taking did not lead them directly into the towering ranges. This would have been an impossible route to try and negotiate, with snow on the ground and still falling.

Jeff did not want to worry the young and eager Tony but had given a sigh of relief when they had come within sight of the truck stop and realised that they did not, thank goodness, have to consider an alternative route to avoid the mountain ranges.

"Well, there may well be an autoroute but certainly not one going the way we want!" Jeff stretched his arms above his head to ease the stiffness in his shoulders. "But I blame myself for that one. That's one thing I should know better about. It's not always a good idea to draw a straight line through a map and head that way. Doesn't always work."

Jeff could have kicked himself. He SHOULD have known better. His years of driving experience should have taught him that at least. "In hindsight it would have been better, and probably quicker, to have gone further down Italy to Brindisi and got a boat across into Greece, then cut back up that way to Bulgaria, or, thinking about it now, the slightly longer way via Trieste, then heading down."

"We will have to plan more carefully next time." Tony agreed. "Make sure we don't get carried away with a panic quick run and do our own checking out. Marco has no idea about these roads so we should not really have listened to his idea of a route. We'll not make the same mistake again! It's put us back a day. I doubt we will be able to get much further now."

Jeff nodded. Tony was right. The run they had planned for a few hours had taken the whole day, winding the big trucks along the badly maintained roads, the snow falling steadily and no direction signs to suggest that they were actually going the right way.

"We live and learn." Jeff was always philosophical about life's twists and turns. He had learned long ago that it was no use grumbling about what had already taken place. No amount of complaining would turn the clock back so Jeff always believed in forgetting what had gone before and could not be altered and making sure the next step was better prepared. "Right now the most important thing is getting something to eat! My stomach thinks my throat is cut!"

Both men were hungry and weary after the long drive and trudged their way through the maze of vehicles, slipping and sliding in the slush under their feet, towards the welcome sight of the grubby-looking café area across the other side.

"Don't know what the food will be like here," Jeff remarked as they stepped inside, "but frankly I don't care, I could eat a horse!"

"Probably will have to." Tony quipped. "It's most likely to be on the menu!"

At least it was warm inside the steamy eating area. They found a place to sit in the corner, catching the eye of the waiter as he nipped skilfully between the crowded tables and ordered the 'meal of the day', which appeared to be a big dish of thick stew with cobs of rough bread to mop up the juice.

"That should do us okay." said Jeff, craning his neck to see if he could see the 'Silver Lady' across the sea of vehicles. "Don't like not being within sight of the trucks though." he added. "You never know what goes on in these places."

But both trucks were well out of sight, tucked away at the back of the truckstop. Even if they had been closer the gathering darkness and the falling snow would have shielded them from view.

The wiry young waiter appeared, carrying a large two handled metal pot with a basket of bread balanced precariously on the top. He plonked the steaming pot down in the middle of the table, lifted the bread basket from the top and deftly flicked bowls in front of Tony and Jeff. He produced a ladle from his apron pocket, dropping it into the pot and throwing two spoons onto the table. He nodded abruptly and left the men to their meal.

"Smells good!" Tony remarked breaking off a chunk of bread and dipping it into the stew.

"Too hungry to care what it smells like." Jeff replied taking charge of the ladle and spooning the stew from the pot, heaping it into the bowls and tearing off bread from the rough brown loaf.

"I was wondering." Tony's ice-grey eyes twinkled at he looked towards Jeff. "I have been driving along considering another truck, possibly another Volvo, and was wondering if you wouldn't mind me having a short drive in the 'Silver Lady' to see how she handles."

He didn't actually hold out much hope of the older man agreeing to part with his beloved truck even for a few hundred kilometres, but thought he would ask anyway.

Jeff broke off another chunk of bread and dropped it into his stew, stirring it round with his spoon. "I was wondering when you were going to ask me that!" he smiled, spooning a juicy piece of meat and bread into his mouth and chewing carefully.

"Almost afraid to ask!" said Tony. "I know how attached you are to her."

"Well sure I am, but if you're thinking of getting Carol to buy another truck you need to know which one you will feel comfortable with lad. Reckon you can take her for spin when we get out of here. We can swap over and you can take my 'Silver Lady' to the border. I reckon it will be a good few hours drive from here so that will give you an idea of whether you like the feel of a Volvo or not. Though I personally, can't think what there is NOT to like about them."

"Hell! Thanks Jeff!" Tony was delighted, and more than a little amazed. "I will drive her with great care, don't you worry!"

"I trust you." Jeff laughed.

"When should we get started?" Tony asked.

"First thing in the morning, crack of daylight. We're agreed we can't get any further tonight." Jeff replied through a mouthful of food. "We are both knackered and out of driving time. Not to mention the fact that we are not sure exactly where we are and it's snowing like hell!"

Tony stretched back in his seat. "Yes, you're right. We'll get a good nights sleep and head off in daylight. Makes more sense. We'll have the whole day to get tipped and loaded up then."

Jeff pulled out his mobile phone and checked for a signal. "No signal," He remarked. He hadn't really expected to get one out in the middle of nowhere with snow falling all around. "Shall we try and find a telephone and tell Carol and Gina what's happened? They must have one here."

Jeff always wanted to speak to Gina. "I'll go and find out and I'm sure we can find someone here who can tell us how far to the border then we can turn in."

He was eager to get back to the trucks. He never felt a hundred per cent easy on strange ground and wanted to get back to the 'Silver Lady', lock himself into the comfortable cab and settle down for the night. Tomorrow was going to be a busy day.

*****

"There must be something about us and rats!" Gina giggled, holding her wine glass towards Katy for a refill.

"What?" Katy tipped the last of the wine into Gina's glass.

The three had thrown the dust covers from the comfortable furniture in the newly heated living room and had feasted on pizza and jacket potatoes, delivered to the door by a young man on a small motorbike displaying 'L' plates.

"Well, remember when we were broken down on the road to San Guistino? We thought there was a rat in the bushes and it turned out to be a dog, a pregnant one at that." Gina reminded her.

"Oh, yes of course." Katy pulled another bottle of wine from one of the many packing cases. "And this time it's kittens! No rats so far though." she laughed. "Never mind, third time lucky."

"Oh, thank you madam!" Carol walked in from the kitchen. "That's a comforting thought! Rats don't particularly bother me but I don't want them moving in here."

"Could you see the mother cat?" Gina enquired.

"No, it's far too dark now." Carol plonked down onto her chair, picking up her wine glass. "I will have a quick look in the morning but they have been managing okay so far so I am sure she will do fine now she has a supply of food. I wouldn't worry, animals are more resilient than people most of the time."

"Can't help worrying about the poor little things though." Katy added, sitting on the rug next to Bruno and leaning her back against the sofa. "Trust Bruno to search them out." She ruffled the big Alsatian's ears as she spoke. "He's so clever aren't you boy!" Bruno wallowed happily in the fuss he was receiving. He adored his Katy and never left her side on her visits home from university.

"How long will we have the pleasure of your company this time Katy?" Gina queried.

"Oh, dunno really. About a week or possibly a few days more," Katy replied. "I have SO much revising to do I just don't seem to be able to settle to it back at my place, always somebody coming or going or making some sort of racket. That's the drawback with shared houses." She turned to flash an infectious smile at her mother. "I needed to get some peace and get it all finished so here I am." She lifted her arms to dramatise the statement. "I could have gone to Andy and Anna's, of course, but I thought I really should come and see my dear old Mum!"

Carol pulled a face at her daughter. "Peace and quiet she says. With all this work going on it's like a war zone at times."

"Oh, you know what I mean! It's not like a house full of people asking questions and borrowing stuff and so on. " Katy pulled her fleece top over her head and tossed it onto the chair behind her. "Phew, this heating certainly works, Mum!" she noted, feeling more comfortable in her thin cotton T-shirt.

"Wonder how far Jeff and Tony have managed to get." Carol remarked glancing at her watch. If Jeff's timings had been correct, they should be across the border and into Bulgaria by now.

"They will telephone as soon as something interesting happens." Gina replied casually, kicking off her cream ankle boots and tucking her legs underneath her as she snuggled into the comfortable armchair.

"Do you think you will be able to expand more now Mum?" Katy enquired, still fondling Bruno who was loving every minute of it. "Get another truck, do you think, and even do some of the driving yourself? After all, that was the plan to begin with wasn't it?"

"Well don't forget the original plan was for me to get a job and drive for someone else actually." Carol reminded her. "I had never dreamed in a million years I would be running my own company."

"With Jeff's help of course." Katy added.

"I doubt that Jeff would have taken the plunge had Carol not dragged him into it though." Gina put in thoughtfully. "He always wanted to be his own boss but caution always got the better of him. It was Carol's enthusiasm that spurred him into it in the end."

"Not to mention the fact that Mum just went ahead and bought the haulage yard which just happened to include Jeff's truck!" said Katy.

Gina laughed. "That just MAY have been a decider!"

"And I do have some interesting news," Carol continued. "Tomorrow I will be picking up my second truck. Another Volvo Globetrotter that will go very nicely with Jeff's 'Silver Lady'. Just hope Tony likes it as much as I do."

"He will, don't you worry." Gina put in. "You never know, he may be relieved to get a truck that doesn't break down every five minutes."

"Wow! Well done Mum, but tell me, exactly how do things work with Tony." Katy asked. "Yes I KNOW you are madly in love with the guy, but how does it work, him driving your truck but also being part of his own family's' business?"

"Madly in love?" Carol's emerald green eyes flashed, she could feel her face flushing. "Honestly, Katy, I'm not sixteen you know!"

"That's debatable!" Katy replied wickedly.

Carol ignored the remark. "It works quite well actually. As you know we originally got the contract to run loads of olives and oil from San Guistino to England. Good for Tony's family and certainly good for us. But, of course, Marco is a very astute businessman and can organise other deliveries for us too. He, of course, will get an agents cut from any deals he gets us."

"Sounds sensible." Katy was trying to keep up.

"Tony, as you know, hated the business side of things and far preferred to be hands on with the growing and delivering side of it all. We decided that he could use my truck, not exactly as my employee, but sort of part of the firm. I still get a good rate for the job but Tony also gets a wage out of it. It works well, as it leaves me free to really get the business up and running this end and sort out this derelict barn of a house. It leaves me free as well to earn money myself at the driving school. Actually I am no worse off financially by staying here and losing some money to Tony as I make it up with my own job."

"Not to mention the fact that Tony drives over to England nearly every week and so can spend time with you!" Katy laughed. "Very astute move Mum!"

"Makes sense business wise too though." Gina put in. "We all talked it over and it seemed the best way to go to start with, although if we get really busy and into supertax status……" she raised her eyes to the ceiling, "things would, of course, have to take a rethink."

"Well before you go off ordering fleets of new trucks…." Katy got to her feet and started collecting the empty pizza cartons. "…maybe we should make some plans about Christmas. It's not that far away now you know."

"What do you fancy doing for Christmas?" Carol asked. "I would love to have you here, of course, but if you prefer to spend it in Derbyshire with Andy and Anna, or go away with friends, you know I won't mind." Carol dearly hoped Katy would want to come to her for Christmas but had always left her daughter free to make her own decisions.

"Oooh! Here *definitely*!" Katy said with enthusiasm, disappearing into the kitchen with the cartons, Bruno at her heels. "Wouldn't miss your first Christmas in your new house for the world." Her disembodied voice echoed through the half empty rooms. "The tree will look wonderful in that huge front room and we can hang lanterns in the garden like we used to in the old place." She re-appeared into the living room with Bruno still dogging her steps. "Will you and Jeff be here too?" she asked Gina.

Gina sighed. "Don't know for sure Sweetheart, but I do know we both would LOVE to be here. A real celebration, but we will just have to see a little closer to the time."

Before Katy could question Gina further Carol cut in. "Why not stay the night Gina?" she asked. "We can open another bottle of wine and play silly board games."

"Oh what fun!" Gina took no persuading. "It's years since I played board games. It will be our own private party."

Carol felt content as she went in search of the packing case which may hold a Scrabble set, or Monopoly. Who could ask for more? She had a wonderful daughter, a true friend, a handsome Latin lover and an up and coming business. She was walking on air.

*****

Carol threw some more slices of bread into the toaster and reached the butter from the fridge. "Tuck in," she told Gina. "There is plenty more where that came from."

Rain was drizzling down miserably, running down the kitchen window as the two friends sat at the table, drinking mugs of steaming tea and buttering toast.

"Katy's still fast asleep." Gina remarked, wrapped in Carol's white towelling bath robe, her hair piled loosely on top of her head, still managing an air of elegance despite a late night and early morning.

"Poor kid needs a good lie in." Carol joined Gina at the table and helped herself to a round of toast. "She always uses so much energy, living life to the full, she needs to recharge her batteries from time to time."

"Who needs to recharge batteries?" Katy appeared in the doorway, hair tousled over the collar of her blue cotton pyjamas, a grinning cartoon dog printed on the front, her fluffy dressing gown flung casually over the top.

"Oh! You're awake! We tried to be quiet so you could sleep in Honey, did we disturb you?" Gina was concerned.

"No, don't worry. I've been awake for ages. Just waited till I heard you two getting the toast on before I decided to put in an appearance."

"Crafty!" said Carol, feeding more bread into the toaster and pouring another mug of tea.

"I wonder how the men are getting along." Gina mused. "I can't believe they went so off course like that. I had honestly expected to hear that they had dropped and reloaded not that they were still on their way to the border."

"Hmm, me too." Carol replied. The telephone call from Jeff late the night before had been a surprise to them. "Jeff is usually so brilliant with his timings you can almost set your watch by when he will arrive."

"Yes I know," said Gina. "Jeff has always been reliable, but this is not his fault," she added defensively. "I think they just got carried away with the urgency of the contract."

"Oh, don't think for one moment I am blaming Jeff," Carol said quickly. "Anyone could have done it. It probably seemed like the best idea at the time. It's not the end of the world though. As long as they get there in one piece everything will work out fine, I'm sure. And if it doesn't.....well it will just be a lesson to us not to be so eager next time. It will be fine, I'm sure."

Her confident tone belied the niggling voice of doubt in her mind. She trusted Jeff's judgement and was pretty sure he would work it out without losing too much time, but neither of them could afford a big setback at this time. Not with the business being so new and both of them having invested so heavily into it.

"Jeff said they would 'phone as soon as they got unloaded. They will have a much better idea of where they are and where the pick up place is for the toys by then. It should all run smoothly after that." Gina sounded confident. Jeff had never let her down all the time they had been married and she had no reason to believe that this was to be any different.

"Well, I'm going to get myself washed and dressed and get off to work," Carol announced. "I am taking the bus this morning as Derek will be giving me a lift to Epping later so that I can pick up the Volvo and bring it home. We can travel in together Gina."

"I could give you a lift if I had a car or was insured on yours," Katy chipped in with a grin. "I am a fully fledged driver now you know."

"Ooh! of course you are!" Gina teased, gathering the plates and cutlery from the table and tidying away. "I would not be surprised if a car was not top of your Christmas present list now."

"Hmm, now there's an idea!" Katy grabbed the last slice of toast off the plate as Gina started to clear the table and crunched into it. "But seriously, I don't think I can afford to run one right now. The insurance is far too high for a poor starving student."

Carol decided it was wise not to get into this conversation. "Actually that reminds me." she said quickly, hanging round the door on her way to the stairway. "I am still running the Chevy on Spyder's insurance. He had a few more months left to run on it so has let me keep it in his name but I must do something about re-registering the car in my name and getting my own insurance. Gina, remind me to do that will you?"

"Sure Kiddo, will do." Gina called back cheerfully, searching in the cupboard for an iron. She had rinsed her blouse through the night before and would never have dreamed of dressing in clothes that had not had full benefit of steam and starch.

Tony turned up the collar of his thick fleece lined leather jacket. The air was icy even though the snow had stopped falling for now. He walked round the 'Silver Lady', checking the tyres, kicking them each in turn to make sure none where low on air. The snow chains were still in place and by the look of things would have more work to do before being taken off.

"It's not good news I'm afraid." Jeff's shoulders were hunched against the cold, his hands stuffed firmly in his pockets as he walked back across the crowded parking area.

"Don't tell me we're further from the border than we thought?" Tony turned his attention from the truck to his friend.

"Depends how you look at it. The border between the two countries is only a few kilometres that way." Jeff pointed. "But the actual crossing point is about a four hour drive! We have to head towards the border line then follow it up and cross at the customs point here."

He produced a piece of paper from his pocket with a rough sketch of a map. "I asked most of the drivers who have any English at all and they all agree, this is the only way. In fact they seem to think we are completely mad to be here in the first place as apparently NOBODY goes this way!"

"Nobody except us." bemoaned Tony. "But nothing we can do about it now. No point in whining, we will just have to tramp on and do the best we can out of a bad start." He started to clear the snow from the wing mirrors and side windows.

"Yes, you're right mate." Jeff conceded. "I did wonder why we were the only British trucks in this place. Now we know! But you're right, the best thing to do is carry on and get across the border into Bulgaria. There is definitely a good road there into Sofia, I double checked that one, and according to the men I spoke to, the Bulgarians keep their roads pretty clear of the snow too so we should be okay then. Plain sailing into Sofia, get this lot dropped off and head for the re-load. After that... pedal to the metal and get the stuff back home."

"You still okay with me driving your truck Jeff?" Tony enquired.

"Sure! Just make sure you have your own passport on you and I have mine in case we get a tug at the border, but you go for it. See how you like my old girl and I'm sure you will soon find a way to sweet talk Carol into another Volvo. Although," Jeff added wickedly, "she may like it so much you will find yourself in the office while she does all the driving!"

Tony laughed. "Right now a nice warm office job doesn't sound too bad at all," he observed taking the keys from Jeff's hand. "Let's get these wagons dieseled up and get under way. I hope your heater works okay!"

"Everything on my 'Silver Lady' works okay, you cheeky young pup!" said Jeff, reaching up to clear the film of snow from the windscreen of the Transcon. "I just hope this old girl isn't a death trap by now after you've spent the last six months gluing her back together with chewing gum and string!"

Jeff jumped into the Transcon and turned the key. The big engine roared willingly into life. "Still trying hard old girl." Jeff had a soft spot for the old truck. He had used it for years when he had first started out with old man Winters and, in a strange sort of way, was looking forward to driving the old 'Fighting Spirit' one more time.

He checked behind to see if Tony was up and running then led the way out of the parking bays to head over to the diesel pumps. It was going to be a long haul to the customs crossing and, at this point, neither of them needed the hassle of running low on fuel.

*****

"So what do you think of our new baby?" Carol gestured grandly towards the new acquisition, standing proudly alongside the ivy-clad wall of the haulage yard, paint-work and trim catching the light in the late winter sunshine.

"I say! VERY nice!" Spyder ran his hand over the paintwork and stood back to admire the Globetrotter.

"It came complete with trailer too?" asked Katy, walking the length of the trailer, not quite sure exactly what she was supposed to be admiring but making the right noises anyway.

"Well, sort of. Mr Manning, the chap I bought it off, said he was buying new trailers so I sort of got one of his old ones thrown in cheap as part of the deal."

"It's in good nick," Spyder commented. "It looks pretty straight to me, and so does the truck."

"All the paperwork and tests are all up to date." said Carol, "So it has obviously been serviced regularly. I have no worries about that."

"Well I don't know the first thing about trucks," Katy admitted, stuffing her hands deep into her pockets to keep them warm. "But the paintwork is nice and clean and there is no rust on those underneath bits that I can see so I suppose that's good isn't it?"

Carol laughed. "To be truthful Katy, I don't know much more than you do really. I just went by Derek's judgement and my own instinct. It drives beautifully though, that's what sold me on it."

"Don't you mean HER?" Katy put in glancing wickedly at her mother.

"Okay cheeky, that's what sold me on HER!"

"Let's get it right," Spyder chipped in. "All vehicles are female. Probably because they are unpredictable and you never know what they are going to do next!"

Carol laughed. "Or more likely that they work themselves into the ground before falling to bits!"

The three made their way back into the welcome warmth of the house and congregated in the kitchen.

"Hmm, something smells good." said Carol, slipping her coat off and hanging it on the back of one of the dining chairs.

"I'm making a bolognese." Katy replied. "I tried to 'phone you to ask if you fancied one but your mobile was off. Anyway, I had a grub round in the fridge and cupboards and found most of the makings for the sauce and you had plenty of spaghetti. I went out for some fresh baked bread though. I love crusty bread to dip in the sauce."

"Thanks Darling, that sounds great. Sorry about the 'phone but I switched it off as I always do when driving, especially in a strange truck. Need all the attention span I can muster for that. Do I have time for a quick bath before we eat?"

"Yes, of course. You go and get a good soak and I will help Spyder clear up. We can relax then and have a nice laid back evening."

"Great! Just what I need." Carol picked up her coat and headed out of the kitchen. She felt happy and content and was looking forward to a long relaxing bath followed by a cosy evening with her daughter.

"I've told Spyder to stay and eat with us too." Katy went on.

Oh well, no quiet evening alone with Katy then. "Oh fine, you're welcome of course but won't Suzie be expecting you?" Carol queried.

"Gone to her Mum's for a couple of days with the kids," Spyder explained. "She's making the most of it before the next one arrives. If it's any trouble...."

"No, don't be silly, just wondering that's all." Carol was quick to put him at ease. "You will have to put up with me slopping around in my bath robe though," she warned, heading across the hallway. "By the way," she added, hesitating at the foot of the stairs, "Have you seen that cat today?"

"Yes." Katy's voice came back from the kitchen. "They're all fine. The mother is obviously feral, we can't get near her, but the kittens seem fine and absolutely gorgeous! Now go and get your bath!"

Carol smiled and set off up the stairs, looking forward to her soak. She failed to notice the tiny red light flashing on the answer-phone in the hallway.

****

CHAPTER SEVEN

"We will have to 'phone Gill and ask her which kitty little David would like," Katy said brightly, handing out steaming plates of spaghetti bolognese. "I had a peek in there today in daylight. There's a black one with a white bib and paws, a little tortoiseshell one and a bright ginger one. All absolutely gorgeous with eyes wide open already."

"Bet he goes for the ginger one," said Carol, curled up in one of the big armchairs, her mass of auburn curls tied back with a band, wrapped comfortably in her towelling bath robe. "He's a 'Tigger' fan as I remember, so I would lay money on the ginger one and no prizes for guessing what he will call it!"

"That will make his day, bless him." Katy remarked warmly. "His little face will light up!"

"Where did you learn this recipe?" Carol asked, tearing off a chunk of crusty bread.

"It's surprising what you can knock up out of very little when you are a penniless student you know!" Katy replied with a grin, plopping down on the floor, her tray balanced on a large cushion across her knees.

"Tell me about penniless!" retorted Carol. "I brought you up on next to nothing. Talk about living off your wits!"

Katy suddenly collapsed into laughter. "Remember the apple pie and gravy dinner?"

"What!" Spyder looked up from his plate. "Is that a Derbyshire speciality or something?"

Carol had burst out laughing at the memory. "Not really. I was always flat broke and looking for a bargain, so called into the little butchers in the town one day to see what there was. I had Katy to make dinner for, and also Andy was coming round to eat."

"Andy was, or should I say still is, Mum's best friend from years back." Katy explained to Spyder.

"Oh, that's the guy who married your old schoolfriend and now lives in your old house?" Carol had often spoken about Andy.

"Yes, that's the one. Well I had both him and Katy to feed so was looking for something cheap and filling and I saw that they had a 'special' on pies. I saw what I took to be Cornish pasties, really cheap in packs of three, so bought a pack. Went home and popped them in the oven to heat up then served them with mashed potatoes, carrots, peas and gravy."

"I took one bite and... ugh!!! I thought the meat was off." Katy pulled a face.

"I hadn't tried mine at this point, as I was busy seeing to Katy and Andy first, so I tasted Katy's and thought the same as she did, that the meat was off. It was only after a few minutes that Andy said he thought it was apple."

"Mum checked on the little label on the packet and sure enough, 'Apple Turnovers' it said, serve hot with custard!" Katy was in stitches at the memory.

"The funniest thing about the whole business, though." Carol went on laughing along with Katy. "Andy said he didn't care as he was starving and ate the lot. His own and ours too, apple, gravy and all."

"Those were the days." spluttered Katy, having a fit of the giggles.

"I sometimes think being broke can be more fun than being rich." said Spyder, finishing his last forkful of spaghetti. "You certainly have more fun ducking and diving and it's always great to look back on."

"Remember the time we helped the farmer dig the potato field and he gave us a whole sack of spuds AND a five pound note" said Katy.

"That fiver was a lifesaver at the time." Carol replied wistfully, remembering back. "And the blackberry picking for jam and crumbles. Remember that big plum tree which hung over the road."

"Not sure whether that was stealing or not, come to think of it." Katy remarked. "You always made sure it was dark before we went there!"

Before Carol could reply, the sound of the telephone cut in to their nostalgia. Katy bounced round in the big chair, sitting on her knees to hang over and reach the telephone from where it sat on a wooden packing case.

"Transcon Haulage," she called cheerfully into the receiver. "What... oh yes... of course. Hey, are you okay, you sound awful.... all right.. I'll pass you on." Katy held out the receiver to her mother.

"It's Tony," she whispered "and he sounds awful!"

"Tony." Carol's happy mood had gone in an instant. "Is everything all right?"

"No, Cara Mia. Everything is not all right." Tony's voice cracked as he spoke.

"Darling, what on earth is the matter?"

"Jeff has been arrested." The words just spilled out.

"What!"

"Jeff. They arrested him at the border into Bulgaria this afternoon. They have taken him away. I don't know where. I don't know what to do to help, I am totally shaken."

He was not alone. Carol herself was shaken to the core. She didn't know what to say, her head was spinning but her mind was a blank.

She fought to get herself together. "Tony, keep calm and tell me EXACTLY what happened. Exactly please, don't leave anything out."

"I don't know much really. I couldn't see. We were at the border, they stopped Jeff and arrested him!"

"No Sweetheart." Carol's calm voice belied her feelings. "Please; EXACTLY step by step. Which border, what time was it, how did it occur?"

"I'm sorry Cara Mia." Tony took a deep breath and tried to keep calm. "We had queued at the border crossing...."

"What was the name of the border?" Carol signalled to Katy to pass her a pen and pad that was lying by her chair. "Spell that please Darling, I will need all the information I can get to try and help Jeff." Carol struggled to keep her voice from shaking.

"Of course." Tony spelt out the name. "I think that's right. It was just gone one o'clock, I DO know that as I had checked the time as we pulled up."

"Well done, that will help." Carol didn't know if it would help or not but was trying every way she knew to re-assure Tony.

"We were all lined up in lanes, waiting to pass through customs. There were dozens of trucks, some going through faster than others. Jeff was in the queue next to my lane and I saw them stop him. But they ALWAYS seem to stop Jeff. It had become a joke between us that they did this." Tony took a deep breath.

"Suddenly there were a lot more border guards than usual. The odd thing was that they did not seem to be paying any attention whatsoever to any of the other trucks, just Jeff's. They all piled round his truck and got him out of the cab. I saw other guards with guns going into the control hut. I was looking back as I passed, trying to see. I think I saw them pull a large bag of some type out of the trailer side box and they took him inside."

It didn't sound good. "What happened then?" Carol asked, still trying to keep her voice steady although she felt suddenly very sick.

"I had already been cleared. I was going to go back and see what the problem was with Jeff but another driver grabbed me. Told me not to be a fool and that they would only arrest me too. He advised me to drive on and wait for a while to see if they let Jeff go. The other drivers told me the same so I drove on, out of the customs post and onto the road. It was a good road and I found a pull-in and stopped there and waited for a while. But there was no sign of Jeff. I waited quite a long time then decided to carry on. After all, what else was there to do?"

"Nothing. You did the right thing." Carol reassured him.

"I stopped a couple of hours down the road at a truck stop and tried to 'phone you but your mobile was switched off and there was no-one answering at your home. I left a message on your answer-phone. Did you not get it?"

Carol felt guilty. "Oh, Darling I am so sorry. I have not checked the answer-phone and I had my mobile switched off as I was driving." Not a good time to mention the new truck. Not under these circumstances.

"It was there I met up with some of the other drivers," Tony continued, his voice still shaking badly. "Everyone it seems, had heard all about it. They told me that Jeff had been arrested for carrying a large amount of heroin across the border. They were keeping him in custody and had impounded the truck."

Carol was horrified. Jeff! Carrying drugs! It was not possible.

"No. That cannot be right. Jeff would never have anything to do with drugs."

"Yes, I know that! I don't know what's happening. It is all complete madness. I am totally lost about the whole thing and worried sick about Jeff."

"Tony, where are you now?" Carol asked, her brain desperately trying to think straight.

"I am at the reload depot." Tony told her. "I didn't know what else to do. I carried on into Sofia, found the drop off point, and dropped the oil. I took a leaf out of your book and found a taxi cab. Told them the address and followed it across the city to where the oil was to be delivered. I told the driver to wait and he then piloted me to the pick up factory."

"Well done Darling. Your mind is still working clearly. I am so proud of you. As soon as you get loaded just come straight back. Let us worry about Jeff this end, there is nothing you can do at the moment."

"I know. That's what makes it so bad. I feel so helpless not being able to help my friend and just carrying on with the job."

"This is Jeff's business as well as ours," Carol reminded him. "He would not want you to sit there and miss the deadlines. Do your best, Darling, and come here are soon as you can. We will have news by then I am sure. If I have anything to report before you get here I will ring your mobile. Please be careful Darling. Get back here safe."

Carol worried that Tony was now out there on his own, on strange ground and with a lot on his mind. Had she realised that the weather was so bad she would have worried even more.

"I will telephone you when I know exactly when I will be getting into England." Tony sounded much calmer now. "But please let me know if you hear anything about Jeff." he added. "And Gina. You must tell Gina. I cannot bring myself to tell her such terrible news about her husband!"

Oh, God! Gina. Carol's heart sank again. "Okay Darling. Leave it to me. Please travel safe. I love you!"

"Those words will keep me safe. Ciao, Cara Mia."

Carol dropped the receiver and sank back into her chair. Her hands were shaking and she felt sick.

"What's happened?" Katy asked quietly. It was glaringly obvious that something was terribly wrong.

"Jeff's been arrested on the Bulgarian border." Carol could hear her own voice ringing in her ears as though it were someone else speaking, the truth of the words suddenly making the whole awful business sink in. "Tony says they accused him of carrying heroin, across the border. They took him into custody and impounded the truck. I don't know where, or for how long they intend to keep him or what the hell we can do to help!"

"Jeff! Drugs! I don't believe it!" Katy was horrified. "It must be some awful mistake, Jeff is so strongly against anything like that. It just *has* to be a horrible mistake!"

Spyder had gone into the kitchen and returned carrying a glass of brandy. "Drink this." He pressed the glass into Carol's shaking hand. She took a gulp, the warm liquid burning it's way into her stomach.

"Of course it's a mistake," said Carol. "Jeff would never do such a thing and certainly not risk all that we are building up together. It's unbelievable!" There was also something niggling at the back of her mind. Something that would not come forward.

"What can we do?" asked Katy, sitting on the side of the chair and slipping a supporting arm around her mother's shoulder.

"The first thing to do is tell Gina, of course." Spyder put in sensibly. "Then get on to the Foreign Office first thing in the morning and tell them everything, then get a solicitor, a good one."

"Yes, you're right, of course." Carol was glad someone was thinking straight. "My mind is in a whirl. Oh!... how the hell am I going to tell Gina?" she took another sip of brandy.

Katy shook her head. "She will have to be told Mum, and you're the only one who can do it, you know that."

Carol nodded. Yes, she was Gina's closest friend. It had to be her.

"I can't tell her by 'phone." Carol got to her feet. "I'll get dressed and drive round there now." Her feet felt like lead as she rose from the chair.

"You're not driving anywhere in that state." Spyder's voice was firm. You sit and finish that brandy and I'll run you round there. If you don't want me to come in I will just sit outside and wait until you are ready. No rush, no pressure. Whatever's right."

Carol smiled gratefully, sipping the brandy. "Thanks Spyder," she said quietly. "I could do with some support right now. I'll just finish this and pull myself together then I'll take you up on your kind offer of a lift. This is going to be one of the hardest things I have ever had to do."

****

"Carol! What on earth…." Gina's heart sank. The sight of Carol's serious face as she stood on the doorstep, coat huddled about her shoulders in the gloomy evening light, told her something was badly amiss.

Carol turned and raised a hand to Spyder, sitting at the wheel of his brightly painted pick up, engine running. He nodded in acknowledgement then drove away, leaving the women alone.

"Gina, Honey. It's okay, but there is a bit of bad news I'm afraid." Carol stepped into the welcoming warmth of the hallway, closing the front door behind her.

"What's the matter? What's happened? Has there been an accident? What!" Gina visibly paled. She led the way into the elegant living room, Carol followed, slipping off her padded jacket and dropping it onto the settee. She took Gina's hand and sat down, pulling Gina down next to her.

"Gina I don't know how to tell you….."

"Just say it for God's sake."

"Jeff's been arrested."

A mixture of astonishment and relief crossed Gina's face. In the last few moments she had pictured Jeff injured, or worse. His lorry, crashed in the mountains or piled up on a busy Autoroute, but arrested! This had never crossed her mind.

"Arrested! What on earth for? It must be some mistake surely. Where was he....."

"Gina, yes of COURSE it's a mistake. It's all very unclear really, I've only just heard myself...."

"How? How did you find out..."

"Calm down, listen." Carol took a deep breath and explained, as best she could, all that Tony had told her.

Gina did not speak. Her mind was in a whirl. Arrested! Drugs! Jeff, HER Jeff... it was unbelievable. She got to her feet and walked over to the polished walnut cabinet, pulling out a bottle of brandy and two glasses.

She poured a measure into each. "Are you driving?" her voice sounded small and distant.

"No, Honey, I'm staying." Carol replied firmly.

Gina at once tipped a further measure into both glasses and handed one to Carol, taking a gulp of the fiery liquid herself before sitting down again next to her friend.

"I must get my head round this." Gina tried to keep her voice steady. Getting into a panic was not going to help Jeff. "We must try to think straight and decide what to do."

"Yes, I know. Spyder was the only one who thought straight right away. He says we must phone the Foreign Office, tell them what has happened and ask for advice, then of course a solicitor, a good one, as soon as possible."

"Oh yes, the best!" Gina glanced at the carriage clock sitting on the mantelpiece. "Of course, we can do nothing tonight, far too late, there will be nobody at work at this time." She was desperately stamping on her emotions, trying to keep calm and logical. "But first thing in the morning, action stations!"

"Absolutely," Carol agreed raising her glass and taking a sip. She felt she needed the calming effect of the brandy but was also aware that they would both need clear heads in the morning. "I telephoned Derek quickly before I came, told him I would not be in work tomorrow. He did understand."

"Was there NOTHING that Tony could have done?" Gina asked desperately, grasping at straws, trying to make some sort of sense out of the situation.

"No, of course not." Carol replied calmly. "It's just as well he didn't try. I think they would probably have arrested him too had he gone back and made a fuss."

"Yes, your probably right." Gina conceded. "I should have realised, it's just so.... well such a... oh Carol! what are we going to do! What if they don't

realise it was a mistake. What if they keep him locked up…" Gina's voice was shaking badly, her hands shaking as she gripped her glass.
"Hey 'what if' nothing. Keep thinking positively. Keep strong. Jeff will need all the help we can give him and, my God, we are going to do all we can, just believe it!"
Gina huddled back into the soft cushions of the sofa, drawing her knees up to her chin and wrapping her arms around her shins. Phoebe jumped up beside her, sensing something was wrong and gently patting Gina's face. "I know we are!" said Gina scooping Phoebe into her arms and holding her close. "And I know Jeff knows we are. It's just such an unbelievable situation! The very notion that Jeff, of all people would have anything at all to do with drugs is absolutely laughable!" She buried her face into Phoebe's soft fur.
"Yes, I know." Carol agreed gently, realising her friend was close to breaking point. "It's beyond belief to think Jeff would be in any way involved with such dealings. But remember Honey, we know Jeff, those people don't. It's going to be up to us to prove it to them and I'm sure we will in no time." Carol's confident tone belied her feelings. She was pretty sure that this was not going to be an easy situation and could honestly not see a quick and easy solution. But right now, buoying Gina's spirits was top priority.
The two women sat together talking late into the night. Every angle and every possibility was exhausted before the brandy and the late hour took their toll.
"We have to try to get some sleep." Carol pointed out as the clock fingers slid past the witching hour.
"Yes I know." Gina sounded like a small child about to break into tears.
"Come on Honey." Carol said gently, pulling Gina to her feet. "I'll share with you tonight. You're not spending the night alone."
They made their way upstairs, weary and drained and fell into bed exhausted with the events of the day.
"Sleep well Kid." Carol spoke softly as she clicked off the bedside light.
Gina did not answer. She had curled into a ball, her back to her friend. In the velvety darkness the tears had started to fall, her body wracked with silent sobs.
Carol understood. She turned, sliding her arm over Gina's shuddering body, and holding her tight as she sobbed herself to sleep.

*****

The stench of urine filled Jeff's nostrils. The strong acrid smell making his eyes water. The journey to the prison had been unbearably cold and uncomfortable, and interminably long. Bundled into the back of a windowless van, handcuffed to a sullen uniformed officer, Jeff had been stunned by the whole train of events.

After reeling from the initial shock, he now understood the severity of the situation though with no doubt.

It had been like a slow-motion dream. An unbelievable nightmare. He had watched with horror as the strange leather bag, one he had never seen before, had been hauled out of the side box of the Transcon. The border guards had opened the bag in front of him to reveal countless plastic bags, all stuffed with white powder.

Jeff was no fool. He knew exactly what the white powder was and the implications it carried.

He had, of course done his best to deny all knowledge of the contents of the bag, of the bag itself in fact, but realistically had held out little or no hope of being believed.

A voice at the back of his mind nagged into his sub conscious. Did Tony know anything about the bag. Why did he want to change trucks? Why then, at that time? Was it Tony that suggested Jeff drive the Transcon over the borderline, or did that just happen that way?

Jeff was confused. He pushed the thoughts away. Thinking of this sort would do him no good. He had to try and think straight.

None of the border guards had spoken a word of English. Either by complete ignorance of the language or by choice, Jeff wasn't sure, but not one word was spoken that Jeff understood. He understood only too well that he had been arrested and for what reason.

He had been handcuffed, shoved into the back of the van, and hauled overland to God knows where, the van eventually pulling up in what was clearly a back street of a big town.

As he had been taken from the van and frog-marched into the building Jeff could hear the bustling sounds of traffic coming from further beyond the solid stone prison. They were obviously using the back entrance. Grim and far from welcoming.

His handcuffs had been removed and he had been given a jug of water then left alone. The smell of damp concrete vied for prominence over the stench of urine. The air, clammy and dismal. He sat on the edge of the hard mattress, not eager to lie down on the damp wadding and trying not to think of bed bugs or worse.

Daylight was filtering bravely through the filthy window. It was surely only still mid afternoon, though it felt to Jeff as if he had been here a lifetime already.

What had happened to the truck, to the load? Where was Tony? What on earth would Gina think. Oh God! Gina! How on earth would she take this. How long would he be stuck here a million miles away from her. How would she find out and what was there to be done. Jeff's mind was alternating from frozen numbness to churning turmoil.

The sound of a key in the lock made him leap to his feet. Two uniformed men entered the cell. One man towered above the other. Huge and thick set with a full black beard and piercing black eyes. His boots, polished to a mirror like shine, encased the largest pair of feet Jeff could ever remember seeing. The smaller man standing behind, like the Giant and the Troll from a child's storybook.

"You, English!" The giant spoke with a thick accent.

Jeff felt relief flood through him. He could communicate at last. The absence of his mother tongue had, somehow, been the worse part of all this horrific business.

"Yes, yes I am! Thank God for someone who speaks English! Can you help me, I have no idea what is going on!"

The big man's expression did not alter. "I do not come to help you, English." The guttural voice was devoid of emotion. "I come to tell you what your charge is and what we will do with you."

"Charge! I know that the border guards found drugs on my truck but I honestly don't know how they got there!" Jeff's heart began to sink once more.

The big man shrugged. "That is not our concern, English."

"What do you mean, not your concern." Jeff was struggling to keep abreast of the situation. "Please explain to me what happens. I have never been arrested before, not in my own country or another so I have no notion as to what happens. Do I get a solicitor?" Somehow he doubted it.

The big man stared into Jeff's eyes. "You are guilty of bringing drugs into our country." he stated flatly. "You will wait here until you see the governor for a hearing in twenty eight days."

"Twenty eight days!" It was an eternity. "Then what?"

"You will be given a sentence and you will stay in this prison until sentence has been served."

"Wait! You speak like I have already been found guilty!" Jeff was horrified.

"You ARE guilty, Englishman!"

"What! Without a trial or anything? How can I be?"

The smaller man was looking bored, he glanced at his watch and spoke quickly to his colleague. The bearded giant raised his hand, signalling him to be patient and wait. The Troll immediately stood to attention.

"Our laws are very plain, very, er how you say, straight on."

"Straightforward." Jeff added helpfully.

"Yes, straightforward. It is against the law to bring drugs into the country."

"Yes, of course I know that." Jeff answered. Surely that law was pretty universal.

"Did they find drugs on your truck?" The big man spoke bluntly.

"Well yes but…"

The man raised his hand for silence. "Did you drive that truck over the border into our country?"

"Well, er, yes but…"

"The drugs were on your truck, you brought them into the country."

"Well if you put it like that I suppose…."

"Then you have broken the law and brought drugs into our country. You are guilty of this crime. There is no other question. You come!" He grabbed Jeff by the arm almost lifting him off his feet and propelled him, as if he were a weightless child, from the small cell.

Jeff's head was spinning. His mind in a whirl, as the two guards marched him along a row of corridors, up a flight of stone steps and along a further stone walled landing, and finally to a large cell with half a dozen men, huddled in thick jackets against the chill air, lounging on bunks or pacing the stone floor.

The big barred gate was hauled back and Jeff pushed roughly inside. The big man pointed to a bunk, high up against the wall. "You sleep there." he stated bluntly. "You will be given a plate and spoon at mealtime. Do not lose this. There will be no other give." He turned to a tall quiet man sitting on the edge of his bunk. "One of your countryman." The big mans voice sounded a little softer as he spoke to the tall prisoner. "You explain for him how things are here."

With that he turned and walked from the crowded cell slamming the gate behind him with the most desolate, hopeless sound Jeff could ever remember hearing

*****

"This is so bloody frustrating!" Gina slammed the receiver back into the cradle. "When do these BLOODY people EVER answer the BLOODY phone!"

Carol walked through from the kitchen carrying a tray of tea and toast. "Well it is only just nine o'clock." She pointed out, setting the tray down on the glistening glass coffee table and handing Gina a steaming mug of tea.

"Exactly! All offices open at nine. But oh no, NOT the British Foreign Office it seems!" Anger and frustration was taking hold of Gina. However hard she tried to be calm and think straight, the fear continued to well up inside her. Fear for Jeff. What was he going through right now? Where was he? Was he cold, hungry frightened? Had he been beaten? Oh dear God, please don't let him be beaten! What were they going to do with him? Fear for herself also. What would she do without Jeff, her rock. What about the business. Jeff's business, their future. Gina felt sick.

"Why don't we try the solicitor first?" Carol asked gently, breaking into Gina's turmoil. "After all, I think we need all the advice we can get before we go making demands from the Foreign Office. It may be the best move."

The night had dragged heavily, and neither Gina or Carol had managed to get much sleep.

"God, I feel awful. This worry is killing me, I even threw up this morning." Gina certainly looked pale.

"Have some toast while we get ourselves together. No point in running off 'half cocked' is there?" Carol was trying hard to think straight and do things properly. Trying hard not to give in to the rising fear of the situation. She had deliberately not dwelled on the problem of the impounded lorry. Gina had enough to worry about with Jeff without Carol sounding selfish about the loss of a truck and what it may do to the delicate beginnings of their business. But nevertheless, it was a problem that had to be faced. Faced and dealt with. The business needed two trucks up and running to pay its way and at this present moment there was only one. Not to mention the cost of losing a truck. Carol silently thanked providence that she had bought the Volvo only yesterday. She knew in her heart that the 'Fighting Spirit' was on it's last legs. Tony would have to use the new one now. With the 'Silver Lady' impounded in Bulgaria he would have to. The old Transcon could not take the strain of all the work.

"What solicitor are we going to use?" Gina's voice broke into Carol's thoughts. "We haven't actually got one as we haven't had to use one. Well, not recently. The business deal was just between us so we didn't bother did we?"

"There is always Mark Cameron." Carol hardly liked to bring Mark's name into conversation at this sensitive time but he was the only person that sprang to mind. "He did say he was branching out into criminal law."

"But Jeff's NOT a criminal." Gina's reaction was volatile. "I don't care what these flaming Bulgarians say he did. He is NOT a criminal!"

"I know that, and YOU know that." Carol pointed out patiently "But THEY don't. And if we are going to have to fight for Jeff in a foreign court we don't want a solicitor that specialises in child maintenance or the like, or arranging mortgage transfers. We need a criminal lawyer, one who knows how to fight for a not guilty verdict. Think about it Gina." Carol's voice was firm. "We need to fight fire with fire. We can't afford to tiptoe around this. We have to go straight for the jugular and start the fight, right now!"

Gina ran her fingers through her fine silken hair. Even after a terrible night she still looked like a delicate china doll, huddled in her cream silken robe.

"You're right of course," she conceded. "But getting a criminal lawyer makes it feel like we need one to defend a criminal!"

"Yes I know, but we have to do it. Shall I ring Mark or do you want to do it?"

"No, you do it. Please. He is the last person I want to speak to right now."

Before Carol could reach the telephone it rang, making them both jump. Gina ran into the hallway and snatched the receiver off the hook.

"Hello Jeff?" Her voice cracked with eagerness. "Oh, Poppa........yes, I'm okay, shocked, of course, but okay." Her voice dropped and her whole body slumped slightly as she held the receiver. "Carol is with me.... Oh, you have spoken to Katy....right, yes, of course. Poppa, I will hand you over to Carol, she is the better one to speak to at the moment....yes, thank you, that's very kind, here is Carol."

Gina handed the receiver to Carol and sat back down on the sofa, tucking her legs underneath her, hugging her knees and rocking gently, head bowed, her fine silken hair falling around her face.

"Poppa, have you heard from Tony?"

"I have, Ducks, bad business all this, very bad business!"

"You're not kidding! I can't believe it, I'm having trouble taking it in. Is Tony all right? I'm worried to death about him out there all alone, considering what has happened to Jeff I fear for Tony now!"

"I know, Ducks, we're not best pleased here either. The lad just phoned me. He asked me to speak to you as he doesn't know when he can get to a telephone again."

"Is his mobile not working?"

"Listen, Ducks, he didn't get to tell you what truck he's in, did he?"

"Er, what do you mean? He's in the Transcon isn't he?" Carol could not take much more confusion.

"Right, let me put you straight now." Poppa said gently. "Tony just told me the whole story, or at least what he knows of it. Before they got to Bulgaria they had stopped for the night at a truck stop and got talking over perhaps getting a better truck on the road, better than the old Transcon you know. Anyway, the boys decided to swap trucks so that Tony could see how he liked driving the Globetrotter. They were thinking that one like it may be a good buy for the future you see."

"So, wait, hold on." Carol was trying to drag her mind together. "So you mean when Jeff was arrested he was driving the Transcon - and it's the Transcon that's been impounded?"

"Yes, that's right, sorry Ducks, it's your own truck they've got over there. Tony's in the Globetrotter. He explained it all to me then suddenly realised that he hadn't told you. Can't blame the lad really, this is all pretty bad for him to take in." Poppa ended a little defensively.

"Of course, poor Darling!" Carol didn't know what else to say, she was almost at a loss for words. It was all too much to take in. She was trying to file all this information into some sort of order in her already overloaded brain.

The old Transcon had been on its way out for a long time so at least it was no real great loss if the old girl had been impounded. The fact that Carol was fond of the old truck was a pity but thinking logically it was a truck that had passed it's sell-by date and the replacement was right now standing in her yard.

"We have to think about Jeff first. The truck will just have to wait." There had to be some logical order to all this mess. First things first.

"You're right Ducks, the main problem is what can we do to help Jeff." Poppa said firmly. "Marco is trying to contact the Bulgarian police to see what has happened and what Jeff has been charged with. Also what we can do about releasing the truck, though that is secondary to getting Jeff home safe and sound."

"Oh, absolutely." Carol was still desperately trying to get her head round it all. "I have to say, although this may sound strange, It is slightly better that it is the Transcon stuck over there. At least Jeff won't have the worry about losing his own truck as well as being in trouble himself."

"That's very generous of you Ducks." Poppa said kindly, impressed with the fact that Carol had not given a second thought to the fact that it was her own truck that was held by the Bulgarian authorities. He liked Carol, and liked the fact that she could, he secretly hoped, one day be his daughter in law."

"And what's more I only yesterday bought another truck. A globetrotter like Jeff's 'Silver Lady'. I was hoping Tony would be pleased. I guess none of us have much choice right now though."

"Well there you are then. A bit of providence in a dark world there, Ducks!"

"Oh, Poppa." Carol suddenly felt very weak and helpless. Speaking to Poppa like this brought on a swell of self pity. She desperately wished that she could pick up the phone and talk to her own father. Dear old Pop. He would have been her rock to lean on. She also felt angry that he was not there when she needed him most. Oh Pop, WHY did you have to die!

"It's okay lass," Poppa said gently, almost as if he could read Carol's thoughts. "Don't go taking on now. It will all work out okay in the end, you'll see."

"I know, I'm sure it will, and getting silly and tearful won't help will it? I've got to be strong to help Gina through this. She is the one we should be thinking about, she and Jeff."

"Good girl." said Poppa. "I know you're made of strong stuff, Ducks. You'll do your best. But...." he added quietly, " ...if you fancy a good cry any time and feel it's all getting too much, then you get straight on the 'phone to us, any time day or night you hear?"

"Thank you Poppa, that's very kind. I may have to take you up on that offer some time, be warned!"

"Speaking of 'phones, that's why Tony can't use his mobile. His charger is in the Transcon, so he has Jeff's one, which doesn't fit his phone see? Not to mention the fact that he has Jeff's clothes bag and Tony's is in the Transcon still!"

"Oh good grief! What a mess!"

"If it wasn't so bad it would be funny, eh Ducks?" Poppa was still trying to raise Carol's spirits. "Well anyway, the lad is over the Border and on his way to Belgrade. He plans to head straight up to through Austria and on to England via the usual route through France. Should take him a good four or possibly five days as the weather is pretty poor, snow a lot of the way, and they'll have closed all the mountain passes so it will be the long way round whatever happens."

"I hope he takes his time. I can't bear the thought of anything happening to Tony too." said Carol, a small knot of apprehension settling in her stomach.

"He'll be okay. Sensible lad my Tony," Poppa said brightly, trying hard, for Carol's peace of mind, to mask his own worries about his eldest son. "Now you go and see what can be done for Jeff your end and we'll carry on doing our bit this end. Chin up, Ducks!"

Carol said her goodbyes to Poppa and went to find Gina. "What on earth are you doing!" Gina was on her hands and knees, cloth in hand polishing the skirting boards in the kitchen.

"I've been meaning to do this for ages. The dirt just builds up you know." Gina carried on rubbing at some invisible speck of dirt on the polished pale wooden kick boards. "And I can't just sit there doing nothing! I'll go mad!"

"Gina, honey, leave that now." Carol gently took Gina's arm and guided her back to the living room, sitting her onto the sofa and plumping up cushions at her back. "Just sit there for a minute, then I'll get us another mug of tea. After that we'll get onto making these 'phone calls, okay?"

Gina nodded like a lost child. She was taking this a lot harder than Carol had expected. Normally Gina was the toughest of the two, despite her delicate appearance. This behaviour was alien to Carol, she had never seen her friend fall apart like this.

"Don't you start going all girlie on me now, Kid, not when we need nerves of steel." Carol tried to make the remark a light-hearted one.

"Yes, of course, you're dead right. The last thing Jeff needs is some soppy woman going all to pieces at the wrong time." Gina got to her feet. "I can't make important phone calls looking like this!" she announced. Carol smiled to herself. Typical Gina.

"I'm off to get a shower and change then I will really feel like kicking some arse!" Gina's cream satin robe swished round her ankles as she trotted up the stairs with determination.

"That's my girl." Carol felt relieved. "When you're showered and done I will tell you all what Poppa told me and we can get stuck in to these 'phone calls.

"Right you are." Gina called back from the landing. "These officials won't know what's hit them. And as for the bloody Bulgarians! How DARE they lock up my husband. They've got Gina Meredith to deal with now!"

Carol smiled. Gina was back on form and now, together, they could make some sense of the whole terrible business.

*****

CHAPTER EIGHT

Jeff was in a state of shock. He looked around the cell, feeling unable to move. He knew he should do something, say something, but what and to whom? He looked around at the other men, staring warily at the newcomer, sizing him up with curiosity.

The tall man, that the guard had spoken to, swung his long legs off the edge of the bunk and got to his feet, walking the short distance across the stone flagged floor to where Jeff was standing, frozen to the spot.

"All right mate?" The man put a hand on Jeff's shoulder. He was tall and thin with long dark hair tied back into a pony tail. A goatee beard and drooping moustache adorned his face.

"Bit strange at first isn't it? You'll get used to it." The London accent was desperately welcome to Jeff's ears as he tried hard to recover his powers of speech.

"Thanks, yes I still don't know what the hell is going on. It's all a bit of a nightmare just now."

"Name's John Miller." The tall prisoner held out his hand. "Stick with me for a while 'till you get to know the ropes in here. It's easy to come unstuck."

"Jeff Meredith." Jeff took the proffered hand, suddenly aware that his hand was shaking badly. "I'm a trucker. Was driving a load into Sofia and got a tug at the border. They say that I had drugs on board."

John led the way across the cell to his own bunk. "You probably did have." He stated simply, gesturing Jeff to sit, and pulling out a small tin of tobacco. "Smoke?"

Jeff stared in disbelief. "I didn't have drugs on board, or at least I didn't KNOW of any drugs, I have no idea....."

"Listen!" said John, raising his hand. "Forget what you were, or were not aware of. This place is about survival, not who is innocent and who isn't! Get it?" he shoved a roll-up cigarette into Jeff's hand and offered him a light.

Jeff drew strongly on the rough tobacco. He had to get something in his system that would stop his inside from shaking and help his brain to relax. He had to think straight. The word 'survive' rang in his head. Yes he would have to survive this. Whatever it took. However he could.

"Thanks." Jeff was trying to make sense of what he was hearing. "So what's the score here. I am totally green when it comes to prisons."

John gave a wry grin. "Weren't we all! The first thing you have to realise is that you're here, and for all intents and purposes you're guilty as sin, same as all of us here."

Jeff looked around. The motley group of men inside the cell were still staring with interest at the newcomer. Jeff felt uneasy.

John leaned back onto the bunk and drew on his cigarette. "The name of the game here is survival. Getting through one day at a time without getting your bones broken. The guards don't need any excuse to break your head with their batons or worse. You will have noticed they are all carrying guns. Believe me, mate, they are not opposed to using them either."

Jeff had noticed. Just another thing to make his nights sleepless. "How long have you been in this God-forsaken place?" he asked.

"Just over four years. John stated bluntly. "Same charge as you. Drugs on board. Guilty as charged, and just like you, had no bloody idea the stuff was there."

"Four years!" Jeff felt the blood drain from his face. How could he be stuck here for four years. What about the business, the truck. What about Gina. He struggled to get the thought of Gina out of his mind. He couldn't bear to think about her right now.

A movement caught Jeff's eye. A young man on the bunk above had stirred from his sleep and sat up. "What's happening?" He asked bleary eyed.

"New cell mate." John answered. "This is Jeff. He has just booked in for an extended stay at the Rat-trap Hilton! This…" he gestured to the young man, "…is Gary, my nephew. Came along for the ride with me and ended up in here to keep me company."

Gary's eyes darted around the cell and back to Jeff. He looked nervous and on edge like an animal in a cage, somehow in contrast to John, laid back despite the circumstances. "Go back to sleep." John told him. "You still don't look right."

Gary wordlessly flopped back down on his bunk, turning his back to the cell and the two men in conversation.

"Not doing well isn't young Gary." John spoke quietly. "Just had a week of sickness and the shits. At least it has kept him quiet. I have my hands full just keeping him out of trouble, his mouth gets in the way of his brain most of the time."

"So tell me, what happens now. Did you get a solicitor, does your family have to help, do you get any legal help through this place? I don't know what to expect."

"First, does anyone know you are here?" It was an obvious question but one Jeff had not considered.

"Well, I was driving in convoy with another one of our guys, I got pulled at the border but Tony was ahead and, as far as I know, has not been pulled. As far as I know he has gone on and either tipped the load or gone back home or.... well I have no idea, they tell you nothing here. In fact you are the only person, apart from that big guy, who has spoken English to me so I am well in the dark."

John rolled another cigarette. "Have you brought any fags in, Marlborough would be good."

"Fags? There was a couple of hundred in the cab but I only have a few with me," Jeff replied. "I don't even have my clothes. In fact I wasn't even driving my own truck!"

"What!"

Jeff told the story of the trip out, of changing trucks and of the arrest.

"Well it makes no difference about the clothes really. You have a warm coat and good boots so that's all that matters in here." John pointed to the high window. A good inch of ice was clinging to the inside of the glass. "Just keeping warm is what matters in here, not fashion or how good you smell. Cigarettes are good though, they are the best currency in here."

"I have some money in my pocket." Jeff remembered. "They searched me and took my wallet but they missed a few bob that I had in my pockets."

"That's good, you may need it." John told him. I suppose that your mate, this Tony, will have 'phoned home and told your family where you are."

"Yes, of course, I'm sure that it would be the first thing he would do."

"You're lucky." John replied. "I had been here over a week before my family was informed."

"A week! Do we get any legal help or anything?"

John laughed. "Listen, mate, this is what happens. Usually they nick you and throw you in solitary on bread and water for twenty eight days. At the end of that period you get a quick cursory hearing telling you that you are, in fact, guilty and you get chucked in here with the rest of us. Then you just have to wait until they arrange a trial to see how many years they will give you, and the trial could be any time they feel like it, sometimes months away. For some reason you managed to miss out on the twenty eight days solitary. The only reason I can think of for that is that they are expecting some high profile prisoners and they want them in solitary more than they want you. I'll find out, I do know a few guards who tell me stuff."

Jeff was still having trouble filtering all this information into his brain. Still could hardly believe it was happening. "I suppose my wife will get a solicitor for me, get the Embassy involved and all that."

"The Embassy will give you a visit, that's for sure. Only 'cos it's their duty though. They will probably not believe that you're not guilty any more than the Bulgarians, and as for a solicitor." John pulled on his cigarette. "You are only allowed a Bulgarian solicitor, probably one who doesn't speak English either."

"What!"

"Yep! This is the way things work here I'm afraid. You can have another solicitor in England but he will have to deal with the one over here."

"Oh, God! It's all a bad dream surely. I still don't believe that there was anything actually ON my truck. They showed me a bag full of stuff but I hadn't seen it before."

John took a deep breath. "Just the same as happened to me mate." He said quietly. "I didn't believe it either but now I understand."

"Understand, how?"

"Well the drugs 'barons' or whatever you chose to call them, are trafficking the stuff on a regular basis. Its' a multi-million pound business after all. But hey, you don't expect them to risk their own necks do you? Or bother to pay mules to carry the stuff when they can get us drivers to do it for them do you?

"What do you mean?" Nothing was making sense, nothing in this whole mess.

"They have tons of the stuff on a daily basis." John said matter of factly. "What they do is hang around in the truck stops, see what trucks are going where and which ones are heading towards the border. They wait until the drivers are in the showers or asleep in the cabs or even just out of sight having a meal. Then they get the stuff and plant it on the trucks, usually doing about a dozen trucks in one truck stop. Then they just wait for the trucks to drive off and carry the stuff over the border. They just follow behind at a safe distance, unnoticed."

"But don't they risk losing it. I got nicked didn't I and the customs guards took the stuff away."

"Aha! now here is the clever bit!" John went on. "To make sure that most of the stuff gets through unhindered they actually make one truck into the fall guy. They phone ahead to the border and tell the guards that there is one truck carrying contraband and tell them which truck it is. Anonymous of course. The guards then pay no bloody attention whatsoever to all the other trucks that are going through that day as they have a definite nick with the one reported, yours in this case, so while they were dealing with you there was probably another dozen trucks going through loaded with the stuff. All the dealers then have to do is follow the trucks over the border, wait for the drivers to stop and sneak the stuff back off. There's loads of drivers out there who have carried stuff across borders and have no idea that they've done it!"

It was all beginning to make sense to Jeff now. He had been used as a tool by the drug traffickers. He remembered the crowded truck stop where they had spent the night. Anything could have taken place there. Maybe Tony had also been planted with the stuff. Maybe he was still driving with it on his truck or maybe he had been 'unloaded' by now.

"What happens if you notice the stuff before they get it off. Or see them doing it."

"That would be very unfortunate," John said gravely. "They would have no compunction against shooting you to get their property back. This part of the world is another way of life, you have to understand this."

Jeff's heart sank. What if Tony WAS carrying. What if he met the men responsible. Was his young friend safe? Jeff dare not think too much, surely his brain would burst.

"How come you know so much?" he asked. This man certainly seemed to know a lot.

"You pick up a lot in here." John answered simply. "They got me in exactly the same way as they did you. I was just as green too, but I had this one to keep an eye on. Felt responsible for him, he being younger than me and my sisters kid at that." He gestured to the younger man curled up on the top bunk. "Not the brightest spark in the firework box, isn't Gary." John lowered his voice. "Reckon I have stood between him and a good beating more than once. Just doesn't know when to keep his mouth shut."

"Maybe the young pup is no great loss. Safer for the rest of us." The heavy German accent made Jeff turn. A fair haired man had obviously been intently listening to the conversation, lounging on his bunk at the side of the cold, damp cell.

"You were young yourself once Hans," John spoke quickly. "You just leave Gary to me, I'll look after him!"

"You should," The German grunted. "I will not!"

John stared at the man for a moment then turned his attention back to Jeff. "We are a pretty mixed bunch in here. Every nationality except Bulgarian."

"Why no local men?"

"They don't get the 'luxury' of this place." John gave a wry smile. "From what I hear their lock up is ten times worse than this!"

Jeff could not for the life of him imagine any place being worse than this damp stinking dungeon. "God help them then." He muttered quietly.

"Amen to that," John agreed. "But the best way to get on in here is to know when to stand your ground and when to tow the line. That's a lesson our young friend here is having trouble getting the hang of. The guards don't respect a groveller but they won't stand any full on arrogance. It's a fine line to tread. For example...." John rose from his bunk and stretched his long limbs, "there is a rule in here that does not allow beards or long hair."

Jeff could not fail to notice that John Miller had both a beard *and* hair long enough to be tied back into a pony tail.

"As you can see, I have both. Why? Because they don't provide us with razors to shave with!"

The rest of the men in the cell, although not been smooth shaven had only stubble and badly cropped hair.

"So what are you supposed to do?"

"The prison barber does all the cutting and shaving. I get away with it because I told them that it was against my religion to have another man shave me or cut my hair."

"What religion is that then?"

"One I made up! It's a game I play with them. They don't believe me really but to be on the safe side they let it go rather than offend a religion."

"I suppose it pays to have a sense of humour too." Jeff remarked.

"You would go mad without one but it's not the easiest of things to keep up in this place."

Jeff had taken a liking to the tall Englishman with the strange philosophy. He felt himself starting to calm down and his mind starting to work more logically.

John spend the next few hours talking to Jeff, explaining the routines of the prison and what to watch out for. He told Jeff about Zhravko Markov, the uniformed giant who had introduced them. This man was fair, as far as the strict prison regime allowed. He had gained the respect of most of the prisoners and had earned a reputation for what passed as fair play in this place. John also warned Jeff not to expect any legal help or advice for at least a few weeks.

Jeff found this the hardest thing to stomach. He wanted a solicitor. Now! He wanted to get to court, be allowed to state his case and, hopefully, be given his freedom. But this did not seem in the least bit likely. Not even a remote hope right now.

His only hope was that Tony had contacted Gina and Carol and that they would be using every method they could to get him help and make some sense out of all this terrible business.

*****

"Barrington, Green Solicitors!" The brisk voice on the end of the telephone announced brightly.

"Good morning." said Carol. "Will you put me through to Mark Cameron's office, please?"

"Can you tell me what it is about please." The brisk voice went on. "I will then see if Mr Cameron is free. He usually only speaks to people by appointment."

Carol was in no mood to be fobbed off by a receptionist, and had no intention whatsoever of discussing their private problems with this woman.

"It is a personal call." She said coolly. "Please tell Mark that Carol is on the 'phone, Carol Landers." She deliberately used Marks christian name to make the call sound personal and not in the least business-like.

"Er, please hold." The brisk voice sounded somewhat put out.

Carol glanced across to Gina who was sitting on the foot of the stairs stroking Phoebe's silken coat. She looked calm and composed, dressed in loosely fitting bronze trousers and a soft cream jumper, her hair swept onto the top of her head in an elegant swirl.

"Good morning, Mark Cameron here."

"Oh, good morning! Mark, we need your help...badly!" Carol came straight to the point.

"Oh, Mrs Landers? er.. Carol" Mark sounded puzzled. "You do sound as bit ruffled. Is this very important? Do you need an appointment?"

"No!" Carol almost snapped down the telephone. "We need to speak to you today. Now...at once. If you can't help us then PLEASE tell us who can. Gina's husband, Jeff, has been arrested and we need a good solicitor right now.. this minute."

"Arrested!" Mark's attention had been grabbed. "Which police station has he been taken to? What is the charge? Is Gina all right?"

"No, you misunderstand me." Carol realised she had not made things clear. She too was rattled and nervous with this horrible situation and was only showing a calm exterior so as not to make Gina feel any worse than she already did. "Jeff was arrested in Bulgaria. He was taken at the border and accused of carrying drugs on his lorry. The Bulgarians have kept him, God knows where, and, as far as we know, impounded the lorry, again God knows where, and we have no idea what is happening or what we can do. Please Mark, we need your help, and no, Gina is not all right as you can well imagine!" Carol threw this last piece of information into the conversation deliberately. If Mark still held any affection for Gina, if in fact he ever had any in the first place, surely this would be a good bargaining tool, fair or otherwise.

"Good heavens!" Mark Cameron's usual calm and businesslike demeanour was obviously shaken. "What a dreadful situation. Gina must be besides herself." That was certainly no understatement.

"Yes. Gina is shaken to the core. We really don't know where to start with all this. I believe we have to contact the Foreign Office or something similar, tell them what has taken place and then go with their advice from there, but of course a solicitor is vital. A good solicitor, of course and you were the first person to spring to mind." A little ego massage at this point would not go amiss!

"Well I am flattered that you thought of me." Mark replied. "I have to admit, this is the first case of this kind that I have been faced with but I can assure you I will give it my utmost attention immediately. In fact, due to the severity of the situation I will put my other cases on hold for the morning and make some enquiries on your behalf at once. The one thing you must do, as you so rightly say, is to contact the Foreign office and give them all the details of the matter that you have to hand. Give me a couple of hours and I will get back to you. Are you at home?"

"I am at Gina's house at this moment," Carol replied. "I will be staying here for now, or at least for the best part of today so that we can try and make some sense of all this. I cannot leave Gina alone at the moment."

"Of course, absolutely." Mark's attitude puzzled Carol a little. Was he being thoroughly businesslike or did he actually feel genuine concern for Jeff's plight.... or Gina's feelings, more to the point. She decided not to worry about exactly what Mark Cameron's motives were, but to just go with the fact that he was willing to help. Any port in a storm, and this was certainly a huge storm!

"Well there we are. Step one on the ladder of the 'Free Jeff' campaign!" Carol announced as she put down the receiver. "Did you get the gist of all that?"

"Yes, pretty much." Gina rose from the stairs and walked into the kitchen, filling the kettle with water and clicking on the switch. It was clear that the kettle would not be allowed to go cold this day!

"The next phone call will have to be to the Foreign Office." said Carol dialling directory enquiries and asking for the number, the toneless automated voice coldly giving her the number as she wrote it down on a small pad on the polished telephone table.

Gina was going through the motions of scooping cat food into Phoebe's china dish and washing the cups ready for their next re fill of tea.

Carol dialled the number of the Foreign Office. "Let me speak to them." Gina announced, taking the receiver from Carol's hand. "I must make them understand that my husband is not the average run of the mill drugs dealer that they probably deal with every day!"

Carol went into the kitchen to pour the boiling water onto the tea. She could hear Gina's voice explaining the situation then a pause, then Gina's voice again, once more explaining to yet another official what had taken place. Her voice getting more and more fraught with almost every sentence.

"But my husband is NOT the sort of man that would be carrying drugs, in this country or any other!" she almost shouted into the telephone. "It must be clear by now that not ALL people who are arrested are automatically guilty, surely you know that….."

"Yes, I do realise that these things take time but…."

"Yes, we do have a solicitor…."

"Yes, of COURSE he practices Foreign Law….." Gina actually had no idea if he did or not.

"I must have some contact with my husband….."

"When? When will you let me know…."

"Then I will telephone the British Embassy in Bulgaria, I will speak to them myself. Please give me the number……"

"No, I don't want to wait. I WILL do it myself……"

"Thank you!" Gina slammed down the telephone.

"Bloody bureaucrats. The man sounded positively bored! Like he had heard it a million times before. "What makes me really mad is all these bloody people who DO go dealing drugs to foreign lands. They get arrested and make a big stink about it when they are as guilty as sin and when someone like my Jeff get arrested nobody believes him!"

Gina immediately started to dial the number of the Embassy in Sofia.

"Calm down." Carol pushed a china mug of hot tea into Gina's hand. "At least we have made some headway. We have got some wheels in motion. "Now we'll see what the Embassy over there has to say."

Gina explained the situation as calmly as she could to the well-spoken British voice on the end of the telephone.

"Well this is a nasty situation, Mrs Meredith. It must be most disturbing and frightening for you." The voice of the Embassy official sounded sympathetic. "But, of course you will have to understand that our powers are very limited here. We will, I assure you, make arrangements to visit your husband as soon as possible, make sure he is all right and well treated, but as for getting him released.... that will not be possible."

No if's or but's, just the blunt statement.

"What!" Gina felt a further wave of nausea sweep through her stomach. "Surely there is something that you can do to help."

"You must understand that this is Bulgaria and, rightly or wrongly, all persons arrested here, whether they be Bulgarian or foreign, are treated under the same laws, which, you must be very clear about, are not quite the same as ours. We will of course, arrange for him to have a solicitor as soon as possible."

"We have already arranged a solicitor for him over here." Gina said quickly.

"Ah, yes well, the situation here is that, by law once again, your husband MUST have a Bulgarian solicitor."

"What! Why is that, why can't he have his own solicitor."

"Once again, the law of the land I am afraid, Mrs Meredith. The local court will appoint a local man to represent your husband. The only way round it is for you to have a solicitor at your end, one who practices Foreign Law, who can negotiate with the solicitor at this end. I know it is all very complicated but this is the way things work out here. And another thing, please don't expect the Bulgarian solicitor to necessarily speak English, so you would be advised to hire a professional interpreter for your solicitor. It will be at your expense, of course, although we will be able to help with interpretation at this end."

"Good grief." Gina's head was spinning. This whole thing was archaic, almost medieval. If it wasn't so serious it would be laughable.

The embassy official assured Gina that Jeff was now 'in their system' and that he would be visited by a member of their office. Not the reassurance Gina was hoping for but she was beginning to realise that this was pretty much as good as it could get for now. She felt drained and exhausted as she replaced the receiver and carried her mug of tea into the living room, flopping down wearily on the sofa, every muscle in her body aching with tension. Every nerve on edge and her mind a complete turmoil of emotions. She had to get through this. Be strong for Jeff's sake. She glanced gratefully at Carol, leaning quietly in the doorway, waiting for Gina to tell her what had been said. The knowledge that she had such a staunch and supportive friend gave her strength. Between them they would cope. Cope with the situation whatever the setbacks and with luck, determination and tenacity, come out on top. "Thanks for this," said Gina, climbing across the big back seat of the Chevy. "I just could not face meeting Mark in my own house, Jeff's house. Not under the circumstances, it just didn't feel right."

"That's okay, Kiddo." Carol turned to look from the front passenger seat to speak to Gina. "I know how you feel, my place will be a lot more neutral and anyway, there may be paperwork appertaining to the truck that Mark may need to see."

Spyder steered the Chevy along the high road and turned into the lane. "Did either of you get any sleep last night?" he asked, carefully avoiding any questions that he considered to be none of his business.

"Not really," Carol answered. "It was all such a shock it was hard to relax enough to get any proper sleep. At least we made the relevant phone calls this morning and started to get the wheels in motion."

"Yes, that was the main thing. Getting things started, and when we speak to the solicitor this afternoon I am sure things will be even clearer." Gina put in, pulling the fur trim of her collar up round her neck and snuggling into the warmth of the cashmere coat.

Spyder asked no further questions as he chauffeured the girls along the winding country lane and into the gravel haulage yard.

The wind whipped across the open space as the three made their way up the big stone steps. Katy had seen them arrive and flung the door open even before they reached it.

"Gina! How are you?" Katy flung her arms around Gina and gave her a warm hug. "Poor you! I've been thinking about you all night."

"Thank you Darling," Gina replied warmly. "It certainly is a terrible business but your Mum and I have made some headway this morning and soon the solicitor will be here and we will then know a lot more of what can be done to help Jeff."

Spyder led the way into the kitchen and put the kettle on. "You will want some privacy when the solicitor gets here," he said. "I can keep out of the way and finish off the varnishing or I can clear off completely, whatever's right," he shrugged. "I don't mind, whichever you want."

"Thanks Spyder." Carol slipped off her coat and took Gina's from her, making her way to the stairs to hang them in the wardrobe. "But there's no need for you to disappear. You know what's happened and there is nothing we have to hide. If you want to stay and carry on then please do."

"Is this *the* Mark Cameron who is calling round, the same solicitor who helped you to buy the house Mum?" Katy enquired. Wise beyond her years, she new a little about Gina's brief affair but had no intention of mentioning the subject, especially with Spyder within earshot.

"The very same." Carol answered, disappearing up the stairs, arms laden with coats.

"Yes, Honey, the very same." echoed Gina, sitting at the kitchen table and fondling Bruno who had pushed his head onto her lap for a fuss. "We decided to meet here as it would be, well, more convenient all round!"

Katy nodded. She understood. "I'll have a quick tidy round in the living room so that you can have a proper talk in there," she announced. "I hope he will be able to help. What did the Foreign Office have to say?"

Gina explained to Katy and Spyder all that she knew.

"It makes us feel so helpless," said Carol coming back into the kitchen. "It's almost as if we should be running round, doing something, instead of just sitting here waiting for something to happen."

The sound of the doorbell broke into their conversation. Katy ran to answer it.

"It's Mr Cameron." she announced formally, standing back and gesturing Mark to enter.

Carol and Gina ushered Mark into the living room. Katy had removed the dust-sheets in an attempt to make the room more inviting and thrown a cloth over one of the packing cases to act as a table.

"I have to congratulate you on the improvements you have made to this old place," Mark remarked politely, looking around. "The value of the property has been significantly increased already."

"Thank you." Carol answered politely. It occurred to her suddenly that only yesterday, her main concerns were re-decorating the house, planning the furnishings and finding homes for three stray kittens, and now today everything had changed. The house, and the repairs and improvements seemed to have paled into insignificance and as for the kittens, well they could have the run of the place for all she cared. These latest developments had overshadowed everything.

Bruno padded into the room, glancing warily at the stranger before sitting protectively at Carol's feet.

"Gina, how are you?" Mark Cameron smiled kindly at Gina. Carol could not tell if this was a professional enquiry or a personal one.

"I am devastated!" Gina said simply. "Totally devastated! I need to know what we can do to secure the release of my husband in the shortest possible time.

"Of course," Mark replied, slipping off his expensive, well tailored overcoat and sitting down, dropping his briefcase onto the make shift table and pulling out some papers. "I understand that Mr Meredith and yourself Mrs Landers…"

"Carol, please." Carol could not be bothered to stand on ceremony.

"…Carol, that you and Mr Meredith are now partners in your own haulage company and one of the company's trucks has been impounded and Mr Meredith incarcerated in Sofia."

"That's pretty much it in a nutshell!" Carol replied.

"Right. I have spoken to the Foreign Office……"

"So have we," Gina cut in. "We didn't get much joy from that!"

"Yes, they told me." Mark answered. "I spoke to them at length and got as many details as possible about the situation and what the legalities are regarding such a case. It appears that your husband, Gina, has been found guilty of transporting drugs into Bulgaria."

Gina went to speak but Mark held up his hand. He was in professional mode now.

"The way the law stands over there is pretty basic. The drugs were on his truck when he drove across the border, so regardless of the fact that he may, or may not, have known of their existence is besides the point. He has, in fact, broken Bulgarian law so is guilty, there is no question." Again Mark held up his hand before either of the girls could speak. "What we have to do now is push for a trial, push as hard as we can so that there will be a trial as soon as possible. If we don't push like hell it could take many months before it even gets to court. Even then it will be academic. He IS guilty so the only question is how many years he will be sentenced to!"

"Years!" Gina felt sick again. The thought of Jeff being out there for a number of weeks was bad enough, but years!…..It did not bear thinking about. "Mark, what are we to do?"

Mark cast Gina a kindly glance. "I will do whatever I can, you know that." he spoke gently. It was clear that he still had feelings for Gina. Carol hoped that this would help their cause and not hinder it.

"So what is our first move?" Carol spoke for the first time.

"We've already made the first move." Mark said. "I have spoken to the Foreign Office, as did you, and also spoken to the British Embassy in Sofia, where I was told that you had already beaten me to the punch. However, I too spoke to them this morning and was assured that Mr Meredith would be visited tomorrow morning by one of their representatives. He will check that your husband is in good health and has not been badly treated. He will also listen to his side of what happened and make sure that a solicitor is placed at his disposal. I took the liberty of telling the official that money was no object and that speed in procuring a solicitor was paramount. I also explained about the truck and made enquiries as to how this can be released."

Carol had almost forgotten about the truck. "I don't really care too much about the truck," Carol cut in. "If we have to spend money I would much prefer that it went to Jeff's defence rather than spend it on releasing the truck."

Mark nodded. "I understand where your priorities lie, but it sometimes is best, and not even more expensive to deal with all the outstanding matters at the same time."

"By the way." Gina had said very little up until now. "Are you registered to practice law abroad." She remembered what she had been told this morning.

"Barrington, Green and Partners is a very well-respected law firm." Mark told her, not without a small glow of pride. "As I told you once before, they specialise in criminal law and as most criminals seem to bolt abroad, then my company had to make sure it was registered for foreign law, so yes, in answer to your question, we are all qualified to represent you, and anyone else for that matter, at home or abroad."

Gina nodded. She was not really surprised to find that the sort of clients Mark's firm represented were probably little less than gangsters. However, she was satisfied with the answer. Maybe a firm of solicitors that earned their daily bread by helping hardened criminals find loopholes in the law was just what Jeff would need.

"Another thing I have for you is the address of the prison that they are holding your husband." He pulled out a piece of paper and handed it to Gina.

Gina stared at the address. Strangely enough she had not imagined being given an address telling her where Jeff was. She had imagined a nameless place in a faceless town, somewhere in a foreign country. To hold the actual address made her hand shake.

"I suggest that you send food," Mark said simply. "I have checked, and it is allowed, in fact expected. Apparently the food served in prison is not exactly, er, shall we say, up to the standard that your husband will probably be used to."

"You mean it is horrible prison food." Gina sounded distressed.

Mark caught Carol's eye. "Well yes, you could say that," he said, not unkindly. "You see it's not quite the same as it is in England., the prison food provided is pretty basic to say the least. So you will be allowed to send a food parcel, along with a letter. I'm sure it will be appreciated. Tins and packets of course. Fresh food will not travel well."

Carol understood what Mark was trying to keep from Gina. This prison was obviously no hotel, and the food, if she had read Mark's expression correctly, was certainly not haute cuisine. Mark rose from his seat. "Tomorrow I intend to contact the prison direct. I am arranging for an interpreter to come to my office, and with his help I will speak directly with the governor and see what can be done."

"I'm impressed," said Carol. "That is certainly getting the ball rolling right away."

"No point in waiting is there?" Mark Cameron slipped on his overcoat in preparation for the cold afternoon air. "I will telephone you tomorrow, as soon as I have spoken to the prison." He nodded politely to both women. "I'll see myself out."

Carol ignored Mark's words and followed him out of the living room. "What do you think of the chances of a quick release?" she asked quietly.

Mark hesitated in the hallway. "Not good," he answered simply. "But, of course, we must not appear negative at this point. We do have Gina's feelings to consider and of course, it's early days as yet."

Carol nodded. It was as she suspected.

"Do you have internet access?" Mark turned as he opened the front door.

"No, not yet," Carol answered. "But oddly enough it was one of the things we had been about to arrange."

"Do it then," Mark advised. "That way I will be able to fire off emails to you as soon as I get information and of course, you will be able to contact the Embassy and the Foreign Office a lot more easily, AND have evidence of doing so."

"Thank you for the advice. That's something we will get under way immediately." She had no idea how she or Gina were going to be able to work the thing but decided to cross that bridge when it arrived. "Thanks for coming Mark, we all feel better now we know we have you working for us."

Katy appeared from the kitchen where she and Spyder had been straining to hear what was being said as Mark swept through the front door and strode towards his silver Mercedes.

"I heard most of it." Said Katy, coming into the living room. "But is it good news do you think. Will he be able to get Jeff out."

"Oh, I don't know Katy." Gina felt deflated. There was nothing more that could be done this day and she felt exhausted. "But at least I have his address. I know where my Jeff is right now." She stared at the paper again.

"If we are allowed to send him a food parcel then why don't we make one up today, get it in the post at once." Carol was trying to cheer Gina's spirits.

"Yes, of course. I will write him a letter as well." Gina started to glance around for pen and paper.

Katy produced a large writing pad and a pen. "Gina, why don't you sit quietly and write a nice long letter to Jeff? Mum and I will raid the cupboards and see what we have. Then we can go down the shops and get it in the post and, at the same time, sort out something about getting a computer. I heard the bit about having one being useful."

"Yes absolutely! I'm sure I have loads of stuff we can send." Carol said cheerfully, almost too cheerfully. She had to keep Gina up and running.

Gina smiled and took up the pen.

"Come on." Carol said quietly to Katy, slipping an arm around her daughter as they went to the kitchen to search for suitable items to put in Jeff's parcel. She glanced round at the door to see Gina, head bent, a stray lock of hair falling over her face, as she started to write her letter. Carol's heart went out to her. She knew that this was going to be a long haul.... for both of them.

*****

CHAPTER NINE

Carol's boots slipped on the soft ground as she clambered up the steep incline through the thickly wooded copse. The trees opened up, allowing her to make her way to the gravel path that led along the river. The wind whipped her mass of auburn curls about her face as she came out of the shelter of the trees. The river gave Carol a sense of peace, winding through the woodland and making its way towards the first of the houses, before becoming wider and bubbling briskly through the more built up area then slowing to a gentle drift through the town park. There, the clear water became covered in algae, not so attractive but good for the ducks and water birds that made their homes on its banks.

She whistled to Bruno who was digging happily at the base of a tree, obviously keenly intent on some delightful scent that was in desperate need of his full attention.

The afternoon was chilly and damp, the smell of rotting leaves filled the air as Carol walked along the winding river bank. She had needed to be alone, to get out of the confines of the house and the smell of dust and paint and to clear her mind. There was so much to think about. She worried about Gina, struggling to come to terms with Jeff's imprisonment. She was also worried about the business. Transcon Haulage was far too new and vulnerable to be able to withstand a big setback. She sat down on a small log and gazed into the flowing water. Bruno joined her at once, pushing his big head into her hands. Tony would be arriving soon, possibly tomorrow morning with luck. She longed to see him, longed to feel his arms around her, to feel safe and cared for. At this moment she felt as though she was the one who must be strong, to support Gina and consider the future of Transcon Haulage. They had to get the new truck up and running. She knew this, but who would drive it? Would she have to go herself and, if so where would that leave Gina. Surely she could not leave her friend to cope alone.

Katy and Spyder had been supportive. Over the last few days she had wondered how she would have managed without them. Spyder, quietly getting on with the job in hand, painting ceilings and running back and forward to the DIY superstore, collecting paint and necessary bits and pieces without bothering to involve Carol in the mundane tasks.

Derek too had been understanding. "Take as much time as you need." he had told her. "There will always be a job here for you when you need it, but for now, you need to get your own business sorted." He had waved away her apologies. "Get your priorities in order girl." he had said. "You have a business to tend to!"

Katy had been exceptional. She had accompanied her mother and Gina to the computer store and given advice, telling them which one to buy and having the knowledge to install it and get it up and running. Carol was beginning to get the hang of it, albeit slowly, but Gina had taken to the complexities of computers as to the manor born, as though it where her lifeline to Jeff. She had listened intently to Katy's instructions and soon had the basics required for sending and receiving emails. She had also learned to search websites for anything that she may find useful in her fight to free her husband.

During one of these searches she had discovered that Jeff was not alone. He was certainly not the only British driver to have been arrested, thrown into jail in some foreign land and pretty much ignored by those in power back home in England. Gina had contacted some of the families, spoken to the wives and mothers and gleaned information about any organisation that may be able to offer help.

Carol sighed and got to her feet, the seat of her jeans now cold and damp through sitting on the rotting log.

Bruno trotted ahead as she followed the curve of the river, heading towards home, the biting wind catching her breath as they rounded the

bend, leaving the gravel towpath and turning into the small patch of woodland to cut through to the lane.

Carol stuffed her hands deep into her pockets as she walked. She would make no further decisions until Tony arrived. They needed to have a long talk. Talk about Jeff, talk about the business and talk about what they must do next.

In her heart she felt that there was no quick answer to getting Jeff a quick release. It had to be faced that he may be in that terrible place for some time and if that was the case then some serious decisions had to be made to keep the business afloat.

How Gina would react was a worry to Carol. She loved her friend dearly but knew, deep down, that she could not stand by and let the business go to ruin. She had to be strong and do what was required to keep the Transcon Haulage going. Keep it going for herself and, in fact, for Jeff and Gina. How long Jeff would be away nobody knew but Carol had no intention of just throwing up her hands and letting the whole thing slide. Jeff would not want that and to be fair, only she was in a position to safeguard the business so that Jeff would have something to come home to. Whenever that would be.

Yes, she had to be strong..... again. Carol sighed. This feeling was all too familiar, she had done it all before. Supported Katy alone and struggled to make ends met. Now she would have to support Gina in her hour of need and also keep the business up and running. Oh well, at least she'd had plenty of practice, so what was another battle to fight? She had done it before so would do it again.

She lifted her head high, the biting wind taking her breath away. It had started to rain but Carol disregarded the raindrops showering onto her face. She whistled to Bruno and lengthened her stride. There was plenty to be done and she had to get on with it. She was not going to let this setback run Transcon Haulage into the ground, she was made of stronger stuff. Transcon Haulage would survive, and by the time Jeff got home, it would be up and running, bigger and better than ever.

Bruno bounded ahead as Carol made her way between the puddles in the rough track leading from the lane to her haulage yard.

Walking through the big iron gates into the yard, Carol noticed how busy the place was beginning to appear. The three driving school trucks, each proudly displaying bright red 'L' plates were neatly lined up against the high brick wall to her left, under the overhanging trees, tucked tightly together to be as unobtrusive as possible. Her new Volvo, complete with trailer, stood resplendent along the wall nearest to the workshop, close to Jeff's old Ford Escort, covered in dust, grime and golden leaves, falling from the trees. Seeing it like that tugged at Carol's heartstrings. She made a mental note to get a bucket and sponge and clean the paint-work. Jeff wouldn't want to come home to a neglected car.

Next to the wrought iron gate leading to the house, her own Chevrolet dwarfed Spyder's brightly painted pick-up truck. She looked across to where her old battered mini was resting sadly outside the big ivy covered workshop. The doors were open and Carol could hear voices coming from inside.

"Having fun?" She enquired, walking into the workshop to find Spyder and Katy busy rummaging around amongst the old furniture that she had taken from the house and temporarily dumped there.

"Oh, Hi, Mum!" Katy backed out from under the cluttered workbench, pulling a heavy cardboard box behind her. "I told Spyder that you had all this old stuff in here and that you said he could help himself." She said brightly, brushing cobwebs from her dark chestnut hair.

"It's still okay isn't it?" Spyder enquired from over the top of a large wooden chest.

"Oh, yes, definitely." Carol replied quickly. "There is nothing here I will be wanting. Not my cup of tea this sort of thing, but I know there are some people who like it."

"You'd be surprised" said Spyder. "There's loads of people about who would find this lot a real treasure trove." He picked up an oddly shaped coffee table and carried it over to where Carol was standing. "Have a look at this!"

Carol looked. The plywood table was shaped like an artist's palette, four garishly bright, coloured rings stood proud from the pale wood, probably for use as drinks mats. The three spindly legs in black completed what was, to Carol, the worst possible example of taste.

"Do you like that then?" She asked carefully, so as not to insult Spyder's taste in furniture.

"Nineteen sixties is this," Spyder replied, turning the item in his hand. "A bit modern for me and Suzie actually, we go for the fifties stuff really but I know many people would give money for this."

"Really!" Carol was amazed. "Who on earth would want that?"

"Collectors actually. Like a lot of this stuff here. Very auctionable." Spyder informed her.

"You mean we could sell it and get money for it?" Katy was immediately interested.

"Yes, if you want to," said Spyder "Do you want me to look into it for you?"

Carol could not believe it. She could certainly do with some extra cash under the circumstances, but remembered she had promised Spyder anything he wanted. "But I said you could have it." she reminded him truthfully.

"But you didn't know it was worth anything then did you?" Spyder replied with equal honesty. "There are one or two bits that I know Suzie would love," he went on. "But to be really honest, some of the stuff is worth quite a good amount and I would not like to fiddle you and take it then sell it on at a profit. I know you could do with every penny at the moment."

"The best thing to do is find out if it really is worth something first." Katy put in practically.

"Yes, you're right Honey." said Carol. "Tell you what, Spyder, you do some groundwork and see what we can get for any of this and whatever it is we can share it, but of course if there is anything you want to keep then dig it out first and put it to one side."

"Well thanks for that." Spyder was pleasantly surprised at his new employers generosity. "Suzie knows all about this auction lark, she is always going to one or another and coming back with interesting stuff on the cheap, but she knows where the specialist ones are too. I will cart all this stuff back to my place and let her have a look. She can take it from there if that's okay with you."

"Fine by me." said Carol, pleased that she would finally see the back of it.

"There is one other thing." Katy leaned back onto the old workbench, hands behind her back.

"Oh yes, madam. I've heard that tone of voice before." Carol always knew when Katy wanted something.

"Well it's just that Spyder says he can fix up your old mini, get it up and running and looking good. If he does, then can I have it?"

Carol looked at Spyder who had quickly turned his back and was innocently busying himself amongst a crate of crockery.

"Oh really! Make it into a super 'custom car' no doubt!"

"Well not exactly spend a fortune," Spyder said sheepishly. "Just get it back to being really nice and standard and get the engine running, nice and reliable. You will find the insurance is cheap too." he added quickly.

"Go on." Carol knew she would have little chance of dissuading either Katy or Spyder from this one.

"As the mini is pretty old, and if Katy is only going to do limited mileage per year then we can get specialist Hot-Rod insurance which is cheaper than the standard sort. It's only a small engine too so it won't cost the earth to insure or to run. I will take care of it for Katy as I know you have a lot on your plate right now."

Carol felt a twinge of guilt. All the recent events had taken precedence over everything and pushed poor Katy into the background somewhat. "Okay, you got me." Carol threw her hands up in submission. "The car is all yours if you want it. Go ahead and do whatever is right, and DO make sure its one hundred percent safe before Katy gets her hands on it!"

"Oh, absolutely, one hundred and ten per cent, I promise!" Spyder grinned happily over to Katy who dashed over to Carol and gave her a hug.

"Thanks Mum, you're a diamond!"

"Yes, I know!" Carol laughed. "Just don't get carried away and forget the auctions." She called to Bruno and turned out of the workshop. Out of the corner of her eye she could see Katy and Spyder giving each other the thumbs up. She smiled to herself and walked up to the house leaving the conspirators to enjoy their treasure hunt.

*****

The heavy barred gate slid back with a groan as Zhravko Markov strode into the cell. "You come!" he pointed to Jeff, sitting on his bunk, reading an old magazine that John had given him.

"Where?" Jeff put down the magazine but stayed where he was.

"You come with me, English!" Zhravko Markov repeated.

"Where to?" Jeff repeated. "Will I get to see a lawyer as I requested?"

The big man hesitated. "There is one of your countrymen from the Embassy. He will speak with you." He looked Jeff in the eye as he spoke. This new man was quiet but strong. Markov had respect for that.

"Thank you," said Jeff, swinging his legs over the side of the bunk and dropping down onto the concrete floor. "Thank you very much, it is good of you to arrange that for me."

He followed Markov out of the cell and along the maze of corridors. "We did not arrange this meeting." Markov said eventually. He was an honest man and would not have the prisoners think that he was available to do favours for all and sundry. "It is your basic right. Your Embassy, they always send envoy to speak to new prisoner. They do nothing more. Just visit, make correct speech then leave."

That didn't sound particularly promising. Jeff stopped and turned to the big guard, looking him in the eye. "You mean my Government will do little or nothing to help me. I am not important enough for them to upset their relations with your country and, as far as they are concerned, a visit from the Embassy will suffice!"

Markov returned Jeff's stare. "All governments work same way."

The thick accent was abrupt but the eyes held some understanding. "They have bigger things to deal with. Money, oil, trade. If one man from their country has to be sacrificed then..... so be it!"

Jeff stood still, taking in the words. "Tell me Zhravko, how many people do you have in here that are truly guilty of the crime they are accused of?"

"Most of them." the answer came with no hesitation.

"Most of them you say, most but not all."

Markov shrugged. "It is not for me to make judgement. I take care of prisoners, take care of prison, I do my work."

"Just for my own peace of mind. Do you believe me when I say I knew nothing of the drugs on my truck and I am totally innocent of this crime."

Markov held Jeff's stare. "Maybe. Maybe not. That is for you and your God to know." He gestured to Jeff to move on. The two men walked in silence, down the iron staircase then along a further corridor, stopping by a big wooden door.

"But you did not say definitely no." Jeff pointed out quietly as Markov pulled open the heavy door and led Jeff inside.

The room was almost pleasant. In stark contrast to the cell he had just left. The walls painted a pale blue, almost matching the heavy duty carpet on the floor. Jeff had almost forgotten what it was like to have carpet under his feet.

A smartly dressed man rose to his feet behind the small wooden table in the centre of the room. "Good afternoon Mr Meredith. James Huntingdon-Smythe, at your service! How are you? Do please sit down while we have a chat." He waved Jeff to the chair opposite him. "Any chance of some refreshment old chap?" James Huntington-Smythe fired the last remark at Markov, a charming smile on his face. Apart from the surroundings, he could have been inviting someone to tea on the lawn in an English country garden.

"I will send coffee." Markov answered gruffly, closing the door behind him.

"Right, old chap." Huntington-Smythe went on, his manner becoming more serious as the two Englishmen found themselves alone in the small interview room. "Tell me as much as you can about what happened."

Jeff realised that there was surprisingly little to tell. He had been crossing the border. He had been arrested. He had been thrown into jail. What else was there?

"Now are you PERFECTLY sure that you knew nothing at all about the heroin on the vehicle?" Huntington-Smythe asked bluntly.

"Absolutely nothing!" Jeff replied with fervour. "How many people do I have to convince of that!"

"More than just me, I'm afraid." The answer was clipped and to the point, but Jeff knew it was exactly right.

"Yes, of course. It's just very hard to stomach being accused of something I haven't done."

"Ah, but you DID do it. You DID drive across the border so technically you are...."

"Yes, yes, I know. Guilty as charged! I DO know that, I've been told about the laws often enough. I just find it hard to come to terms with the fact that I can't bloody well do anything about it! When do I get a trial or see a lawyer?"

"Well, we have had lengthy conversations with your dear lady wife, your business partner and the solicitor they have enlisted to help you. A very, er, well known firm. Well known for defence cases actually."

The man's tone puzzled Jeff but he decided not to cloud the issue in hand by asking why. "I was told that I could only have a Bulgarian solicitor," he remarked. "One that probably wont speak a work of English at that!"

"Yes, that is the law here, but your wife has arranged an English Solicitor to work with him, and an interpreter."

Gina! Oh, God bless her..... and Carol too. Jeff could hardly bear to think about Gina. It was far too painful to think about his beautiful wife in this horrendous place.

"It's good to know I will be having some decent representation." he tried to keep his voice level and his mind on the case in hand. "I also have a business to run. The business is very new and I need to be there, doing my share, working, driving the truck, not sitting in here rotting away!"

Huntington-Smythe leaned forward, his voice lowering. "I advise you to listen very carefully to what your own solicitor advises. Heed his advice well. Remember, this is NOT England!" He sat back, his manner reverting back to the original brisk persona. "Well then, where has that coffee got to?"

Jeff could not help but wonder if this was an act. Would this man go back to his office, toss his papers on the desk and go off to dinner, not giving a second thought to the case. Was this purely a duty call, then, duty done, forget all about it.

The door swung open and a small, hunched man of indiscernible age walked in carrying a tray with a coffee pot and two thick mugs, a bowl of olives and a basket of bread. The man's hawk-like eyes darted from Jeff to the Embassy official and back again. It was hard to determine if the man was young or old, his skin sallow despite the obvious dark pigment. He put down the tray, glanced furtively around the room and left.

"Eat and drink while you can," Huntington-Smythe said quickly, pouring coffee into a mug and pushing it across the table to Jeff. "The food in here is little better than pig-swill as you have probably already found out!"

Jeff had found out. The main meal of the day was always some sort of stew. A thick layer of oil floating atop a watery mess of what appeared to be boiled cabbage leaves with rice. One day there had been a piece of meat amongst the soggy vegetable mush, but that had tasted highly dubious. The hard bread that was provided struggled to soak up the mass of water and oil. Jeff had hardly eaten the first day, his stomach being turned by the sight and smell of the stew, but hunger had taken a hold and common sense told him he could not go without food indefinitely. His stomach revolted at the first 'meal' and he had thrown up, but gradually he had got used to the foul oily mess presented at each meal. His bowels, however, had not. Frequent trips to the tin buckets in the corner of the cell had become the norm, the smell mingling with the stench that already hung heavy in the air.

"It is perfectly acceptable for your family to send food parcels old man." Huntington-Smythe went on. "It's the only way to supplement the diet here. In fact you must understand the way things work over here. When someone is arrested and locked up it is normal procedure for the man's family to be responsible for providing their food, clothing, blankets etc. Technically it is not the prisons responsibility to actually feed its prisoners."

Jeff was astounded. "You mean anything we are fed is at the discretion of the prison?"

"Well, not exactly. They do realise that they can't starve you all to death so they do provide the basics."

"You mean that disgusting oily soup stuff?"

"Exactly, but to them that is staple food. They believe that oil is good for you so they ladle it on with gusto. But of course, it is certainly not to our western tastes so it is best to get some food sent in, even convenience packaged food will do you well."

"Yes, I realise that." Jeff replied. He had been given some flavoured packet noodles, made up by John Miller. Not the sort of thing he would ever have considered eating under normal circumstances, but here, in this place, the taste had been as nectar.

"What time scale am I looking at before I can hope for a release from here." Jeff asked directly. He needed to stick to the main point.

Huntington-Smythe cleared his throat. "Well that, of course, depends entirely on the outcome of the trial you know."

"No, I don't know." Jeff said bluntly. "I haven't had a trial yet and don't know when there will be one."

"I will make sure you get a visit from your Bulgarian solicitor as soon as possible. I will also speak with your solicitor in England again, probably later today."

"You will 'phone him?"

"No need. I have a feeling that he will contact me. He already has telephoned me and tells me he will do so again later today. He seems to have the bit between his teeth on this case." Huntington-Smythe got to his feet, glancing at his watch. He obviously wasn't comfortable in this place. "Sorry old chap, got to dash. I hope this little chat helped make things clearer."

Jeff realised that Huntington-Smythe had said absolutely nothing of any use. It was clear that the Embassy was simply going through the motions and he was probably just another irritation to their routine. He got up from his chair and followed Huntington-Smythe to the door. Zhravko Markov was standing in the corridor.

"Thank you so much." The British official said politely to the big man. Jeff wondered why on earth the English had developed this habit of thanking people for absolutely nothing. He felt deflated and alone. If he was going to get out of here, it would not be with the help of the British Embassy, that was for sure. He would have to rely on the lawyer that Gina had found. It was his only hope. The only other alternative was to get used to being here. The thought sent his senses reeling. John Miller had been here for over four years. Would Jeff also be here that length of time. Suddenly he felt sick. Was it the realisation of the situation or was it the revolting oily stew gripping his insides. Whatever the reason Jeff's spirits hit rock bottom. As he followed Markov along the echoing corridors he glanced up at the high narrow windows, covered in ice and grime. Would this be the only sight of the outside world he would have for the next few years. He felt he would rather die!

*****

"Thank you so much Michelle. You have been more than understanding. I will get into the shop within the next couple of days......no, don't worry, I don't like letting you down and I think work, and being in the shop, will be more therapeutic than sitting here worrying about Jeff." Gina swished the clean yellow duster around the telephone table as she spoke. "No, we have heard nothing more, but I will be speaking to our solicitor again tomorrow so fingers crossed that he may have good news.... yes.....thank you Michelle.... goodbye."

Gina replaced the receiver and walked briskly through to the kitchen.

She had cleaned every inch of work surface and polished the tiles until they gleamed in showroom condition. She had turned every room inside out in a cleaning frenzy. Exhausting her body and venting her frustrations on any stray speck of dust or encroaching cobweb.

Phoebe swished hopefully round her ankles reminding her distracted owner that her pet was in fear of wasting away.

"Sorry sweetheart." Gina bent to stroke Phoebe's silken fur. "I nearly forgot you, didn't I?" She reached into the cupboard and opened a packet of cat food for the hopeful feline, depositing it into a china dish and setting it down on the plastic feeding mat neatly tucked into the corner of the spotless kitchen.

The doorbell made Gina jump. She was not expecting any callers and certainly did not feel in the mood for a chat.

"Mark!" The last person Gina expected to see standing on her doorstep was Mark Cameron.

"Hello Gina." Mark's voice was soft, the flicker of a smile on his lips. "May I come in please, I need to have a private chat with you?"

Gina hesitated. This would be the first time she had seen Mark alone since the end of their affair. If you could call it an end. She had simply discovered that Mark was seeing his secretary and had cut all contact. She had never officially ended the affair. Never told him it was over, but, after six months, it would be hard to presume that he had not gathered this.

"Is this about Jeff?" Almost lost for words, it was the first thing that sprang to mind.

"Yes, it is. May I come in?" Mark repeated.

"Oh, yes. I'm sorry." Gina led Mark into her living room, politely taking his coat and inviting him to sit. There had been a time, not so long ago, when she would have flung herself into his arms, their passion leaving no time for polite conversation. Not so now.

"Gina. I needed to speak to your privately, for a number of reasons." Mark got straight to the point.

Gina sat down on one of the big comfy armchairs facing him, a respectable distance between them. "Mark, I know what has gone on between us could cause embarrassment." She cut in. "But I want your assurance that what went on between you and I will make no difference to the way you handle this case and that you will do your absolute best to secure Jeff's release from that dreadful place."

"Gina, I am a professional. Nothing will cloud my judgement on a case, rest assured." Mark replied. "But there are one or two things we need to set straight."

Gina didn't need this. Was he hoping to re-start the affair. Could he be trusted to work on Jeff's behalf, or would it suit his needs to have Jeff out of the way and a clear path back to her bedroom.

Almost as if he could read her thoughts Mark reassured her. "Firstly, there can be no denying that you and I were once an item." He spoke quietly but with confidence. "However, I realise that you ended the relationship for your own reasons and I will not push you on this. I always knew that you never had any intention of leaving your husband."

How wrong he was. Gina had given it much thought at the time. She had been besotted.

"I always knew that one day you would turn tail and run, as you did. I don't blame you. You are a lovely lady and not the sort to be dishonest to your husband. You did what was right in the end and I admire you for it."

Mark had no idea that Gina and Carol had seen him with his secretary in the pub garden, holding hands in deep conversation. Gina decided not to mention it. This was not the time and, to be honest with herself, she didn't care any more. Jeff was her only concern. She loved him and wanted him home.

"Is this what you came to talk about?" she asked, giving nothing of her feelings away.

"Partly." Mark replied. "Partly because I wanted to clear the air as we will have to be working closely together and partly because I wanted to assure you that I have no intention of trying to win you over again or ask you to pick up where we left off."

"Thank you for that." Gina said quickly. "I really am now happy and settled with Jeff and nothing would encourage me to have another affair. I actually feel guilty for what we did anyway."

"Please don't." said Mark, his eyes meeting hers. "What we had was what we wanted at the time. It didn't hurt anyone and you ended it. Let us look forward and draw a line under it. Okay?"

"Okay." Gina agreed, feeling somewhat relieved. "I just want to concentrate on this awful situation with Jeff."

"Well that's the other thing I need to speak to you about. Speak in private, as what I have to say is not exactly, how shall I put it, 'politically correct." Mark sat back on his seat, glancing around as if he thought someone might overhear. "The brutal truth is that we can do very little to help your husband."

Gina felt sick to her stomach. She said nothing, simply rose from her chair and walked over to the rosewood cabinet, reaching out the brandy and two glasses.

"Only a very small one please." Mark held up his hand as Gina poured out the brandy. "Driving you know."

Gina handed Mark a small measure of the soothing drink and curled back into her chair, taking a sip of her own brandy, feeling the fiery liquid working its way into her system, settling the fluttering in her stomach. "You mean we are not going to be able to get him out of there as quickly as we had hoped."

Mark shook his head. "To be brutally honest, if we go through official channels, do the right things and wait for a trial, Jeff will not have any hope of returning to England for probably around five years."

Gina was horror stricken. "Five years! No! That just can't be true. Oh, Mark, I can't BEAR it. Five years." Tears started to well in her eyes and the room swam. What on earth would she do. How would she cope without him. How would Jeff cope. His life, his business. Oh god, this surely was a nightmare and she would wake up, Jeff at her side and realise it was all a dream.

Mark was unsure what to do. He wanted to gather her up in is arms, hold her tight and reassure her, but felt that this would not be appreciated nor appropriate under the circumstances. He cleared his throat. "Gina please, don't get upset. I haven't finished, please listen to me."

His voice brought Gina back to reality. "What more can you say? You've just said that official channels will take years. What else can we do? It all sounds so hopeless."

"This is the whole point." Mark continued patiently. "I am a solicitor, so officially, I can only advise you about the legal and proper way of doing things, but as a friend….." he hesitated and caught Gina's glance. "As a friend I can tell you that there is a more straightforward method of securing Jeff's release."

"What?" Gina would grasp any straw that was offered.

"Buy him out." Mark stated simply. "As I explained to you earlier, foreign countries work a lot differently than here in England. You can buy him out if you have enough behind you!"

"What!" Gina repeated. She could not understand. Was it as simple as it sounded. Surely not.

"Let me explain." Mark leaned back into the soft cushions of the sofa and took a sip of his brandy. "If there is enough money involved then Jeff's freedom can be bought. It's not entirely unusual, it has been done before, although the wording on the release documents do not always put the matter quite so bluntly."

Gina's head was spinning. She could hardly take it in. BUY Jeff out! It had not entered her head that this could be done.

"Of course." Mark went on. "It's not called bribery, you understand. It's classed as, well shall we say, negotiation. There is a possibility that you can pay Jeff's 'fine' and when that is done, then he will be released. Be warned though, it differs from country to country and also from prison to prison actually. You will have to be very careful how you approach the subject. Definitely not through the Embassy!"

Gina regained the power of speech. "How can this 'negotiation' be put into progress?" she enquired.

"It's a matter you will have to bring up directly with the prison authorities I believe." Mark informed her. "But of course arrangements have to be made to get him home and things can, I'm afraid, change by the minute or by the whims of who you are dealing with at that particular time. You must understand though, I cannot assist you in any way with this sort of dealing. All I can do is to carry on as normal, going through the usual channels and dealing with Embassy officials and the Foreign Office. In fact." Mark set down his glass. "In fact, this conversation Gina, has never taken place, do you understand?" Mark held Gina's eyes with a serious gaze. "It's just some food for thought, another approach for you to consider."

"Yes." she answered quietly. "Yes, I do understand and thank you Mark, you have been very kind."

Mark got to his feet. "Kind? Rather unprofessional I'm afraid, but needs must when the Devil drives and all that." He flashed Gina one of his charming smiles. "I must go. Caroline has invited guests for dinner this evening, but tomorrow I will be speaking once more to the Embassy and possibly, if it has been arranged, with Jeff's Bulgarian solicitor. I have an interpreter on call."

"Thank you." said Gina. "There is one other thing you can try and arrange for me though," she added. "I want to know if I can visit him. Go over there and see him, see that he is all right and speak to him. Can that be done?" Her eyes implored Mark to help her.

Mark sighed. "I will make enquiries, although it's not the best place to visit on your own you know."

"Let me worry about that." Gina was still a strong lady. She knew the dangers of travelling alone but her need to see Jeff outweighed everything.

"Okay, leave it to me and I will let you know what can be arranged." Mark could see that Gina was not to be swayed on this.

"Thank you." Gina said once again as she walked Mark to the front door. For a brief second he hesitated and Gina thought for a tiny moment, he may bend and kiss her. She took a small, almost involuntary, step back.

"Goodnight." Mark read her body language.

"Goodnight Mark, and thank you for everything." Gina closed the door, and leaned her back on the solid barrier between herself and the outside world. She could hear Mark start the engine on his Mercedes and drive away. At one time, she reflected, she would have watched him leave, waiting until he was well out of sight before coming back inside. How things changed. She sighed and walked back into the living room. What Mark had just told her had completely thrown her.

She needed to think, think hard. She needed to find the right person to help her deal in underhanded methods. She needed to see Jeff.

She needed another brandy!

*****

CHAPTER TEN

The loud blast of air horns woke Carol from a deep sleep. It was barely dawn, darkness still cloaking the outside world beyond her bedroom window, the morning chorus not yet beginning.

She leapt from her bed, now fully awake, and flung the window wide. Peering through the gloom into the haulage yard she could see the 'Silver Lady' turning slowly, manoeuvring into place alongside her twin sister, the new Volvo Globetrotter.

Tony had arrived. At last! Carol's heart leapt as she pulled on her towelling robe and ran from the room, clicking on the lights as she hurried along the landing and down the stairs towards the front door.

Bruno was already on sentry duty, sniffing at the door with interest at the prospect of such an early arrival. Both Carol and Bruno vied for position as she pulled open the door. The early morning air was cold and damp but Carol paid no regard as she ran, barefoot down the big stone steps towards the yard.

Tony looked weary and unkempt as he dropped down from the high cab, locking the door and heaving his large canvas bag over his shoulder.

"Darling!" Carol felt all the worries and tension release at the sight of him. "Darling, thank God you're all right."

Tony dropped his bag and held his arms wide as Carol rushed across the gravel towards him, gathering her close and burying his head into her auburn curls. "Cara Mia! It's all right. I'm fine, just worn to the bone that's all." He held her close for a moment then released his grip, sliding his arm around her waist and guiding her back towards the house. "Hey, look at you, running barefoot on this hard ground."

"I hadn't noticed," Carol had not given it a thought. "I'm just so glad to see you at last. I was so worried about you, after what happened with poor Jeff it must have been horrendous for you out there!"

Tony dropped his bag inside the hallway and slammed the front door. Again he took Carol into his arms and held her close. "Oh, you smell so good!" he murmured, bending to kiss her full on the lips.

"You don't actually," Carol observed, coming up for air. "A mixture of sweat and road dust." she laughed. "But I don't care right now. As long as you're here. Safe and with me!"

"I didn't bother stopping as often as I should have," Tony admitted. "I just wanted to keep tramping on and get here to you as soon as humanly possible." "Thank you Darling." Carol kissed him again, disregarding the staleness of his mouth and three-day stubble. "I didn't realise how much I needed you 'til I heard you pull in just now. Oh Tony!" Tears welled up in her eyes. This last week of being strong for Gina and holding everything together suddenly took their toll and Carol melted against Tony, allowing herself the small luxury of a moment's weakness.

"Hey, come on, Cara Mia. This is not like you." Tony led Carol gently into the living room, sitting with her on the big comfortable sofa. He pulled her close to him and leaned back, stroking her hair.

"Sorry." Carol snuggled into his chest. "It's just been such an awful strain."

"Yes I know." Tony continued to stroke her hair. "I know very little myself, only what happened at the border and what little news others had heard." Tony tried to stifle a yawn. "I telephoned Marco after I had spoken to you and, of course, he said he would immediately get on to the authorities and try to find out where we stood about the load and the truck. I have not spoken to him since then as I have been concentrating on getting this load back here and myself back to you."

"I understand, Darling. It must have been terrible for you."

"Cara Mia, I am worn to the bone. Let me take a shower and get some sleep. Later we can talk properly." He tilted her chin. "Go back to bed and wait for me there. I will be able to speak more clearly after a few hours rest."

Carol kissed him again. "Of course Darling, go right up, there is plenty of hot water, I'll take us up a hot drink, that will make you feel better." She felt slightly guilty that she had not considered the fact that Tony had probably been driving most of the night to get to her. But she delighted in the fact that she could lay for an hour or so, locked in his arms, thinking of nothing but themselves before beginning the task of working through the events of the border arrest.

Her heart went out to him as he walked slowly, head bowed, up the big staircase. It had taken five days to get back to England. The weather and the terrible circumstances taking their toll. But he had managed well, better than could have been expected and still had showed patience and understanding. Any doubts that she had ever held about her feelings for him had flown away. She knew that she loved him. Totally.

Carol made two cups of coffee and took them upstairs to the bedroom. Tony, fresh from the shower flung himself under the still warm covers and took a sip. Carol joined him, sitting together in bed it felt cosy and familiar.

"I need to get a little sleep," Tony said wearily, sliding down under the duvet and resting his head back on the pillow. He flung out an arm and Carol tucked in besides him, resting her head on his shoulder.

"Rest as much as you need, Darling," she said softly, turning towards him and cuddling up close. She needed to feel him close to her after all the trauma of recent events. "We can talk later."

Tony turned and kissed her on the lips. A shudder slid down her spine as his hand caressed her back. "It's just so good to have you here, next to me, safe and warm," she murmured. Tony didn't answer. Exhausted he had fallen asleep in her arms.

It was almost noon before Carol was awakened by the sounds of activity downstairs. She could hear the voices of Spyder and Katy drifting from the big front drawing room below. Spyder was obviously getting stuck in to finishing off the painting of ceilings. Tony stirred at her side, his eyes opening as he adjusted to his surroundings.

"Hello again, Cara Mia." he said huskily, stretching and easing his arm from under her neck. Although it had been delightful to fall asleep locked together in a close embrace, the muscles in his arm were complaining. Carol sat up, stretching and shaking the sleep from her eyes.

"Good heavens, look at the time," she was never one for lying in bed under normal circumstances. "Katy and Spyder must have been up for hours."

"They obviously haven't missed us though!" Tony's startling grey eyes had regained their sparkle. He reached up his arm over Carol's shoulders, pulling her back down next to him. "If they haven't missed us yet then another half hour wont make any difference will it?"

Before Carol could answer he had raised onto his elbow, leaning over her, kissing her passionately. Carol had no objections as his hands slid over her naked body and she melted to his advances.

*****

"I suppose we should put in an appearance." Carol sighed, still glowing from their lovemaking. "Katy and Spyder will be wondering what the hell we are doing up here!"

Tony laughed. "I have no doubt that they are perfectly clear on what we are doing, Cara Mia!" He brushed her face lightly with his fingers.

"Tony! I hope not." Carol's cheeks flushed red.

Tony laughed again. "Oh, you English. How prudish you are. Is it not normal for people to make love, especially when they have been apart for so long?"

"Well yes, I suppose. But... well... we don't always BROADCAST it you know! And anyway, you are English too don't forget!"

"Yes, Cara Mia, by birth I am as English as you are, but by heart I am now Italian and feel very much as all Italians, that making love is a wonderful thing and not to be hidden behind drawn blinds and never discussed unless in hushed tones!"

"Tony! You can't mean that people in Italy do it publicly and talk about it to all and sundry!"

Tony laughed at Carol's flushed face. "No silly one. Not at all. In fact in Italy making love is treated with far more respect than it seems to be in England, it's just that we are open about what we do, though that is not to say we do it in public you understand. Poppa and Mamma often go for a 'lie down' in the afternoon. We know they are not sleeping but why should they? They are deeply in love and want to be together. How can that be bad?"

"Of course, it's not bad." Carol swung her legs out of bed and reached for her bath robe. "I've always been a little shy about things I suppose. Silly really."

"It's not silly." Tony sat up, running his fingers through his mass of jet black curls. "I think it is charming to have a lady who is so modest. I love you for it, Carol Landers!"

Tony pulled on his jeans and reached inside his carry bag for a clean shirt. "Go and shower, my lovely, I will go downstairs and meet the workers. Tell them that we have not deserted them entirely!"

Carol pushed her feet into her slippers and made for the bathroom, feeling like a truant schoolgirl at this late hour. She heard Tony's steps pass the door and go downstairs. How self assured he was. Younger than she, but years ahead in confidence and maturity. As always, she doubted her own attraction. Tony was young, handsome, kind and gentle. Not to mention sensible and trustworthy. She glanced in the bathroom mirror as she slipped the bath robe over her shoulders and onto the floor. Her auburn curls had frizzed in the steam, her face still flushed from lovemaking. What on earth did he see in her she wondered. Italy was full of beautiful young girls, all looking for a good husband. Why on earth had Tony fallen in love with her, a truck driver living a thousand miles away? It hardly seemed to be the ideal match for one such as Tony.

Carol remembered that Tony had once been engaged. He was to have married Maria, a suitable Italian girl. Had tragedy not struck and Maria had not been killed in a horrific road accident then no doubt he would have been married by now, probably with children. What had she, a thirty four year old truck driver with a teenage daughter got to offer him?

She decided to brush these thoughts from her mind. She loved him and by all tokens it appeared that he loved her. "Take it for what it is." Gina had told her many times. "The man loves you, you ass, just believe him for God's sake and stop fighting it. Enjoy it!" Carol knew her friend was probably right and she should just take things for what they were instead of trying to analyse everything. She had no idea of her own attractiveness, her sex appeal. Tony was totally in love with her. That was clear to everybody.......except Carol herself.

*****

"Morning Mum!" Katy looked up from a pile of note papers and reference books, an impish twinkle in her eyes. "Tony and Spyder are in the yard admiring the new truck," she announced. "He asked whose it was so....well we just said it was yours. Couldn't not say really, could we?"

Carol had dressed hurriedly but carefully, in fresh pale denim jeans and cream jumper, her hair piled loosely on top of her head and held in place with a wide velvet band. Coral lipstick and a touch of green shadow on her lids highlighted her emerald green eyes and fresh complexion. The effort did not go unnoticed on Katy who decided against remarking upon it.

"What did he say when you told him?" Carol plonked down on the arm of the settee next to Katy's flurry of paperwork, trying to appear casual.

"Seemed quite pleased actually. Said it was a great looking truck and he and Spyder went straight out to admire it. You know, toys for the boys and all that. Looked happy enough about it being yours though. Surprised you didn't tell him already!"

Carol got to her feet. "He was utterly shattered when he got here. Poor love, too tired to talk even, just went out like a light."

Katy opened her mouth to offer a mischievous quip about them having all morning to talk, then thought better of it. "Well he looks fine now so you had better go and see how he likes the new 'baby'." Katy put down her books and stretched. "Anyway, now you're both up and about I'll put some bacon under the grill. We can all have a sandwich. Breakfast for you two and lunch for Spyder and me!"

"Cheeky!" Carol stuck out her tongue at Katy and made for the door. She could hear Spyder and Tony chatting animatedly outside.

"Hey you two." Carol called as she crunched across the gravel towards them, Bruno bounding ahead. "So, Darling, how do you like her?"

"Now this is more like it!" Tony called back enthusiastically, standing back to get a better look. "What made you take the plunge on this one then?"

Spyder winked at Carol and made his excuses, walking back to the house.

Carol stood close to Tony. "Well to be honest, Darling, it's been a thought I have had for a while now, but I didn't want you to think I was ungrateful for all the work you put into the Transcon, keeping her going and all that. But this one seemed so right I thought I'd better take a chance and buy it. The old Transcon can't go on forever and now... well she's stuck in bloody Bulgaria with poor Jeff."

Tony ran his hands through his dark curls. "Jeff. Yes, we will have to talk about that in detail. It's bad Cara Mia, very bad." A gust of wind made Carol shiver. Tony slipped his arm around her as they turned for the house. "You must bring me up to date on what's taken place. I know very little. Been driving me mad not knowing what's happened. Just needed to get back here as soon as I could and speak to you." He glanced at his watch. "I must leave soon, get this load of toys delivered."

"Not before you've eaten," Carol remarked. The smell of grilling bacon was drifting temptingly in the air as they walked into the kitchen.

"Mum, I hope you don't mind. Gill rang earlier and I told her she could pop round with the little ones to choose a kitten. I didn't like to say she couldn't. In fact I didn't mention the Jeff business at all. Didn't think you wanted it public knowledge just yet."

"Thanks Darling. You are right. Let us keep it just amongst ourselves for now. If the boys want to come round and see the kittens that's okay. Life must go on as normal as possible. We can't let this awful business take over our lives to the exclusion of everything. When are they arriving?"

"After playschool, about three I think." Katy was piling bacon between thick slices of fresh bread and handing round the sandwiches.

Tony had forgotten how hungry he was and fell upon his well filled 'doorstep' sandwich. "This is good!" he announced, chewing gratefully. "What kittens?"

"Those kittens!" Katy pointed. From the kitchen window they could see the three small balls of fluff venturing from the old privy and exploring the nearby bushes. "We should really pick them up and bring them inside.

Handle them to make them friendly, otherwise they will grow as wild as their mother."

"Wild ones can never be tamed." Tony mumbled through a mouthful of bread and bacon. "But the little ones will soon get used to being handled. But tell me, what headway has been made with the Jeff situation?"

Carol brought Tony up to speed with all she knew. "It seems so hard to get anybody to do anything concrete though." she ended. "I suppose he is just another statistic to the Foreign Office and the Embassy guys."

"There is one thing that could make matters even worse." Tony said seriously, finishing his last mouthful and pushing his plate away.

"Surely things can't get any worse than they already are." said Spyder, gathering up the plates and piling them into the sink. "The poor man is locked away and the truck is stuck out there. What can be worse?"

"Jeff is the CPC holder is he not?" Tony asked. "He holds the 'O' licence, the Operators licence that allows this business to run. With him locked away is it still valid? Is the business still running legally? Can you carry on in his absence?"

"Oh God!" Carol groaned. "I hadn't given that a thought! I really don't know. I have no idea of the legalities of the situation. I suppose we had better ask Mark as soon as possible."

"Mark?" Tony looked curious.

"Oh, he's our solicitor," said Carol. "His name is Mark Cameron." Carol decided that no further explanation was necessary.

"Oh, right, better to find out as soon as you can, Cara Mia. This thing could have far reaching consequences for us all."

Carol felt thoroughly deflated. She wondered how bad things could possibly get. "I'll come with you to deliver the toys," she announced. At least a ride in the truck and Tony's company may be some sort of compensation. They could also talk more on the way.

Tony smiled. "Thank you, Cara Mia, I will enjoy your company, the ride here has been long and lonely. When we come back this evening I must speak to Marco. I have to find out what he has learned about the Transcon and our load of oil that they impounded. Though I doubt we will ever see the load again. Also find out what arrangements he has made for the next load. We must not let customers down, it is bad business."

"But you need a couple of days break." said Carol "You can't do it all yourself. With two of you doing the runs we were tight, but now Jeff's not here…." She knew she had to help now.

"I did have one good break," Tony said simply. "Although sometimes you can get away with it, technically it is not allowed to drive trucks across some places on Sundays. I was unlucky and got pulled over and told to stop. Actually I waited 'til it was all clear and made some more headway down the back roads, but I did get a chance to rest up a while. But I do need to speak to Marco about the Transcon and about Jeff." Tony went on "Tell him everything you have told me and find out what action he has been able to take. My little brother has many connections, I doubt if he has been sitting idle. He will have been trying every angle to get our load back and maybe by now he may have spoken to someone who can help Jeff too."

"Do you really think so." Carol felt hope rise once more.

"I'm not sure, but as our family business is so closely connected with yours, I know we are all in this together. We are one truck and driver down now, remember, and now is when the olive picking season really gets under way. There will be lots of work to be done, and we need all the help and ideas we can come up with."

Carol knew he was right. They needed more than help. They needed her back on the road.

*****

Gina pulled the soft cream drapes across the big front window, shutting out the cold dark evening outside. She felt the need to indulge herself, spoil herself and feel comforted.

She had soaked in a sweet smelling bath until her skin had started to wrinkle, cleaned and re-polished her toenails and fingernails and wrapped herself in a soft towelling robe. She needed to forget everything right now, just for this evening. If not she felt her brain would burst.

Gina was made of strong stuff but this situation was taking its toll and she recognised the need to relax, get herself on an even keel, all the better to deal with the future. Nothing ever came of getting hysterical and weeping copiously and doing absolutely nothing. She would relax this evening and start afresh in the morning. Renewed in body and spirit.

She had made herself a bowl of the ultimate 'comfort food', mashed potato with egg and melted cheese with chocolate ice cream to follow. There was an interesting documentary about the Great Barrier Reef on the television, soon followed by a gripping Lynda la Plante drama. She would curl up in the glow from the fire, eat her food from a tray and wallow in the television programmes.

As she stepped towards the kitchen to take her bowl of cheesy mash from the oven, the telephone rang briskly. Gina sighed. Should she answer it or ignore it? She did not feel in the mood for light conversation, but was this about Jeff? Even so late in the day it may be him, telephoning to say it was all a huge mistake and that he was free and on his way back to her. Gina snatched the phone from the cradle.

"Hello, Gina here!"

"Ah, Gina! At last. It really is *far* too inconvenient to keep telephoning you and getting no reply." Her mothers irritated tone snapped down the wires. Oh no! NOT her mother! Why had she not left the damn thing to click onto answer-phone!

"Oh, hello, Mummy."

"Why you can't think to pick up the 'phone and dial once in a while is really just bad manners, Gina! You certainly were not brought up that way. DO have some consideration dear!"

Gina bristled. "I do have other things on my plate at the moment Mummy," she said sharply.

"That's as maybe." Unfazed, her mother's voice trilled on. "But Christmas has *got* to be fully arranged. There is far too little time to dally." Christmas! Gina didn't want to think about Christmas. Not a Christmas possibly without Jeff. She opened her mouth to tell her mother that Christmas was the last thing on her mind at present but was not given the opportunity.

"I have had to take the arrangements upon myself..... as always! We will be celebrating here. You two must be here by ten thirty on the twenty fifth, which will give us time for drinks before the other guests arrive. You will then be able to help me in the kitchen, Gina. Dinner will be for eight people. So that's settled then!" It was more like a command than an invitation.

It was all too much for Gina. "No it is NOT settled!" Gina snapped into the receiver. "Jeff and I will NOT be coming for Christmas. We have made other arrangements!" There, she had said it. Told her mother that she would not be fitting into her carefully made plans.

"What! What other arrangements. Gina how terribly selfish of you!" SELFISH! Gina had heard enough. Her mother had only ever thought about herself, or appearances, or materialistic things for as long as Gina could remember, and to accuse her now of being selfish!

".....I have no idea how I am going to tell Daddy what you have just said!" Her mother's voice grated on. Gina was angry and close to tears. She felt like slamming the telephone down there and then. "....Arthur! Speak to your daughter!" As usual, when all else failed, her father was being summoned to deal with his wayward daughter. Gina took a deep breath and held back the tears. She could hear her father's steps approaching the telephone.

"Gina?"

"Oh Daddy!" On hearing his voice it was all too much. Gina burst into tears.

"Hang on." Gina heard the living room door close with a click. Her father could not be overheard. "Princess, what on earth is it. Has Mummy upset you so much?"

"Oh, Daddy." Gina repeated. "It's not just her it's...... Oh, Daddy something awful has happened!" The tears were coursing freely now down Gina's cheeks.

"Princess, you wait there, I'm coming right over!"

"No, don't! Mummy will want to come and she is the very LAST person in the world I want here, and DON'T tell her that anything is wrong!"

"Darling! Give me some credit." Daddy had no intention of telling his wife anything..... anything at all if it could be avoided! "I will be there.....alone, right away, okay?"

Gina felt better. "Thank you Daddy. I DO love you!"

"And I love my little princess, so cheer up. Daddy's on his way!"

Gina put down the phone and blew her nose on a pretty pink tissue. Daddy was on his way. All would be well. But that was when she was a little girl. Daddy put everything right. But she doubted that even Daddy could fix this awful mess.

*****

"Did Gill come round with the kids this afternoon?" Carol asked between mouthfuls of beef stew cooked by Katy. The three were dining cosily from trays in the living room. Carol and Tony relaxing after an afternoon of battling with the London traffic.

"Oh, yes." Katy replied. "The kids were chuffed to bits with the kittens, though Frank Junior is still happy for half shares in Bruno and took him for a 'walk' round the garden while David was deciding which kitten to have!"

Carol laughed. "Was it a difficult choice then?"

"Of course it must have been!" Tony put in, finishing his last mouthful and setting down his tray. "Children take these things very seriously you know, especially when faced with a choice of three!"

"Surprise, surprise, he actually chose the ginger one!" Katy informed them.

"And called him Tigger, I suppose?"

"Well no, Thomas O'Mally actually!"

"Thomas O'Mally! Really? Why on earth would he call a kitten Thomas flaming O'Mally?" Carol giggled.

"Hey, come on Mum, stick with the plot. 'The Aristocats' of course." Katy gathered up the trays and walked them through to the kitchen.

Carol had a vague recall of the well known cartoon. "Wasn't he black and white?" she called after Katy's disappearing form.

"I thought he was a tabby," Tony put in. "Goes to show how much we all think we know. Bet the children could tell us every colour and every name!"

Katy laughed, returning with a tray holding fruitcake and coffee. "I did suggest he called him Tigger but he told me not to be silly and that Tigger was a different shape and what's more he was back at home sat on his bed!"

"So there! That was YOU told," said Carol between giggles.

"It gets better." Katy went on. "The black and white one is now Digger and the little tortoiseshell is Cinderella!"

Carol's eyes widened. "Dare I ask why?"

"Cos 'Digger' was digging a hole at the time, so that makes sense and Cinderella has the same colours as Cinderella's patchwork apron in his book! Obvious really!"

"Oh yes, of course. Quite obvious! Why didn't I think of that!"

"Spyder came up with a sensible thing though." Katy tried to stop giggling enough to be serious. "Suggested calling the local Cat Protection place and says they will catch the wild mother cat, get her neutered then put her back. Can't have her keep producing kittens wholesale can we? I reckon you could just put some food down outside for her and leave her be after that. She will no doubt be fine. Oh, and Spyder says he and Suzie will probably like 'Cinderella' when she is a few weeks older."

"Really! I thought they had the baby due in a few weeks. Won't it be too much work?"

"Oh no, she will be a present for Suzie's mum it seems who is a real cat person and would absolutely adore her. But I think you are going to have to keep 'Digger' though, Bruno has taken to him like you just wouldn't believe."

"Really, has he, how so?"

"He just seems to love him. Licks him at every opportunity and has even picked him up and carried him into the house, lying down with him between his paws!" Katy walked back to the kitchen to see if the kettle had boiled.

"Bruno always liked cats, come to think of it," Carol remarked. "Remember when he was a puppy he was always cuddled up with Buster."

"Oh yes, of course, he and Buster were inseparable."

"Buster?" Tony asked.

"Buster was our cat in Derbyshire," Katy explained. "He was black and white too actually, but he was getting on a bit when Mum moved down here so we let him stay there and live with Andy and Anna. He's still going strong though. Oh, nearly forgot, Gina rang. Says she will speak to you tomorrow as she is trying to have a relaxing night and get herself together a bit, poor love."

Carol felt immediately guilty. She had been laughing and happy while her friend was alone and still anguishing over Jeff. No doubt Gina was also worried about the future. Her own future and the future of the business. Carol knew what she had to do. "How many loads of toys are available from the Sofia factory?" she asked.

Tony glanced up from the paperwork he was sorting in preparation for speaking to Marco. "Marco will know," he answered. "Why do you ask, I'm not sure if we will be doing it now under the circumstances. Maybe just stick with the German runs."

"The Sofia factory is one load short of the ordered oil," Carol pointed out. "And we are one load short of toys for the London delivery. We can't just drop out on good orders, it will give us a bad name, so it's pretty obvious, I must get the other truck on the road," she stated. "We need two trucks up and running and as we have the 'Silver Lady' and the new Volvo then there it is. No question really, it's now down to me, we can't let the firm run into the ground just because Jeff isn't here right now."

"You can't drive to Bulgaria!" Tony said sharply.

What! Carol had never been good at being told what to do - or what not to do. "I beg your pardon!" Carol's emerald eyes flashed and her voice had an edge that did not go unnoticed by either Tony or Katy but before Tony could reply Katy stepped in diplomatically.

"I think what Tony means is that it would be unwise for a lady on her own to drive over there. Isn't that right Tony?" She put down her writing pad and glanced over to where Tony was crouching, ruffling through the papers spread out on the top of one of the packing cases. He caught her eye then looked across to Carol, sitting in one of the big armchairs, her hands cupped round her coffee mug, her emerald eyes flashing with emotion.

"Exactly. It would not be a good idea for you to do that, Cara Mia. I thought you were only considering Italy or Germany. Not Bulgaria!"

Carol was bristling with indignation. "I did my first run without asking advice and managed to get there and back in one piece. Why should anyone try to tell me where, or where not, I should go to now. Also let us not forget that this is MY company and I certainly have every right to make sure it stays running and to drive my own truck wherever I please!" She was angry. She had not struggled to come this far to be told what to do by anyone, even Tony.

Tony realised that he had definitely struck a raw nerve and came to sit next to Carol. "Sorry, that certainly came out very wrong. All I meant was that driving to Bulgaria is not like driving across France or Italy. The roads are unmade in places and very lonely. Bandits run rife out there and some even carry guns. The police will do little or nothing to help foreign drivers. I would fear for your safety Cara Mia."

"Put it this way." Katy, also worried about her headstrong mother, cut in quickly and tried to clarify Tony's words. "If there was someone trying to steal a load or rob a truck and he had the choice between a big beefy male trucker and a petite lady driver, which one do YOU think he would consider to be the easiest target?"

"Robbery may not be the worse thing to consider," Tony added. "Women are targets for rapist whereas men are not."

Carol knew they were right. It still rankled that she should have to make different decisions and alter her way of life because of her gender. "I know what you are trying to say," Carol said honestly. She did not want to argue with Tony. They saw little enough of each other without spoiling things with a row. "But don't ever try to tell me what I can, or cannot do. I make my own decisions!"

Tony sighed and threw up his hands. He admired Carol's determination and fighting spirit. He did not want to change her. He loved her for what she was.

"Anyway, we could travel in convoy." Carol was softening slightly after her initial bout of indignation. "What could possibly happen if we were together? I suggest that we arrange two loads of waste paper from the factory here as usual, load up together and run to Florence.

We then go on to your place and load up with the oil, run on to Bulgaria to unload, pick up the toys from the factory and straight back here. What can go wrong with us both together?"

Tony did not answer. He and Jeff had been together and look what had happened there. "I will telephone Marco." He said diplomatically. He knew Carol was not to be deterred once she had made her mind up but he was far from happy.

*****

"Come on Princess, you let it all out." Arthur Greenwood held his daughter close as Gina wept copiously. "I can't remember the last time I saw you cry!" Gina was sitting on his lap, weeping piteously, her body wracked with sobs. Somehow it was making her feel better. Her father holding her close as he had done when she was tiny, and her tears releasing the pent up anguish inside.

She sat back, wiping her eyes with a tissue. "Oh, Daddy, I am sorry to do this to you but I think I must have needed to let it all out. I'll be okay now." Gina kissed her father on the top of his balding head and slid off his lap. "Honestly, look at me, a grown woman sitting on Daddy's knee!" a wry smile making its way through the slowly drying tears.

"Grown or not, you're still my little Princess!" Her father adored her and felt guilty that his beloved daughter had not found it possible to confide in him at once. But, of course, there was his wife, Gina's mother. She would certainly be able to dine out for months on the story of her daughter's unsuitable husband being locked away for drug trafficking in hostile lands! Arthur liked Jeff. He was a man after his own heart. Honest and hard working, and more than that, he loved and cared for Gina. That was more than enough for him to like and respect the man.

"Pour me a brandy, Princess. Let us make the most of your mother's absence and tell me what I can do to help."

Gina reached the brandy glasses from the cabinet, pouring her father a generous measure. Mummy would not have approved! "There is nothing you can do Daddy," she handed him the glass. "I have a solicitor and Carol is also helping. We are doing everything we can and have done everything we can, …. except there is one other road to be explored." She explained about the mysterious conversation with Mark.

"That sounds about right to me!" Arthur said bluntly.

"What! Do you think that is normal!" Gina was taken aback.

"I have travelled widely, Princess, seen many countries and seen many, er, shall we say, different customs. This is probably just one of them." He leaned forward and took Gina's hand. "You will need money," he said gently. "Whatever it is just tell me. You have it. Understand!"

"Oh thank you Daddy." Gina hugged her father close. "I have some savings so I may be able to manage but thank you SO much anyway. I WILL ask if I need it." she drew back. "But what about Mummy?" The last thing she wanted was her mother bringing in to all this.

"Don't worry Princess." Arthur Greenwood smiled. "As far as Mummy is concerned, I am round here trying to talk sense into you about Christmas. When I go home I will just tell her that you have made other arrangements and will not budge. She'll get over it. In fact it will be another drama for her to wallow in and gain another sympathy vote from the other old biddies down at the bridge club. She won't hear a word about this business from me, I can assure you!"

As Gina waved her father goodbye and closed the door, she felt so much better. Was it from all the pent up tears she had released or was it that she had been able to unburden herself to her father. Whatever the reason, she felt better. She felt more positive than she had done all week and strode purposefully into the kitchen to rescue her cheesy mash from the oven. The great Barrier Reef and Lynda la Plante were awaiting her.

*****

CHAPTER ELEVEN

"What are you two doing?" Carol asked, as she and Katy hauled grocery shopping out of the capacious boot of the Chevy.

Spyder was sitting in the cab of the new Volvo and Tony in the cab of the 'Silver Lady', the doors wide open on both trucks despite the driving rain and bitter wind.

"Come and see," Tony called back as Carol and Katy ran past the trucks and into the house with the shopping.

"I wonder what on earth they are up to now," Carol remarked, dropping the heavy bags onto the kitchen floor.

"Dunno. Go and see while I unpack and put away," Katy suggested.

Carol zipped her coat up to the neck against the cold and ran back to the trucks, climbing into the 'Silver Lady' and sitting next to Tony.

"I know you are determined to do the drive, Cara Mia and to make me personally feel happier Spyder provided us with these CB radios that he had tucked away in one of his garages."

Carol looked blank. "What do they do then?"

"There are two radios and hand speakers, one in this truck and one in the other. We can speak to each other as we drive along!"

"Hmm, nice." Carol still had no idea what possible use being able to chat while driving could be. Not to mention the fact that it looked like she would have to hold the speaker in one hand and drive with the other.

"They have a range of a good couple of miles, so if we lose each other, we can still keep in touch. Supposing one or other of us was in trouble, we could call for help."

Ah, so that was what it was all about. Tony thought she needed keeping an eye on. She considered giving a sharp comment about the radios but decided that it was hardly worth the argument. Anyway they just may be handy in an emergency, supposing she broke down again. Yes, okay, they just MAY be a good idea. "Thank you Darling, that's very thoughtful!" She decided to take the line of least resistance. She could not bear the thought of having to drive all that way with tension between them. "I will leave you and Spyder to finish fitting these, er, things, while I go and telephone Gina. I have to tell her what we have decided to do, she is part of all this after all."

"Of course." Tony agreed. "Give her my best wishes when you speak won't you."

Carol gave him a peck on the cheek and jumped out of the cab, running through the rain to the house.

"Guess what those two have come up with now!" she announced to Katy as she divested herself of her wet coat and kicked off her boots. "We now have CB radios installed in the trucks."

Katy giggled. "Oh, no! It gets worse! It will be like that film, you know, what was it called? All those American truckers calling each other 'Plastic Duck' and 'Smoking Bandit' and stuff!"

"Convoy!" Carol replied with a groan. "Oh, PLEASE! Please don't tell me I will have to have a 'handle'!"

Katy collapsed with laughter. "Yo! 'Mothertrucker', one-nine for an eyeball from 'Sexy Curves' do you copy!" Katy was in fits of giggles, using a ketchup bottle as a microphone.

"Good grief!" Carol groaned. Well, don't expect me to use all that sort of garbage. Why can't people just speak properly as they do on the telephone?"

"I suppose you can." Katy was still finding the whole thing totally amusing. "But you have to have a call name though."

"Why?"

"Well suppose you just shout 'Tony' down the mike. There may be a dozen or more 'Tonys' driving along within a five mile radius. You have to get the right one, you know!"

"Hmm, suppose." Carol was still not convinced, it all seemed pretty childish to her. "I'm going to phone Gina." she announced, leaving Katy to talk to her sauce bottle and unpack the groceries.

*****

"Carol! You're driving to Bulgaria?" Carol could not work out if Gina's tone was that of surprise or horror.

"Oh, for heavens sake, Gina. Don't YOU start telling me what's safe and what's not. I had that yesterday from Tony, and I wasn't standing for it! This is my firm, mine and Jeff's and I have no intention whatsoever of letting it go down the pan just because Jeff is not here at the moment!" Carol picked her words carefully when mentioning Jeff.

"Hey, don't get all defensive on me, Kiddo, I wasn't suggesting for one moment you should not go." Gina said quickly. "I think it's wonderful. I can come with you and see Jeff!"

What! Had she heard right? Gina wanted to come along. Carol immediately worried that it would all be too much for Gina, travelling all that way then maybe not being able to see Jeff when she got there. But after her own outburst at Tony last evening for having the temerity to suggest that she not go out there, then what right had she to preach to Gina.

"How do you know that you will be allowed to visit?" Carol asked carefully.

"I spoke to Mark the other day," Gina answered. "I told him I wanted to visit Jeff and he said he would arrange it." She deliberately did not mention the other delicate subject that Mark had spoken about. She would use that information if and when needed.

"And has he?" Carol asked. "It's a long way out there if he hasn't arranged it, and, according to Tony, bloody cold as well."

"When are you leaving." Gina skirted the issue.

"Monday morning first thing is the plan." Carol answered. "That will give us plenty of time to arrange the loads and don't forget that there is that flaming Sunday driving ban around Paris for heavy trucks, so Monday is sensible. Also, Tony has to confirm with Marco that the toys are still available from the Sofia factory. We were, after all, supposed to collect two whole loads last week but, due to what happened, of course, we only took the one. Tony seems to think there will be no problem, as the manufacturers need to shift the merchandise, but it is worth checking out anyway, just in case they have already made other arrangements, used another haulier perhaps, but Tony thinks that is unlikely. But all being well, the plan is to load up both trucks with waste paper on Monday morning then set off for Dover. Get the ferry Monday lunchtime with luck and get over to Florence by Wednesday evening. We drop the paper at the processing plant as we did the last time we went, then head off to San Guistino and spend a night, or even two if there is time, with Tony's family, before getting under way with the olive oil to Sofia.

"Monday. Hmm, that gives us plenty of time to prepare." Gina was sounding more positive than she had done since Jeff's arrest. "I can make arrangements for Phoebe to be fed and get on to Mark about the visiting arrangements. I won't take no for an answer!" She needed to speak to Mark about the other matter too.

"Okay Honey, I will let Tony know what's happening and as soon as I know exactly when we are leaving I'll let you know. It will be great to be travelling together again!" Carol was beginning to look forward to Gina's company on the trip. Maybe it would be for the best that they travel together. She doubted whether Tony would be so pleased though!

Carol walked back into the kitchen to find Tony and Spyder warming their hands round hot cups of coffee made by Katy. "Well you can stop worrying about me being on my own in the truck." Carol announced. "Gina is riding along with me!"

Tony took a long sip of his coffee. "That's good." he replied carefully. "It will be good for you to have her along, help to navigate like last time." Inwardly he felt that now he would be responsible not only for Carol but for Gina as well but thought better of voicing his opinion. Carol was watching his expression closely, but his face gave nothing away.

"Yes, that's what I thought," said Carol. "To be honest my first thought was to try and put her off, what with it not being the best place to drive to, then decided it was far too hypocritical to even think that way so welcomed her on board instead!"

Tony decided against passing any remark.

"Well I am happier about it anyway!" Katy put in. "For what it's worth it makes me feel ten times better knowing that you will have Gina for company. She has her head well screwed on does Gina!"

"Oh, and I don't I suppose, Madam!"

"Not always!" Katy replied with a grin. "You can't deny that one really can you Mum?"

"No, suppose not." Carol poured herself a coffee and sat down at the kitchen table, scratching Bruno behind the ears. "How long will you be staying here, Sweetheart?" she asked Katy.

"Well I had planned on about ten days originally but that has gone on a little so I can't stay much longer. But what I can do is go back to Uni', pick up some more course work and come back here to study if you need me to look after the place."

"No need for that, Darling, I don't want you to upset your studies. You just get on with things as normal. Spyder, will you be okay about being in charge here in my absence?"

Spyder felt a glow of pride to have this trust settled upon him. "Of course! Too right I will be okay! I can just get on with the painting and stuff and feed Bruno. Will you want him to go for a walk as well, I don't mind?"

"Thanks Spyder, that will be great. If you don't mind giving him a short walk once a day to keep him happy, just don't let him off his lead, he may take advantage of you! and, of course, keep an eye on the kittens. If you do have any major problems, don't forget that Derek will be in the yard each day taking his trucks out. He won't mind giving you a bit of moral support if you need it, or helping you out with anything he can."

Spyder gave a mock salute. "Okay Boss. No probs, will do." He was delighted and proud to be so trusted. "You can ask Gina if she wants me to feed her cat as well, I wouldn't mind."

"That's great Spyder. It will surely be a load off my mind knowing that everything back here is in good hands."

"When we've finished this coffee perhaps you would like to have a demonstration of the CB radios." Tony suggested. "You will have to decide on a radio name so that we can keep in touch."

"I reckon Mum's handle should be 'Mothertrucker'!" Katy put in with a giggle. Carol raised her eyebrows.

"Fine. That will do." Tony grinned. He could see Carol was less than impressed. "I will be 'The Owl.'"

"The Owl! Where did you get that from?" It was the last thing Carol had expected.

"A nickname Marco used to call me when we were little. His eyes were dark and mine, obviously are very light so Marco decided to call me 'Owl' when we were children. It just came into my head so whatever, it will suffice!"

"Owls don't have grey eyes! Katy pointed out.

"Marco used to draw blue dogs and pink cats at that time so I suppose owls with grey eyes sound pretty normal!"

"Okay, Mr Wise Owl. Come and show me how these flaming things work." Carol set down her cup. "Better get the hang of it now before I make a complete fool of myself out there on the road."

Katy grabbed her coat and Spyder also made for the door. Obviously her first lesson was going to be a full family affair!

*****

It may have been mid afternoon or later, Jeff could not tell. The grimy window was covered in thick ice and the single light bulb that hung limply from a long cord connected to the high ceiling bravely glowed a gloomy, shadowy light in to the room for the duration of the day.

The cell gate rattled open and the Troll pushed two boxes into the cell.

Without a word he stepped back and slammed the door.

The usually sedentary Hans leapt from his bed and darted towards the boxes.

"Don't get over excited 'Adolph'!" John said quickly, striding across the floor towards the boxes and crouching down to read the labels. He turned towards Jeff. "Deliveries for us I believe." he announced. "No luck this time my friend," he said to the German. "I reckon your sausage is still in the post!"

Jeff walked quickly over to join John. Sure enough one of the boxes had his name on it. He instantly recognised Gina's handwriting and his heart gave a lurch. Gina had touched this box, written on it and now his hands were touching the paper and cardboard that she had touched. It gave him a strange sensation. The boxes had been opened and thoroughly rummaged through before being sent to the cell, that was evident. "Do you think it's all here?" he asked as he and John carried their treasures back to their bunks.

"Yes, probably," John replied pulling packets from his box. "My Doll always writes a list of what she has put in so they know this and know it will be obvious if they have nicked anything!"

"Sensible," Jeff replied. As he rummaged in the box his hands fell upon a letter. Disregarding the rest of the contents he pulled open the folded note and read the letter, drinking in every word that Gina had written. 'Don't worry Darling…….. the very best solicitor……..no expense will be spared….. I love you, miss you……' Jeff's stomach tied itself into a knot. He was a strong man, but reading this letter from Gina, his emotions boiled over.

He sat quietly, holding the letter for a moment then turned to the contents of the box. Packets of soup, noodles and dried fruit. A bag of porridge and a box of Oxo cubes. There was also a plastic bag with malted milk drink inside. Gina had taken it out of the glass jar and tipped the contents into a bag to save space and weight, enclosing a piece of paper with 'Ovaltine' written on it. She had also sent dried milk and packed the items between some thick woollen socks and warm underwear. There was a novel too, the sort that Gina knew he would enjoy. She had thought of everything. Jeff glanced over to John's bunk. He too was sitting quietly, re-reading his letter.

Gary hung over the edge of his bunk. "Anything in there for me?" he asked , his speech slurred like a drunken man.

"Don't worry young un," said John, looking up from his letter. Doll always makes sure you are not left out, she always sends enough to share though I reckon it wouldn't hurt for your lot to send a parcel once in a while!"

"Why should they!" Gary answered sullenly. "I wouldn't be here if it wasn't for you."

John ignored the remark. Gary was getting worse by the day. Sullen, moody and unpredictable. This place seemed to be taking its toll on him.

Jeff stepped in diplomatically. "Well at least we can have a decent meal. I never thought I would look forward to a big bowl of porridge for dinner but right now it sounds wonderful!"

"It's surprising what you enjoy in here." John replied, sifting through the packets in his box. "I get one of these most weeks so I feel I'm lucky. Though it grieves me to think of Doll going short so send it over to me."

"Has she been sending them all the time you've been in here?" Jeff asked.

"She sure has." John replied, not without some pride. "What she does, is go out a couple of evenings a week with a friend of hers and they walk round the lorry services with leaflets about me and a collection box for money to help send the food across. She hasn't given up on me yet! She even went on a march to Downing Street with a petition, along with a load of other drivers. Got herself on the telly, but no joy from the MP's though. They don't give a stuff about us drivers!"

Jeff nodded. He hoped that Gina would not be reduced to picketing lorry parks and petitioning for his release but in all truth it was just the sort of thing he could imagine her doing.

Look out Downing Street, if Gina got the wind under her tail!

*****

Gina had the whole weekend to prepare. The butterflies started fluttering again in her tummy. Maybe this time next week she would have seen Jeff. Seen him and spoken to him, made sure that he was all right.

She had telephoned Mark as soon as his office had opened this morning. After speaking to Carol the night before she had hardly slept. She would be travelling over to Bulgaria. Over to where Jeff was. She wanted to make sure that arrangements would be made in time for her to visit him. Visit him and possibly secure his release. But she dare not think so far ahead. She must keep telling herself that it may not be possible to get into that awful place and actually see him and that her attempts to buy his freedom may possibly be in vain. But she intended to try. Try with every ounce of strength, cunning and tenacity she could muster.

Mark had given her all the advice she needed. Take cash, he had told her, but keep it well hidden and don't tell anyone about it. Gina wondered if that included Carol. Maybe she should keep it secret, even from her friend. If Carol knew that she was carrying such a large amount of cash maybe she would worry. No, it was better if she kept it to herself. Stowed the money well out of sight and told nobody that she had it. Nobody until the time was right and it was needed. English money was good everywhere. Cash was always the best bargaining tool. For a moment Gina considered again the thought that the prison would not consider her offer. Mark had been quite clear. She had to find the right person to deal with. This arrangement was not exactly to the book, as it were.

Mark had offered to make tentative enquiries. If he could not find the right person to deal with then at least he would be able to warn Gina who was NOT approachable on this matter. Gina decided not to think about it until she got there. She prided herself on being a good judge of character and was sure she would know who to deal with when she met them. But this was all new ground to her. She had never moved in underground circles and was totally green to anything less than aboveboard dealings. She gritted her teeth mentally. She had to be strong and get through this. And get through it she would. If Jeff was not released and had to stay locked away then it would not be for want of her trying.

Gina decided to clean the house from top to bottom. Armed with an arsenal of cleaning equipment she attacked the house with a fervour of determination. She wanted it spick and span on her return. She also prepared her travelling bag's and planned what clothes to take. The weather out there would be bitterly cold and she would be travelling by truck, but that, to Gina, was no excuse to look less than presentable. When she met Jeff she would, as always, look her best.

*****

The weekend had flown by. Carol had spent the last few days impatiently waiting for Monday morning, wanting to get the trucks loaded up and on the road. The weather had been less than kind. Lashing rain, biting winds and snow flurries had not invited the less than toughest to venture outside.

The kittens had shrewdly moved into the house, their mother, still wary of human contact had decided to take up residence in the old privy, venturing forth for food and the occasional sortie around the garden. The youngsters, in contrast, had taken the best option and moved into the warmth of the kitchen, lying in luxury in a wooden box lined with an old towel. Digger, however, preferred the luxury and warmth offered by Bruno's thick ruff and was to be found, most of the time, burrowed comfortably in the placid dog's coat.

"What day will you be going back to Uni?" Carol asked, folding an extra warm sweater into her roomy sports bag.

"Wednesday," Katy replied. She was sitting on the bed, a thick comfortable cardigan on top of her pyjamas watching her mother pack and prepare for the long haul across the Continent down to Bulgaria. "I'll get my train ticket this morning after you have left. Spyder said he will give me a lift to Euston on Wednesday morning. I will be keeping in close touch with Spyder so that he can keep me informed if anything happens."

"Happens? Like what?"

"Oh you know." Katy tried to sound casual. "News of Jeff or anything!" She chose not to get on the wrong side of her mother by mentioning that she was worried for her safety on such a trip.

"Hmm, or in case I come unstuck and get into bother out there I suppose!" Carol had known Katy far too long to be fooled by her casual demeanour.

"Okay, and that as well, if you want the truth!"

Carol stopped her packing and came to sit next to Katy, slipping an arm around her shoulder. "Thank you for being so considerate, Darling," she said. "I DO appreciate it you know, but one day you will go dashing off to places that I will worry about you visiting but that's life I'm afraid. In the end we are all free to make our own decisions and make our own way in life. Don't forget you plan to go back-packing round Nepal in the not too distant future, and believe me, I won't sleep well at night until you are back here home and safe!"

Katy considered her mothers words. "Yes, you are right. I am sorry but we are allowed to worry about each other aren't we? Wouldn't be natural if we didn't. I do love you Mum!"

Carol hugged Katy close. "I know, Darling, and I love you, more than you'll ever know."

"Am I interrupting?" Tony stopped in the bedroom doorway.

"No, that's fine. We were just sorting one or two things out." Carol gave Katy a squeeze and got to her feet. "Mustn't forget toothbrush and stuff." she announced, heading for the bathroom.

"You will keep an eye on her won't you Tony?" Katy said quietly.

"Don't worry, Katy, I will guard her with my life, even though she would not appreciate me doing it!"

Katy laughed. "She has always been tough as old boots, has my mum!"

Tony laughed. He knew Carol was strong, but comparing the woman he loved to old shoe leather was not something he could picture.

"What are you two laughing about?" Carol came back with an armful of toiletries.

Tony winked at Katy. "Just remembered that you may need more than one pair of boots. It is snowing like a Christmas card in Bulgaria."

"Yes, that's right." Katy was quick to pick up on Tony's ploy. "There's nothing worse than cold wet feet you know."

Carol did not believe a word of it but held her tongue. She knew whatever it was about it would be with her best interest at heart.

*****

The early morning was still dark and bitterly cold as Carol and Tony walked across the yard to give the trucks a last minute check and stow their bags into the big roomy cabs. Carol turned the key in the ignition, feeling the engine turn over and roar into life. She sat for a moment or two, gently revving the engine, listening to the irritating buzzer on the air tank gauge, cutting through the dawn silence at it warned of low air. She kicked the accelerator, blasting more power through the system helping to build the air up in the holding tanks. The buzzer stopped suddenly. The tanks were full. All systems were up and running and the truck ready to roll. Carol glanced at her watch. Almost twenty to six. Gina should be here very soon. She checked that the heater settings were on full blast then dropped down from the cab and slammed the door. The engine could run for a while and send warm air round the more than spacious interior of the cab.

She walked over to the Silver Lady where Tony was gently revving the engine waiting for the air buzzer to stop whining. Tony pointed towards the gate. "Here comes your passenger." Carol looked behind her. A mini-cab was jolting over the ruts in the short drive leading towards the big iron gates. Carol waved as the cab drove towards the trucks.

Gina stepped out and paid the driver. She was dressed warmly in a dark brown woollen coat with a thick fur collar, knee boots and a Cossack hat with a thick band of fur pulled down round her ears. Carol smiled. Her friend would look good for any occasion and under any conditions, whereas she herself, wore thick boots and socks and a warm padded jacket over her warmest jeans and sweater.

Tony leaned into the back of the cab and pulled out two matching, pale tan leather bags, walking over to the Globetrotter and stowing them on the lower bunk. Gina watched him carefully. "Thank you Tony." Her breath sending clouds of steam into the frosty morning air as she spoke. "Are we all ready to go then?"

"We have time for one quick coffee with Katy while the truck heaters do their stuff then we will get off. We need to get the waste paper loaded then get straight off down to Dover. The ferry is already booked, so there should be no hold ups."

"Don't leave the lorry door unlocked." Gina said quickly.

Carol looked around the deserted yard and down to the silent lane. "Don't seem to be any thieves about." she remarked, a little puzzled at Gina's sudden security consciousness.

"All the same," Gina was hesitating before walking to the house. "I do have both my cases in there and yours too."

Carol shrugged. "Okay, if it puts your mind at rest." She walked back to the cab and switched off the engine, taking out the key and locking both doors.

"Thank you." Gina sounded relieved. "Best be on the safe side."

They walked briskly to the house for their final cups of warming coffee.

*****

"This all seems a little familiar." Carol remarked as she clicked the gearstick into a lower gear to hold back the truck with the heavy trailer as she negotiated the steep hill dropping down into Dover.

"Hmm, know what you mean." Gina replied, glancing out of the window towards the busy docks, solid with trucks waiting to be loaded onto the ferries that would carry them to France. "The last time we did this though, the weather was a lot nicer."

The rain had eased to a fine drizzle, the heavier downpours swept away by the lashing wind. "I hope this wind doesn't affect the crossing." said Carol. She was not a great fan of being stuck aboard a floating lump of iron in heavy seas.

"Doubt it," Gina said casually. "They are built to withstand the British weather. I heard they just roll over and bob back upright again if they capsize."

"Wonderful!" Carol was far from impressed by this snippet of information and was hard pushed to believe it anyway. She had a vague recollection that some lifeboats may do this trick but had little faith in channel ferries being capable of performing such a feat. She decided not to shatter Gina's illusions by querying her theory. She glanced in her mirror to see the 'Silver Lady' two trucks behind, following her down the hill. She slowed down further as the traffic in front started to bottleneck, every one, cars vans and trucks, heading for the port. The last quarter mile was usually in crawler gear as each driver filtered through the dock gates and lined up, ready to take their turn onto the ferry. It occurred to Carol that maybe the Tunnel would be a better option and that taking the ferry was mostly due to force of habit. She would consider that option in future. "Have you got the paperwork ready?" she asked. Gina had naturally taken up her position as chief organiser where the papers were concerned and had also taken charge of the maps. Gina was invaluable as a navigator, although Carol knew that she would simply follow Tony's lead when they eventually disembarked on the French side.

Eventually they found themselves in the lane required for their ferry. Tony had managed to pull in directly behind them and jumped out of the cab, paperwork in hand, and walked over to the girls. "Just get this lot sorted then all we have to do is wait to be loaded on," he said as he pulled the cab door open. "There will be time to call into the 'Wheelhouse' for a coffee and a snack if you want to. Otherwise we can eat on the boat."

"I'll stay here." Gina said quickly. "If you don't mind that is," she added. "I don't want anything so you two go on and I will see you when you get back." She handed Carol the relevant papers.

"Okay Kiddo. You stay and put your feet up, we won't be long." Carol said kindly. "I wonder if Gina is feeling okay." she remarked to Tony as they walked away from the trucks. "I thought she would have been glad to get away from the truck and stretch her legs."

"Or at least use the toilets." Tony put in. "I know I certainly need to find them!"

Carol laughed. "I thought it was women who always needed to find a loo!" she teased.

Tony pulled a face at her. "Don't be so sexist! We men do have occasional rights you know!"

As they reached the door of the 'Wheelhouse' café a familiar voice rang into Carol's ears. "Hey, lady driver! How's it all going?"

"Good grief, Jack Daniels!" Carol smiled broadly and held out her hand to the big burly man with the booming voice. Carol and Gina had met Jack and his wife in a café, high in the Italian mountains during her first trip in the summer. Carol had not expected to bump into him again so soon. "Nice to see you once again, and where is the lovely Mrs Daniels?"

"Oh the old girl is knocking about here somewhere." Jack boomed. "Probably locked in the ladies toilets doing her lipstick or something. "You heading out or heading back? and where's your mate this time?" He was looking curiously at Tony.

"Oh, Gina is waiting in the cab. Saving her energy for the trip I reckon."
There was still something about Gina's behaviour that was bothering Carol.
She made a note to ask her friend exactly what was the matter.

"Still working for that Winters lot are you girl?" Jack enquired.

Carol laughed. "Not exactly Jack." She introduced Tony and explained,
briefly, her change in status. "So you are now looking at the proud owner of a
haulage firm."

Jack gave an appreciative whistle. "Well done girl, I hope it all works out
well for you. I heard that there was a lot of bad luck with that old Winters
firm."

"How so?" Carol asked cagily.

"Well that young guy, you know Nick, the one Mags and I told you about on
the last trip. Got arrested didn't he, that very trip I believe. Locked up for
drug smuggling." Carol did not want to get into this conversation. Jack was a
lovely man but discretion did not seem to be his forte. Whatever reached his
ears seemed soon to be public knowledge around the trucking world.

"Yes that's true Jack." She began to edge towards the 'Wheelhouse' door. "I
reckon he got what he deserved though."

"Agree with you on that girl." There was no getting away from Jack at this
point. "There's too much of it about." He pushed open the door of the café
and held it for Carol and Tony to step through, following them into the
steamy atmosphere. "I said to Mags only the other day, I did. Lock 'em all up
I said, or shoot em. They're no good those drug runners. No good I tell you!"
Before either Carol or Tony could reply, they were rescued in the shape of
Mags Daniels appearing from the direction of the Ladies. "Ah, here she is,
the old girl." Jack boomed cheerily, his voice carrying to the ears of anyone
who happened to be within a mile radius. Carol smiled at Mags, asked after
her health and introduced Tony, all the time desperately trying to think of a
reason to edge herself away from the conversation. She did not have any
wish to explain about Jeff or the current situation.

"Cara Mia, we must really get our business attended to, and there is little time
to refresh ourselves before the journey." Tony came to the rescue.

"Yes, of course, we really must get on. Lovely to see you both again." Carol
smiled at the cheerful pair as she and Tony made their escape in the direction
of the toilets. "Gina and I met Jack and Mags on the way to Italy this
summer. It was those two who inadvertently told me that Nick, my then so
called boyfriend, was driving along with another girl in his cab," Carol
explained. "He had no idea that Nick and I were supposed to be an item, but
it certainly did me a favour finding out like that. But Jack is a terrible gossip.

I don't think he knows about Jeff so just hope and pray they are not on the same boat as we are." she added under her breath.

"You are bound to meet someone who will know the story of Jeff, Cara Mia. You will just have to learn to stand your ground and hold your head up. Do not forget that Jeff is your friend and we must never turn our backs on our friends."

"I would never turn my back on Jeff!" Carol said indignantly. "What makes you think that I would?"

Tony smiled at her, his diamond grey eyes boring into hers. "There is more than one way to reject a friend, Cara Mia." he said. "If anybody asks about Jeff just hold your head up and tell them where he is. There is nothing for you to feel bad about. You are not ashamed of Jeff are you?"

"No! Certainly not!"

"Then do not be ashamed to be his friend. This situation is not of his making. Not his fault that he is there. Be brave and be honest. Never be ashamed."

Carol did feel ashamed. Ashamed of herself for wanting to hide the situation. She looked up into Tony's dazzling eyes. Younger than she, but years ahead in maturity and understanding. She was proud to know him, proud to love him and proud that he loved and wanted her, faults and all. Already she felt stronger. If anybody mentioned Jeff, she would simply tell them that a mistake had been made. Tell them with truth and conviction and give them no reason to think that she herself may think otherwise.

*****

Carol pulled the Globetrotter forward as far as she could. Stopping only a foot short of the truck in front before clicking on the handbrake and switching off the engine. The noise of other vehicles, still with engines running, pounded the girls eardrums, the smell from the exhausts filling their lungs in the confined space of the ferry hold.

"Let's get ourselves out of here and into the lounge." Carol said with feeling. She hated to be confined in this enclosed space in the bowels of the ship and wanted to be upstairs, in a position to be able to walk outside onto the deck or at least see through a window.

"I'll just put a cover over these bags." Gina had scrambled from her seat and was busily tucking her smaller travelling case well down under the mattress of the lower bunk. "I never trust these places one hundred per cent, you know."

"I thought it was pretty safe down here." Carol answered. "Nobody is likely to be prowling round, searching out our bags and nicking our smalls in a place like this!

"Well, anyway, better safe than sorry." Gina smoothed down her tailored trousers, and slipped a soft woollen cardigan over her shoulders. The boat was usually quite warm so her thick, lined coat would not be necessary.

Tony had parked the 'Silver Lady' almost directly next to Carol's Globetrotter. "That is very convenient." he remarked. "Do you want me to lead the way when we come off the boat or would you prefer to go in front." Tony was being nothing if not diplomatic.

"Oh, you go first if you don't mind, Darling." Carol squeezed past the tightly parked trucks as the three made their way to the iron steps leading up to the comfortable lounge areas. "I am still not entirely au fait with the directions and certainly not half as experienced as you are so yes please, if you don't mind leading we will be glad to follow."

"Save me map reading all the way." Gina put in. "I can sit with my feet up and enjoy the ride."

Tony smiled and held the door open for the girls to step through into the passenger area of the boat. "First stop the drivers lounge I think." he said. "We can get a good meal down us while we sail then make the most of the travelling time when we drive off the other side. The food is not like Mamma cooks but it will surely fill our bellies so that is all that matters."

"I'm really looking forward to seeing Mamma Gina." said Gina, her manner immediately becoming animated with anticipation, "I so much enjoy helping in that fabulous kitchen."

"Mamma is always in her kitchen," laughed Tony. "Even when we are all finished eating, we still find Mamma in there. She always seems to find something to do in there. It is her own little palace where she reigns as queen."

Carol laughed. "I sometimes envy Mamma her lifestyle. Happily cooking huge amounts of food, looking after her family and making everyone happy." They had reached the drivers' café and were standing in the queue, trays in hand.

Gina wrinkled her nose. "Not quite what Mamma would cook, I agree, but I am suddenly starving so what the hell. If it is on a plate I will stuff it down!"

Carol and Tony had to agree. Breakfast seemed to be a long way in the past and they had a long drive to look forward to. A full belly was suddenly top priority.

*****

"God! I will be glad to get off this flaming boat!" Gina felt decidedly queasy. The crossing had been rough, churning her stomach almost from leaving Dover. "I could have well done without Jack Daniels booming at me all the way through lunch too!"

"Hmm know what you mean." Carol replied, as the girls sat in the cab of the Volvo, waiting for the boat to dock and open the big ramps to allow them onto French soil. "He seemed to be very understanding about Jeff though."

"I wasn't sure what to say at first." said Gina. "It hadn't occurred to me for a moment that we would possibly bump into anyone we knew, or anyone that knew Jeff and have to explain the situation. Still, I suppose I will have to get used to it. I am certainly not going to look ashamed and hide away. If anybody chooses not to believe that Jeff is innocent then that is entirely up to them. We know the truth so that's all that matters to me!"

"I think we put our point across adequately," Carol replied. "Both Jack and Mags were a bit speechless to begin with, but I was surprised to hear what Jack said. You know, about it being common practice for drug dealers to hide drugs on any truck at random. It seems the usual thing to use strangers to smuggle the stuff over borders. I couldn't believe it when he said that there are dozens of British drivers locked up in foreign prisons, stuck there for ages, usually without trial and little or no recognition from our government!"

"Yes, I know. At least it proves that there are lots of innocent drivers caught in this way and that not all are bad people or guilty men. They don't even know it is THERE when they are driving along. Oh, it's so WICKED, I feel so angry that my Jeff has been used in this way!"

"I know, Kiddo, it's bloody frustrating, but calm down. Getting worked up won't help, it will just make you feel ill." There was a slight bump as the ferry touched into the dock. "Not long now." Carol remarked. "Do you still feel sick?"

"Not too bad actually. I really don't understand it." Gina's tone was cross. "I usually travel so well, and I NEVER get travel sick. I usually have the constitution of an ox, but just lately I have been getting a funny tummy for any or no particular reason."

"Nerves." Carol stated bluntly. "You have had a terrible shock after all so it's bound to manifest itself some way or another. However strong you intend to be, your nervous system does exactly what it pleases."

"Hmm, suppose!" Gina rubbed her tummy. "It feels a little more settled now, I'm just hoping nobody starts an engine too soon. That smell in this confined space is enough to finish me off completely!"

There was a loud clang and a rattle of chains as the big loading ramps were lowered onto the dock, followed with an eruption of engines as all drivers turned their ignition keys and fired up their vehicles. One by one the lorries rolled off the boat and into the port of Calais. Tony sitting tight behind Carol's trailer as the two heavy trucks rolled slowly across the port and through to the customs' check point. Luckily they were waved through with little waiting time and Carol led the way out of the docks towards the main Autoroute. She pulled over at a wide point in the road, allowing Tony to overtake, pulling out immediately after him and driving directly behind as he piloted the way to the Autoroute heading towards the south and Italy.

Carol relaxed at the wheel. The big truck was pulling beautifully and she felt safe and confident with Tony leading the way. She was looking forward to the journey. Looking forward to meeting Tony's family once again and enjoying their company. She was also feeling slightly elated to be back on the road, proud to be driving her own truck and hauling her own load across the Continent. In the back of her mind she had a tiny niggle of apprehension about the second part of the journey. Driving across strange ground to Bulgaria was a challenge she could have well done without but she decided to worry about it when she needed to and not let it cloud the whole of the trip.

"At least it's stopped raining." Gina said, peering up at the grey sky, "But it's still terribly windy."

"Let's hope that eases off before we get on the Autoroute." Carol replied. "It's hard work keeping this thing in a straight line when the wind catches the side of the trailer, though I don't think it's as bad as it was. I do believe it is easing up quite a lot." she mentally crossed her fingers that it was not just wishful thinking. She still had that mad dash round the Peripherique to contend with. She had only driven it once before, she and Gina travelling together, sitting tight to the tail lights of a friendly British driver, piloting them through the disorganised and often lunatic traffic of the Paris ring road. Possibly the worst part of the journey and only a couple of hours ahead. Still, this time she would be following Tony so she intended to stick close and follow his lead. She had made it in one piece the first time as a rookie driver, so this time at least she would be ready for it.

The plan was to get through Paris and stop for the night a few kilometres further south. They would be out of driving time and it would be almost dark. They would have done enough for one day.

Carol glanced in her mirror. "Jack and Mags are a couple of trucks behind us." she remarked.

Gina leaned forward to peer into her wing mirror. "Hmm, they will be behind us until we take the road off towards Dijon, then will carry on to the next junction, I think. They are bound for Spain, aren't they? "Yes, Barcelona. Nice quick trip, there and back within the week.

Mags was saying they had booked a villa down there for three weeks over Christmas for the whole family."

"They are very close, aren't they." Gina mused. "A bit loud for my liking but there is no denying that they are meant for each other."

Carol did not reply. She was keeping an eye on a small white Fiat that seemed to be totally oblivious of the heavy trucks that it was trying to cut in between. "Prat!" Carol touched the brakes to avoid shunting the Fiat into Tony's tail lights, and gave the driver the full benefit of a loud blast from the Volvo air horns. She was rewarded by a universal gesture from the drivers window as the Fiat slowed then swerved violently to the left, cutting across three lanes of traffic and disappearing onto the distance. "And we haven't even reached the Peripherique yet!" she remarked ruefully.

Gina giggled. "You certainly have found your feet since your first trip," she said. "That sort of thing would have worried you to death a few months ago. Are the mirrors set all right for you?"

"Could do with your one pushing out a little." Carol replied. She considered Gina's words. Her friend was right. She was not in the least ruffled by the Fiat's antics, unlike her first trip abroad in the summer. She remembered gripping the wheel until her knuckles shone white, sweat seeping from the palms of her hands as she negotiated the heavy traffic, all seemingly travelling at excessive speed and all on the wrong side of the road!

"That okay?" Gina was leaning out of the window, pushing the big wing mirror into position.

"Yes, tons better thanks. Must remember to adjust the things before we get off the boat next time. You certainly need to re-angle them for driving on the right."

Gina wound up the window again, blocking out the cold rush of air and the roar of traffic. She sat back in her seat, smoothing down the creases in her trousers and slipping her warm cable cardigan over her shoulders. "I feel a little tired," she remarked. "Must have been the early start. I can hardly keep my eyes open."

"Why not lie on the bunk and have a nap then?" said Carol. "We have a few hours to drive yet and I don't need you to navigate, I will just follow Tony."

"Thanks Kiddo, but I won't lie down, I'll just put my head back and have a little doze. Sorry if I'm not being much help."

"Don't be so silly! You have a doze, I'm fine!"

Carol glanced quickly at Gina. She had always been amazed by Gina's strength of character and boundless energy. This business with Jeff certainly seemed to be taking its toll. She could not ever remember Gina showing any kind of weakness or getting tired through something as simple as an early morning start. Gina curled her head into the thick soft wool of her cardigan and closed her eyes. Carol drove on in silence. The rain had stopped and the wind had eased as the signs for the Autoroute appeared on the gantry above her head. It would now be a straight drive for a couple of hours, down to the outskirts of Paris. She relaxed in her seat and clicked the gearstick into an easy cruising gear. She was starting to enjoy the drive and all apprehension of the trip had faded into the distance. She felt safe and insulated, high up in the big cab and decided to take each mile as it came. She had been on this route many times before, with Nick to start with, then driving herself with Gina as navigator. It was familiar ground and, for the first time since obtaining her Heavy Goods Licence, did she actually feel confident, actually felt that she knew what she was doing and knew she was doing it right. It was a good feeling and Carol held onto that feeling as Gina slept and the Globetrotter effortlessly ate up the miles, rolling down the Autoroute towards Paris.

****

CHAPTER TWELVE

The lights of Paris, twinkling ahead, told Carol that they were nearing the dreaded Peripherique. She took a deep breath in preparation for the mad, headlong dash round the multi-laned ring road, skirting the city. The lights drew ever closer until they surrounded the trucks into their midst. Gina stirred, blinking as she opened her eyes. "Where are we?" she asked sleepily. "Just coming up to the Peripherique." Carol replied without taking her eyes off the road, making sure she kept close behind Tony's trailer. Under normal circumstances a safe gap with plenty of braking distance between herself and the vehicle in front was Carol's rule of thumb. But not now. Under these driving conditions she needed to sit as close as she could behind Tony and follow his lead through the unbelievable devil-may-care driving of the Parisians.

"Sorry to have dozed off on you like that. Fat lot of company I am," said Gina, stretching and making the effort to gather her wits.

"No problem, Kiddo. You must have needed it and anyway, I was quite happy, just toddling along nice and easy. That's the end of the easy bit for a while though." she added. "Here comes the 'cannonball run'!"

Blasting of horns seemed to be the accepted mode of making way through the headlong rush around Paris. "If their horns broke I doubt if any of these people would bother to take their cars on the road." said Carol ruefully as yet another car came dangerously close to the big trailer, trying it's best to edge between the trucks before giving up on the exercise and blasting the drivers with both use of horn and Gaelic profanities out of the window before accelerating madly in an attempt to overtake.

"It's starting to get a bit dark too." Gina remarked casually. It never ceased to amaze Carol that her friend could stay so calm and unruffled under circumstances such as these. Gina may have been coasting down an empty country lane for all the notice she took of the drivers hurtling along the giant ring road. Carol didn't answer, she was using every ounce of concentration for the drive. Her mirrors were her lifeline as seemingly insane French drivers, whose well-focused, sole ambition appeared to be to get from point A to point B in record time, hurtled around the big truck, like terriers snapping at the heels of a bull. She was determined to keep close to Tony's tail lights, watching which direction he was taking. When Tony signalled, she signalled, when Tony changed lanes she sat close behind. She felt as though her eyes were burning as she noticed the turn off that they would be taking to head down towards Italy. It was with some relief that they left the mad rush around Paris and headed out onto the road to Dijon.

"Phew! That drive never gets any better does it!" Carol remarked, relaxing into her seat and easing back to a respectable distance between herself and Tony.

"No, it's always been the same." Gina seemed as usual, totally unperturbed. "Shall we see if this radio thing works and say hello to Tony?" she reached up and started to fiddle with the switches on the CB.

"I'd completely forgotten about that!" said carol. She still did not have any idea what possible use the contraption could be.

The CB crackled into life as Gina found the 'on' button. "Tony, you on radio?" Gina called into the microphone.

"You're supposed to say. 'Owl, Owl, do you copy', Carol reminded her."

Gina pulled a face. "What rubbish! Tony, are you on radio?" she insisted.

"Hello Gina." Tony's voice crackled back over the air-waves. "I take it you are not well versed in the art of CB speak!"

"You mean all that ninety nine and copying and stuff?" Gina answered. "No, I am most certainly not! Where are we stopping for the night, anyway?"

"Another hour or possibly a little longer then there is a nice place to shower and eat. We can sleep there and set off nice and fresh in the morning. Carol, how was the Peripherique?"

Gina held the mike towards Carol. "Bloody awful as always!" Carol replied bluntly. I will be glad to see a cup of coffee and a ladies' loo I can tell you!"

"Can you hang on 'til we get to the rest stop?" Tony asked.

"Yes, not desperate, get your foot down and we will see you there."

"See, that wasn't so bad was it?" said Gina, hanging up the microphone.

"Except that every driver within a five mile radius now knows that I want to go to the loo!" Carol retorted.

"Hmm, that will be a good lesson in thinking before you speak next time." she giggled. "Good fun though, isn't it!"

"If you say so." said Carol, pressing her foot gently onto the accelerator as the trucks picked up speed along the Autoroute. The first day of their trip was almost at an end. Carol wondered idly what the rest of the trip would be like. Bulgaria. She had never even given the place a thought before but now it loomed large in her mind. What was it like? What was the journey going to be like? Would they actually get to see Jeff, and was there any chance that the Transcon would be there? She had hardly given the old Transcon a thought, but now it suddenly came into her mind. It was, after all, her own truck. She really should do something about trying to get the old girl back. If there was anything left of her to get back, that is.

Dusk was drawing in as Tony signalled to leave the Autoroute and pull into a well lit service station with ample parking for the many trucks that pulled in for a well earned break or an overnight stay.

"Thank goodness for that!" said Gina. "I am starting to get as stiff as a plank sitting here."

"Know what you mean." Carol replied with feeling. Her bottom was starting to get numb and her shoulders were aching. "Can't think why my shoulders are stiff." she commented. "The power steering on this truck is perfect and the road is straight so why am I feeling so bloody stiff?"

"Tension." Gina said simply. "It's all the concentration. You should make a point of dropping your shoulders every so often. Eases them up a bit. Jeff always used to do that."

"Good point." said Carol, shifting the Volvo into a low gear as she followed the 'Silver Lady' into the big parking area. "Remind me to try that tomorrow. Right now I feel like I could do with a good massage!"

"Won't get that here I'm afraid." Gina laughed. "But the food will be okay. We can have a couple of relaxing drinks at the bar as well. I'll give your shoulders a rub before we turn in, I take it we are stopping for the night here?"

"Yes, I reckon so." said Carol. "We are pretty much out of driving time so let's get some rest and start off early in the morning. We should, by rights, make it to the Italian border by tomorrow evening then straight down to San Guistino the day after." She pulled the truck forward at crawling pace having spotted a suitable parking spot.

Looking quickly over her shoulder to check the distance she slipped the Volvo into reverse and slowly inched the big trailer round between

two other parked trucks and eased back until she was directly in line between the two.

"Well done." Gina praised her friend's skill. "Tony's parked over there." she said, clambering over the bunk, in search of her case.

Carol reached down her own washbag from the upper bunk, slipped it into her roomy shoulder bag and rolled a towel under her arm. "You don't want your case do you?" she asked, puzzled. "You'll only need your wash things and a towel for the showers. We can get cleaned up, dump the towels and stuff back in the cab then go for dinner feeling nice and fresh."

"Not sure if it's safe to leave it here." Gina looked apprehensive, holding the smaller of the two cases across her lap.

"There is a compartment under the lower bunk." Carol remembered. If you lift up the mattress then pull the wooden support underneath, there is a storage compartment if that makes you feel better."

"Is there really!" Gina immediately scrabbled and hauled the mattress up, finding the empty storage compartment below. "Must be custom made." she remarked. "I have never seen this sort of arrangement before."

"Dunno." Carol replied casually. "I just noticed it was there when I was giving the truck a good coat of looking at after I bought it.

"*Very* handy!" Gina sounded delighted as she stuffed the small case tight into the corner of the storage compartment and covered it with a blanket. "Just make sure the doors are well locked Kiddo, won't you."

"What on earth have you got in there. The crown jewels?" Carol remarked light-heartedly. She found Gina's behaviour totally out of character, but after the strain she had been under, a change of behaviour was hardly not without understanding.

"Well you never know who is around these places." Gina replied quickly. "After all, look what happened to Jeff!"

Carol decided against replying and locked the cab doors securely before the two girls walked over to meet Tony who had found a parking slot almost opposite theirs. "How was the drive Cara Mia." he asked, slamming the cab door closed and turning the key in the lock, his diamond grey eyes alight with the exhilaration of the drive.

"Fine, just a bit stiff that's all." Carol eased her shoulders and stretched her legs. "The Peripherique gets no better, they must all be totally mad, especially the ones who drive it daily. Surely there must be loads of fatalities!"

"You should try driving through the centre of Naples!" Tony laughed, Marco calls it C'armageddon! If you don't get squashed flat by some death-race driver you can sit in a huge traffic jam getting slowly poisoned by carbon monoxide while you play a game called 'spot-the-car-without-a-dent' but you don't win many points because there are not many dentless cars to spot!"

"I think the Paris run will do me for now." Carol replied ruefully. "I feel absolutely shattered now!"

"Nothing a good meal and a night's sleep won't sort out." Tony smiled as the three walked towards the café area. Carol had to agree. She was looking forward to a good meal, a couple of drinks and a good nights sleep.

*****

Jeff was chilled to the bone. The small window, high above his bunk was covered with a thick sheet of ice. He had slept fully dressed with his jacket on for over a week now. The thin excuse for a blanket that was provided by the prison was little more than a token covering.

"Got any hot water to spare mate?" John Miller walked over to where Jeff was sitting on the edge of his bunk waiting for the tiny tin pan to boil on the small primus stove. John had 'bought' the stove not long after his incarceration using cigarettes as currency. The tiny stove had earned its weight in gold these past years.

"When this thing eventually boils." Jeff replied. "What have you got?"

"Packet of rice with bits in and a tin of sardines," John replied. "My Doll will have posted another parcel by now so we won't go short. Odd we both got parcels on the same day, but handy though."

"I got pretty much the same as you except that Gina, typically, threw in some clean socks and pants." Jeff replied giving the pan a shake in the hope of hurrying the boiling process. "God its bloody freezin' in this place. I'm sure glad of the socks. If you need socks then have a pair, I can always ask for more!" Jeff pulled out his box of groceries from under his bed. "There is a packet of dried veg in here." he

noted, "and a packet of rice, so if you like we can mix the whole lot together and see how it comes out."

"With sardines on top!" John pulled a wry face. "Can't see us looking forward to this sort of thing at home, but here it's better than that bloody oil-in-water-with-cabbage they give us every day.

Jeff glanced around. The thick set German was lying on his bunk staring at the ceiling. The two Romanians were playing some sort of card game on one of the bunks. Gary was nowhere to be seen. "Where's the kid?" Jeff asked.

"Haircut," John replied. "Seems to spend more time at that bloody barbers than he does in here with the rest of us."

"He don't look right." Jeff remarked. "Saw him this morning in the showers, he looked real ropey, though cold showers in this climate make ME feel ropey so I reckon I'm in no position to make judgements." The showers were pretty much an ordeal. The shower building across the exercise yard had bare stone walls and floors, freezing to the touch and a large, glassless window, overlooking the yard, which allowed the biting wind to whip into the building and the snow to drift onto the shower floors. It certainly did not encourage even the hardiest to disrobe and stand under the blast of freezing water. By the time the men had rubbed themselves to almost dryness on the thin pieces of towel, the clothes that they had discarded were now stone cold and had to be re-warmed by what little body heat they had left.

"Not looked right for weeks hasn't that lad." John agreed, ripping open the packets of dried rice and veg and mixing them together before dividing them into two bowls while Jeff poured on the barely boiling water. With the sardines balanced sparingly on the top of the rice, the two men set to with their spoons. The idea was to eat it quickly in the hope that the hot food would warm them through, a theory that did not always work.

The rattle of the cell gate heralded the entrance of Gary, returning from the barbers. "Okay Gary?" John called over as the thin young man walked unsteadily towards his bunk. Gary did not reply, his only acknowledgement a raised hand before he fell onto his bunk and turned his head into the pillow.

"Want some food Kid" Jeff asked. No reply. Jeff and John exchanged glances and continued with their frugal meal.

"The kid not need food after where he has been." The voice of the German, sneeringly announced.

"And what's that supposed to mean 'Adolph'!" John snapped back.

"Don't tell me you don't know. The man who gets his own way all round the prison doesn't know what the barber can do for you. That why you have long hair Miller, frightened to visit the barber and get what the rest of them get. Maybe you don't trust yourself to go!"

"What the hell is he on about?" said Jeff, finishing his last mouthful.

"Ignore him." John gave the German a look of disdain and returned to his food. "I'm not getting drawn into a fight to please that smug bastard. He would like that."

Jeff glanced at the sneering German then back to John. He could see his friend was angry but holding his cool. "Yeah, ignore him, it will be time for the exercise round in the yard soon. That should cool him off, in fact cool us all off more bloody likely!" It was cold enough in here without having to brave the snow, now lying thick on the ground in the cobbled yard.

Before John could reply the barred gate rattled wide again and Zhravko Markov strode into the cell. "Jeffrey Meredith, the Governor will see you. Now!"

"The Governor? What the hell does this mean." Jeff had seen the Governor of the prison once only, briefly on his first day. "I hope it's good news and not trouble. Any ideas Markov?"

Markov said nothing as Jeff got to his feet and followed him through the cell gate.

"Don't mind me, Dear!" John called after him. "Just go off and enjoy yourself, leave me to do the washing up! Grounds for divorce is this you know!" Jeff chuckled. It amazed him how John had kept his sense of humour in this place for so long. A sense of humour that certainly kept Jeff's spirits aloft during these last weeks.

****

The Governor of Zatfora Prison was a small bespectacled man of indeterminate age. At first glance he reminded Jeff of a village postmaster, sitting behind his huge wooden desk strewn with papers.

"You will be getting a visitor." Govorner Balenko got straight to the point.

"A visitor? Another visit from the Embassy already. I seem to be very popular!" This seemed like good news to Jeff. Perhaps things were getting under way to get him out of there.

"Your wife." Governor Balenko stated bluntly. "Your wife will be calling to the prison in some days time. You will be granted permission to see her but you will see her in the presence of either myself or Markov and the presence of a British Embassy prison visitor."

Jeff's mind whirled. Gina! Coming here, to this place. How on earth was that possible. Who would she be coming with. Surely not alone. What airport was she landing at. Where would she be staying. A million questions raced through his brain.

"You will, of course, show her that you are in good health and that you are well cared for in our country." Governor Balenko was still speaking. "There will be witnesses to the conversation to make sure that no propaganda is passed on and no bad lies told about the conditions here."

"Of course." Jeff had no idea what to say, or what to think. "Of course, Governor, I will be very pleased to see my wife and I can assure you that I will say nothing to disgrace your country or your prison, which, I must add, is a credit to your administration!" No harm in buttering the biscuit as old man Winters always used to say. Governor Balenko grew another inch behind his desk. Jeff almost glimpsed a shadow of a smile, fleetingly passing across the hawk like features. "May I ask when exactly my wife will be visiting?" Jeff asked politely.

"Five days, six days maybe. We will tell you when she arrive."

"Well thank you for that news Governor. It has made my day very pleasant." Jeff was going through the motions of saying the right things but inside his head was spinning. He wanted to bolt back to his cell and impart the news to John. Surely this could only be a good thing.

"You will see your lawyer again very soon. You will also see British Embassy official. He will speak to you about visit from wife. Not all prisons are so understanding as this." he added with a sense of importance. "This prison understand you will want visit from family persons. You will tell them how well you are treated." This was not a remark, Jeff noted, more of an instruction.

"Of course, Governor, I will explain that I have been treated fairly although you must not be offended if I do not seem more than willing to enjoy your hospitality for longer than I have to! Do we know when I will be sent for a proper trial? I would like to know exactly how long I may have to be under your roof."

Governor Balenko's eyes flickered to Markov and back again but gave nothing away. "Things have been suggested that there may be ways to settle your conviction. Ways that may hurry the legal procedure. Beyond that I say no more. Markov, return the Englishman to his cell." There was no further discussion to be undertaken. The tone of Governor Balenko's voice had made that perfectly clear. Jeff was now thoroughly confused.

"What's going on Markov?" he asked as the huge man escorted Jeff down the myriad of corridors back to the cells.

"There have been questions asked about the price of your release." was the simple answer. "Beyond that I can say nothing."

Jeff decided that there was no use in pursuing this line of conversation. He would have to wait until he could speak to his lawyer. Not the easiest of conversations. The lawyer had no English whatsoever and the translator was hardly a linguist, but maybe they would know something and be able to throw some light onto the matter. He would just have to wait.

As if reading his mind, Markov stopped in his stride, turning towards Jeff. "And it is not for discussion! Discussion with other prisoners or Embassy visitors only slow down any proceedings in these matter."

Jeff met Markov's gaze. "Okay, I understand." he said – though in truth he had no idea whatsoever what the hell was going on.

*****

It was with great relief that Carol drove out of the waste paper plant on the outskirts of Florence. "The smell in that place is unbelievable!" she remarked opening the window a little to breath in the fresh afternoon air.

"Don't think it was quite as bad as it was in the height of the summer." Gina countered.

"Well, only by a tiny degree, I suppose. Still couldn't stand having to work in it, day in and day out, though could you?"

"Yuk. Would hate to have to, though I suppose the people here have got used to it, they don't seem at all bothered by it and all seem happy in their work."

Carol drove slowly through the busy narrow streets of the industrial area then turned onto a wider road leading to the Autostrada. "Tony won't be very far behind," she remarked. "They had almost finished unloading him when we pulled out so he may even catch us up before we get to San Guistino." The smell of the factory had not encouraged Carol and Gina to wait for Tony to be unloaded.

"Don't know about that," Gina replied. "This truck is certainly a flying machine. Pulls a lot stronger than the 'Silver Lady' to my mind."

"Yes, she certainly pulls well and the acceleration is brilliant. Not too bad on fuel either. I can't tell you how glad I am I bought it, in more ways than one. She's an absolute angel!"

"Know what you mean. Lucky you got it when you did or we would have been stuffed about doing this trip and lucky you got such a great truck. Jeff may even be envious when he sees her, your 'Flying Angel'!"

Carol smiled but passed no comment. She wondered how long it would be before Jeff got the opportunity to actually see the new truck or his beloved 'Silver Lady'. She mentally crossed her fingers that it would not be too far into the future but, at the back of her mind she had to be realistic and face the fact that it may be years before Jeff could return to England. These thoughts, however, she kept to herself.

She had no intention of destroying Gina's hopes of a quick release for her husband.

"Wonder what Mamma Gina is cooking up for dinner." said Gina, almost thinking aloud. "I can't wait to see everybody again can you? It seems ages since Marco's wedding. What a great few days that was."

"Absolutely!" Carol agreed. The wedding had certainly been something to remember. "I bet Mamma is cooking up a storm as we speak. She sure does love her visitors, doesn't she?"

"Hmm, but I reckon she cooks like that all the time. A real traditional, Italian cook." Gina said wistfully. "The heart of the family is the kitchen out here isn't it, so cosy and traditional. Real family values. I think that it's a lovely way to live, I don't think we English pay enough attention to the important things in life. You know, like all the family sitting together round the dining table in the evening eating loads of wonderful food and not caring a tinkers cuss if they get fat or not. Nobody in Italy seems to care if their good lady wives are as fat as bacon pigs or thin as reeds. I think they have the family thing far better organised than we do."

"Depends how you look at it." Carol replied thoughtfully. "At least in England we women have lives of our own. We can go off to the pub or to a club or even on holiday alone whereas over here it's marriage, babies, then kitchen. I know there are exceptions, but as a general rule, that is the norm. Don't think I would like it."

"Pity we can't get a happy medium and combine the two really." Gina had visions of a perfect world. "Gosh, I'm feeling tired again. Can't believe I have been so weary lately."

Carol glanced over at her friend. "Perhaps it may be wise to visit the doctor when we get home." she suggested. "You may be a bit run down and in need of a tonic. Better have a check up, a nasty shock can do all sorts to your system and you will need all your strength to help Jeff fight for his rights."

"Yes, I think you're right. I probably am run down a bit. Not been sleeping well at all although I'm tired all the time. I know I'm not eating properly. Keep feeling a little nauseous too. Not at all like me really, I am usually as strong as an ox constitution wise. Nothing seems to do me much harm, I've always been lucky like that."

"Not far to go now." Carol pointed ahead. The sign for San Guistino pointed the way off the Autostrada and up into the hills. She glanced in her mirror to see if Tony was behind, but so far no sign of him. No matter. This was familiar ground to Carol. She slowed the truck and dropped into a lower gear, turning off the Autostrada and onto a fairly good road leading to the foothills of the Apennine Mountains. The incline started off quite gently but got steeper and the road narrower as they progressed. Before long Carol spotted the familiar side road which would lead them directly to San Guistino and the friendly welcome of Tony's family.

Gina wound down her window, taking deep breaths and drinking in the glorious scent of the woodland around her. Sun was filtering through the trees, even this late in the year it warmed the inside of the cab but in the distance, tall mountains, glimpsed through breaks in the trees, were heavily covered in snow, their peaks glowing pink in the afternoon sun.

"It sure is beautiful here." Gina remarked wistfully. Do you think if you and Tony get married you will give it all up in England and move in here?"

Carol shot a surprised glance at her friend. "Crikey, that's a bit forward thinking isn't it. We haven't even discussed marriage yet, never mind where we would live. Don't rush me girl, give me a chance to breathe!"

"I smell wedding cake already!" Gina said devilishly

"Well don't sniff too hard just yet! There are loads of things I want to do, want to *achieve* and achieve on my own before I decide to share my life with anybody yet. Even Tony, as much as I adore him."

"There you are. You DO adore him, you DO love him so you WILL get married." Gina was on a matchmaking mission. "The question is, where will you live? Go on, think about it. Humour me!"

"Okay." Carol sighed. "We will keep my house and the yard and have another home built here in the hills so we will never get bored of where we are. There! Does THAT satisfy you?"

Gina thought about it. "Hmm, sounds good. The best of both worlds. You have my personal seal of approval on that, well done!"

"Thank you! Now can we change the subject away from weddings BEFORE we reach La Casaccia, and definitely NO mention of that sort of thing in front of Mamma Gina and the girls. They will have me up the aisle before I have chance to think straight!"

"Okay promise." Gina was satisfied that she had the answers she wanted. "Ooh, look! Isn't that the spot where we found little Toby?" she pointed to a clump of peach trees.

"Could be," Carol replied, although it could have been anywhere along this road where they had broken down in the summer, found the stray dog and been rescued by Tony.

"I'm sure it was." Gina was positive. "You should put a plaque up there to say that is the place where you met Tony!"

Carol glanced over to her friend. Gina was grinning broadly. "For one awful moment I actually thought you were serious!" she said.

Gina spluttered with laughter. "Sure had you going for a moment though!" she said wickedly. "Changing the subject, when we get to La Casaccia, we can 'phone home and see if Spyder is managing okay."

"And if Katy got back to 'Uni' all right too," Carol put in. "Hope we haven't put on Spyder too much, he has all the responsibility of my place and yours as well so he has his hands full. I reckon he can manage okay though. He's a great boon to have on board."

"Oh yes, a real poppet!" Gina agreed.

They rounded a steep bend and up ahead could see the big wrought iron gates leading into La Casaccia. Carol gave a blast on the air horns as she approached, slowing to a steady crawl as she threaded the big truck and trailer through the gates and along the gravel track towards the house. "That's odd," said Carol. "Where is everybody, the place is usually hanging alive with kids!" she pulled the truck round to the front of the barn, clicked on the handbrake and killed the engine.

"Mamma Gina won't be hard to find." said Gina flinging the cab door open. "She will most definitely be in the kitchen, when is she *never* in the kitchen?"

A small brown dog appeared from the depth of the barn, curious to see who had arrived. "Toby! Hello girl, look Carol it's little Toby!"

Gina crouched down to fondle the little dog's head and suddenly found herself surrounded by wagging tails. "Hey, she looks so well!" Carol joined Gina amongst the throng of eager tails and lolling tongues. "And how the puppies have grown, they are as big as their mother now."

"Nice to see her so fat and well after the state she was in when we found her. I am sure she would have died if Tony had not brought her here and taken care of her. And young Paulo seems to do so well the animals." Carol remarked as the two girls disentangled themselves from the eager puppies and headed for the house. "I am sure he will follow his dream to become a vet, he seems to have the dedication." The kitchen door was, as always, standing open as Carol and Gina approached. "Hello!" Carol hailed the house.

"Buena, Buena, you have come! I hear-a no engine! Come, come!" Mama Gina's ample frame flooded through the door, her rotund figure shaking with every step as she swooped towards the girls, arms outstretched. Carol and Gina braced themselves as Mamma descended the wooden steps from the veranda and hurtled towards them, arriving in a flurry of aprons and enveloping them in an enthusiastic embrace.

"Hello Mamma, how lovely to see you again." Carol gasped for breath as Mamma Gina crushed them with enthusiasm.

"Yes, Mamma we have been looking forward to seeing you all of the journey!" Gina mumbled into Mamma's plentiful bosom.

"Ah, Bellissima." Mamma held the girls at arms length, giving them time to breathe. "You look-a so well, so brave, I WEEP-a for you, for Jeff. Ah, morte morte, I feel I DIE when I hear of Jeff!" Tears sprang profusely from Mamma's eyes as she shepherded the girls towards the sanctuary of the kitchen. Gina gave Carol a sidelong glance. They had expected Mamma Gina to go overboard with emotion. She always did. Mamma wept when someone died, when someone got married, when a child was born or simply if a visitor arrived. Mamma certainly wore her heart on her sleeve and did not believe in hiding her emotions.

"Thank you Mamma, that is very kind of you to think of Jeff like that." Gina put her arm, as best she could, around Mamma. "But be brave. I'm sure it will all work out all right in the end. We will see Jeff very soon and I am sure he will be home before long."

As always, a huge pot was simmering on the big double cooker which took up most of the far wall in the gloriously rustic kitchen, a tantalising smell drifting from the steam. Little Christo, all of five years old, was perched on a high wooden chair at the huge scrubbed table in the centre of the room, his tiny fingers carefully wielding a large knife to chop small green apples and pile them into a bowl.

"Hello Christo!" Gina bent down to kiss the little boy's dark curls. "That is a very big knife for a small boy isn't it?"

"I help Mamma." Christo beamed happily at the visitors. Oblivious of the worried look on the girl's faces as they watched him chopping the apples.

Mamma Gina picked up immediately on the girls thoughts. "Ah, in my country we learn very quickly to use-a the tools," she explained. "Keep child away from sharp knife it will cut-a the hand first time it touch one. Teach child to use knife right and poof! No trouble!"

There had to be some kind of credibility in this theory. Little Christo certainly had all his full contingent of fingers and there was no blood in evidence in the bowl of chopped fruit. A huge cake with a mound of cream, topped with an adornment of glace cherries stood proudly amidst the clutter of the big table, next to a huge platter of dissected chickens. Evidence that the chicken was indeed fresh were a pile of feathers in a box under the table.

"Where is everyone else?" Carol asked, seating herself next to Christo. "We expected to see the other girls all here helping you."

"Is olive picking season." Mamma explained, reaching a big jug of peach juice from the crowded dresser and making space amongst the homely clutter of cooking preparation scattered across the table. "Olives must all be picked very quick and go to 'frantioio' for making oil or to bottle store so everybody go to fields. All family and neighbours, everybody, they pick. Then we pick-a the neighbours olives. Everybody help everybody."

Christo pointed to the cake. "Paulo and Georgio - compleanno!" He announced.

"Oh my goodness. A birthday. I'm sorry, we did not know." Carol felt guilty

Mamma Gina shrugged nonchalantly. "No problem. The boys, they are nine, they are happy with cake and kisses. They have all-a they want!"

"See!" Gina put in, digging Carol in the ribs. "It is all so lovely, relaxed and friendly here. I can't see how you can resist!"

Carol cast her a withering glance. "Do you need any help with dinner Mamma?" she asked.

"No need, no need." Mamma poured peach juice into tall cups and set them in front of the girls. "All is prepared. Bread in oven, pasta ready to cook and-a the sauce already cooking. Poppa and others be back soon, ready to eat." Mamma bent to check the temperature of her oven. Satisfied she turned back to the girls. "Antonio? Where is Antonio? He travel with you no?"

"Yes, Mamma, he will be here soon." Carol answered. "We were unloaded first so could not wait to come up and see you!"

"Ah, Bella!" Carol's kind words were rewarded with another crushing embrace from Mamma Gina, only to be rescued from certain suffocation by the sound of the 'Silver Lady's' engines approaching through the gates and getting closer to the house. Mamma at once, flurried to the door. Her first born had arrived home and needed the full benefit of her greeting.

*****

"Get a doctor! For Christ sake a doctor NOW!" John screamed the words franticly through the bars of the cell gate.

Gary convulsed again, froth pouring from his almost blue lips. Jeff held tight onto the writhing body in a desperate attempt to stop him from falling from the high bunk.

"Help! Help! Where the fuck is everybody! Get a doctor!" John was bellowing into the deserted corridor.

The sound of boots approaching then Zhravko Markov appeared, reaching his keys from his belt and swinging the gate wide. "Get a doctor!" John repeated. "Gary's fitting, he needs help quickly, DO something!"

Markov did not speak. His big frame crossed the cell in three strides and he pulled Gary from the bunk. "You come!" he commanded John as he carried the writhing body from the cell closely followed by John Miller. By this time a small army of guards had arrived to bar Jeff's way and re-lock the cell door in his face.

Jeff was stunned. It had all happened so fast. Gary had returned from the showers, looking glassy eyed but fairly cheerful for a change then suddenly.........

"The young pup get too much for his own good this time!" Hans' voice was flat as the German lounged on his bunk, a vantage spot to watch the activities though making no move to help.

"What?" Jeff shook his head. What on earth was this man on about now? The boy had taken ill had he not?

"Don't tell me you know nothing about it, driver. You are in here for carrying the stuff. Where do you think it goes when you drop it off?"

Jeff was trying hard to make some sense of what the German was saying. His mind was split between concern for the young Englishman and his new friend and trying to take in what Hans was sneering about. The two Romanians were in animated conversation, obviously discussing the excitement. Although Jeff had never heard them utter a word of English and he understood no Romanian, the content of the conversation was obvious.

Jeff flung himself back onto his bunk. What the hell was going on? "Okay Hans, what is your take on the situation. Forgive me for sounding thick and stupid but I have no bloody idea what you are talking about!"

Hans swung himself down from his bunk and reached for his box of stores, pulling out a bottle of juice and taking a mouthful. "I find it hard to believe you are so naïve, Englishman." He said, screwing the top back onto his bottle and stowing it safely back into the box. "The young pup visit the barber more than any in here no?" Jeff nodded. Gary certainly seemed to spend a lot of time wandering to the barbers or the showers, certainly more than the rest of the cellmates. "He gets more there than a clean chin."

It was slowly beginning to dawn on Jeff exactly what the German was talking about. "Drugs!" You mean he has been getting drugs. In here!" Surely that could not be possible. He himself, was locked up for the mere suggestion of being guilty of handling drugs and now this man was telling him that they were freely available inside the prison itself. The double standards were all but unbelievable.

"Aha! The realisation has settled!" Hans eased himself back onto his bunk. "Yes, drugs. Probably heroin. Did you not see signs?"

Jeff shook his head. He had never had any dealings with drugs so would not have recognised the signs if they had jumped out and bitten him. "No," he said quietly. "I don't know anything about drugs. Only what I read in the papers. I never suspected a thing. Just thought the lad was ill, under the weather. Food poisoning or something."

Hans sneered. "You will learn." he said. "You have plenty of time to learn."

Jeff did not reply. There was nothing to say. He climbed back onto his bunk and pulled out a pouch of rough Bulgarian tobacco. That was easily obtained in here and all thoughts of giving up smoking had flown out of the window. He needed all the help he could get to keep sane. But heroin.....! Please God that he would never be tempted to go there. He finished rolling his slim cigarette and lit the end, drinking in the soothing smoke. He did not know how long he would have to wait before John returned to tell him how Gary was faring.

Jeff had not meant to doze off. Maybe it was the rush of adrenaline, followed by the shock of the German's revelations, but he had been sound asleep before being woken by the rattle of the cell gate.

"You okay, mate?" It was a pointless remark but Jeff had no idea what else to say as John, head bowed made his way across the cell.

For a moment John said nothing, reaching for his pack of tobacco and rolling himself a cigarette. All the others sat in silence, eyes on John, waiting for him to speak. "He's dead!" It was a simple statement but it rang like a shock wave through Jeff's brain.

"Dead! Good God mate, I'm so sorry." What else could he say.

*****

Chaos reigned at the long trestle table on the veranda. The evening was cool, but Poppa had fired up the huge stone 'chimenea' built onto the outside of the kitchen wall to take off the chill well enough not to warrant eating inside the farmhouse. Not that the crowd of diners would have fitted into Mamma's kitchen, large as it may be. Everyone who had helped with the olive picking had returned to the farmhouse to eat making the evening meal into a raucous occasion. Claudia, Carlotta and Sophia, Tony's sisters, chattering incessantly in a mixture of Italian and English as they helped three year old Maria with her pasta, the pretty child, lively after her afternoon nap, happily covered in sauce, while Christo, very grown up, wielded his own fork and spoon. Poppa, Tony and Marco were discussing the harvest with more than a dozen neighbours who had joined them for the feast. Carol noticed with amusement, Claudia's eyes travelling constantly to a dark-haired young man sitting opposite her. His eyes returning the silent compliment in mutual regard. Sixteen year old Sophia, already beginning to feel the stirrings of adulthood, flirted outrageously with any of the olive skinned boys who caught her eye for a moment, while Carlotta, the quietest of Mamma's daughters, smiled shyly at any of the boys who spoke to her but seemed to prefer to help Mamma ferry an endless parade of dishes and tureens to and from the table.

Paulo and Georgio sat resplendent in new clothes. So much for congratulations and kisses! Guliana had accompanied Marco to the city today and had returned armed with parcels of clothes for the boys, carefully chosen from the selection of shops in the city centre. Marco himself had carried in a huge box filled to the brim with a selection of extravagantly wrapped bonbon's and chocolates which, of course, delighted the nine year olds even more than the carefully chosen clothes. The boys excited chatter centred around which one of them had picked the most olives today, both of them rushing to the fields directly after school to help with the harvest.

Carol and Gina were sitting with Guliana, Marco's new wife, who was delighting in relating all the details of the birth of her sister's child and how she missed the 'bambino' now she had returned to be with her husband.

"Never mind." Gina told her. "Maybe soon you will have your own bambino to care for." Guliana was obviously desperately broody and could hardly wait for the happy event. Fat, olive-skinned babies were an Italian treasure.

Carol glanced over to Tony. He was leaning back in his chair, looking totally at ease amongst the throng around his family table with a glass of wine in his hand. Gina's suggestion that they would marry and live this sort of life brushed quickly through her mind. It was a good life, without doubt, and a happy one. She felt she had choices to make but did not want to rush into any decisions. She wanted to take Transcon Haulage to the top. Take it there herself, through the sweat of her own brow. Only when Transcon Haulage was a success would she consider changing her lifestyle. Tony certainly had made no move to rush her into anything. He caught her eye and flashed her one of his devastating smiles. Carol's heart leapt as she smiled back. A moment of intimacy between them despite the crowded table.

"More escalopes!" Mamma Gina bustled through from the kitchen onto the veranda bearing a huge platter of chicken escalopes. Thin slices of chicken, beaten with a mallet and coated with Mammas own recipe. "Claudia, you help bring-a more pasta, our guests may be hungry!" Claudia did not break her stride in keeping up with the conversation as she left her seat and followed Mamma into the kitchen, returning with another bowl of pasta, her voice still chattering on.

"Claudia is such a chatterbox! It amazes me how she can talk in Italian, switch to English then back to Italian again without even taking breath!" Carol remarked.

Gina laughed. "They all do it, have you not noticed, even the little ones. It must be wonderful to be so at ease in both languages."

"I know," Carol replied. "Even little Maria and Christo. We speak to them in English and they answers back perfectly then when Mamma or anyone speaks to them in Italian, off they go fluently. They don't seem to notice the change, do they?"

Only Guliana struggled with her English but insisted on practising on the girls who always did their best to help.

Gina leaned across to speak to Marco. "Have you managed to contact the prison?" she asked quietly while Carol's attention was distracted in helping Guliana with her English pronunciation.

Marco nodded. "Both yesterday and today I speak with the Governor of the prison. I will tell you everything after dinner. I think you will be satisfied with what I have discovered."

Gina's heart leapt. "You mean it is okay to do as we discussed?"

Marco glanced around. "I think it's better that we speak in private later. You tell me that you don't want Carol or Tony to know what you have in mind."

Gina nodded. She would explain to Marco what her reasoning was later. She knew that the less she told Carol about the situation, the less her friend would have to worry about on the long journey. She nodded to Marco. "We will have a proper chat after dinner then Marco, thank you." Marco flashed her one of his most charming smiles. Almost identical to Tony, with a mass of dark curls, olive skin and dazzling white teeth, the only thing setting him apart from his elder brother were velvety brown eyes.

Gina looked around the table at all the happy, animated faces. She sat back, glass in hand and thought of Jeff. What was he doing right now? Had he eaten well? Was his bed comfortable and was he safe and well? She felt a pang of guilt for enjoying herself this evening and not knowing how he was or what was happening to him. But she knew Jeff well. He was strong and surely by now he would have been informed that she was on her way. He would be happy to know that, and probably happy to sit and read the book that she had sent him and

wait for her to arrive. Surely nothing truly dreadful could happen. Could it?

*****

CHAPTER THIRTEEN

Carol woke to the sound of voices outside her window. She and Gina had slept in the big airy room at the side of the house overlooking the apple orchard and the barn. There was never any suggestion of her sharing a bed with Tony. Under Mamma's roof traditional respectability was adhered to at all times and both Carol and Tony accepted this without question. They had, however, managed to slip away from the throng of diners after dinner and had strolled, hand in hand, through the olive groves, a lantern to light their way. Carol thought it all terribly romantic as Tony kissed her in the moonlight, hidden from prying eyes by the peach trees and apple trees in the enclosed orchard.

They had left Gina in deep conversation with Marco. Carol knew that Marco had been making enquiries about Jeff and hoped that he would be able to ease Gina's worries with what he may have been able to discover. It had been late, and Gina was already asleep by the time Carol crept back into the bedroom, climbing carefully into the big carved bed so as not to wake her friend. Gina needed all the rest she could get to keep her strength and sanity.

The morning was aglow with shafts of gentle sunshine, filtering though the fine, hand made lace curtain and gleaming on the snow capped mountains in the distance. The window was ajar, a gentle breeze wafting the lace and carrying the scent of winter jasmine into the room. There was no sign of Gina save for the dent left in her pillow. Carol slid out of bed and walked over to the window, pushing it wide and drinking in the fresh mountain air. A group of brown hens were pecking nonchalantly in front of the barn and Amico, the children's rather ancient pet donkey, was snuffling lazily in the orchard. She could see beyond the road to where Poppa and the others were walking to the olive groves, keen to begin the day's work, picking the trees bare of the ripe fruit, ready to send to the presses or to the bottling plant for export or for use at their own tables.

A movement near to the barn caught her eye. Gina and Marco were passing by her window, talking together. Gina must have risen early, Carol had not heard her leave the room. She sat for a moment watching her friend speaking closely with Marco. The conversation must, of course, be about Jeff. Carol wondered if Marco had heard anything through his enquiries. He had widespread contacts and Carol often wondered how one so young could have such a far reaching network.

Carol watched idly as Gina and Marco walked over to the 'Flying Angel' and opened the door. Gina clambered inside then re-emerged, a moment later, jumping down from the cab and slamming the door. Carol was slightly puzzled about her friends apparent obsession about checking that her bags were safe. But, she understood, shock took people in different ways, and perhaps Gina had been affected with insecurity after Jeff being arrested.

She stretched and reached for her towel and washbag. It had been arranged that the trucks would be loaded today and they would set off for Bulgaria almost at once. They had discussed the route in detail the night before. Driving from San Guistino along towards Trieste then working their way down to Ljubljana, Zagreb, Belgrade then on to Sofia. It would be a long haul and the weather may not be good. It had been decided that to aim for a first night at the Italian border would be a good goal. All the way there would be mountains, valleys and, to Carol, uncharted territory to cross. She was not sure whether she should feel nervous or excited.

She walked across the landing to the roomy, marble floored bathroom and spun the taps to fill the enormous bath. Carol wondered idly where on earth Poppa had come across such a huge bath, but then thought maybe all Italian families had family sized baths in their bathrooms! She would indulge herself with a leisurely wallow, wash her hair and begin the day fresh. It was the start of another adventure and Carol intended to face it fully prepared.

*****

"Now, you take care Ducks." Poppa Copeland gave Carol and Gina a hug as they prepared to leave. "And don't you forget what we was talking about last night." He wagged a finger at Gina. "Anything you
want, anything at all, you just pick up the 'phone and ask. We all think very highly of your Jeff here and want to see him back safe and sound."

"Thank you Poppa." Gina suddenly wanted to cry. All the kindness she had been shown made her emotions rush to the surface. She gave Poppa a tight hug then jumped into the cab, slamming the door shut. She glanced sideways to see Marco, dressed for the city, standing by his car. He caught her eye and nodded. Gina smiled and nodded back. They had an understanding.

Carol turned the key in the ignition and the Volvo leapt into life. Poppa had come back from the fields to wave them off, holding little Christo and Maria in his arms, safely away from the big trucks as they pulled away and headed through the gates towards the hilly road. Carol and Gina waved to Mamma and Poppa out of the window as they turned out of the gates, heading for the packhouse. Up in the high fields they could see the olive pickers, pulling the ripe fruit from the trees and heaping them into baskets, working as they must have done for many years in the past, still the old ways, tried and trusted. The girls waved out of the cab window as they climbed higher into the hills, Tony's sisters waving in return before continuing with their work.

"I bet Claudia is still chattering!" Carol remarked with a smile as the olive pickers disappeared into the distance.

"And I bet she will be working as closely as possible with that handsome young man that she couldn't take her eyes off last night," Gina replied.

"Hmm, and I reckon you smell wedding cake again, don't you?"

Gina stuck her tongue out, sniffed and turned to look out of the window.

*****

The workers at the packhouse had the load ready and were expecting the two Transcon Haulage trucks. Carol reversed slowly onto the loading bay next to Tony and waited as the fork lift truck heaved palette after palette of olive oil onto the trailer. The owner of the packhouse was an old friend of Tony's family so Marco had pre arranged for the load to be ready and waiting and, as usual, the produce from La Casaccia took top priority, over any other trucks that may be waiting. Not that there were any other trucks in evidence. Transcon Haulage seemed to be the only company scheduled for load this day. "We won't set our sights too high today," Tony said as he watched the fork lift trucks do their work. "But we should be able to get a good head start and get to Udane before having to park up for the night."

"Where is Udane?" Carol asked. "I thought we were going to Trieste." This was all new ground to her.

"I gave Triesete as a reference point because you know where it is, Cara Mia, but Udane is just a bit further up the map and the point we will be heading to. It's pretty much the last place in Italy before we cross over the border at Gorizia into what used to be Yugoslavia and is now Slovenia. We may even make the border before having to stop for the night. I reckon it will be about nine or ten hours drive. Don't forget that this is also pretty new to me too," said Tony. "Although I came back that way after I left Sofia last time, I was just following my nose really what with all the worries I had on my mind. But I have spent the last few months picking the brains of any other drivers who have travelled more widely than I, so that way I did have a vague picture of what to expect." He flashed Carol a smile. "We will learn together!"

Carol wondered if this was the best idea, both of them embarking onto strange territory, then remembered her first trip. There had been plenty of drivers heading in her direction and each one of them had been happy to give help or advice. She decided to cross the bridges of worry if and when needed.

"I've been through there." Gina stuck her head out of the cab window. "Jeff drove to somewhere out there some years ago, the name escapes me at the moment, but I remember passing through the border just past Udane. It took ages to get cleared!"

"Gorizia," Tony put in helpfully.

"Yes, that's it….. I think!"

"Apparently it is a lot easier now," said Tony. "A lot of their borders have come down what with all these countries wanting to be one big Europe. A bad thing in some ways but good in others, especially if it gets us across borders more quickly."

"You reckon we will get to Sofia within four days?" asked Carol. She was not sure that this was not going to be a tall order. It seemed an awful long way on the map.

"Yes, I'm sure we will." Tony sounded confident. "But we will just have to do our best and see what happens. It took me five days to get back to England from Sofia didn't it, but we are not that far away from here so let us see shall we?"

"Wonder what the weather will be like?" Carol remarked, peering up at the sky. The early morning sunshine had retreated back into the clouds and the day was getting dull and decidedly chilly.

"Bear in mind we will be going into the mountains," said Gina. "It may be snowy or foggy or anything up there. You can never tell with mountains!"

That was surely true, thought Carol. The mountain weather had a habit of changing direction within moments.

A shout from the bald headed foreman brought their attention back to the trucks. "That's it." said Tony "All done and ready to roll." He walked over to the foreman and shook his hand, taking the papers for the loads.

The two trucks set off in convoy, pulling out of the packhouse, onto the road and starting the long trip to Bulgaria.

Gina hung out of the window, admiring the stunning view of the mountains. Her emotions were a mixture of apprehension, excitement and worry as they made their way up the winding road to traverse their way through to the coastline then turn towards Venice. "Oh, I really love it in this part of the world." For the first time since Jeff's arrest, Gina sounded her old self. "I had such a lovely evening with the family. Everyone is so relaxed and happy."

"I noticed you and Marco were having a good chat." Carol changed into a lower gear to negotiate a steep bend in the road.

Gina glanced sideways at her friend then returned her attention back to the view from the side window. "Yes, we did have a good chat. He has been doing his best to be helpful." She quickly changed the subject. "Did you notice the pig!"

"Pig? What Pig?"

"There was a fat brown piggy in the orchard. The boys brought him in to the barn for the night."

"Not another pet surely."

"Er, no actually. Marco said it was the 'Christmas' pig."

Carol shot Gina an amazed glance. "You mean they actually have a pig running around the orchard then *eat* it at Christmas!"

"Well at first I was a little taken aback, actually meeting the poor thing, then realising it was for the pot but, as Marco explained, it is a terribly hypocritical way to think. I mean, when did WE ever turn down a bacon sandwich or a slice of ham?"

"Hmm, suppose you're right, but we never MET those pigs did we?"

"Marco says the pig has a great life, running round the orchard, digging for apples then sleeping all night on nice clean straw, then come Christmas, Poppa gets his gun, walks out to the barn and, boom... instant table meat. Piggy never even knows what's happened!"

Carol gave the subject a moment's thought. "You know, I think that is FAR better than what we do. Go to the supermarket and buy a faceless piece of meat that has probably been crammed into awful conditions is some factory farm somewhere and never had a good life. Probably carted miles to a terrifying slaughterhouse too, before being killed. The farmhouse pig certainly gets the best deal!"

"Marco also said that Mamma uses every tiny bit of the carcass too. She makes a sort of brawn out of the head and does something with the ears, cut into strips and all crispy. Apparently that is the kids favourite bit. She uses the trotters for soup and all the other bits too. She sure doesn't waste anything."

"Gina shut up! You are making me hungry!"

"What! After the huge breakfast that Mamma made us eat. Pig yourself!" Gina laughed. "I wonder why we couldn't get hold of Spyder last night," her mind wandering to the previous evening.

"Don't know," Carol replied. "Wasn't too surprised that he was not at my house, considering the time of day but can't think why his mobile was switched off. You don't think there is anything wrong do you?"

"No, very doubtful. After all what on earth COULD be wrong and if there was a problem, he has the number of La Casaccia and would have left us a message and he also has your mobile number too."

"The mobiles are sometimes less than useless in these hills though." Carol put in. "But we'll give it another go when we stop for the night. I personally am much happier with payphones anyway. At least they work!"

Carol was not too worried about the lack of contact with Spyder. She had no doubts that he was perfectly capable of looking after her property and the animals in her absence. If not, she would never have given him the responsibility.

*****

Jeff lay on his bunk staring up at the grey ceiling. The events of the night before had thrown a sombre atmosphere into the cell. There had been questions, of course. Each man had been, in turn, hauled up in front of the Governor. The same questions thrown at each of them. Had they noticed the young Englishman's state of health. Had he eaten anything sent in from a food parcel that could have 'upset' his digestion. John Miller had given the Governor blunt answers. Gary had died of a drugs overdose. That was clear to him and anyone else that had seen the convulsions and the vomiting, the foaming from the mouth. He had been silenced at once. The doctor had examined the body and given his verdict. Heart failure. Heart failure due to an undiscovered medical condition.

John had been incredulous, but his attempts to disagree were met with stony silence. Stony silence, then the suggestion that he was under, for the best translation, severe strain, not himself, not thinking straight. The death of his relative had caused him to temporarily lose his mind. He could be prescribed tranquillisers, that may help his frame of mind. The suggestion that young Gary had obtained drugs in this well run prison was tantamount to propaganda, slandering the good name of the institution. Maybe a week in solitary confinement may improve his memory.

John was not stupid. He agreed that, yes, he was very much under strain. Yes, the unexpected death of his nephew was indeed a tragedy and, of course, his lunatic ramblings about drugs were a consequence of his grief. No, he did not need tranquillisers, he would soon 'pull himself together'. Satisfied, the Governor had ordered him returned to his cell, but a guard, constantly outside the cell, was obviously listening for any subversive comments that may be passed amongst the prisoners.

Jeff had been grilled in the same way. Asked his opinion on the cause of Gary's sudden demise. Truthfully he had explained he knew nothing of the young man's condition. Had no idea what had caused the convulsions and gave the prison officials the satisfaction of accepting their verdict. Heart failure due to undisclosed medical condition. He knew the truth. John knew the truth, so did the Romanians and the German but nobody spoke a word about it. There was nothing to say. Gary was dead. The Death Certificate authenticated and signed. Arrangements were already being made with the Embassy for return of the body to England. There was nothing that discussion would do to change the situation. So they got on with the business of survival in silence.

Jeff reached under his bunk and pulled out his box of belongings. He took out the letter from Gina and read it for the hundredth time. Gina was coming to see him, but beyond that he had heard nothing. He had no idea when she would arrive so had asked for a visit from Huntingdon-Smythe. This request had been met with opposition. For no reason Jeff could think of, he was told that this request would be considered 'in due course'. When Jeff had questioned the reason for not being allowed an immediate visit he was told simply that visits were at the discretion of the prison and he had already seen the man from the Embassy so would have to wait, for how long they did not say.

Jeff put this stalling down to the death of Gary. The prison obviously did not want anybody speaking out of turn. He wanted to write to Gina, but if she was coming to visit then what would be the point?

He glanced over to where John was laying on his bunk. "You all right mate?" Jeff asked, his voice cutting through the silence in the cell.

"Yeah, fine." The sarcasm in John's voice spoke volumes. "But life goes on, eh." He swung his long legs off the bunk and onto the floor. "Fancy a game of chess?"

Jeff nodded. A game of chess would be good. The sort of game that taxed the brain, but needed no conversation. Under these circumstances, ideal. He sat up and pulled his box from under the bed to use as a table.

John walked over with his chess board and pieces. "Black or white?" he asked.

"Nothing in here ever is, mate, is it!"

John half smiled. He understood exactly what Jeff meant.

*****

The windscreen wipers swept monotonously across the screen, clearing the dismal view as the two trucks passed under the Autostrada gantry pointing directions to Venice, Trieste and Udane.

The tinkling of Carol's mobile phone broke the monotony of the drive. "Grab that for me will you Kiddo." Carol asked, not wanting to take her mind off the road.

Gina fished the small mobile from the depths of Carol's shoulder bag and clicked the answer button. "Carol's phone!....... Oh, Hi Spyder, everything okay?....... no Carol is driving at the moment.....Oh, how wonderful! ....Congratulations!.......Oh, that is really lovely.....yes, of course.... We did try to ring you last night...... of course, no wonder.....Oh, great, Carol will be pleased....yes, ...no,..... I don't that will be a problem do you?......oh, really, good idea, that's a good plan..........yes I will tell her, you take care now, bye Spyder." she clicked off the phone and returned it to Carol's bag.

"Come on, do tell, what was that all about?" Carol slowed down as the traffic got heavier with trucks and cars pulling off in different directions at the turn-offs to the various cities.

"No wonder Spyder was unavailable last night." Gina beamed happily. "His wife, Suzie, had a little girl yesterday, Jade Victoria, she weighed in at seven pounds and all is well. Spyder is delighted, his first daughter after two boys. He sounds like a dog with two tails."

"That IS good news! I bet he is thrilled to bits! A little girl, how lovely! I hope he isn't finding all the work too much with a new baby to visit and everything."

"Doesn't seem to think so. He says Suzie is coming home in a couple of days, all being well, and her mum has moved in to help with the kids and will be staying for a few days to give her a hand when she gets home. Also, when mum-in-law does go home, she is taking Cinderella with her, so that's one kitty down already. Spyder also said that the cat charity man has been round with a big net and captured mother cat and hawked her off to be snipped, so there won't be any more litters of kittens in your outside loo from now on!"

"All this positive news in one 'phone call." Carol laughed. "Can't be bad!"

"Oh yes, and Katy telephoned Spyder and told him that she would be home again in a few weeks for Christmas and, er, that she would be bringing a couple of friends with her as well for the holiday. It seems that some of them have no homes to go to, so Katy is taking care of that!"

Carol raised an eyebrow. "I wonder exactly what Katy's definition of 'a couple' is?" she mused. "You and I know it means two but with Katy....."

Gina giggled. "Spyder also seems to have taken that piece of information on board too. He says he will concentrate on getting the bedrooms painted and in order so that visitors won't be a problem." Gina smiled. "I think it sounds lovely, a house full of people at Christmas, all sitting round a big table and enjoying the day. I am only praying that Jeff will be home by then." She turned to stare out of the window. "And to HELL with my Mother. We will definitely be with you! All of us together toasting the future!"

Carol said nothing, but suddenly Poppa's 'Christmas Pig' did not sound like such a bad idea after all!

*****

The sun had stayed in hiding for the duration of the day, a miserable drizzle falling relentlessly throughout the whole of the drive. It was well past dusk and darker than usual, due to the grey skies and thick cloud, as Carol followed Tony into the parking area of the border crossing at Gorozia.

The two trucks parked up in the waiting area and Carol switched off the engine. "One thing I do know I want is the ladies loo!" she said, reaching behind her for her jacket in preparation for the cold and rain outside.

"Me to!" Gina replied rummaging in her roomy, soft leather shoulder bag and producing a small mirror and lipstick, applying a quick sweep of the crimson cosmetic to her lips before attempting to leave the vehicle and face the world. "Want a dab?" she offered the lipstick to Carol.

"Thanks, no need to look like a couple of old dogs if we don't have to is there?" Carol applied a coating of the lipstick then slipped on her jacket.

Tony had parked next to them and walked over to the cab. "What do you want to do Cara Mia?" he asked standing at the open cab door. "Do you want to get the papers in, get across the border then sleep the other side, or shall we leave it all until morning and do it then?"

Carol glanced at Gina who shrugged. "Leave it to you, Kiddo," Gina said. "You are the one who is driving, I'm just along for the ride."

"Let's go to the loo, have a drink and see how long it is likely to take," Carol suggested. Personally it would suit me to get across tonight. Will give us a head start in the morning. If we wait, it may take ages tomorrow and bite into the day and we don't need that do we?"

"My thoughts exactly," Tony replied. "We will go that way then. Let us hand in the papers and find out how long the wait will be."

The three walked over to the first window to show their passports, then handed in their paperwork to the control officer in the second window. "How long to wait?" Tony asked in Italian. The guard shrugged and pointed to the clock on the wall behind him, sweeping his finger round the face. "One hour?" Tony asked. The officer nodded.

"That's not too bad, is it?" Carol remarked. "If he is to be believed of course, though at least we will have time to go to the loo, I am in serious need right now.

The girls ran across the short distance to the toilets. "Not much here to attract the visitor is there." Carol remarked as the girls made use of the sparse facilities.

"Glad we ate at Udane," Gina put in, washing her hands in the not-too-clean sink. "This place is not at all inviting is it?"

Carol looked round to see if she could see Tony as the two girls came out of the toilets and hurried back towards the truck. "Wonder who that is," she remarked, spotting Tony, strolling back towards the 'Silver Lady' in conversation with a tall, bald-headed man with a goatee beard.

"No idea." Gina pulled her fur-lined coat around her, huddling against the inclement weather. "You know what these drivers are like. They will talk to anybody that will talk back!" She pulled open the cab door, climbed quickly inside and fished around for her box of tissues. There were some small muddy marks on her suede boots that needed to be removed.

"According to that guy I was just speaking to," said Tony, arriving at the side of the Volvo, "It is always pretty quick here. Apparently it is hardly more than a formality these days."

"That's good," Carol replied. "As soon as we get through, we can park up and relax for the night. I, for one, am completely shattered!" Nice early start in the morning, yes?"

"Can't believe it is only a couple of nights and we will be in Bulgaria," said Gina. "Then I can see Jeff."

Tony climbed into the cab with them. "Gina, are you sure that the arrangements have been made for your visit.

"Mark said that he had informed the prison of me wanting to visit and been told it was okay. He also spoke to the Embassy about it and I also emailed the embassy... twice... to tell them I was coming. So if they don't know by now that I am on my way then......" she threw her hands in the air. "Then they must be both blind AND deaf!"

"But did you get the okay. Did they say that you *could* actually visit Jeff?" Carol was dreading Gina being disappointed on her arrival at the prison. "Have you any written permission?"

"Nothing in writing actually," Gina replied, "But I telephoned them and told them approximately when we would be arriving and they said to contact them straight away and that they would arrange a hotel. Mark also spoke to them and told me that I had been given permission to visit, and also Marco has spoken to the prison and told them that I am coming, so they should have the message by now, although...... I just MAY have to pay a fee to see Jeff."

"You mean you will have to give them money or they won't let you see him!" said Tony, puzzled. This did not sound right.

"Not necessarily," Gina continued, her head bowed as she concentrated on rubbing at the stubborn mud specks on her boots. "But if there is any hold up or problem then offering money to help with 'administration' it appears, helps smooth the way."

"Well, as soon as we get there, speak at once to the Embassy as they suggested. You have brought all the telephone numbers and everything, haven't you?"

Gina smiled. "Oh, yes! I have brought absolutely everything that I need!"

Carol cast her friend a sidelong glance. She had a strong feeling that Gina was not telling her absolutely everything, but could not for the life of her imagine what her friend could be keeping to herself. Carol said nothing. When Gina was ready to tell her then she would. Until then she would allow her the privacy she was entitled to. She would be there with support when needed and felt sure that very soon this support would be called upon.

"Hey, any of you lot fancy a hot drink?" The bearded, bald headed man that Tony had been speaking to strolled over to the cab. "Charlie has got his pot on the boil and we wondered if the ladies would fancy a coffee."

"Oh, that's very kind," Gina answered at once. "That would be lovely. Shall we bring our own mugs over?"

"Yes, you'd better. Charlie only carries a couple and never washes 'em up too often." The tall man grinned. "I'll tell him we got visitors, okay, see you over there."

"That's very kind isn't it?" Gina remarked buttoning up her coat once more.

"Yes, a coffee will be nice," Tony replied. "Pass an hour anyway."

"We've got some cake here we can take to share." Carol grubbed about in the supplies box for some generous wedges of rich fruit cake provided by Mamma Gina.

The three walked over to the big yellow Scania where they could see a rather overweight man with a shock of grey hair sitting in the cab and the bald-headed man standing alongside.

"Pile in everybody." The large man swung the cab door wide. "Plenty of room inside!" The roomy Scania cab was spacious enough to accommodate Carol, Gina and Tony on the lower bunk and the two drivers on the front seats.

"This is a great arrangement you have here!" Carol was surprised to see that between the two seats in the cab was a small sink and cooker fitment.

"Invaluable these things. An old 'Middle East' cab this. Charlie here would waste away if it wasn't for his mobile kitchen!" said the bald-headed man, his eye on the cake that Carol was holding.

Charlie grinned. "Had this for years and wouldn't part with it. Have you met my mate Matt," he asked waving a hand at his lanky friend.

"Pleased to meet you both." Tony shook hands and introduced Carol and Gina.

"We have plenty of cake here to go with the coffee." Carol handed the cake over to Charlie. "It was home made by Tony's Mamma, who is the world's best cook!"

"Well you obviously all know each other," Matt remarked. "So what are you two ladies doing in this neck of the woods? Don't often see lady drivers on this run do we, Chas?"

Carol glanced at Gina who shrugged nonchalantly. She was well past caring who knew about Jeff and cared little for their opionion anyway. Carol explained, briefly, the situation.

"Banged up in Sofia you say." Charlie handed out the mugs of coffee. "That's bad luck, Darlin', getting your man taken like that. Too much of it going on, I reckon." He wielded a large knife as he spoke, slicing the cake into manageable portions.

"Jeff would not do such a thing!" Gina snapped pointedly. "I am absolutely sure he is a victim in all this and it's some terrible mistake!"

"I'm sure it is," Charlie went on smoothly. "Have you any idea how many of our boys this happens to? Dozens of 'em, that's how many. And how many do our Government help? Not a bloody one that's a fact."

Gina calmed down a little. "I had no idea," she said a little lamely. "I thought Jeff may be the first one. The first innocent one that is"

Matt threw his head back and laughed out loud. "Sorry missus, but that's almost funny. There have been guys out there, without trial mind you, for bloody years. About time something was done that's what we think don't we Chas?"

"Too right. How did it happen, do you know."

"I was there at the time," said Tony. He related the tale as best he could for the two interested listeners.

"Hmm, planted, definitely planted." said Matt firmly. "Without a doubt. Planted on the border he was. Wouldn't be surprised if you weren't carrying too, Mate, just got lucky and got through. You wouldn't even know you had the stuff on board. They probably followed you through and grabbed it back off the minute you were out of sight of the cab!"

"That's what we heard before." Carol said, amazed that these men were so casual about the whole thing. They had heard it all before and it seemed like common knowledge that this sort of thing took place. They were also taking it on face value that Jeff was, indeed, innocent.

"You would, Love," said Matt. "It's a common practice. Now take my advice. Whenever the truck has been out of sight, like now for example, never just drive off. Check the bloody thing from nose to tail. And never forget to do it."

"What if you find something?" Gina queried. "That's a problem in itself, I should imagine."

"Sure is," Charlie answered. "What I would do is just pull the stuff off and drop it on the ground and drive away...... quick! Don't open the bag, don't fiddle with it and don't make a fuss. Just dump it and go!"

"Trouble is, they are sometimes watching you, see, and if you find it and try and take it to some official or the like, they will have a knife in your back before you know they are there."

"What if they don't see you take it off and go to retrieve it and find its not there. They may think you have still got it." Tony added.

"Yes, Mate, there is that too. I've only come across it once and I just pulled the bag off the underside and dropped it were I stood. Drove off like the devil I did but heard no more. Still it's a dangerous old job and no mistake."

Carol glanced over at Gina who was sitting quietly staring into her coffee mug. "You okay Kiddo." she asked.

"Yes," Gina replied. "I just hadn't realised how widespread this thing was, with drivers being locked up, willy-nilly all over the place."

"Chin up love." Matt noticed Gina's sorrowful face. "At least your old man has got a visit from his pretty missus to look forward to!"

Gina smiled. Yes she would be seeing Jeff soon. She would keep that thought at the forefront of her mind and keep focused. Keep positive and be strong for Jeff. They would be across the border within the next hour or so and another country nearer to seeing him. It was a thought that kept her spirits high as she waited for the time to pass.

*****

A loud banging on the cab door woke Carol and Gina from their sleep. Carol reached over and pulled aside the cotton curtain covering the cab window.

"Good morning, Cara Mia." Tony was cheerful despite the early hour. "If you two ladies have had enough sleep we can get an early start."

Carol yawned and nodded. "Give us a few minutes, Darling. We have to gather our wits."

Tony smiled and walked away, back to the Scania where Charlie had the ever-boiling kettle ready to pour morning coffee.

"What's the weather like?" Gina asked pulling her sleeping bag up round her chin. "It's so nice and warm in here!" The night heater was doing its work well, warming the cab to a cosy temperature.

"It's not raining," Carol replied, wriggling out of her sleeping bag and peering out of the window. "But it looks pretty cold out there. I think it's going to snow soon."

"Oh, wonderful news!" Gina replied sarcastically, unwillingly pulling down the zip on her sleeping bag and sitting upright. She reached for her cosmetics bag and set about cleansing her face and brushing her hair, winding it up on top of her head and fixing it in place with a large clip comb. "Matt and Charlie said last night that we should be able to make it down to a place called the National Hotel, or something, near Belgrade by tonight." she said. "Charlie says it's a good place to stay and we can either sleep in the cabs or in the hotel itself. He and Matt both agree that the food is great there, so that's something to look forward to."

"Oh, really? I must have missed that bit of the conversation." Carol put in, pulling on her jeans and a thick sweater.

"Not surprised. Gina grinned. "You and Tony went off in a little world of your own at the bar. Matt, Charlie and I just had to get on with it, without the pleasure of your input!"

Carol grabbed her hair brush and tried to beat her rebellious curls into some semblance of order. "I hadn't realised how nice it would be to travel with Tony," she said, giving up with the hairbrush and dabbing on a quick coat of lipstick. "It's an odd thing, but when I am in England and he is travelling, the time seems to fly and I just look forward to seeing him at weekends, but this last week has been lovely."

"Maybe you should think about travelling together all the time." Gina suggested. "Or would that take the edge of it and become boring do you think."

"Not boring, I hope," Carol put in quickly "If two people are in love or get on very well they should never get bored of each other's company, should they? We never get bored with each other do we?"

"No, suppose you're right, we don't do we?" Gina finished her morning make up and reached for her case of clothes. She selected dark brown trousers and a cream cable sweater. She pulled on her fur topped suede boots and reached for her jacket. "All ready for morning coffee…. and the loo!"

"Now that is one thing I would appreciate in a truck." Carol remarked as she locked the cab door before walking over to the Scania. "A built-in loo would be absolute bliss don't you think?"

Gina laughed. "As long as we didn't have to empty it ourselves!" she said.

"Hmm, yes, there is that." Carol had to agree. "Not the best job in the world after a week away, I shouldn't imagine!"

"What isn't the best job in the world?" asked Charlie as he swung the cab door open for the girls to join them.

"Emptying toilets!" said Gina, moving up along the bunk next to Tony as Carol climbed in next to them.

"What! What on earth brought up that sort of conversation before breakfast." Carol laughed. "Don't ask." Charlie decided not to. What women found to talk about had always been beyond him.

Charlie handed round mugs of hot coffee and croissants with chocolate filling. It was cosy sitting in the big cab with a hot drink and croissants to dunk. A good way to start the day.

"It looks like snow," Matt observed, peering up at the threatening sky. "I reckon we will still make it to the Nationale before bedtime though, what do you reckon Chas?"

"No problem." Charlie gathered up the cups and swiped around his own pair with a tissue, stowing them back in his supplies box. "The sooner we get started though the better, you never know what hold ups there may be. Nothing is set in stone on these trips is it? You both dieseled up?" he asked.

"Yes." Tony replied untangling himself from the bunk. "We filled up last night just before we pulled into Gorizia so we will be fine for a while."

"Well, we can't go anywhere 'til we have visited the ladies," Carol stated firmly, sliding off the bunk and opening the door. Shall we meet you back here in fifteen minutes, Tony, then we can set off?"

"We can all go off in convoy." Matt suggested. "Always safer in numbers I reckon, but it's a good run down the old Killer Road to Belgrade so we should just be able to go nose to tail all the way."

"Killer Road!" Carol was not sure she liked the sound of that.

Charlie laughed. "Oh, don't you worry, Girl, that was the old name for it when there were loads of mad drivers running cheap duty-free's back to the east, in cars that were fit for nothing but the scrap heap and drivers that had not slept for days. You will be fine in your truck, Love, don't you worry, it's a good straight road, no problems!"

"Okay, I believe you….. I think!" said Carol, fastening up her coat against the cold. "Actually, I am beginning to wonder when things WILL go wrong," she remarked to Gina as they made their way towards the services to make the most of the last toilets they would see for a while. "So far things have gone so well it is almost beginning to worry me."

"Hmm, know what you mean." Gina replied, following Carol through the door of the ladies toilets. "It almost makes you want something TO happen so that you know it will be over and done with, but hey, look on the bright side. Maybe the fates are with us and nothing will go wrong at all!"

"Oh, Gina. I wish you hadn't said that." said Carol, crossing her fingers for luck.

*****

CHAPTER FOURTEEN

Carol pulled the Volvo gratefully into the services. The snow was falling heavily and it had made her eyes ache, peering through the windscreen. They had been driving for hours, longer than they should, disregarding the tacho's registering their every mile. They were close to the outskirts of Belgrade and both Carol and Gina were desperate for sleep.

After Ljubjana the road had been good. Good enough to be boring, Carol had begun to think, as she travelled mile after mile, following the other trucks on the busy through route across the Continent. They had cruised through the borders with little or no waiting and with only one short break for a leg stretch, coffee and cake, it had been a relief to see the signs heralding the entrance to the former Hotel Nationale on the outskirts of Belgrade. Carol clicked the Volvo into a lower gear as the she slowed to follow Tony into the big pull in. The Hotel Nationale, grandly named, was the respite stop for all the drivers travelling the old middle-east route for many years. The parking area was vast and, much to Carol's relief, there was more than enough empty parking space to accommodate the small convoy.

"Wow! This looks impressive!" Gina was delighted with the first sight of the Hotel Nationale. "Honestly I would KILL for a hot soak but I suppose there are just showers here but hey, who's complaining? As long as there is hot water I will be in heaven!"

"I'm with you on that one." Carol was now feeling totally exhausted as she pulled the Volvo into a parking spot, clicked on the handbrake and killed the engine. Her eyes stung, her bottom was numb and her shoulders ached. "I must remember what you told me about dropping my shoulders." she said, rolling her neck from side to side in an attempt to ease the nagging ache.

"Sorry!" said Gina, half standing in the footwell and rubbing her bottom. "You must remind me to keep reminding you. God! My bottom feels completely square with all this sitting. I keep changing position but it hasn't helped much. Poor old you. You can't even wriggle about like I can!"

"Tell me about it!" Carol swung the door of the cab open to be greeted by an icy blast of air. "Bloody Hell, it's freezing out there!"

The two girls climbed stiffly from the cab, their boots crunching on the layer of freshly fallen snow. The other trucks in their group had all parked close by and the girls walked over to the 'Silver Lady' and Matt's truck, parked next to each other.

This weather is a bit of a surprise." Matt stuck his head out of the cab. "It is usually a lot milder around Belgrade, but this is a place I think will meet the approval of you ladies!" He dropped down from the cab and locked the door. "There is hot water galore and the best food you will find on this whole trip, and cheap too."

"Trust you to think of the cost, tight wad!" Charlie was shrugging on his coat as he walked over to join them. "With a bit of luck you will see this bugger buy a drink, if you don't blink and miss it!"

"If this place is as good as you say it is, then the first drink is on me," Tony put in, joining the group. "I have never even heard of the Hotel Nationale before. I must have sailed straight past last time, though I don't know how I ever missed it!"

"There you go, Mattie boy, you got out of buying the first round yet again!" Charlie chuckled as they made their way over towards the welcome sight of the restaurant.

"A drink first, then eat, then a hot shower before bedtime for me," Matt announced. "Let's get the priorities in order!" Personally, Gina would have appreciated a shower and a change of clothes before sitting down to dinner but was far too tired to disagree.

The bar in the Hotel Nationale had certainly, at one time, been a grand affair. Now it had gone sadly downhill, like an elderly matron still desperately clinging to her once glamorous youth.   Right now, Carol and Gina cared little about the décor, all they wanted was a drink and a moment to relax. "There are rooms available to spend the night if you prefer to sleep away from the cab, Cara Mia." Tony slipped his arm around Carol as they stood at the bar. Carol glanced up into his eyes, there was nothing she would have liked better than to snuggle up in a warm bed with Tony next to her.

"I don't want to sound like a wet blanket, Darling." she said, "But I will have to run it by Gina. I feel terribly responsible for her at the moment, and she is far from being herself. She may not want to be alone."

Tony sighed.   He did understand what Gina was going through and totally understood the staunch friendship between the women, but, right now he hoped for a little time alone with the woman he loved. "I understand Cara Mia." he said, not unkindly. "I realise what Gina is going through. We all feel responsible for Jeff, but maybe she will not mind having a single room to herself for one evening." He finished the sentence on a hopeful note.

Carol reached up and kissed him on the nose. "I will pop over and speak to her while you bring the drinks over. I will see how she feels about it."

Gina had made herself comfortable at one of the round tables in the lounge area. "Tony's just bringing the drinks." Carol announced, sitting down next to her friend. "It seems that there are rooms available for the night here and at very reasonable prices too. We were wondering if we should have a night away from the trucks, what do you think?"

"I think that's a great idea," Gina replied enthusiastically. "You and Tony can have a romantic night in the middle of nowhere and I can have a lovely long soak in my room and pamper myself for the night. Sounds wonderful."

"Gina, you are wonderful! Carol hugged Gina spontaneously as Tony, Matt and Charlie walked over to the table bearing trays of drinks.

"Why?" asked Gina in a surprised tone. "What have I done now!"

Carol smiled up at Tony as he passed the drinks round the table. "Gina thinks that getting a couple of rooms is a great idea. She is going to pamper herself for the evening, so we will have to make our own amusement!"

Tony's diamond grey eyes flashed. "I am sure we can think of something to entertain ourselves, Cara Mia." he said, laughing as he saw Carol's cheek flood with colour

"Honestly! You two are worse than teenagers!" Gina put in, picking up her glass. "Here's to everybody." she said. "I feel this will be a most pleasant evening."

"It's stopping places like these that take the grind out of the job." Carol remarked sitting back and sipping her drink.

"I'll drink to that!" said Matt.

"You'll drink to bloody well anything!" said Charlie.

*****

Dawn was hardly breaking as Carol woke and stretched luxuriously in the comfort of the big double bed. Tony was till sleeping soundly at her side as she slipped quietly from under the covers and made for the small bathroom. She ran the shower for a moment to make sure the water was the right temperature before stepping under it and closing her eyes as the hot water streamed over her body.

She felt relaxed and happy and ready for the day ahead as she wrapped herself in a thick fluffy towel, winding her mass of curls into another before stepping back into the bedroom.

"Good morning, Cara Mia." Tony mumbled sleepily from the depths of the bedcovers.

"Good morning, Darling!" Carol sat down on the side of the bed and ran her fingers through Tony's thick black curls. He grasped her hand, turning onto his back and pulled her down towards him, kissing her full on the lips. The bed covers had slipped down and Carol buried her head into the soft covering of hair on his firm chest.

"Hey, come on you," Carol laughed, attempting to pull away. "We have a long drive ahead of us and breakfast to get through yet!"

"And many days before we can enjoy each other once more Cara Mia." Tony mumbled huskily, stroking Carol's damp shoulder.

"Well, you do have a point," Carol admitted, her resolve weakening as she breathed in the warmth of his body. "It's very early after all."

She swung her legs onto the bed and slid back under the covers. "Another hour won't make a difference will it?" she whispered.

Tony did not reply. He just turned, ran his hands down her spine and kissed her passionately.

*****

"Oh, good afternoon!" Gina called across the dining room as Carol and Tony walked into breakfast, hand in hand.

"And what time do you call this then?" Matt glanced at his watch, tapping it with his finger.

"Time they got an alarm clock." Charlie put in with a grin.

"Sorry!" said Carol, colour once more flushing her cheeks. "I did wake up early then sort of…. well dozed off again."

"Yeah! Right! We believe you don't we Chas!" Matt gave his pal a dig in the ribs.

"Easily done when you're in a warm bed for a change," Charlie put in diplomatically. "Well, you haven't missed anything yet. We've only just got down here so let's get breakfast shall we?"

Gina flashed Carol a wink as she and Tony took their places at the table. "It's still nice and early so don't worry." she smiled "How far do you think we will get to today?"

"All the way into Bulgaria, no problem." Matt answered. "Of course, we will be leaving you at Nis. We are heading towards Skopje while you carry on through Nis, following the river and heading through the gorge. Now that's an interesting drive and no mistake, but you'll make it okay. We can stop a few kilometres before Nis for a break and we will say goodbye to you there."

"But we will be thinking of you." Charlie added, catching the eye of the waiter and beckoning him over.

"We will be sorry to lose you," Carol said truthfully. "You have been great company."

"So have you, Love, so have you." Charlie patted her hand. "And you, Darlin' you make sure you get that old man of yours out of that pokey quick smart, you hear. There's far too many of us British drivers banged up over there for little or no reason. Bloody Government don't give a stuff either. Frightened of upsetting their counterparts over there, they are. Couldn't care less that they are ripping lives and families apart." He gave a disgusted grunt and took charge of the coffee pot.

"Thank you Charlie." said Gina. "It is nice to know that so may people believe that Jeff is innocent and not just getting what he deserves."

"I know, Love." Charlie added. "It's very easy to pass the buck and say there's no smoke without fire, but I've known lads go over there and get locked up and they don't even know what they have supposed to have done. Now in England, we have all these toe-rags, muggers, paedophiles and the like, getting away with murder with our soft laws!"

"Oh, here we go!" Matt groaned. "Don't let him get on his soapbox or we will never get away."

"Yeah, sorry." Charlie agreed. "I do get a bit political at times, but I get so mad about injustice, you will bear with me on that one, Love, won't you?" He directed his last remark at Gina

"Oh, absolutely!" Gina agreed with fervour. "I know, without doubt, one hundred and ten per cent, that my Jeff would NEVER in a million years touch anything like drugs. He is SO much against them it is ludicrous to think he would do it, so yes, I DO get mad and angry when I think of the injustice!"

"We all know Jeff is innocent." Tony put in. "If he were not, we would feel it, but we know he is a good man, and all my family is willing to support him, and Gina of course."

"Good lad. That's what we need. More people to stand up and be counted." Charlie reached into his pocket. "Here," he handed Gina a card. "When you get back to England, get in touch with me. Any help you want I will be willing to give. I have a big mouth and I'm not afraid to use it, 'Bout time things improved for us drivers!"

"Yeah, and me." Matt took the card from Gina and wrote his telephone number on the back. "You let us know how things go won't you?"

Gina felt quite moved. "Yes, she said. I certainly will, and right now I am going to call the Embassy in Sofia and tell them that I will be arriving this evening. I am not going to give them the excuse that they were not prepared for my arrival or anything!" Gina left the table and walked over to the telephone booths.

"I hope she is not shot down in flames." Carol peered after Gina's disappearing figure. "She has set her heart on this trip. It will kill her if they won't let her see Jeff."

"Heaven help them if they try!" Tony put in. "She will tear them apart, I believe, if they obstruct her path."

Carol thought he was probably right, but she could not help being anxious as she waited for Gina to return.

"Well, what did they say." Carol could see Gina had a smile on her face so it could not be all bad.

"They were very kind." Gina slid back into her seat. "I spoke, eventually, to a very nice man who told me he had visited Jeff and knew him. He told me that he has prepared the papers I will need for the visit and has even arranged for a hotel directly across the road from the prison so that it will be convenient to get there. Isn't that kind?"

It occurred to Carol that it was the least that they could do but decided against saying anything. "Yes, it is, very kind." she agreed.

Gina pulled a piece of paper out of her bag. "This is the address of the hotel." she held out the paper. "The man I spoke to in the end, something-Smythe was his name, said he would have the relevant papers there, ready for us to pick up when we arrive. Oh, I told him that you would be with me, Carol, I hope that's all right and you won't mind being with me. I haven't upset any plans have I?" She glanced between Tony and Carol.

"Our only plan is to get you to see Jeff and see what we can do to help." Tony was quick to put her at ease. "When we arrive we must drop the load then find the re-load warehouse. After that you and Carol can get a taxi cab to the hotel and I will stay and do the business with the trucks. It is not a problem. We must all do what is best for Jeff. That day will be for you, Gina."

Gina was almost moved to tears. She spontaneously flung her arms about Tony and gave him a kiss on the cheek. "Oh, I am so lucky to have such good friends."

"Not lucky Kiddo." Carol put in as Gina took her seat again. "You and Jeff deserve all the help you can get. You would do the same for us, we know that."

Gina felt that headway had been made. A weight had been lifted from her shoulders and she was definitely on her way to see Jeff. She would see him tomorrow. It was not a huge length of time and she was sure it would fly by.

*****

The small convoy of trucks rolled out of the parking area of the Hotel Nationale and accelerated onto the Autoroute. Charlie led the way, followed by Matt, then Carol, with Tony bringing up the rear. It felt safe and cosy to be sandwiched between the friendly trucks, and Carol relaxed into the journey despite the gently falling snow, hypnotically swishing onto her windscreen.

This was the final run. At the end of the day they would be in Bulgaria. There they would have much to do. Gina sat silently watching the scenery swish by her window. The snow had covered the trees and hillsides with a blanket of white, the mountains, well into the distance, towered majestically, wearing their glimmering white robes, reaching to the clouds above.

"It appears that we are heading straight into the mountains," said Gina, pulling out the map and running her finger along the thin line that denoted the road on which they were travelling. "And it looks an awful long way on this map too, the pages are bigger."

Carol raised an eyebrow but said nothing. Occasionally, Gina's logic, for one so usually sensible, was beyond her. "We are supposed to be stopping for a break just before Nis," she said. "Charlie and Matt both know it so we just follow them in. Actually this is getting quite boring, just sitting behind another truck all the way down the country and back. It doesn't feel like I am actually putting in any effort at all, or being at all independent if you know what I mean."

"Only you would think a thing like that." Gina sniffed. "What do you think the men do, eh?" She pointed ahead. "Look at Charlie and Matt. Stuck together like glue all the way from England it appears." Tony and Jeff set off together, and would have come back together if all had not gone pear shaped, and how many other drivers have we met on our travels that go nose to tail in pairs or, even threes and fours?"

Carol thought about it. "Yes, suppose you're right," she conceded. "It's just this stigma about women drivers I suppose. We can't just get the job done and forget it, we have to PROVE, beyond doubt, that we can do it without the slightest bit of help whatsoever!"

"That's silly!" Gina retorted. "The old cry about women drivers used to be 'what would you do if you had a flat tyre Girlie'? Well it's quite obvious what we would do. Call out the breakdown services just like all the bloody men do. You don't see a trucker, even the beefy ones, standing at the side of the road heaving dirty great wheel braces about and hauling two ton wheels onto the thing, do you?"

Carol had to admit it was not a sight that she had noted on a daily basis.

"Thing is," Gina went on. "It's only the ones with an insecurity complex that it bothers if you think about it. Most of the guys we have met have been fine haven't they? Both on this trip and the last one, you showed them you knew what you were doing and they just treated you like another driver didn't they?"

"Yes, you're right." Carol agreed. They had met some friendly people on their travels and most of the truckers had been just as willing to help Carol as much as any other rookie driver.

"The thing is Kiddo, you should not be so sexist!"

Carol looked at Gina in amazement then burst out laughing. Yes, she was being sexist. The very thing that she was ready to accuse the men of, she was actually guilty of herself. She made a mental note to meet all new drivers, male of female, on a level footing and either like or dislike them for their own personalities and not for their gender. If she was offered help and advice she would take it and gratefully, but if she was met with a negative attitude she would ignore it and carry on. Gina's innocent remark had given her food for thought.

*****

After a brief stop for coffee and to say their farewells to Charlie and Matt, they had driven on and were soon approaching the outskirts of Nis, the wide road following the banks of the river towards the town. With a loud blast of air horns, Charlie and Matt turned off towards their destination leaving the two Transcon Haulage trucks to carry on, skirting the city and heading on their way towards the Bulgarian border. The mountains, towering into the sky, like huge monoliths, covered in white cloaks were an impressive sight as Carol steered the truck along the winding road, a huge gorge, cutting through the mountains gave the impression of swallowing the trucks into its mouth as they made their way forward.

The route took them through a succession of tunnels, carved through the rocks, water constantly dripping through crevices in the arched roof onto the vehicles passing beneath.

"It's very claustrophobic in here!" Gina remarked, peering up at the dank walls of the tunnel. "I wonder how long they have been built and if they are still safe."

"Thanks for that!" Carol replied wryly. "I was trying not to think about exactly how many tons of rock are hanging over our heads right now."

"Hmm, that's why I have never been keen on going in the Channel Tunnel train." Gina said thoughtfully. "There is a hell of a lot of water over the top of you in there isn't there?" Daylight shone up ahead as they drove out of the first of the tunnels and continued to wind their way along the river. The sides of the mountain were, at times, worryingly close, with overhanging rocks appearing so low that on occasion they were inclined to duck as they passed underneath.

"Don't know why we are ducking our heads down." Carol pointed out. "We have a good few feet of truck above us but, my goodness, they look low!"

Gina giggled. "Just can't help it can you," she laughed. It's like when you go into a car park under the low barriers, you still duck even though they never touch the roof of the car."

"Self preservation instinct," Carol replied, slowing down and dropping a gear to negotiate a particularly tight bend. "Wonder how far ahead Tony is."

The two Transcon Haulage trucks had been separated on the wider road leading towards Niz. Tony was now at least three vehicles ahead as they followed the road towards the border. "Don't know," said Gina reaching for the CB speaker. "Hello, up ahead, where are you Mr Owl?" she called into the microphone. Crackling and static was the only response. "Hello, Owl, do you copy?" she tried again.

"No use under all these rocks and stuff." said Carol. "They probably cut out all the radio waves for miles around. I do know one thing though."

"What?"

"I am absolutely DYING to wee! I don't know whether I can hold on 'til the border, I am pretty desperate. It must be all this cold weather and water all over the place."

"Gina looked around. "God knows where we can stop so that you can go!" she said. "There doesn't seem to be any signs for rest stops or anything. Just look out for a pull-in, nip out of the truck and do what you have to, it's not as though this bit of the road is particularly busy, so I doubt if anyone will see you!"

"I am fast getting to the stage where I don't care if anyone does!" Carol replied grimly. She gritted her teeth as they continued on their way, keeping a hopeful lookout for any sign of a relief stop. The road wound its way endlessly along the foot of the mountain with no hope of a respite pull in or, in fact, any place at all that may offer a momentary stopping place. Eventually, the big rocks seemed to start edging further away from the side of the road, giving way, at first, to shrubs and bushes then trees, as woodland started to pan out on one side.

"There is a wide bit up ahead." Gina pointed out helpfully. "You can just pull in, nip out for a piddle, then carry on before anybody notices."

Carol, at this point was past caring about being noticed or not as she pulled the Volvo to the side of the road, making sure that the outside wheels were still on the hard surface. The last thing they needed right now, was for the truck to get bogged down and be unable to drive on.

"It's a bit creepy!" Carol noticed as she cut the engine. Dusk had started to fall, casting shadows through the trees, the woods almost tinkling with the winter sounds of ice and snow. "And don't they still have wolves out here?"

"Not sure," Gina answered, peering through the woods. "Isn't that Transylvania? They have them there I think."

"Not sure, but even that can't be too far away from here and they travel a lot!"

"Well don't get out then," Gina suggested. "To be on the safe side, just do it in here, there is an old pan you can use, look!" she brandished an old aluminium saucepan that had been stored away in the top locker.

Carol pulled a face. "Well, okay, and it is bloody cold out there!" she noted. "But this will be a bit of a production whichever way you look at it!"

Gina giggled. "Oh, go on! Get on with it. Just take your boots and jeans off and we can sling it through the window. Yellow icicles! That will give the passers by something to talk about." Carol suddenly noticed that there were no passers by. They were, for the moment the only travellers on the road.

She kicked off her boots and slid out of her jeans and gratefully made use of the saucepan. "God, that's a relief,!" she sighed, sliding the almost full pan over from her seat and reaching for her jeans. "I don't think I could have gone much......."

Suddenly the drivers door was swung wide. A leering, bearded face with a set of rotten teeth appeared right besides them. Carol, for a moment was frozen with shock. She vaguely felt another, or possibly more than one, person by the side of the truck, but for a second was stunned.

A sudden flash of movement brought her to her senses as the contents of the saucepan flew across in front of her, hitting the leering face full on. The man yelled and reeled back as Gina flung herself, full length, across Carol and whacked the dripping head hard with the saucepan, before grabbing the door handle, slamming it shut and clicking down the lock.

The dishevelled man was shaking his head and wiping his face with a grubby sleeve as another man ran forward, trying to pull the door open.

"Drive!" Gina yelled, bringing Carol out of her state of shock. "Drive will you!"

Carol turned the ignition and roared the engine into life, slamming the gearstick forward and dropping the handbrake. As she did so, a battered grey pick up truck shot round from the back of the trailer and veered in front of them. Carol did not hesitate, she gunned the engine, firing the big truck forward, directly towards the pick up. The driver, at this point, realised the error of such a move and tried to drive out of the way. Too late. The front of the Volvo slammed into the rear corner of the battered vehicle, spinning it like a child's toy into the carriageway. Carol slammed the accelerator once more, straightening up in the road and caught the vehicle once more as she careered past, sending bits of metal and glass flying in all directions. Building up speed, as best she could on the winding road, she glanced in her mirrors, to see the pick up, or what was left of it, hanging at a precarious angle over the edge of the road. The only thing holding it in place, the heavy duty safety barrier, with three bewildered would-be robbers, trying to work out their next move as the 'Flying Angel' disappeared into the distance.

"Good God! Did that just really happen? Where the hell did they come from?" Gina peered back through the mirrors to see if she could still see the remains of the pick-up and its occupants.

"No idea." Carol was still pretty shaken. "But dare I ask what the hell you threw at him!"

Gina snorted. "Your pee of course! Good, hot, fresh and England's best! Serves him right, got him slap bang in the face, great shot!"

"Then hit him on the head with the pan for good measure!" Carol reminded her. "My God, Gina, you are so quick-thinking! I was stunned for a moment, I dread to think what would have happened if you hadn't thought fast like that!"

"Oh, I didn't think!" Gina replied. "It just sort of happened. You had moved over to get your jeans, and the pan was just there so..... whoosh... all over the evil little rat! I had to get the door shut and locked so, as I still had the pan in my hand, I clumped him with it for good measure!"

Carol realised that she was careering along a most precarious road at a speed that was not her usual careful progression. She eased of the throttle a little as the adrenaline subsided. "I can't believe that just happened!" she said, taking a deep breath. "And I can't believe I am driving down this bloody road in my knickers and bare feet!"

Gina giggled. "Oh, yes, I hadn't noticed. Do you want to stop and get dressed?"

"NO! I am certainly not stopping again." Carol was trying to curb the urge to collapse into slightly hysterical laughter. "I will just have to put up with it until we reach the border crossing. Then I will get dressed quick sharp before Tony wonders what the hell we have been up to!"

Before Gina could reply the sound of Tony's voice crackled over the CB. "Hello, back there, Carol, Gina, do you read me? Are you okay?"

Gina reached up for the microphone. "Hi, Tony, yes we are fine, aren't we Kiddo?" she held the microphone to Carol's lips.

"Yes, Darling, absolutely fine! Just trotting along as usual! Just past some signs saying 'Pirot'," she was still fighting down the urge to giggle.

"That is good to know, Cara Mia. I have just passed through there so we are not too far apart." Tony's disembodied voice crackled on. "I just wanted to speak to you, although I realise there is nothing that could possibly happen to you, as long as the truck is running well. I will see you at the border."

It was all too much for Carol and Gina. The giggles took hold and it was all Carol could do to keep the truck on a straight route, driving, in bare feet and half dressed, on towards the border.

*****

As the 'Flying Angel' rolled towards the border, Carol and Gina had regained their composure. Up to a point, that is, as Carol was still in a state of semi-dress. It was well past dusk as they arrived, slowing to a crawl and swinging into the parking area to prepare to present their papers. No sooner had Carol clicked on the handbrake and killed the engine, she scrambled quickly to climb back into her jeans and pull on her boots. "Just glad this heater works so well," said Carol as she finished dressing. "My bum would have been frozen to the seat otherwise!" They both climbed down from the cab and at once went to the front of the truck to inspect the damage they expected to find after the collisions with the pick-up.

"I can't see any damage at all!" Gina peered at the front of the 'Flying Angel'
"There is a small scratch on the corner, but apart from that, I think there is
very little evidence of a collision!"

"I know these older Volvo's are built like tanks," Carol put in looking
closely, "But actually I think I caught them sort of front on, so it was a
straight shunt and the second time I got them with the corner of the trailer."
Both girls went round to look. "No!" Carol remarked with surprise. "No
evidence that I can see. Luckily for us, in case there is any come back."

"Come back! What are they going to say. 'Please your honour, we tried to
rob-rape-murder these women but they wrecked our pick-up instead! I don't
think so!"

"Hmm, you're probably right," Carol conceded. "But I will feel better when
we are over the border and tucked safely away in Sofia." As she said the
words, it seemed a contradiction in terms, considering that Jeff was 'tucked
away' in Sofia, and not willingly.

"The 'Silver Lady' is just over there," Gina pointed across the parking area as
she espied Tony's truck. "No sign of Tony though,"

Carol looked around. "He's over there," she pointed towards a group of men,
standing next to the custom's offices. Carol gathered up the relevant
paperwork and she and Gina walked over to join them.

"Ah, Cara Mia!" Tony smiled broadly as he caught sight of the girls walking
towards him. "We have just been discussing how quickly the service is
moving this evening," he said, stepping towards Carol and kissing her lightly
on the cheek in greeting. "I have already presented my papers, so if you hand
yours in we should be through the border and into Bulgaria within the hour.
If that is the case, we can be in Sofia in no time, which will be good as it is
Saturday now, so If we do not get unloaded tonight we will have to wait with
full loads until Monday morning."

Neither Carol nor Gina had any intention of mentioning the fracas on the road
to the border. To begin with, they had decided that to mention it to Tony
would have worried him unnecessarily and, apart from that, knocking the
locals pick-up trucks of the road may be deeply frowned upon in this part of
the world, depending of course on whose story the local officials wanted to
believe. After all, they were not at all sure
what the motives of the men had been. It had all happened far too quickly to
establish whether the motive were robbery, or worse. A still tongue was
always a wise thing.

*****

After clearing the border, it was a surprisingly fast run to the outskirts of the city of Sofia. The light was beginning to fade as they trundled into the main streets of the city, the evening traffic busy with the usual hustle and bustle, familiar to all cities throughout the world. Tony had a rough idea of where the drop off point was for the oil and made his way, almost directly to the industrial area on the far side of the town. The loading bays were almost deserted as the two trucks rolled into the yard. It was clearly closing time and the workers were preparing to leave for the evening. Tony and Carol walked over to the main office and presented their paperwork.

"Unload tonight?" Tony asked hopefully, glancing around as he saw workers, obviously making no move to unload, and clearly wanting to get away and back to their homes and families.

The foreman shook his head. "Monday," he managed in English then something in Bulgarian that neither Tony nor Carol could understand.

"Go and get a pack of Marlborough out of the cab," said Tony. "Maybe they will speed things along a little." He signalled to the foreman that some sort of remuneration was forthcoming as Carol ran back to the truck and pulled out a pack of two hundred cigarettes, hurrying back to the office.

Tony held the cigarettes out to the foreman. "Tonight?" he asked again waving the Marlborough under the mans nose. The foreman glanced at the trucks, then the proffered cigarettes. He shouted to a couple of men passing by the door, making their way out of the factory. The men waited, while the foreman spoke to them then both looked at the cigarettes. At once, they removed their coats and waved towards the loading bays.

"Sorted!" said Carol, as she and Tony hurried back to the trucks to drive them on to the bays. "Amazing what a little bribery can do isn't it?"

Tony grinned. "I have Jeff to thank for that nugget of information. He always said that tobacco was the best currency. The bosses get the hard cash but the workers like their own little 'perks'"

"Thank goodness for bad habits, that's all I can say!" Carol replied as she jumped back into the cab.

"What's happening?" Gina enquired as Carol manoeuvred the Volvo into position for unloading. "Are they going to unload us, even at this time?"

"The cigarette bribe worked its charm!" Carol replied. "So that will save us a great deal of messing around in the morning. I reckon we should get ourselves unloaded then go straight on to the pick up place. From there we can get a taxi to the hotel that the Embassy has arranged for you and make our arrangements to get to the prison in the morning."

"Where is the pick up place?" asked Gina. "Is it far from here?"

"Just the other side of town I believe," Carol replied. "I reckon we should get a taxi to pilot us across there then the same cab can take us to the hotel. Makes sense."

"Yes, it does." Gina replied. "Perhaps the foreman here will phone for one for us."

"Well if you can get across to him exactly what we want I am sure he will. He speaks no English at all so good luck!"

Gina smiled. "Oh, don't worry," she said climbing down from the cab. "I always manage to get my point across!"

Carol had no doubt whatsoever that Gina would come up trumps.

*****

The taxi cab piloted the two trucks quickly round the city to the address that Tony had written on a piece of paper. On arrival it was clear that the warehouse was closed for the night, which was as expected. The evening rush of traffic had began to subside in and around the city so it was clear that most workers had finished their days tasks and gone home to their families.

The taxi driver pointed through a pair of big double gates, into a cobbled yard. Loading bays stood along the far wall with their shutters closed down and locked.

Tony climbed down from the 'Silver Lady' and signalled for the cab driver to wait and walked over to Carol's truck. "We had better get inside and parked up for the night." he said. "Then I will stay and keep watch here while you and Gina go to the hotel and see what arrangements have been made for visiting Jeff."

"Will you be all right here alone, Darling?" Carol asked.

Tony laughed. "Of course I will! I have travelled alone before, you know, and there is another truck over in the corner, the light is on in the cab so I take it that there is another driver here to keep me company."

"Well if you're sure that it will be all right, I will get parked up then Gina and I will take the taxi to the hotel, wherever it is!"

Carol swung the Volvo into the yard and reversed onto the nearest loading bay. That way it would save Tony the job of juggling two trucks when the time came to load. Gina pulled her cases from the truck and made her way to the taxi, handing him a piece of paper with the address of the hotel.

"We will ring you as soon as we know what is happening." Carol said as she kissed Tony goodbye.

"Do not worry, Cara Mia, I understand that this is of the utmost importance and may make a lot of difference to Jeff if all goes well."

"How are you feeling?" Carol asked as the taxi sped through the brightly lit streets of the city.

"Nervous as a kitten!" Gina replied. "I've tried not to think of it as much as possible but now.... now that we have actually arrived I just don't know what to expect." The taxi turned into a wide street, away from the busy centre and the hustle and bustle of town. Trees lined one side of the road, which seemed mainly to be made up of hotels, the type usually frequented by business persons. Certainly not seedy or cheap, but definitely not expensive and upper crust as the sort preferred by the more discerning tourist or wealthy patrons.

"This is it I think." Gina checked the address on her notes and fished in her bag for Euros to pay the taxi. "It doesn't look too bad does it?"

"Very nice so far." Carol replied, pushing open the big glass doors into the foyer. "I have no idea how we are going to communicate that we are already booked in though." she added, as they approached the front desk.

Gina took charge. "We are from England." she stated clearly. "British Embassy have made booking, yes?"

"Good evening." The manager's English was accented but obviously good, and far better than Carol and Gina's none-existent Bulgarian. "Your booking was made by Mr Huntingdon-Smythe." he smiled and reached under the desk. "He charge me with giving you papers, yes?" he handed Gina a large brown envelope and reached a key from the hook. "Your room, Madame, I hope you will be satisfied with our service." He gave a small bow as he handed Gina the key.

"Thank you." Gina was a little taken aback that it had all been so easy. The girls picked up their bags and made their way to the lift. "I hope there is a bath in this place," Gina remarked. "First thing I want to do is have a good soak then relax and read every word on these papers."

"Yes, I hope there is a bath too." said Carol as the lift doors opened. "It does seem to be a reasonable standard hotel, so they usually have baths as well as showers."

The hotel room exceeded all their expectations. It was huge by almost any standards. Two wider-than-normal single beds stood against the far wall opposite a huge old fashioned sofa and matching lounge chairs. Above the dressing table was an enormous, elaborately gilded mirror and the double windows were dressed in splendour with swags and tails of floor length velvet.

"Very nice!" Carol swung her bag onto one of the beds. "This is all very grand. Didn't look it from the outside though did it?"

"Hmm, yes it is rather splendid isn't it?" Gina agreed. "Obviously one of the old style hotels, probably family run and been the same for a million years," she opened a door in search of the bathroom. "I say! The whole bathroom is marble through here! Very Cleopatra! And there is a shower and abathtub too. Brilliant!"

Gina spun the bath taps on to full. At once a loud banging sound reverberated around the room making the girls jump.

"What the hell is that?" said Carol, the thudding almost drowning her voice.

Gina giggled. "I thought this place was too good to be true!" she said. The plumbing obviously is as old as the hotel." She turned off the taps with the bath only half full. "I reckon it is their way of saving on the hot water," she suggested. "Nobody could spend too much time with that racket."

"Well, you go first and save me the water," Carol walked back into the bedroom. "We could wake the dead with that noise."

"Never mind. At least we can have a soak, and it's hot too," Gina picked up her smaller case and closed the bathroom door, gritting her teeth and turning the taps on once more to fill the big tub to over halfway.

"That's good," Carol yelled back from the bedroom. "And at least there is an electric kettle with milk, tea and coffee sachets," she added. Carol always believed in getting the priorities in order.

Gina did not reply. She had taken her toiletries from the top of her case and had pulled the wooden panel slightly away from the bath. She tucked her case underneath, out of sight and replaced the panel. Only now she was ready to undress and slide into the hot water.

*****

"Well that was a complete waste of time!" Gina plonked the papers down on the side table and leaned back in the big chair. "Of course, I should have realised that it would all be in Bulgarian, I just didn't think." The girls had both enjoyed a long bath and were relaxing with cups of coffee.

"So we actually have no idea what they say or what we are supposed to be doing with 'em." Carol put in. "Are there no clues at all?"

"No, none whatsoever. Only this explanatory note from this Huntingdon-Smythe chap. All this says, is to go to the prison at twelve noon tomorrow and present these papers. So I reckon that's what we will have to do!"

"Okay, then that's what we will do." Carol said simply. She glanced at her watch. "I suggest we get dressed and go and see what the food is like here and, of course, sample the Bulgarian wine. I'll ring Tony and tell him what is happening, then an early night, what do you think?"

Gina agreed. She just wanted this night over with and for tomorrow to come as quickly as possible. Then she would see Jeff. Beyond that thought, her brain could not reach.

*****

CHAPTER FIFTEEN

The gates of Zafora Prison were cold, and forbidding. The icy wind lashed Carol and Gina's faces as they approached. They rang the bell and waited. There was no sign of life in the courtyard within the gates that they could see. A voice through the intercom spoke gutturally in Bulgarian. "We have a permit to visit," Carol spoke into the tiny grill above the bell. Silence. Another burst of Bulgarian then a click. The women waited.

"What's happening?" Gina's voice was low.

"They are probably deciding whether to let us in or not," Carol replied.

A uniformed guard appeared from the side of the building. Bearded and stern he grunted at the women and slid the small panel at the side of the big security gate open and gestured them inside.

Gina pulled the paperwork from the Embassy out of her pocket and held them out to the guard. "We are here to see Jeffrey Meredith." she said slowly, pointing to Jeff's name on the paperwork. The guard grunted and walked towards the building, opening the door and ushering the girls into a stone corridor with doors, all closed, along its length. He walked down the corridor without a word followed by Carol and Gina and stopped outside one of the doors. He pulled the door open and signalled them to wait inside before closing the door behind them and leaving them alone. The two friends looked around. The room was small and sparsely furnished with a desk and three chairs, the floor covered with a plain grey carpet. A large window, high in the wall, let the light, strangely grey from the winter sky, fill the room. "It seems fairly normal for a prison," Carol remarked, trying her best to keep Gina's spirits up although she had no idea what prisons were supposed to look like, never having being in one.

"Wouldn't know," Gina replied bluntly. "I don't usually frequent these places."

Before Carol could reply the guard returned with another uniformed official. The man was huge, well over six feet tall, with broad shoulders and a full beard. His eyes, so dark, almost black like pieces of coal, glinted at the two women.

"You have come to see the English." It was a statement not a question.

"Yes!" Gina answered eagerly. "Can we see him, we have written permission from the British Embassy." she reached in her bag for the papers.

The man's eyes passed from Gina to Carol and back again.

"Arrangements have been made," said Zhravko Markov. "The prisoner will be brought. You will speak for fifteen minutes. A witness from the Embassy will be present for the time of the interview."

"From the Embassy?" Carol enquired. "Is this normal procedure?"

"For this prison, yes," Markov stepped towards the door. "You wait."

Carol knew that Gina had wanted a private moment or two with Jeff. She had planned to wait outside the small interview room but now there was to be another person present. It was hardly the meeting Gina had looked forward to.

"Maybe it is a good thing that the man from the Embassy will be here," she said, trying to sound encouraging. "It may help to get his take on things."

"It would have been nice to have Jeff to myself after all this time," Gina replied. "But it doesn't matter, as long as I get to look at him, see he is all right and speak to him."

Time dragged at snail's pace as the girls waited nervously for the appearance of Jeff, or the visitor from the Embassy. The sound of clanging gates and muffled voices drifted occasionally from the corridor outside. Each sound making Gina's heart leap, expecting it to be Jeff. After what seemed an interminable time the door was flung open and Zhravko Markov once more strode into the small, chilly room, a tall, well dressed man following in his wake.

"Ah, good day ladies, good day! James Huntingdon-Smythe at your service!" The Embassy official beamed broadly and extended his hand in introduction. "Thank you kindly Markov, SO sorry for the delay old man, but here we all are now so let the dog see the rabbit eh? Shall we get our man in here then?"

It was clear that the big prison officer had little regard for this overly cheerful civil servant as he left the room without a word, clicking the door firmly closed behind him.

"Now listen ladies," Huntingdon-Smythe's tone had lost the gung-ho edge it had held while the big Bulgarian official had been present. "You will only have a very short time with your husband Mrs Meredith so if there is anything important that you need to say, then please, do not waste time."

"Nothing specific," Gina answered, her mind in a daze. What *did* she want to say? What could she say? Nothing about what she was planning, not in front of all these others. Right now she just wanted to see Jeff. Touch him and make sure he was still alive and well.

"Good, just a visit then. I regret that it is the custom here for myself or someone like me to be present but please just ignore me as best you can.

When they have returned Mr Meredith to his cell we can talk for as long as you wish, there is no hurry and then I will stay for a short time as I need to speak to the prison authorities regarding solicitor's visits, etc."

Before Gina had the chance to reply, the door swung open and Jeff walked into the room. Gina gasped. She had not been prepared for the sight she beheld. Jeff was thin and gaunt, his hair unkempt and curling round his collar, a half inch growth of stubble on his chin. It was not hard to detect the stale smell about him as he approached.

"Darling!" Gina leapt forward and flung her arms around Jeff's neck, disregarding his unkempt appearance and less than palatable smell.

"No contact!" Zhravko Markov snapped, slamming the door closed. Gina jumped back.

"Come and sit here old man!" Huntingdon-Smythe pulled out a chair, cheerfully waving Jeff to sit. "Thank you, Markov. There will be no more breaches of etiquette I assure you. Not with you and I to keep an eye out eh!"

Jeff and Huntingdon-Smythe sat on one side of the small wooden table and Carol and Gina took their places opposite. Markov stood behind them with his back firmly to the door. It occurred to Carol that there was no way that they could possibly have made any attempt to rush through the door to freedom even if that had been a consideration. The yards of winding narrow corridors were in themselves a maze to confuse and the presence of the huge uniformed man would have certainly dampened any thoughts of an escape.

"Darling, how are you?" Gina leaned as far as she dare across the small table. Jeff smiled. "I'm fine, my love, just missing your cooking that's all." He was determined to look as positive and cheerful as the circumstances would allow. His main worry was that Gina would be struggling to cope in his absence. The last thing he wanted to do was alarm her. "To be honest the food in here is lousy and the food parcel you ladies so promptly provided has certainly made a difference. Keep them coming love, they are something to look forward to."

Jeff made no mention of the terrible fate that had befallen his young cell mate. That would have been too much to have to try and explain. He wanted to tell what he had heard about an early release, but was frightened of raising Gina's hopes, only to have them dashed if this did not come to fruition. Anyway, he had heard nothing about it from the Embassy as yet, so decided to keep quiet.

"Oh, I will, Darling, I will send parcels every day if necessary," Gina was determined not to burst into tears at the forlorn sight before her. She desperately wanted to tell Jeff that she had brought money, that she was going to try every means within her to get him out of this place but could not. The presence of Huntingdon-Smythe stilled her tongue. Also, what if it could not be done. She could not bear to raise Jeff's hopes in case her plans did not work, and she still had no idea whom she would have to deal with in this matter.

"Carol, how is the business coping?" Jeff needed to know. "The Transcon is still stuck out here and the load…..well God only knows where that has gone but I doubt it will be still on the trailer."

"Don't worry Jeff. We have it all in hand," Tony has been terrific, he got the first load and brought it back, shaken though he was after what had happened," Carol tried to sound more positive than she felt. "I have bought another truck, and it's up and running. Tony and I are both on the road so that's fine for now."

"The new truck is great!" Gina tried to sound up-beat and raise Jeff's spirits. "She can even outrun the 'Silver Lady'! We call her the 'Flying Angel'!"

"So you two have driven here, come by truck?" Jeff did not like the idea of Carol and his Gina being out here in a truck after what had happened to him.

"Tony is here as well," Carol put in quickly. "The trip was really uneventful and pleasant." She lied, "We have the re-loads arranged and will be travelling back in convoy too. But don't you get any ideas of resting up here too long though. We need you back on the road too!"

Jeff smiled wryly. "Okay, Ginger Nut. I'll just have a short break here then I'll get back out there on the road so you can work me to death!" Jeff had not lost his sense of humour.

Carol wanted to ask about the Operators licence being in Jeff's name and how the business stood with his incarceration but held back. This was Gina's moment and it was for her to speak to Jeff.

Carol turned to James Huntingdon-Smythe and engaged him in quiet conversation while Gina spoke to Jeff. They only had fifteen minutes together so Carol attempted a low profile although privacy was hardly possible.

The time flew by, although Carol had glanced at her watch and noticed that the statutory fifteen minutes had stretched to nearer twenty five. "Time finished. You come now." Markov spoke gruffly although his voice was not harsh.

"Okay Zhravko," Jeff replied familiarly. "Do I have your permission to kiss my lovely wife goodbye?" Markov nodded curtly.

Jeff walked round the table towards Gina. "Chin up my lovely," he said quietly and kissed her gently. "It will all work out in the end you'll see," He stroked Gina's silken hair and nodded to Markov who opened the door, standing aside as Jeff walked through then following him into the corridor, closing the door behind them.

Gina sat down heavily once more on the hard wooden chair. Her heart was breaking. "We have to get him out of here!" she announced desperately, lifting her eyes imploringly to Huntingdon-Smythe.

"I do understand how you feel Mrs Meredith....."

"No! No you DON'T understand how I feel! Nobody can understand how I feel. Not unless the person you love most in the world is locked up in this place and you can't do anything to help them. No, Mr Huntingdon-Smythe, you have NO idea how I feel!"

Carol did not speak. There was nothing she could say that could be of any use so she held her silence.

"I apologise Mrs Meredith." Huntingdon-Smythe tried again. "I do realise of course that this is a terrible situation for you, and for your husband. We are of course trying to do the best we can but things take time here. I can only apologise. I will be staying back here when you leave and speaking further with the Governor. We need to get a trial date sorted out as soon as possible to find out what the sentence will be."

"But my husband is innocent!" Gina's voice quavered as she spoke.

The Embassy official sighed. He had heard it all before. "Let me explain." He tried to sound patient as he spoke. "Bulgarian law is very simple and clear cut. The law states that 'it is illegal to carry drugs into Bulgaria', that is the bottom line."

"Yes, but..." The man held up his hand.

"There are no 'but's' I'm afraid. Your husband was driving his truck, was he not?"

Gina nodded. "And he crossed the border into Bulgaria, yes?" Gina nodded again. "This is where his truck was searched and the drugs were found?"

"That's what happened," Gina agreed. "Nobody is denying that, the question is...."

"There is no question here." The man stated firmly. "Your husband is guilty of carrying the drugs into Bulgaria, it's as simple as that I am afraid!"

Gina was lost for words. There was nothing to say. The British Government was obviously not going to chance compromising its position in a foreign land for the sake of one man. "But what about a trial?" Carol asked. "You said something about a trial. If he is already supposed to be guilty then what purpose does a trial serve?"

"The fact that he is guilty is without question here," Huntingdon-Smythe went on. "The trial is really just a formality. The best we can hope for is that some doubt is cast onto whether Mr Meredith was aware that the drugs were on his truck or not."

"So if they believe him they will let him go." Gina felt hope rise in her chest.

"Sorry." Huntingdon-Smythe shook his head. "The best we can hope for is a reduced sentence."

Gina felt sick again. "Reduced to what? From what?" Carol asked. "We know nothing of what to expect"

"Around twelve years is the usual sentence." Gina felt the room starting to spin. "But if he can prove...... and it will be extremely difficult to prove... that he knew nothing of what he was carrying, then it may be reduced to seven years."

James Huntingdon-Smythe's eyes looked sympathetically at Gina, sitting frozen to her chair and desperately trying to control the urge to vomit. What if her plans did not come to fruition. Jeff would have to spend years in this place.

"What we usually do in these cases is ask that the sentence be served in a British prison, which at least will allow your husband to be taken back to England. But as our laws are so lenient in comparison to Bulgarian law, they usually insist that at least five years of the sentence is served in this country."

"I have to get her out of here." Carol stated. Gina looked ill and this conversation was not helping. "You will speak to Jeff before you leave won't you?"

"Yes, then I will make some arrangements and try to get a lawyer to him some time tomorrow. I will be in touch as soon as we know something." He was looking at Gina, ashen and shaking. "Take your friend back to the hotel." His voice softened. "I think she needs to rest."

Carol thanked him and helped Gina to her feet. "Come on Kiddo, let's get you back for a lie down. You need to eat as well."

Gina did not answer as Carol led her towards the door and the long corridor leading outside. There was surprisingly no sign of any prison guards. "Just follow this corridor to the door." Huntingdon-Smythe advised. "There will be someone in the yard to let you out."

"I would have expected someone to escort us out, going by the strict security in here." Carol remarked.

"Oh, the security is certainly here. Believe me!" The Embassy official shook their hands and walked the opposite way down the corridor as Carol and Gina walked towards the door leading to the courtyard,

The cold air met them in a rush as they walked outside, into the concrete yard.

"Carol! My legs just won't...." Gina slumped to the ground. Carol grabbed her arm in an attempt to break her friend's fall as Gina collapsed onto the cold concrete.

"Gina! Gina!" Carol knelt down and lifted Gina's head onto her lap. The icy wind making her ears ring. Desperately she looked around. The burly, bearded prison guard was striding towards them. Carol desperately hoped that it was not against Bulgarian law to faint on prison property.

"I'm sorry." Carol looked up helplessly as the big man arrived at her side. "My friend, she is not well, I must get her to the hotel."

Without a word the bearded man bent down and lifted Gina effortlessly into his arms and began to walk towards the gate, shouting an abrupt instruction to the young guard who immediately punched in the code on the gate panel and swung it wide to allow them through. Carrying Gina as though she were weightless, the big man strode across the busy road towards the hotel. Carol almost had to run to keep up. "This hotel you stay?" It was the first time he had addressed them.

"Er, yes..... thank you!" Carol was not sure how to react. Was he doing a genuine good turn or was it his official duty to clear swooning ladies from his prison yard.

Carol opened the big glass doors into the hotel foyer and Zhravko Markov strode through, turning slightly to angle Gina's small frame clear. "Get key!" he instructed, showing no signs of depositing Gina onto her feet. Carol ran to the desk and demanded her key from the curious hotelier.

Gina had come round but was not sure what was happening. "It's all right, Kiddo." Carol tried to assure her as they entered the lift. "This kind man came to our rescue." She fervently prayed that the 'kind man' was not going to demand favours for helping them and desperately wished she could think of the right things to say to relieve him of his burden before they reached their room.

"I'm sorry to be such a problem," Gina had regained a little of her composure as the lift began its journey. "I think I may be able to stand now."

The big man gently lowered Gina to her feet, keeping his arm about her for support.

"It is hard on the woman when her man is taken." His voice struggling for the correct English words but the tone was gentle.

"It is a shock more than anything." Carol tried to explain. "This ladies husband has never been known to do wrong."

An inclination of the head but no answer.

"You have been very kind." Carol continued. "What is your name?"

"Markov." The man replied. "Zhravko Alexandrou Nikolia Markov."

"I am Carol Landers and this is Gina Meredith."

"The English is lucky man!"

"Not right now!" Gina said weakly. "Locked in a cold cell for something he did not do."

The lift doors opened and Carol led the way to their room. At the door she hesitated. Zhravko obviously intended to accompany them inside.

"Thank you once more for your help." Gina looked up at the tall man, still supporting her with an arm about her shoulders.

Markov removed his arm and gave the hint of a bow. He glanced to the number on the door, "This evening. Be here. I may have something to offer you."

Gina shot him a desperate glance. "You may be able to help Jeff, help us?"

"There are ways of making things move faster, as, I believe, you already know Mrs Meredith." His eyes were steady on Gina's face as he spoke.

Carol took a step towards Gina, protectively standing close. This did not go unnoticed by Markov. He stood back. "Please do not misunderstand." he said curtly. "Both you women are safe as long as Zhravko Markov is your protector." He almost stood to attention, inclining his head smartly in salute.

"Thank you." Carol was still not entirely convinced. "I am sure we both appreciate having you as our champion."

"How can things be made to move faster?" Gina remembered what she had been told by Mark Cameron and Marco. "If it can be done by paying Jeff's 'fine' then that will not be a problem. Can you find out for us if this is possible."

"Oh, Madam, it is more than possible," Markov replied.

"How much?" Gina spoke directly.

Markov was impressed by her strength and tenacity. "It will have to be discussed." he said bluntly.

"With whom?" asked Carol, taken by surprise by this sudden turn of events.

Markov ignored the remark. "There is a truck involved is there not?" he asked.

"Yes, a Ford Transcontinental, complete with trailer and a load of olive oil. Or at least it did have a load of olive oil when Jeff was arrested. Carol put in. "Why do you ask?"

The big man looked Carol directly in the eye. "I will come here to this room tonight." he announced.

"You will have news for us?" Gina looked hopefully into the coal black eyes.

"Tonight," was the only answer. Zhravko gave a curt nod of the head, turned on his heel and strode back to the lift.

Gina's legs still felt weak as she walked across the room, slipping off her coat and sliding onto the bed, leaning back on the pillows. "Oh hell! I feel like such a weakling, passing out like that." She was beginning to regain a little of her colour.

Carol grasped Gina's boots and eased them off her feet then tucked another cushion behind her friend. "Hey, be fair on yourself." She filled the small electric kettle with water from the bathroom and switched it on. "You can't always be a tower of strength, we all get knocked for six sometimes." Her first concern was to see that Gina was all right, but the words spoken by Markov kept spinning around in her head.

"But this is not a good time to go all weak and swooning female!" Gina stated, angry with her own weakness. "Not now when Jeff needs me and needs me to be strong and support him. I have to think straight and do what's needed to get him out of there."

"That's my girl!" Carol poured the boiling water onto the tea bags. "I don't think I've ever seen you in such a state."

"Can't remember ever being in one."

"I always thought you were the strongest." Carol remarked. "You certainly pushed me all the way when we drove to Italy in the summer."

"Yes, but it's easy to be strong for someone else. I held up well in front of Jeff I think." Gina got to her feet and crossed over to the dressing table, peering into the mirror and pulling a face. "Oh good heavens! I look awful."

Carol raised her eyes. "Gina! You NEVER look awful! If you weren't my best friend I would hate you! You look good whatever happens!"

Gina managed a smile. "Thanks, but I don't ever remember feeling this peculiar. I have never passed out in my life. You know I've had my share of nasty shocks but I have always kept my head. I just feel completely out of control at the moment. And all fluttery inside."

"It's allowed!" Carol said firmly, passing Gina a mug of strong tea. "Drink this, there is nothing like a good old cup of tea to put things right. The British way you know."Gina smiled and took a sip. "Yes, it is so very British isn't it? Some neighbour knocks on your door with a huge tale of woe and the first thing we do is put the kettle on!"

"If you hear someone has died you rush straight into the kitchen and put the kettle on." Carol was trying to keep the conversation on a simple level until Gina was feeling more herself.

"Can you imagine if war broke out." said Gina. "The surge of electricity as every householder switched their kettles on would cause a blackout!"

The girls laughed together.

"That's more like it!" said Carol. "Now start to think positive and we can try and work this whole mess out. What the hell do you think that Markov person was talking about. Quicker ways of getting Jeff out. Do you know what he was talking about?"

Before she could reply, Gina's face paled. "Oh God! Here I go again." She ran into the bathroom.

Carol could hear her throwing up, retching violently. "Hey, this is not good Kiddo." she called through the half open door. "I am going to go down to reception and see if there is an English-speaking doctor around."

"No, really." Gina re-emerged from the bathroom. Her face ashen as she flopped weakly back onto the bed. "I don't think I could stand being poked and prodded by some 'quack' who may not be up to standard."

"I am going to ask anyway," Carol stated firmly. She was worried about her friend, so far from home and clearly unwell. Before Gina could voice any further objections she left the room and ran down the stairs.

Gina closed her eyes. This, she did not need. It was bad enough having Jeff locked away a short walk from their room without her feeling so utterly wretched. She had to get herself together for the meeting with Zhravko Markov this evening. He seemed to be the man who knew what she wanted to do. After a few moments rest she felt slightly better and took another sip of tea.

"Apparently there is a doctor nearby who speaks good English," Carol announced, returning to the room. "They made a telephone call and told me he will be here almost at once."

"Must be better service than the National Health at home then," Gina remarked wryly, easing herself back onto the pillows, holding her cup of tea. "You are either dead or cured by the time you get an appointment there!"

"Hmm, maybe quicker, but let us not judge until we see the standard he works to shall we?" Carol had no intention of delivering her friend into the hands of some dubious doctor in a foreign land. She would monitor the consultation closely.

About twenty minutes later Carol answered the door. "Good afternoon. There is a lady sick here?" A surprisingly young man with surprisingly good English entered the room. "I am Doctor Kutrov." he said by way of introduction, setting down his universal doctor's black bag and slipping off his thick full length coat.

"I am sorry to bother you." Gina said weakly. "But I have not been very well today."

"Ah, typical English!" The young doctor smiled. "Always apologising for being sick. Remember, without sick people we doctors will have no work! We are pleased to see sick people. That is what we do." He strode across the room and took Gina's hand, smiling into her eyes. "Now Madam, tell me what the problem seems to be." His manner had turned strictly professional.

"It's my tummy Doctor." Gina began to feel trust creeping in. "I get terrible flutters and I have been sick a lot lately. I actually fainted today!"

"That could be stress though." Carol put in and explained, frankly, the reason for their visit and what had taken place that day.

Doctor Kutrov nodded gravely but passed no remark, simply taking Gina's temperature and blood pressure. After sounding her chest he stood back. "Which part of England are you from?" He asked casually, making notes in a small notebook.

"London." Carol answered. "Do you know it?"

"I studied in Manchester and London during my training." the Doctor replied. "I spent seven years in England altogether. I returned to my country only last year. There is a need for good doctors here." Both Carol and Gina felt relieved that this young man seemed more than qualified to attend to Gina's needs. "Please lie flat Madam, I need to feel your abdomen. You have no objections?"

Gina shook her head and slid down the bed, lying flat as instructed and resting her head comfortably on the pillow while Doctor Kutrov pressed her tummy. "Are you taking any supplements?" he asked. "Any vitamins or iron?"

"No," Gina replied. "I have never needed anything like that. I eat healthily and exercise well so I am usually in good health."

"But now you are pregnant you will need to take a little more care."

"What! Pregnant! I'm not PREGNANT!....... am I?"

Doctor Kutrov stood back, glancing from Carol to Gina. The looks on both the women's faces told him that this was certainly the last thing either of them had expected to hear. "Yes, Madam, you are indeed pregnant, and I am pleased to be the first to give you the happy news. You do, of course, want the baby do you not?" He looked Gina in the eye.

"Of course she wants the baby." Carol was the first to speak. "It's just such a shock..... and under these circumstances too. You must understand that we had no idea. If we had, I doubt we would have taken a chance on riding all this way by truck."

"You came here by truck?"

Gina explained briefly how they had come to be there. "I had no idea," she said quietly. Her eyes still wide with the shock of the news. "No way would we have endangered my baby by travelling overland in a bumpy truck. I want this child desperately!"

Doctor Kutrov laughed. "No child ever was hurt by travelling a little. Bumpy ride or otherwise. He is well tucked up and safe inside the

womb, only his mother will feel the bumps and the discomfort, don't worry about your child, Madam, he is warm and safe!"

Gina looked relieved. A moment ago she had no idea that she was carrying a child. Now, knowing that Jeff's baby was growing inside her, it seemed of the utmost importance to make sure that the baby was safe and in no danger from the rash behaviour of its mother.

Doctor Kutrov gathered up his bag, slipped on his coat and wrote out his bill. "There is no need for any drastic action." He smiled at Gina. "Eat well, don't drink and don't smoke and you will have a healthy happy baby." Carol gave him the money. "And see your own doctor when you get home. He will make all the necessary arrangements for both you and your child. Good luck, Madam." He turned at the door. "And may God be with your husband. May he speed his return home to see his wife and child." With that he stepped into the hall and closed the door behind him.

Carol ran over to the bed and flung her arms around Gina. "Oh, Gina! A baby! Oh, this is wonderful news!"

Gina did not reply: her mind in a whirl. There she was, pregnant in a strange country, with a dangerous drive between here and her home. Jeff languishing in a cold dank cell and no suggestion of when he may be home. Please God that she would not have to give birth and look after the baby entirely alone! Please God that Jeff would be home to see his baby born and not be locked away until the child was possibly school age!

"Yes," she said eventually. "Wonderful news!" She managed a smile. Whatever happened now she had this baby to think about, and think about its welfare she would, with or without Jeff, this child would want for nothing. This was Gina's silent vow. A vow she intended to keep.

*****

"At least the mobile 'phones work here," said Tony, ringing from a small café near the factory and had no trouble getting through to Carol's mobile. "Is everything all right, Cara Mia, have you seen Jeff?"

Carol explained about the visit. She omitted to mention the visit from the doctor, or the strange conversation with Zhravko Markov. "Gina has to meet with an official from the prison regarding Jeff's sentence." she picked her words carefully. "The meeting will be some time later today, here in the hotel."

"A meeting you say," Tony sounded pleased. "Do you need me to come and be with you during this meeting or will it be a private matter between Gina and the prison authorities?" Tony was slightly puzzled that an official meeting would take place in the hotel and not the prison itself, but this was Bulgaria. Nothing was unusual here.

"No!" Carol said quickly. "No thank you, Darling. I feel that Gina would much prefer it if the meeting were as private as possible. I will leave her to speak alone, I think. Were you planning on joining us for dinner?"

"To be truthful, Cara Mia, I do not feel inclined to leave the trucks unattended in this place for any length of time. If you don't mind, I will eat at this café then spend the night in my cab." This suited Carol more than Tony could know.

"Oh, Tony that is fine by me. Whatever you think is best. But, of course, I must stay here for Gina's meeting. Moral support and all that. I just feel awful that you are stuck out there alone."

Tony laughed. "I am not alone, Cara Mia. There is another driver here, also waiting for load so I have a friend for company. We will eat together and pass the time."

"Oh, that does make me feel better." said Carol truthfully. "I don't want you to think I am neglecting you, but you do understand that this meeting may be very important for Gina."

"Let us hope that there will be something positive for her to hear, but prepare her for the worse, Cara Mia, you know and I know that this could be a long sentence for our friend."

"Yes, Darling, I know." That was the truth, anything could happen and she and Gina were probably as much in the dark about future events as Tony was right now. "But after coming all this way, we must take every opportunity we can to help Jeff."

Of course," Tony replied. "Without question. If Gina has been granted another meeting with one of the prison officials, then of course that is of

paramount importance. You do what you must and we will meet here in the morning when the lorries will be loaded and
ready to go."

"Okay Darling, as long as you will be safe, stuck out there in a deserted warehouse yard. If you don't think it is safe to stay there overnight then to hell with the trucks, just get a taxi cab and come here to the hotel." Carol's conscience urged her to make the offer, but a voice in the back of her mind told her that it was far better for just she and Gina to be privy to the meeting with the mysterious Zhravko Markov this evening.

"I will be fine, Cara Mia, but are you all right, two ladies alone in that hotel. It is not a well known tourist area after all."

"Oh, don't worry Tony, it's very nice here and we don't plan to go out on the town or anything. After the meeting, just a meal in the dining room then back to our room for the evening."

Gina gave Carol a knowing glance as she said her goodbyes to Tony and clicked off the mobile. "I hate keeping him in the dark." Carol remarked, dropping the mobile back into her shoulder bag and returning to her own bed and flopping full length.

Gina felt guilty. "I have not been entirely honest with you either, Kiddo."

"Why? What have YOU got to hide!"

Gina took a deep breath. "Mark told me one or two interesting things about the Bulgarian penal system," she said. "It seems that if I have enough money I can pay the prison to have Jeff released."

"Go on!" Carol wondered exactly where this was leading.

"He told me that money talks, very loudly it seems. Of course, he is not really in a position to do things er, shall we say, not exactly in line with the established code of practice, so he gave me lots of advice and then I spoke to Marco and told him what I had learned. Marco, as we know, has many contacts and I personally think not all of them are on the right side of legal, but that is by the by. Marco made some enquiries and spoke to the prison personally. He had more than one conversation with the Governor himself and it turns out that there is a price that can be paid to get Jeff an early release."

Carol was astounded. Surely this was the sort of thing that you read about in books but hardly believed it could happen in real life. "What do they mean by early?" She asked. "A couple of years, a couple of months? and has any of this been spoken about in the Embassy. Does that Huntingdon-Smythe character know anything about this?"

Gina shrugged. "Doubtful about Huntingdon-Smythe." she said. "I kept looking at him to see if he knew anything about it, but he seemed completely oblivious and just kept on about trial dates and the like. You see, both Marco and Mark told me not to chat about it and told me to keep it as much to myself as I could. I didn't say anything to you because I really did not want to compromise you in any way as the whole thing seems a little shady to me! Sorry Kiddo, I hope you understand."

Shady! Now there was an understatement! "I'm not sure if I understand anything at the moment," said Carol. "But how much money are we talking about and how much time do you have to get it to the prison. How will you pay it? Banker's draft, cheque? There is all that which must be taken into consideration."

"Cash!" Gina said simply. "That is one of the reasons I didn't tell you. I have brought the cash with me. I thought that if you knew I was carrying lots of money, then you would worry and I thought you had enough on your mind without worrying about me carrying a load of cash about!"

Aha! So THAT was why Gina had been so keen to keep her small case close to her. She had secreted the money in there. "The little case! Is that where you have been keeping the money?"

"Yes, that's right." Gina said slightly shamefacedly. "I have been worried sick about being robbed and losing it, but both Marco and Mark seem to think that cash on the nail is the only way to go with this deal. It's all very cloak and dagger isn't it."

To say the bloody least, thought Carol, still trying hard to take all this information in. "Exactly how much cash have you brought?" she thought she may as well ask at this point.

"Twelve thousand pounds."

"Twelve thous……..! Jesus, Gina! You've carried all that, all this way. Is that legal, taking money in and out of the country like that?"

"No idea." Gina replied simply shrugging her shoulders. "Haven't given it a thought and don't really care. If it gets Jeff out of here then I would pay double, though that is all I could lay hands on at the time."

"How on earth did you manage that amount?" Carol was still more than a little stunned.

"Well I emptied my saving account, you know my own little account that I was thinking of diving into for the BMW, then Daddy gave me another two thousand and then Marco, he gave me another two thousand in Euro's when we were at La Casaccia!"

Carol was wide eyed. She had always known her friend was strong and resilient but this beat all that had gone before. "Kiddo, you amaze me!" was all she could say on the subject. What else WAS there to say! "I need a drink! I say we go down to the bar and get a stiff drink and order something to eat. I don't know how I will manage the food, but I could certainly do with a drink right now!"

"Oh hell!" Gina suddenly shot upright on her bed.

"What now!" Surely another revelation was not possible. "What's the matter?"

"Drink! I have been pregnant for weeks and not known about it. I have been having a brandy whenever I felt like it, not to mention wine and the odd G & T. Oh, God Carol, what if I've damaged my baby!"

Carol laughed reassuringly. "Hey, don't be silly, the baby will be fine! It's not like you've been out on the razzle getting absolutely slaughtered night after night, is it? Anyway, I always used to have a night cap when I was pregnant with Katy. In those days nobody told us not to. Katy is fine and I am sure your little one will be healthy and well, as fit as flea when it arrives. Don't worry, babies are tough little things you know."

"Even so." Gina got to her feet and headed for the bathroom. "No further alcohol will pass my lips until this child is well and truly in my arms. Then there will be a celebration to remember!"

*****

CHAPTER SIXTEEN

"What time is it?" Gina asked again.

Carol glanced at her watch. "Just gone eight o'clock." she replied. "Do you think we should wait here or go back to the room." The girls had eaten an evening meal in the small hotel dining room cum bar. There had been a few other diners in the quite hotel and a small group sitting at the bar. All were Bulgarian as far as the girls could make out. Probably city workers or travelling sales persons but certainly they were the only British in evidence.

The meal had been excellent. Thick vegetable soup followed by a casserole of meat and potatoes with an alcohol-rich, fruit filled cake to follow. Bulgarian cuisine was certainly to be recommended Carol had remarked. She had suddenly remembered that she was very hungry and cleared her plate gratefully, whereas Gina had picked nervously at the food until reminded that she needed to eat for two, so had made a further effort.

"Well, he did say he would go to the room," Gina reminded her. "So I think we had better be there don't you?"

Carol agreed and the two friends made their way back to their room to wait. Gina peered into the elaborate mirror above the dressing table and applied a further coat of lipstick then set about re-brushing her hair then winding it up onto the top of her head in a neat roll. "Do you think I should change my clothes?" She asked. "I want to look businesslike when Mr Markov gets here."

"You look fine." Carol assured her. "You always do!" Gina wore a cream woollen skirt, skimming the tops of her calf length beige suede boots. A rich brown cashmere sweater with a wide neck complimented her pale skin and golden hair. Carol had worn her light blue jeans and cream sweater for dinner. Casually dressed, she had still been the subject of admiring glances from some of the other diners. Her mass of auburn curls framing her face and accentuating her emerald green eyes. She wondered if Markov would be alone and if this were, indeed, a real and proper arrangement. She could not help but worry that something could go sadly amiss.

"This will be a really good story to tell the little one when it is old enough." Carol tried to keep Gina's mind occupied. "His, or her Mum, dashing through the snow in a truck to rescue Daddy, and fighting off robbers!"

"And Auntie Carol driving the truck in nothing but her Marks and Sparks best!" Gina added.

A gentle rap on the door made the girls leap to their feet. They shot a quick glance at each other as Carol stepped over to the door and pulled it open. Zhravko Markov's huge frame all but filled the doorway. "Ah, Mr Markov, do come in." Carol tried to sound as formal as possible under the circumstances but could not help wondering how Tony, or in fact Jeff, would feel had they known what was happening.

Markov, no longer in uniform looked slightly less intimidating than he had on first sight. His long, black overcoat covering a thick sweater and rough woven trousers. His cossack-style hat covered in a thin film of snow. "Good evening." He nodded politely to the women.

"Please sit down, Mr Markov." Gina said politely, indicating one of the antique chairs in the corner of the room and wondering if it would hold his considerable frame. Markov lowered himself into the chair which creaked ominously, but stood its ground.

Carol, British as ever, plugged in the small kettle. "Tea or coffee, Mr Markov?" she asked. She almost giggled as she spoke. Who on earth would believe the situation they were in, and here she was, politely offering a choice of beverage.

Markov shook his head and turned his eyes onto Gina. "I have come to discuss the position of your husband," he announced.

"Please, what have you to tell me about my husband?" Gina eagerly got straight to the point. "I believe that there may be a way to, er, pay his fine, and so allow him to leave your prison."

"In this country," said Markov, "There is always a way to pay for a crime and not spend time and money on prison service."

Now that was a novel way of putting it, thought Carol, having switched off the kettle and sitting on the bed watching the proceedings.

"Let us not waste time. You want to pay for your husband's release. This has been discussed and this will take place if you can pay the right price."

"What is the right price?" Gina did not care what it was, she only prayed she had brought enough.

"Two thousand English pounds." Two thousand pounds! Gina had brought twelve. Surely this trivial sum could not be what all this awful business was about.

Markov misread the look of astonishment on Gina's face. "Two thousand pounds is the price you must pay for your husband. That is not a large sum for the life of a man, no? That is the price!"

"Yes, of course." Gina gathered her wits. "It is a small sum to pay for the release of my husband. How does this transaction take place?"

Markov raised his hand. "There is further transaction that must take place." The girls cast each other a glance. Was this the joker in the pack? They waited. "The truck." Markov carried on. "There is a truck that was impounded when the driver was taken. The price must be paid for this truck also." Carol opened her mouth to speak but did not get the chance. "The price for the truck is two thousand English pounds!" Gina was very tempted to point out that her husband was worth a lot more than an old truck that was on its last legs, and Carol herself felt very much like mentioning that, given the choice, she would never dream of paying two thousand pounds for the old Transcon in England, let alone Bulgaria! But both girls said nothing. "And for further expenses in handling this matter, another two thousand pounds!"

"Is that it then?" Carol put in, trying hard not to let a note of sarcasm creep into her tone. "Please forgive us if we sound a little mistrusting, Mr Markov, but what exactly do we get for this six thousand pounds?"

"You get truck and Englishman."

"Yes, I understand what you have said Mr Markov." Gina cut in, casting Carol a withering look. "What my friend means is, exactly how will this all take place. When will my husband be released, and what arrangements will be made to get him home? Also the truck. How will that get back to England. Will we have to collect it or will it be sent. I do apologise Mr Markov, but as you can see, we have no experience with these sort of dealings at all and, at the moment, we are entirely in your hands."

Carol was impressed with Gina's cool demeanour. "Yes, I do apologise. We really don't have the faintest idea about these things. We would be very grateful if you could explain it all to us." She decided to take a diplomatic leaf out of Gina's book. "To be very truthful, Mr Markov, I do not feel that we will really need the truck. We only really want Gina's husband back."

Markov glanced at the two women in turn. He took a deep breath. "The Englishman *and* the truck. It is one deal only!"

Gina shot Carol a panicked look. "Okay, fine, we take the truck as well," she said quickly. How must we pay this money and whom do we have to see about it? How long will it take?" Gina wondered if she had to wait and see other officials. Was Markov just the first person in a line of solicitors and prison dignitaries.

"You will pay the money to me, now. If not, I do not know if this arrangement can take place!" He looked into Gina's eyes, seeing the surprise on her face. "I apologise for the speed of this transaction, Madam." His voice softened, "But there are things you do not understand and this arrangement *must* take place at once. It was explained you bring money, no?"

"Yes, of course." Gina stood up. "You must excuse me for a moment Mr Markov, I must use the bathroom, I feel a little weak." Gina left the room and walked into the bathroom, locking the door behind her.

Carol walked over from the small table and sat on the bed facing Markov. "Tell me, Mr Markov. You say two thousand pounds for Jeff, two thousand pounds for the truck and two thousand pounds for expenses. Would you tell us please what these expenses are. Flights home for Jeff? Carriage for the truck? Please, we would like to be clear on what we are spending our money on."

"The expenses are necessary," was the simple reply. "Things must be put into place. People must be paid for their services. This is the arrangement." He was certainly a man of few words and even less explanation. Carol had a hundred questions spinning round in her head but the tone of Markov's voice and the look in his eye told her that further questions on this subject were a complete waste of time. The subject was obviously closed.

Gina pulled her small case out from behind the bath panel. She sat on the toilet seat and opened the case, grubbing down inside the silk lining and pulling out a brown envelope. She quickly pulled out a sheaf of notes, all bound into bundles of one thousand pounds, secured with elastic bands. She took the Euro's and five bundles of the English money and carefully lifted the lining of the case, pushing the money safely back inside. She replaced the cosmetics and personal items then placed the rest of the notes into the envelope, slid it into an elasticated pocket in the lid of the case and snapped it shut. She flushed the toilet noisily and ran the hot water tap, the pipes making a loud banging noise as the water rushed though the old pipes into the basin.

"I am so sorry." Gina walked back into the bedroom carrying the small case. "I suddenly felt sick again. I think it must be the tension!" She sat down on the side of the bed next to Carol, opened the case and took out the brown envelope. "It is fortunate that the sum of money you require was not more." She handed the envelope to Markov. "That is every penny that I brought with me. I did not expect it to be so much, but......" she shrugged and indicated for him to open the envelope. "Shall we count it, Mr Markov? I would like to make sure that you are satisfied that the amount is correct!"

Markov flicked through the wad of notes as though they were playing cards. "Is all there. You are honest lady." he reached into his inside coat pocket and pulled out some folded papers. "This is the agreement that will release your husband and the truck." he said, opening the papers onto the bed and pressing out the creases with his hand. "You must sign one sheet, here, and you......" his eyes moved to Carol, "....must sign here." He indicated the places to sign.

"But it is all in Bulgarian!" Gina pointed out. "We have no idea what it says. We could be signing anything!"

"Bulgarian legal papers always in Bulgarian!" Markov pointed out, not unkindly, Carol noticed. "I will read for you if you wish but all legal papers use many words but say very little."

Carol sighed and picked up the pen that Markov had produced from his pocket. "It is the same in England, I'm afraid." she said as she scribbled her signature on one of the papers. "We will just have to trust you on this."

Gina took the pen and signed the other paper. "There, is that it? What happens now."

"Nothing more for you to do." Markov got to his feet. "You are to leave Sofia tomorrow, yes?"

"Well it seems that the trucks will be ready for leaving tomorrow so, yes, that was the plan." said Carol.

"Then that is what you will do. You will go to your truck and go back to England."

"When will Jeff be coming back….. and the truck." Gina put in as an afterthought. She had, after all just paid out more for the Transcon and 'expenses' than she had for her husband.

"Soon." Markov got to his feet.

Gina looked stunned. "But can you not tell me exactly when?" Her voice started to crack a little.

Markov hesitated, then sat down again facing Gina. To her surprise he took her hand firmly in his. "Soon, very soon." His eyes met hers with a level stare. "Believe, Madam, that I am honest man and I will not take this money and go, poof, into the night! There is more things you not know, but I give word of Zhravko Alexandrou Nikolia Markov that your Englishman will be with you, very soon. You drive back to England and speak of this to no-one until you hear of me!" With that he rose to his feet, stepped over to the door and left without a backward glance.

Gina and Carol were stunned. "What on earth…..?" Carol did not have the slightest idea what she wanted to say or, indeed, if there WAS anything to say.

"It's all done now, no going back," said Gina, staring at the closed door. "Shall I put the kettle on?

Carol burst out laughing. Not the kettle again. Whether it were the incredulity of the situation, or whether the tension had manifested itself into hysteria, neither knew, but the peels of their laughter could be heard the length of the hotel corridor. Luckily, Zhravko Markov had already stepped silently out of the building into the blackness of the night and melted into the shadows.

*****

Gina had hardly slept, tossing and turning most of the night. On the odd occasions when she had drifted into a light sleep she had been troubled with strange dreams. Jeff, holding out his hand to her, but when she reached out, she found her hand grasped by Zhravko Markov. Dawn was breaking, filtering gloomy light through the window as she lay, staring at the uninspiring ceiling. Quietly she slipped out of bed and pulled the curtain aside to stare across the square toward the imposing walls of the prison. The square itself was still, almost silent. The odd car, driven by the enthusiastic early riser, swung past the hotel, its tyres leaving tracks in the newly fallen snow. Gina tried to catch any glimpse of activity around the prison but her view into the yard was obscured.

She shivered and made her way across the room and into the small bathroom, closing the door quietly before turning on the taps. The enthusiastic plumbing leapt eagerly into action and rattled and banged noisily as luke-warm water poured enthusiastically into the deep iron bath. Gina considered boiling a dozen kettles to achieve a hotter soak but decided against it. The effort would have been less than rewarding, so she settled for an unsatisfactory dip in the tepid tub. She sponged over her body and washed her hair quickly, the water cooling faster than she had hoped. Stepping out of the tub, she wrapped herself quickly in towels and wound her hair in another. She needed a hot drink, the bath had not given her the warm glow she was accustomed to achieving after a hot soak.

"Morning," Carol's sleepy voice was muffled under the covers as Gina re-entered the bedroom.

"Sorry, Kiddo, did the plumbing from hell wake you?" Gina asked shaking the kettle to see if there was enough water for two hot cups of tea.

"Not really, I always wake early anyway," Carol replied, sliding the covers from over her face and twisting into a sitting position. "Ooh, it's not warm in here this morning, is it?" Carol pulled the covers up around her shoulders and snuggled into the still warm pillow.

"I think the heating comes on at intermittent intervals." Gina replied. "I don't think they expect their guests to rise so early here."

Right on cue. the familiar rumbling of the plumbing leapt into action, shuddering through the pipes as the hotel heating system clocked on for its morning shift.

"Well that sounds promising." Gina spoke up against the racket. "The water will probably get warmer now if you are thinking of taking the plunge."

Carol glanced at her watch. "It's not even six o'clock yet!" she remarked with a yawn. "There is plenty of time. I say we sit here and drown ourselves in hot tea until the room gets really warm before doing anything TOO adventurous, although I see you have already had your morning wake up call."

"Should have waited," Gina replied, plopping tea bags into the thick pottery mugs. "Didn't think about the hot water not being on as yet. I didn't sleep too well actually."

"Not surprised!" Carol answered, hugging her blankets. "Yesterday was certainly a day to remember. How is baby?"

A happy smile swept across Gina's delicate features. "Oh, Carol, I just can't take it in. Part of me is just so excited. Totally elated at the thought that, at long last, I have this tiny baby growing inside me. It's all so wonderful, then...." she broke off to pour the water onto the tea bags. "Then I remember that Jeff is in prison and... well... you know... what the hell is going to happen next!" She passed Carol a mug of tea and perched on the edge of the bed to drink her own.

"Yes, I know. Typical isn't it. One good thing happens but you're not allowed to enjoy it to the full because of a bad thing that always seems to get in the way." Carol sipped her hot tea. "But don't get too down, Kiddo. You never know, if that Markov person is true to his word, then Jeff might even be home before we are!" The Transcon crossed Carol's mind quickly. She still had no idea whatsoever how that transaction was going to pan out. She decided not to think about it. The money had been paid and as long as Jeff got back to England in one piece, then really, she didn't give two hoots about the old truck. Even so it would be nice if she did in fact get the old girl home again.

"Oh, Carol, I dare not even think that way. Today we must leave and really I've no idea if the transaction we entered into last night is even legal. It's like something out of a bad 'B' movie!"

"Well, there is nothing else we can do." Carol took Gina's hand supportively. "We will just have to carry on and put our trust in fate."

Gina nodded. "Yes, I know. I will just have to think positive. I really DO believe that it will work out, don't you?"

"Yes, I do!" Carol said positively, although deep down she was not so sure.

"What time did Tony say for us to meet him?" Gina asked.

"He said ten o'clock would be okay. That will give us time to have breakfast, pay the bill and get a taxi to the warehouse," said Carol. "No point in rushing is there?" She wondered if Tony had spent a comfortable night in the truck. She felt slightly guilty that she and Gina had spent the night in the hotel. Hardly five star, but a solid room with sanitation none the less.

The chill was starting to leave the room as the heating, in the form of bulky wide-piped radiators did their work. "Time for a quick dip, I think." Carol swung her legs out of bed. Today was going to be another long haul, all the way to Belgrade.

*****

Carol and Gina made their way to the hotel reception to settle their account. "I wonder if they take plastic," Carol remarked as they rang the bell for service.

The small, dapper manager bustled almost at once to the call of the bell. "Ah Madame and Madame!" his deeply accented English greeting them with a professional smile.

"We wish to settle our bill." Carol smiled politely at the businesslike manager.

"Bill? Account? The account is paid, Madame! Paid in advance by British Embassy!"

"Oh!" The girls had not expected this. "Oh, really, we did not realise. Thank you. Will you please telephone for a taxi cab for us?" Carol asked.

The manager immediately picked up the telephone, ordering the cab with an air of importance. "Taxi will be here at once," he announced.

They thanked him and walked towards the door to wait. "I certainly did not expect the hotel to be paid for by the Embassy, did you?" Gina remarked.

"No, I didn't," Carol replied. "I thought they had done their bit by arranging it for us, but don't let's knock it. A bonus paid for by our own taxes certainly makes a change!"

"What exactly are we going to tell Tony?" said Gina, almost thinking aloud.

"Hmm, I was wondering that too," Carol replied peering out of the glass doors. "Ah, here is the taxi."

The girls picked up their bags and ran quickly into the waiting cab. The city street was now alive with rushing vehicles, honking horns and suicidal pedestrians, leaping from one side of the road to the other with little or no evidence of a crossing routine and certainly no suggestion of the Green Cross Code.

"I think the best thing to say is to stick as much as possible to the truth," Carol suggested as they climbed into the cab and handed the driver the address of the toy warehouse. "Just say that we met with prison officials, paid a 'small' fee for administration purposes, signed the relevant papers and are now waiting to hear what happens next!"

"Well apart from the 'small' bit regarding the fee, that IS the truth isn't it?" Gina replied. "Yes, that will do, that's what we will tell him. No point in long drawn out explanations. I really am not up to going into detail right now."

"Apart from that, he will think we are mad. Entertaining mysterious men in hotel rooms and handing over large sums of money. You must admit it sounds completely barmy when you say it like that!"

"Yes, the abridged version is much simpler!" Gina agreed. "Oh, and another thing. Would you please keep it secret about the baby, just for a while Kiddo?"

"Yes, of course, whatever you wish." Carol understood that it was early days, and many expectant mothers wanted to make sure the pregnancy was safe before making announcements.

"Thanks for understanding." said Gina. "It's just that, after all this time, I really want Jeff to be the first to know!" Carol smiled. Of course, Jeff should, by rights, be the first to know. She would keep Gina's confidence without question.

The taxi swept through the centre of Sofia, running for a way along the banks of the river Iskur, then turning away from the far-less-than-blue river, weaving in and out of the traffic of the more upper class part of town. The shops in this part of the city, obviously expensive and the haunt of the more well-heeled and discerning citizens. Christmas preparations were clearly in evidence. Brightly coloured lights festooned the streets and the shops, elaborately decorated as in Paris or London.

"Wonder if they have Father Christmas here," Carol remarked as the taxi blasted it's horn, pushing through the city traffic.

"Well I noticed a sleigh with reindeer in one shop window." Gina replied, "So it looks like the old boy does the rounds here as well! It's quite a comfort to know that we all do the same thing at the same time of year. Almost joins us all together." Gina could not help but think of Jeff. Would he still be here, in this city, or in his own home for Christmas day. The driver swung to the right, speeding the girls through the leafy parkland of the city for a short time before continuing to the industrial area, approaching the place where they had left Tony and the trucks, driving into the loading area of the factory and stopping directly behind the 'Silver Lady'.

"Good morning, Cara Mia." Tony jumped down from the cab and walked over to meet them as they paid the taxi. "Good morning Gina, how did your meeting go. Any good news of Jeff?"

Gina told him the story that she and Carol had agreed. "We've done our best and now we must wait and see." She pulled her coat collar round her ears against the wind. "The only thing to do now is get back to England and see what the next move is to be or what news the Embassy will have for us."

Tony nodded. He had a feeling that things may not be as straightforward as Gina obviously hoped for but would say nothing that would shatter her hopes. "That all sounds very positive, do you not think?" he said, doing his best to sound as though he believed that Jeff could be released any day now.

Carol slid her arm though Tony's. "How was your evening Darling?" she asked, still feeling slightly guilty. Firstly, for spending the night in a comfortable room while he played guard dog on both trucks and, secondly, for not being absolutely truthful about what had taken place.

"I had a most interesting evening, Cara Mia!" Tony replied. "I went for a meal and a drink with Yann." He indicated a truck, still with curtains drawn, standing a few yards from the two Transcon Haulage trucks. "He is from Gouda, in Holland."

"Where the cheese comes from!" Gina cut in.

"Yes, he did mention the cheese." Tony laughed "But he drives regularly to Sofia, so knows all the places to visit. We ended up walking round the city, night time sightseeing, very interesting, it is a beautiful city to visit."

"Oh, really!" Carol gave him a playful dig in the ribs, flashing her emerald green eyes into his. "Exactly how interesting? I hope you were not tempted to sample the flesh pots of Sofia while I slept alone, in my own little bed!"

Tony threw his head back and laughed. "There are lots of pretty girls working in the many bars in this city, but none, Cara Mia, to compare with you!" He hugged Carol close to him.

"There is a picture that I just cannot see!" Giggled Gina. "Tony visiting flesh pots! It just does not seem to ring true!"

"No," Tony agreed. "That is certainly not my idea of evening's entertainment. That apart, I needed a good night's sleep to be fresh for the drive this morning. We are now loaded up and ready to go. I have all the papers signed and ready, so, now we are all here, shall we set off?"

"Ready when you are my love." Carol kissed Tony quickly on the lips before walking over to the 'Flying Angel' and flinging her bag up onto the seat.

Gina climbed into the passenger seat and slipped off her coat to avoid it being crushed. "We are both so lucky to have such lovely men," she said spontaneously.

Carol leaned out of the window and took the papers from Tony, watching as he smiled broadly at her before walking over to the 'Silver Lady' and climbing inside. "Yes," she said. "We are lucky. Very lucky."

A few gentle flakes of snow were falling as the convoy of two trucks swept out of the city limits and headed towards the main through road, heading back towards the border. "After this trip," said Carol, "I doubt if anything will ever worry me again, travelling wise."

"Well, we have sure had just about everything possible thrown at us." Gina replied, swinging her legs up onto the dashboard. "You can certainly call yourself a trucker now, without a doubt."

"Hmm, suppose so. Carol replied, "And you, Gina Meredith, will soon be calling yourself a mum!"

"Oh, yes, I KNOW!" Gina's eyes lit up once again. "Oh, Carol I just can't believe it is really happening at last. I just want to tell Jeff, tell him he's going to be a daddy at last. Oh, Carol, he will be a wonderful father. If it's a boy, he will take him to football matches and car racing and, of course, take him out on the truck. He may be a truck driver just like his daddy - and if it's a little girl he will spoil her absolutely rotten. Pretty dresses and dance lessons and….."

"Hey, slow down! What if *she* wants to be a truck driver - just like her Auntie Carol?" Carol pretended to sound indignant. "Now, who's being sexist?"

Gina giggled. "Okay, I'll give you that one," she said. "She, or he, can be anything they want to be and Jeff and I will support her, or him, to the hilt! As long as the child is happy and healthy, that is all I ask for."

Carol smiled. Gina's happiness was a joy to behold, although she knew her friend's state of mind was fragile and could turn to fear and worry for Jeff at any moment. There was so much left unsettled right now. Silently she wondered exactly what the plan would be when they got home. So much was left hanging in the air. Would Jeff be released: Would the Transcon ever get back to England: What would be the best thing to do about the business. If Jeff stayed imprisoned for any length of time, then she would have to take the bulk of the runs on her own shoulders, she and Tony. She may have to take the CPC course herself to keep the business legal and running. She wondered if they could afford to employ another driver. What would become of her job at the driving school. That would surely have to take second place to keeping Transcon Haulage up and running, that was for sure. She also had Spyder's wage to pay. She desperately wanted to keep him on, he was a real find and she had grown to like and trust him. To let him go would be a terrible blow to both of them. If Jeff had an early release, could things go straight back to normal again. So many questions with no answers right now.

She decided not to think about it. Just get on with the job in hand and worry about tomorrow when tomorrow arrived. She still had the important things in life, a true friend, a wonderful lover, a lovely daughter and a trusted employee. She had more blessings to count than most people, so she intended to keep focused on the good things in life. She pressed her foot on the accelerator as they met the run onto the Autostrade. The morning was coming to an end, and they had a good day's drive ahead.

*****

"At least it's stopped snowing for a while." Gina leaned towards the window to peer up at the sky. "But it does look fantastic, all white and pretty with the sun shining through, doesn't it?" Carol had to admit that the woodland on either side looked like a fairy tale. The mountains beyond, peeking above the tall tress, their snow capped peaks glowing gold as the sun's rays lighted upon them.

They had travelled mainly in silence, each with their own thoughts. Gina, of course, thinking of Jeff. Was Zhravko Markov as good as his word, she wondered. Although, on the face of it, the transaction had seemed decidedly shady, she could not help but feel that it was 'kosher'. For some reason, she had a strong conviction that the big man was on the level and that Jeff's release was imminent. Exactly why things had taken place as they had, she had no idea. Perhaps all dealings in Bulgaria were conducted in this way for all she knew, but somehow she doubted it. Still, she was convinced that all would be well, as though a tiny guardian angel was sitting on her shoulder reassuring her.

Carol was thinking along pretty much the same lines, although she had slightly less blind faith in the proceedings than Gina obviously had. She had held her tongue on the matter. Seeing Gina's face, alive with anticipation since the transaction, was almost, in itself, worth the money. She just hoped and prayed that her friend's hopes would not be dashed, and that she would not discover that Markov had disappeared, taking the money with him.

They passed through the border with little waiting, and made their way forward, leaving Bulgaria, and Jeff behind. Gina felt that part of her was still locked in that cold depressing place with Jeff.

Passing the point where they had been involved with the attempted hi-jacking, the girls both got another fit of the giggles, once more picturing the stunned look on the face of the man who had been treated to the full benefit of Gina's aim with the saucepan. This time, there was no sign of any battered pick-up trucks or ruffians, lurking in the woodland and Carol certainly had no intention of stopping.

Approaching once more, the first of the claustrophobic tunnels that ran through the deep gorge, Carol slowed, glancing in her mirror to see Tony, tucked in behind her, keeping apace mile after mile. "Funny how you seem to be taking the lead now," Gina remarked. "At one time you just automatically followed behind Tony."

"Not really," Carol replied. "We just sort of take it in turns to go lead driver. For one, it breaks the monotony and for seconds, it gives the tail-end-Charlie a break from the pilot's job. Works out well for both of us, although it may have been a little more convenient if he had been behind us on this stretch during the outward journey. Those guys would probably not have popped out of the woodwork like they did!"

Gina smiled. She knew that Carol was now fully confident. Driving on her own merit, taking equal responsibility with Tony or any other driver that may join them. She said nothing. Carol just had not noticed her confidence growing as it had, and her ability as a driver evolving into what could be classed as experienced.

Gina yawned lazily and stretched her arms as Carol steered the truck through the first of the dripping tunnels, the water from the roof running down the windscreen in tiny rivulets. Gina reached up and pulled the CB mike from the clip. "Hello back there, Mr Owl!" she called into the transmitter. "Everything okay behind?"

"Hi there, 'Flying Angel' crew!" Tony's voice crackled over the wire. "Everything is absolutely fine back here, just tramping along enjoying the ride." Gina fell silent. In the background she could hear music. Tony was playing tapes on the 'Silver Lady's stereo. She could just catch the melody above the noise of the engine and the crackle of the radio. Lionel Richie. One of Jeff's tapes. For a moment her mind swam and she shut her eyes tight. She was, for a few moments, transported. She was sitting in the passenger seat of the 'Silver Lady', Jeff at her side, driving across the Continent, late at night. The twinkling lights of distant cities reminding her of a million stars, and Lionel Richie serenading them in the darkness.

"You okay, Kid?" Carol noticed the sudden silence.

"Oh, yes, I'm okay," Gina replied quietly. "Just had a moment of deja vu, that's all!"

Carol did not ask any further questions. "The end of the first tunnel's in sight," she said.

The light at the end of the tunnel! That was, metaphorically speaking, what Gina was wishing for.

"I think it may well be!" Gina replied.

*****

The snow had dutifully held off for the duration of the day, much to Carol's pleasure. Despite the fact that it cloaked the expansive scenery with a fairytale magic, it certainly did not lend itself to an easy drive through the mountain gorges and thickly forested areas that the trucks had to progress through, steadily heading north towards home. An enthusiastic burst of sunshine had lightened the day for a short period, glistening on the trees and mountain peaks, before disappearing once more as dusk began to set in. "I am looking forward to the Hotel Nationale this evening," said Carol as the 'Flying Angel' swallowed up the miles. They had stopped briefly for coffee and a short break some hours back and Tony had pulled out in front, taking his turn in the lead.

"Only because it gives you an excuse to share a bed with the lovely Tony!" Gina replied wickedly.

Carol flashed her friend a smile. "Well, yes actually, if you must know. I am looking forward to cuddling up with him again. We certainly don't see enough of each other to miss out on opportunities to be together."

"You make the most of it, Kiddo." Gina said meaningfully as the signs for the Hotel Nationale came into sight. "You never know in this life if, or when, things will change. You enjoy every minute you can!"

*****

They lost no time in parking the trucks in the spacious parking area of the Hotel Nationale and booking rooms for the night. Both Carol and Gina were looking forward to hot baths and a change of clothes before making their way down to dinner.

"Tell me, Cara Mia." Tony dropped their bags at the foot of the bed and kicked off his boots before swinging his legs onto the bed and relaxing against the pillows. "How exactly did this meeting go with the prison officials in Sofia?"

Carol glanced over her shoulder as she went into the bathroom and started to run the taps. "Pretty much as I told you." She hated not being absolutely truthful with Tony. "There were some papers to sign and a fee to pay and, well that was pretty much it really." She walked back into the bedroom, pulled off her jeans and sweater and unzipped her bag in search of her toiletries.

"You forget, I know you very well, Cara Mia. I have strong feelings that things are maybe not so simple as you say!"

Carol sighed. Tony was certainly no fool. "To be perfectly truthful, Darling, I personally don't think it is straightforward myself, but what can I say? This is Gina's business and if she wants to try every possible method of obtaining Jeff's release then we must allow her to try, without putting negative thoughts into her head."

"So, you have misgivings," said Tony, his ice grey eyes fixed on Carol.

"Oh, yes, without a doubt! I have loads of misgivings. The whole thing was like a surreal dream, not really happening, but as I said before, Gina has the last word, so what could I say?" She briefly ran through the events of the night before.

"So what exactly was this 'fee' that Gina had to pay?"

Carol pulled a face. "Altogether, six thousand pounds!"

Tony's face did not hide his surprise. "And for that amount of money, what guarantees were you given?"

"We signed a couple of pieces of paper." answered Carol. Yes, it did sound insane, put like that.

"We? You did not have to sign any papers yourself did you?" Tony enquired.

"Er, well, yes I did. The Transcon was part of the deal!"

"The Transcon! Surely that is in the hands of the Customs."

Carol shrugged and walked back into the bathroom, divesting herself of her underwear and sinking into the tub. "It was all part of the deal. This Markov guy made it perfectly clear that it was Jeff plus the truck or no deal. What could I do? Say I was not going to go for it? Hardly possible, especially when Gina had the money ready and didn't bat an eyelid about handing it over. Honestly, Darling the whole thing is completely beyond me." She decided against mentioning that Marco had provided Gina with two thousand pounds worth of Euros into the bargain. She would leave that to Marco to explain if, or when, the subject arose.

Tony followed her into the bathroom and took a seat on the bidet, leaning forward and putting his chin in his hands. "The only thing we can do is be there to support Gina if none of this is above board and the money, and this mystery man are never seen or heard of again." What else could he say? The money had changed hands and, as Carol had pointed out, it was, after all Gina's money and Gina's business. All they had to do as her friends, was be there to pick up the pieces if it all went horribly wrong. Carol slid her head under the water then surfaced with a rush.

"Sorry we did not explain things more fully when we first met up earlier," she said apologetically. "But to be honest, Gina is a little fragile and was not up to too much explanation this morning."

Tony nodded. He understood what Gina was going through and had no wish to make things worse. "Okay, Cara Mia, Gina will have my support, of course, and let us trust and pray that the man you spoke to was as honest as he would have you believe." He rose from his makeshift seat. "Pass me the soap, I will wash your back. Then we can go and meet Gina for dinner."

Carol passed the soap and sponge. "Shame to waste all this water on one person," her emerald eyes flashed. "I think it's far better for the environment if we share!"

Tony did not need to be further persuaded.

******

CHAPTER SEVENTEEN

The clang of the cell gate swinging open jarred Jeff from his sleep. The night was pitch black save for the low lamps in the corridor outside the cell. He raised himself up on one elbow, peering through the gloom to see the unmistakable bulk of Zhravko Markov step through into the cell. The shadowy shape loomed over towards him.

"That you Markov?" The voice of John Miller called across from the other side of the cell. "What's up? What's going on?"

"Not for you to know." Came the guttural response as Markov neared Jeff's bunk. "You come!" It was a command not a question.

"What, me! Now, where?" Jeff swung his legs off the bunk and onto the floor, wide awake now and alert. This unprecedented arrival in the middle of the night did not bode well.

"What do you want with him. Where is the Governor." John Miller had crossed the cell and was standing in front of Zhravko Markov. "He's done nothing wrong!"

Jeff's heart missed a beat. He had heard hushed whispers about a 'torture' room. Men being taken from their cells and never returned. Please God this was not going to happen. He got to his feet. "What is all this about Markov, I have broken no rules. Tell me where we are going!"

Markov hesitated. He was not used to being questioned. His word was taken as law by all in the prison. But this time it was different. "I cannot tell you. Not here." he glanced around at the other cellmates, now mostly awake and curious. He turned towards John Miller. "You not worry about this English. No harm is coming to him. You go back to sleep, you say nothing, you do nothing, I say nothing more!" His voice was quieter now, almost an undertone.

Jeff got to his feet. Whatever the reason he realised he had no choice in the matter. Wherever they wanted to take him or whatever they wanted to do, he was completely at their mercy. If he made a fuss he would probably just be carried out and things could possibly be the worse for him. It could also implicate John too, he was not the type of man to stand by and watch a friend dragged away without trying to step in and probably end up beaten to a pulp for his troubles. "It's okay mate." Jeff pushed his feet into his boots. "I'll go along and see what this is all about. Probably nothing but I'll tell you about it in the morning. Don't lose any sleep over me." He attempted a grin that was irrelevant in the darkness before following Zhravko Markov out of the cell, stepping through and waiting as the iron gate was swung back into position and locked. John called something after them as they walked down the long corridor but Jeff did not catch the words. The corridors were surprisingly empty. No guards were in evidence as Jeff followed the big uniformed man in silence through what seemed like miles of steps and narrow passages then more steps. His sense of direction had been lost as all the corridors looked identical, with narrow windows, too high to see out of and so to get any perspective of where they could possibly be. He could bear it no longer. "Come on Markov. What the hell is happening. Where are you taking me?"

"We are leaving." Came the blunt reply.

"Leaving! You mean leaving the prison. Then were to?"

Markov stopped suddenly, turning towards Jeff. "Home Englishman." He had reached a heavy wooden door and pulled a key from his pocket, turning it in the crunching iron lock and pushing the door wide. An icy blast of air hit Jeff in the face as both men stepped through into a narrow alley running between the prison and the perimeter wall and leading directly to the big cobbled yard. Snow crunched under Jeff's boots as, lost for words, he followed Zhravko Markov along the alley and across the prison yard. The wind was biting and whipped through Jeff's thick jacket as they rounded the corner of the building, snow falling in flurries and lashing into his face. But to Jeff the fresh night air smelt like sweet nectar after the foul stench of the prison. He totally disregarded the cold and drank in the freshness of the night, filling his chest and dispelling the stale prison air from his lungs. They had reached the gates. Again not a soul in sight as Zhravko Markov tapped in his personal code and tugged open the smaller inner gate, gesturing Jeff through, then following, clanging the gate shut behind him and striding across the almost deserted street. Across the road Jeff noticed a row of parked vehicles. For a split second a small flash of light from one of the vehicles caught Jeff's eye. He turned, trying to focus his eyes in the poor light. He thought he could see a figure sitting in one of the cars. A figure wearing spectacles, glass lenses to reflect the light from the street lamp. But perhaps not, he could have been mistaken. Jeff had given up trying to make sense of the situation or trying to speak to Markov about it. He simply followed where the big man led.

Across the wide street, past the small cheap hotels and the larger more exclusive one on the corner then round, into a small alley way behind the shops. Markov produced a set of keys from his pocket and walked over to a small blue car, battered and rusting, parked alone in the alley. The door opened with a groan. "We go!" Markov folded his considerable bulk into the driving seat, his head almost touching the roof of the tiny vehicle. Jeff climbed into the passenger seat as Markov switched on the ignition. The grating noise of the tinny engine crashed through the silence of the night. Turning again and again before groaning unwillingly to life, the whole vehicle shaking precariously as the ill tuned engine spat and misfired before lurching forwards as Markov shoved it roughly into gear.

Jeff's mind was racing. "Okay Zhravko, we are going, but for Chrissake, WHERE the bloody hell are we going?!" He considered opening the door and leaping out but thought better of it. To begin with Markov was driving through the narrow streets at a ridiculous pace and secondly he had no idea where he was or what his next move would be.

"We go to get your truck Englishman."

"My truck." Jeff was suddenly aware that he was beginning to echo Markov's words with each statement. "Do you mean the Transcon? I have no idea where that is. Do you?"

"Yes. It is not far from here. At a factory with a full load to be transported to your country."

Jeff was incredulous. "You mean we are going to pick up my truck and you are letting me go! Letting me go and carry on with the job I came here to do in the first place. Am I free now?" It all came out in a rush.

"We are not out of Bulgaria yet," was the only answer that came from the stone faced giant.

Before Jeff could question him more, they rounded a corner and slowed, then turned into a deserted factory yard. The factory was in darkness. The only signs of life was the snow, ground to a slush by the many trucks that had visited the loading bays that day. The yard was empty save for one truck, Carol's Transcon, the old 'Fighting Spirit', standing alone, complete with trailer, covered in a fine cloud of snow. Jeff's heart leapt. She looked undamaged, or at least from what he could see, the old girl looked pretty normal. Two men appeared from the shadows as the small battered car carrying Jeff and Markov pulled up beside the big truck. Markov stepped out of the car. "You wait!" he snapped over his shoulder to Jeff.

Jeff waited. The two men approached and spoke quickly to Markov in Bulgarian. Jeff strained his ears to hear. He caught the word 'diesel' and 'papers' but beyond that there was nothing he understood. Sitting in the darkness of the car he saw Markov obviously questioning the men closely, opening the cab and glancing through a sheaf of papers. Eventually he reached into his inside pocket and drew out a leather folder. Straining his eyes to see, Jeff saw him hand a block of bank notes to one of the men who counted it suspiciously. The transaction was obviously satisfactory as both men nodded, inclined their heads and stood back.

Markov waved Jeff to come forward. Jeff scrambled out of the car and almost ran the few yards to the Transcon. "You drive!" Markov we certainly a man of few words.

Jeff stood his ground. "What about the engine. What about oil, water anti-freeze, diesel?" The old truck would not get them more than a mile without the proper care required to run in these freezing conditions. Markov, for the first time, looked a little taken aback. Again, he spoke quickly to the two men who nodded furiously, waving their arms and pointing at the Transcon. Jeff walked round the old truck, checking that all was as it should be, pulling out the long dipstick and peering into the gloom to see the oil level. A stab of light made him jump. Markov had shone a bright flashlight onto the dipstick. The oil level was perfect. Jeff returned the dipstick and wiped his hands on his jacket. He had wiped everything else on it for the last few weeks so what was a little oil? He checked the water. Full to maximum and obviously with anti freeze. Following the beam of light from Markov's torch, he checked the wheel nuts and looked over the suspension. Surprisingly, no obvious defects met his inspection. As satisfied as he could be under the circumstances, he walked round to the driver's door and climbed into the cab. A feeling of relief and exhilaration flooding though him as he started the engine, the familiar wine of the air brake system buzzing in his ears as the air tanks began to fill. He checked the fuel level. Full to maximum. He gave Markov the thumbs up sign. Markov nodded. He was satisfied that these men had done the job they had obviously been set to do and tossed the car keys to them. They scuttled away like rats from a storm, clambered into the tiny car and careered out of the factory yard.

"Okay. Now you drive!" Markov was certainly a man of few words and fewer explanations.

Jeff had had enough of this. He turned the key and switched off the engine, silence enveloping them as they sat in the deserted yard, the snow gently falling about them. "Not before you tell me what the hell is happening!" He turned to face the big man sitting statuesque in the passenger seat. "For the past few weeks now, and for no fault of my own, I have been arrested, handcuffed, trundled overland in conditions I would not inflict upon animals, locked up in a stinking, freezing cell, spoken to in a language I cannot understand and now route marched through the middle of the night with not so much as an attempt at an explanation! Now you want me to drive my own truck, loaded with God knows what and to where? Markov, I swear I will not move as much as an inch without a proper explanation! I've truly had it up to here with all this cloak and dagger stuff!" Jeff's usual patient nature had snapped, the frustration of the situation giving him the strength to stand up to this giant of a man in the middle of the night in this deserted place.

For a second Markov did nothing, then turned to Jeff, his coal black eyes staring directly into Jeff's. "Yes, you have right to know, I apologise."

Good grief, that was a first! Jeff said nothing.

"Your wife visited you, yes?" Jeff nodded.

"I met with her and spoke about your imprisonment. She has paid for your release."

Jeff was totally shocked. "You mean Gina *bought* me out? Why was I not told. Told at once." How dare these people keep this information from him. If, in fact it were true. Could freedom be bought so easily?

"Arrangements had to be made." Was the simple reply. "Before the arrangements were complete it was not for discussion."

"So tell me. What exactly has taken place. What is the story with this truck and what the hell are we doing here in the middle of the night. Surely this is not the usual hour that prisoners are released in your country." Jeff was still suspicious about this cloak and dagger activity. Something did not ring true to him.

Markov sighed. "No." He said simply. "Most unusual, but there are circumstances."

"Go on."

"Your wife paid for your release. Under usual circumstances, after payment made then there is hearing in two, maybe four weeks. Then papers signed, then further payment taken for aeroplane to take you back to your country. Transport arranged to airport. Very long business you understand."

That sounded more like it, Jeff thought. "So what has happened to make it different for me?"

"Further enquiries were made about truck. Your partner, Mrs Landers, yes, she own truck?" Jeff nodded. "I tell her that truck must be part of deal for release. I need this agreement personally."

Ah, here we go now. Here comes the nitty gritty of the matter. Jeff began to see a pinprick of light amongst all this skulduggery. "So why would that be?"

"I must go to England."

Jeff was a taken aback. No smuggling. No underhand dealings. Just a lift to England. Surely not. "If you wanted to go to England then why did you not just book yourself on a plane and fly over, whenever you wanted to?"

"Not so easy." Markov reached into his pocket and pulled out a packet of cigarettes, offering one to Jeff and taking one for himself. The flash of light from his match breaking through the velvety black of the night.

"I am Russian, not Bulgarian. I work many years in high position in government in Moscow. Powerful position, my word never questioned. Times change." he drew hard on his cigarette. "One day I find that I am in danger, my position not as strong as it once was. If I stay in Moscow I know I will not live. I will vanish without trace. So, I leave. Leave quickly and travel to Bulgaria. Nobody in this country know who I am except my friend, governor of prison. So here I work. Here I feel safe, but no longer. Word has reached me that certain people know where I am and who I am, so I must go. Already I have been traced. Two men from my country have already arrived. They are in my prison in solitary confinement, but we cannot hold them for long. England will be safe for me. Your government will be pleased to have me there, I am sure."

Jeff was stunned. Markov, a Kremlin official, probably privy to state secrets, known to the British government and now sitting next to him in the old 'Fighting Spirit'. It was beyond belief. Jeff led a simple life, things like this just did not happen in his world. "I see!" he said, simply for want of some sort of reply. "But that does not explain why we are sitting here in this truck and what is expected to happen next!" Although it did explain why he had been whisked out of solitary so quickly. Obviously the men from Moscow were priority for the cell more than he!

"Your wife pay further money to release the truck. She also gave me money for expenses. I must go to England, so we go together. I make arrangements for release of truck, also make arrangements to get truck loaded with goods for England, that way we travel as two friends, working together. Who will question that."

"The bloody border guards for a start!" Jeff replied quickly. "What the hell is on this truck. Is the load exactly what it is supposed to be and what was all that business with handing money over to those two shady looking characters. What have they got to do with it? Are the papers in order, have we both got our passports. I'll be buggered if I am going to get arrested at the first border we get to and sent straight back to your cosy prison! This is not just a spin in the country on a Sunday afternoon, Markov, this is a bloody long drive through many countries and it has to be done right!"

"You are right to question." Markov conceded, flicking the end of his cigarette out of the window. "For too many years my word is not questioned. I am used to this. I apologise once more. We must be friends yes?" He held his hand out towards Jeff.

After a moments hesitation Jeff clasped Markov's hand firmly. "Colleagues for now." he said. "Friendship must be earned."

"You are right." Markov nodded. He had learned respect for this Englishman. He reached into the leather case and pulled out the paperwork, handing it to Jeff. "The men I pay had collected truck from compound. I charged them with filling tanks with diesel, checking engine in good order and driving to this place to load with children's toys. One of your comrades, Marco Copeland, businessman from Italy, no? He arranged for this load to be available."

Marco! So he was also involved. For some reason this did not entirely surprise Jeff and it made sense. Marco arranging for the load rang true.

"We drive through night. I guide you quick way through city to main route, then sleep. We work five-hour shifts. You drive from here, five hours, then you sleep, while I drive on to Belgrade. We stop to eat there, then change once more, yes?" said Markov. "That way, quicker time to England, no?"

It sounded okay to Jeff. The quicker they got back to England, the better it appeared to suit both of them. He was flicking through the papers, checking all was well. "It all seems to be in order, but if you don't mind, I will just check the load to make sure that we are carrying exactly what it says on the paperwork. You can't blame me for being extra careful considering what has happened to me." Jeff climbed down from the cab into the freezing cold night. He would check every inch of the truck and the load if necessary. Only when he was satisfied would he start the engine and begin the drive. Also there were many more questions he wanted to ask. But they had a long drive ahead of them so there was plenty of time for that.

*****

Light was filtering through the blinds as Carol woke and rolled over in the comfortable bed. Tony was still sound asleep, his crop of black curls buried in the soft pillow. Carol slid out of bed and filled the kettle with hot water from the bathroom and clicked it on to boil before turning on the shower and stepping under the refreshing blast of water. Gina's spirits had been high the previous evening. She had chatted animatedly about Jeff's imminent return to

England and neither Carol nor Tony had uttered a word of negativity on the subject. There was little they could say about it anyway. Travelling as they were, there was no point of contact that they could use to confirm or deny Jeff's whereabouts. That would have to wait until they reached England once more. Only then could they start to find out what was actually going on. Carol switched off the shower and wrapped herself in a towel, walking back into the bedroom. Tony was awake and standing in his shorts, pouring hot water into coffee mugs. "Good morning, Cara Mia." he said lazily, passing Carol a mug of black coffee and taking his own back to the bed and tucking his legs back under the covers to drink the reviving liquid.

"'Morning Darling!" Carol was feeling wide awake now, the shower having livened her senses. She drew the blind aside and peered at the sky. Grey. "Another overcast day out there!" she remarked, joining Tony under the covers as they drank their morning coffee. "But hey, there is no real rush. We are, after all, our own bosses so there is no deadline to meet is there?"

"Only the moral one that we must, for the sake of the credibility of Transcon Haulage, deliver on time as promised and, of course, there are still the German orders to fill." Tony reminded her.

Good old Tony! Carol thought. Keeping her feet firmly on the ground if ever she let her head get too high into the clouds. "Yes, of course, you are right, and thank you for reminding me. We can't afford to lose any contracts now, especially with all this business of Jeff being as yet, unresolved."

Tony put down his mug and gave her a kiss. "You are doing well Cara Mia. I know of no other woman who has done so well in this sort of business. I am deeply proud of you, and proud that you are my 'amore'."

Carol was taken aback. It had never occurred to her that Tony had so much respect for the way she was running the business. "Well thank you Darling." she said, a little lost for words. "Thank you very much for those words of encouragement. And while we are passing compliments to each other, I hope you realise how much I value your help and advice and how greatly I appreciate your support."

Tony smiled. "I know you do, even if you do not always put it into words." He kissed her again. "But right now I think it is time we went down for breakfast. This journey is still far from over and an early start is worth much more than a late finish Cara Mia."

Reluctantly Carol slid from under the warm covers and reached for her clothes.

*****

Gina was nowhere in evidence as Carol and Tony walked into the dining area. "She surely can't still be sleeping." said Carol, looking around as they seated themselves at the breakfast table. "I knocked
loudly enough on her door, and it's not as if it's terribly early is it?"
Gina appeared from the direction of the hotel lobby, a big smile on her face. "Good news," she announced joining Carol and Tony at the table. "I just telephoned Spyder!"
"Oh really," said Carol "I take it everything is fine at home?"
"Thought I'd just give a quick ring while I waited for you to come down, just thought I would enquire if Phoebe was okay and everything, seems rude not to show an interest seeing as we left him dashing from house to house, feeding pets and the like."
"So what's the good news?" Carol reminded her.
"Spyder said that yesterday, those bits of yours went into the auction rooms." said Gina . "And you will never believe it, but that awful table, you know the one like an artist's palette…."
"Yes, I know, do go on." Carol was at once interested.
"….well it sold. And guess how much for!"
"I can't guess! Horrible thing that it was. Oh, I don't know, fifty quid or something silly like that?"
"One thousand pounds!" Gina announced with great aplomb.
"A thous…. Gina, are you sure, that can't be right!"
"That's what Spyder said it went for." Gina insisted. "One thousand pounds exactly. Apparently it was a specialised auction with all sixties stuff and the table was designed by some well-known person of the day it seems, Spyder told me the name but I can't remember it, but I don't suppose you really care, do you? The rest of the stuff sold too, so altogether you got one thousand, six hundred and fifty pounds. Not bad for a load of old unwanted junk was it?"
Carol was astounded. Lost for words for a moment. She gathered her wits. "Well, what can I say!" She managed to splutter. "Yes, absolutely, marvellous news! About time we had something really positive for a change. Of course, I promised Spyder half shares in any cash the stuff brought, so he will be chuffed to bits. Be able to spoil that new baby to death this Christmas, along with the two boys."
Breakfast was a cheerful affair after receiving such good news. Carol made a note to hold this surprise bonus money in abeyance, in case Gina needed

financial help, should her efforts to secure Jeff's release come to nothing. There was still that dark cloud hanging over them.

It was not without effort that the three picked up their bags and left the comfort of the breakfast room, making their way outside into the chill morning air and walking over to the twin Volvo's standing together in the lorry park. Carol unlocked the 'Flying Angel' and checked the oil and water before switching on the ignition. The cab would not be cold, as the night heater had been ticking gently overnight, so a cosy interior would welcome its passengers. Gina climbed into the cab and stowed her bags neatly, settling herself for the journey. Tony and Carol, as always, did their daily walk around the trucks, checking lights and tyres and the obligatory search round any nooks and crannies that may have tempted unscrupulous persons to hide away unwanted cargo.

Satisfied that all was well, Tony kissed Carol briefly on the lips. "Be safe Cara Mia." he said, as he always did. "We will have one short stop this day, then I see no reason why we will not make it across the Austrian border and get to the truck stop at Vienna by tonight."

Carol did not answer. She was staring across the lorry park, hardly able to believe her eyes. The old Transcon - her own 'Fighting Spirit' - was rocking it's way slowly over the gravel towards her, the unmistakable figure of Zhravko Markov at the wheel.

*****

For a moment Carol felt that she was in a dream. Surely it was another truck, one identical to the 'Fighting Spirit' and the man driving, just another heavy, thick set man. It was just not possible. As she was trying to gather her wits, the cab door of the 'Flying Angel' flew open and Gina leapt down from the cab, running towards the Transcon as it slowed to a crawl in search of a parking space.

"Gina! Wait!" Carol found her voice and ran after Gina.

Zhravko Markov saw the approaching women and stopped the truck with a loud hiss of the handbrake. Carol caught up with Gina and grabbed her arm. "Wait, Honey. Hang on a minute, we don't know what's going on yet." That was certainly true. Amazed as she was to see was the Transcon, absolutely the last thing she had counted on was seeing Zhravko Markov driving it.

Markov himself was taken by surprise. He had not expected to drive into the change over location and come face to face with the people he had been dealing with. It was a big country and it was hardly likely that drivers would find each other without prior arrangement. However, he was used to snap decisions and circumstances changing within moments. He could deal with it. "Good morning, Madame's!" He swung the cab door open as Gina and Carol approached. "We had not expected to have the pleasure of your company so soon."

"We?" Gina was standing close to the cab trying to see inside. "Mr Markov, please explain to us what you are doing here." she was desperately trying to sound cool and in control.

"We're here to get a good breakfast, Darling, that's what we're doing here!" Jeff's sleepy head appeared over the bearded giant's shoulder.

"Jeff!" Gina could not believe her eyes. She stood, rooted to the spot, her head spinning. She stayed there for what seemed like an age, as Jeff, almost in slow motion, swung his legs off the bunk, opened the door and dropped down from the cab, grabbing Gina in his arms and crushing her to him.

Carol looked up at Zhravko Markov. The big man looked tired and drawn. "You will be taking breakfast Mr Markov?" She asked politely.

"Yes, we stop to eat, then change drivers." Markov said gruffly, searching his brain cells in order to make the best of this unexpected situation. It was not what he had planned, but it was too late to change and maybe, just maybe, it would not be a disadvantage. He climbed down from the cab and stretched his back, aching from being cramped behind the wheel. "We eat then drive on!" he announced. He could not afford to delay here too long.

Jeff, his arm still firmly around Gina walked round the cab. "As soon as you have parked up, we can go and get some food inside us," Jeff said to Markov. "Tony, how are you boy?" He held his hand out to clasp Tony's hand.

"Stunned right now," Tony replied, clasping Jeff's hand. "Stunned, but delighted to see you." He cast a curious glance towards Markov.

Jeff caught his thoughts. "Don't ask, boy. Far too complicated." He turned towards Markov. "Well come on, my friend, I know you are as hungry as I am right now. Get the old girl parked up and we can get breakfast. You want to set off as soon as possible do you not?"

Markov did not answer. He climbed back into the cab and jammed the gearstick into reverse, swinging into a parking space, switching off the engine then climbing down from the cab.

Carol approached him as he locked the door. "I have to say it's a wonderful surprise to see you.... and the truck so soon, Mr Markov." she said quietly.

"I must thank you for being so prompt with the...... arrangement, although I did not expect you to deliver the vehicle yourself!"

Markov looked into Carol's huge emerald eyes, looking for signs of rebuke or hatred: there was none. "I tell you that it necessary that truck and prisoner are one arrangement." He said bluntly.

"Yes, but....." Carol's words trailed off. She sighed. "Never mind." she said. "Let's just go and get you something to eat."

"That sounds good, eh Markov?" Jeff called over from his conversation, still holding tight to Gina. "We eat, then I do some driving while you get your rest. That suit you?"

Markov nodded. He was hungry and knew food was important. Tony walked ahead and spoke quietly to the desk clerk. They had already checked out of the room, but, as written on the bill, the room was still officially paid up until eleven o,clock and it was still early.

"Take this," Tony held out the room key to Jeff. "I could not help but notice that you may appreciate a shower after your journey." He was too polite to tell Jeff that he could smell him from a good few yards distance. "Mr Markov, if you and our friend wish to freshen up we will order your food to save on delay."

Jeff glanced across to Markov, the big man's eyes giving nothing away. "I think we had better take advantage of the offer, Zhravko," he said, his voice steady as he held Markov's eye contact. "I do believe my friend is trying to tell me that I am conspicuous by my body odour. I don't think either of us need to draw unnecessary attention to ourselves, do we?"

Markov realised that this was indeed, the truth. "A shower will be good, for both of us," his voice, for a moment, sounded weary as he accepted the offer.

"Darling, please order us something really wonderful for breakfast while my travelling companion and I get the smell of the road off our persons." Jeff did not want Gina to follow him and Markov to the hotel room. He needed to speak to the big man alone.

Gina realised what Jeff was thinking. "All right, Darling, but please don't be gone too long. I can't bear to have you out of my sight for a moment longer than is totally necessary." Gina released her hold of her husband's arm for the first time since she had clasped him in the truck park. Jeff kissed her on the nose.

"Do you have clean clothes with you?" Tony was not sure what the circumstances were of Jeff's arrival at the Hotel Nationale, but had noted he carried no luggage.

"Just what I stand up in, Lad," Jeff shrugged. "But if you have some clothes to spare I would be grateful. I reckon they would fit me without a problem now that I have lost a pound or two!"

"Is there anything you need, Mr Markov?" Tony asked.

Markov shook his head. "No, but thank you."

Tony nodded and made his way to the 'Silver Lady' to collect a clean wardrobe for his friend. He had asked no questions as to the circumstances of Jeff's sudden appearance. He had said nothing about the big bearded man that was his travelling companion. There was plenty of time for that. Plenty of time when they were safely back in England and Jeff was once more in his own home.

Jeff and Markov waited at the foot of the staircase. "That young man is the elder brother of your contact, Marco Copeland," Jeff explained.

Markov nodded. He already knew. It was his business to know these things.

"There is everything you need my friend," said Tony. "There are towels and shower gel in that bag too. We will wait for you both in the dining room." He nodded and left Jeff and Markov to make their way to the room.

"I know you want to make as good a time as possible, Markov," said Jeff as the two ill matched travelling companions headed up the staircase. "But you have to admit that I stink something awful!"

"Yes, of course. What you say is right. We must both shower and eat food. That way will have more strength for journey."

Jeff turned the key in the lock and walked into the room. Luxury after what he had endured these last weeks. "I take it you don't mind if I go first?" Jeff walked into the bathroom and wasted no time in pulling off the foul smelling clothes, the stench of the prison still clinging to the fibres. He stepped into the shower and twisted the dial to full. The bliss of hot water, running down his body and stinging his face with the pressure was a pleasure that words could not have described. Jeff stood for a moment, his face turned up to the fine jets, raising his arms and leaning his palms on the tiled walls as it suddenly struck him that it was all actually happening and was not another cruel dream from which he would wake. He poured Tony's shower-gel liberally over the top of his head, ceremoniously cleaning the last of the prison from his skin, cleansing himself from head to toe.

"My God, that was wonderful!" Jeff wrapped a towel around his waist and walked back into the bedroom, flinging himself full length onto the bed. Markov was standing by the window, looking out onto the lorry park. "If it means anything at all," said Jeff. "Everything we spoke about in the cab will go no further, and just for the record, I have no intention of bolting the minute you step into the shower."

Markov turned, his black eyes boring into Jeff's face. "It is of no consequence!" He held the Transcon keys in his hand. "I can travel alone." He shrugged. "Although the truck, your truck, would have to be collected from Dover. I have no plans to take it further!"

Jeff smiled. Markov was no fool. From the little Jeff had learned, Markov was an expert in keeping control. "Speaking of which," he said, "Do you have any plans when you actually get to England. Have you any place to stay?"

Markov strode across to the bathroom. "I shower, then we eat!"

Jeff sighed. Having a conversation with Zhravko Markov could, at times, be harder than pulling teeth.

*****

"Darling, I want to travel with you!" Gina hung onto Jeff's arm as they walked back to the trucks. "You driving, with me sitting besides you, just like we always did."

"Zhravko," Jeff turned to speak to Markov as they arrived at the side of the Transcon. "Do you have any objections if my wife travels with us until we change over again? It would mean a lot to both of us."

Markov glanced from Jeff to Gina. "Madam, if you wish to accompany your husband then so be it!" He gave a slight bow, almost clicking his heels as he did.

"It will only be for a four hour-stretch though." Jeff put in. "I am not really up to a long haul at the moment. By that time I will be needing some sleep myself so you, Markov, will have to take the wheel again while I crash out on the bunk."

"Then you will enjoy your wife's company until then." The big mans deep voice was not without feeling.

"Oh, Mr Markov, you certainly have lived up to being our knight in shining armour!" Gina's face lit up as she clung to Jeff. "If you want to get some rest, I promise I won't chatter on and disturb you!"

Markov glanced at Carol and raised an eyebrow. Quickly Carol caught on to his train of thought. "If you would like to travel with me until the next stop, then your company would be welcome, Mr Markov," she said quickly."Thank you. Your company will make a pleasant change." Markov spoke politely. "I take it your husband will not object to you taking a passenger?"

Tony laughed. "I am not the lady's husband.....yet!" His eyes lighted on Carol's face. "But you are a welcome sight, Mr Markov, and any one of us will be happy to have you as a travelling companion."

A flicker of what could almost be taken for a smile swept across Zhravko Markov's face as he opened the door of the 'Flying Angel' and climbed into the cab. Tony kissed Carol lightly on the cheek. "Take care, Cara Mia," he said in a whisper. "If you find yourself in difficulty then call me on the radio at once!"

"I don't think there will be a problem, Darling. Mr Markov obviously just wants to get to England." The mysterious Zhravko Markov had always been the perfect gentleman.

"We plan to make our night stop in Austria this evening." Tony called up to Markov. "It is about eight to ten hours on a good run. Then our second night will be well into Germany. After that, straight through to England, all being well."

Markov nodded. This was not a problem for him now. He was out of Bulgaria. His countrymen were still in solitary confinement and would stay there until every single day of their statutory twenty eight days without prison. He was not expected to be on duty for another four hours. "Austria will be a good place to stop."

Markov's coal black eyes met Tony's "I believe the Weiner Snitzel is excellent."

Tony left it at that. Carol and Gina had explained a lot of the story to him in the dining room while Jeff and Markov had been using the hotel facilities. He knew that Markov was the contact that the girls had dealt with at the meeting in the hotel. They had explained the price that had been paid and the deal they had agreed. It was clear that this man had kept his word, a lot faster, in fact, than anybody had expected. But still, at the back of his mind there was something that he did not understand. Why on earth had this man taken the money, then was actually driving the truck himself, along with Jeff, all the way to England. Surely that was not normal Bulgarian procedure for releasing prisoners. He felt slightly uneasy about the man travelling in Carol's truck, and would much preferred it if Markov had travelled with him on the journey but decided to say nothing. There were too many unanswered questions at the moment so he would watch and wait.

Just one more thing: "Jeff!" Tony called, holding the keys of the 'Silver Lady' out towards Jeff. "Will you want your own truck back my friend?"

Jeff turned, his arm still around Gina. "No, lad, you keep her for now. You have obviously done her proud these last weeks and I think it best that Zhravko and I continue sharing the truck we are now familiar with, but thanks for the offer."

Tony nodded and pulled open the door of the 'Silver Lady'. They were ready to get under way. So far, since leaving Sofia, there had been no fresh snowfall. The snow that was already on the ground, a dirty brown slush, thrown onto the sides of the Autostrada by the passing vehicles. Only the trees and hills kept a covering of startling white, the cold weather slowing down the thawing process.

After only a few miles, Carol realised that Zhravko Markov was not the world's best conversationalist. She decided to concentrate on the road ahead and leave the big man to sit back in his seat, watching the countryside sweep by.

Carol tried again. "Have you made any arrangements for accommodation in England, Mr Markov?" She asked politely. "Do you know anybody there?"

"I know people." said Markov. "But accommodation can be easily arranged can it not?"

"Oh, yes, I suppose so." Carol said quickly, glad of a breakthrough in the silence. "Depends where you will be heading."

Silence.

"We are going to London, or should I say, just outside London." Carol continued hopefully. "If you were planning on going there, we will be pleased to give you a lift as far as we can."

Markov sat in thought for a moment. "I visited Edinburgh some years ago," he offered.

"Oh, really," Carol was surprised that he had given her any information at all at this point. "I have never been to Scotland. I believe it is very nice."

"I stayed in a small village outside the city." Markov went on. "It was many years ago and it was business trip, not holiday." He had considered his words. Giving this small snippet of information would do him no harm. It would do Carol no harm either. His countrymen knew of the contact house in the tiny Scottish hamlet. His main consideration, right now, was getting to England and making contact with an old friend. There he hoped to live a quiet life. Things had not been good for him for some time now and this was his lifeline. "I intend to travel," he said. "I will travel for a time then decide where I will choose to stay."

He would not be returning to Scotland. He would leave his travelling companions at Dover, possibly with mention of Portsmouth or some other coastal town. He would then make his way directly to the railway station and board a train to London.

Carol glanced over to the big man, sitting stiffly in the passenger seat. There was more to him than met the eye. Her intuition told her that to question him was useless and he would only tell her what he wanted her to hear. But whatever his reasons for wanting to get to England, it had suited their purpose in getting Jeff out of prison. For that she could wish no ill on the man. He had a right to his privacy. Just one more question. "Is Jeff officially free now?" Carol asked, not taking her eyes from the road ahead, following the 'Fighting Spirit' as Jeff drove, leading the way back home.

Markov also kept his gaze directly ahead. "Governor Balenko will, by now, have sent the paperwork to relevant authorities." His voice was matter of fact. "By the time your friend reaches his destination, all will be official. Debt paid. Release registered."

"It will be safe for him to travel abroad again? No sentence hanging over his head?" Carol glanced at the immobile figure next to her.

"Perfectly safe. The Englishman will be more free to travel than many men!" Markov's own personal world was shrinking., but was no immediate panic any more. He had crossed the border and, as far as he knew, nobody was aware, as yet, that he had even left the prison. Governor Balenko would make sure of that. Markov and Balenko had many years of history together and the Governor was one of the few men Markov trusted.

The men who had found him would then be moved to another prison. There was to be no way of them asking questions, possibly connecting the Englishman's release with his own disappearance. It would be many weeks, possibly months, before they would be tracked down by their superiors and released..... if indeed they ever were.

"Thank you Mr Markov. That is all we need to know." Carol did not ask any further questions. She did not need to. Jeff was free and they were all on their way back home. In a few days they would be back in England. By now Gina would have told Jeff about the baby and no doubt be making excited plans for the future. Carol's own future was looking clearer now. Transcon Haulage was out of danger and they were driving on to a promising future. There were still the German orders to fill, but she and Tony would do those runs with ease. Jeff needed a long break after his ordeal and Carol was looking forward to the journeys, she and Tony, travelling together, cementing their relationship. Then it would be Christmas, a time of celebration, family and friendship.

This Christmas would be one to remember. Each of them had something to celebrate and plenty to be thankful for. Yes, it would be very special

*****

"I'll get the door, you get the 'phone!" Carol called to Katy as she closed the oven door. Both the turkey and the leg of pork were roasting nicely, surrounded with potatoes and parsnips. The smell of the roasting meats, drifting through the house, tantalised the appetites of the occupants.

"Merry Christmas!" Gina, wearing a full length crimson woollen cape with a white fur trim looked every bit the Victorian Christmas lady as she stepped into the welcoming warmth of the hallway, Jeff following her through, his arms full of extravagantly wrapped presents. "Hmm, something smells wonderful!".

"Merry Christmas to you as well!" Carol hugged and kissed Jeff and Gina in turn. "Come on in, both of you. I have just checked the turkey and all is doing nicely so we can all relax in the living room and open a bottle of wine."

"Sounds good to me," Jeff smiled as they walked through into the spacious, newly decorated, drawing room at the front of the house. An enormous Christmas tree stood over by the window, resplendent in silver beads and silvery baubles, twinkling fairy-lights giving the tree a magical glow and an elegant glistening star reaching almost to the top of the high ceiling.

"Carol, the tree looks divine! Very designer but straight out of a Victorian novel!" Gina slipped off her cloak and relieved Jeff of the presents, carefully depositing them under the tree, along with the selection already tastefully placed under the lower branches. "And the presents look lovely too. It's like being a kid again," she smiled up at Jeff. "All these lovely surprises just waiting to be unwrapped, and the room looks absolutely delightful!" She glanced around, admiring the newly decorated room. The cream walls and carefully hand painted ceilings had certainly lived up to the picture mentally painted by Spyder at the start of his renovation plan, giving the perfect canvas for the large, comfortable sofas and polished side tables. The logs, burning in the fireplace, crackling gently, giving off a soft pine aroma to add to the seasonal atmosphere. Sprigs of holly and ivy hung in swags around the mantelpiece with huge red bows to hold them in place.

Carol moved over to the gold-inlaid rosewood cabinet and selected glasses to pour mulled wine for her guests. "Let's toast a few moments peace until the chaos of dinner," she said, handing out the drinks and joining Gina on the sofa. "Let's drink to the future and the happiness of us all!"

"Amen to that!" Jeff raised his glass.

"On this occasion, just a small sip, then back to the mineral water for me!" Gina announced, chinking her glass onto Carol's and Jeff's before taking a sip. "I think we deserve a celebration don't you?"

The door flew open and Katy, eyes alight with excitement burst through, followed by Bruno and Digger. "That was Andy on the 'phone," she announced. "Anna has had a little girl, late last night. Your God-daughter has arrived!"

"Oh, how lovely," Carol was delighted with the news. "A Christmas baby, what have they called her?"

"Carol-Anna! Don't you think that is just lovely?" Katy clapped her hands with delight. "I can't wait to go and see her, I bet she is absolutely adorable. I must tell the others! Katy shot out of the room, Bruno and Digger dashing after her as she hurried through to the back room where her friends, all six of them, were playing board games and drinking cans of beer.

"That is a lovely name." said Gina. "You must be delighted to have her named after you! She will call you 'Auntie Carol no doubt!"

"I will be 'Auntie Carol' again soon." Carol reminded her. "How is your little bundle of joy progressing."

"Oh, wonderfully well!" Gina beamed. The doctor says all is well and baby is due around the middle of June. A summer baby will be lovely. I can have all those lovely pure white cotton lace covers on the pram. It will look beautiful!"

"Oh, yes it will, and the baby will be beautiful too. It can't not be beautiful with you for a mum." Carol smiled as a peal of laughter erupted from the other room. "Katy's friends are all in the back room," she explained "Happily playing games and waiting for dinner. Her 'couple' of friends actually materialised as six altogether, but what the hell, the more the merrier eh? We will have to utilise the kitchen table," she announced. "Drag it through into the dining room and tag it onto the end of the dining table for dinner. That should just about do it!"

"Don't worry, we can put a huge white sheet over the whole lot and red napkins." Gina, as always, had a plan for elegant dining. She had brought hand made gold crackers and tiny table presents, elaborately wrapped in gold foil and swirls of bright red, pencil slim ribbon.

"Jeff, Gina, Happy Christmas!" Tony, his hair still wet from the shower walked into the room. "I walked Bruno this morning and got a little muddy," he explained. "But I am now ready to enjoy the celebrations." He kissed

Carol as she handed him a glass of mulled wine and settled himself close to her on the roomy sofa.

"The Christmas cake is very special," Carol announced. "It has been provided by Mamma Gina. We brought it back with us when we came home a couple of days ago so that is something to look forward to!"

"I take it there were no problems with the German runs then?" Jeff enquired. After a few weeks forced rest he was beginning to feel restless.

"The runs went well didn't they Darling?" Carol glanced over to Tony. "The orders will be regular from now on, starting again in the new year and Marco has plenty of re-loads lined up for us too." She took another sip of wine.

"I hope there will be enough work for us all in the new year," Jeff remarked to Tony. His feet itching to get back on the road. France, Belgium, Italy, Germany. None of these places would be a problem to him, he knew them well, but he had promised Gina that Bulgaria, or countries of that ilk would not be on his list of travel plans.

"There is as much work as we can handle." Tony replied. "My brother is very industrious and seems to know every pack-house and factory that could be of any use to us. We will be glad to see you back behind the wheel, my friend."

Jeff pulled out a small pack of cigars. "Join me in a celebration cigar Lad?"

"No, thank you," Tony smiled amiably. "But a refill of wine for us all I think!"

Jeff lit his cigar and settled back comfortably, leaning into the soft cushions. He took a relaxing pull from the smooth cigar, the soft smoke swirling gently into the air, the scent mixing with the smell of wood-smoke from the fire and the spices from the mulled wine. Real Christmas aromas. He closed his eyes for a moment, his thoughts drifting to John Miller. What would he be doing right now?

Jeff had sent a food parcel. A box filled with seasonal cheer. He had enclosed a short note:

'Back in England. Sorry had no time to say goodbye and thanks for being a friend when I needed one. I won't forget you.'

There was really nothing else he could have written. He had given his word to Zhravko Markov that the circumstances of his release would not travel back to the prison. He could not make any real promises to John, but he intended to do all he could to help.

He had received a short letter in reply, thanking him for the food and wishing him well. John also told him that there had been a 'mistake' with the return of Gary's body to England. Due to an 'administrative error', the body had been cremated in Bulgaria, just the ashes returned to the family. There was now no possibility of a post mortem to prove that drugs had been in evidence. The letter finished by wishing Jeff a Happy Christmas, telling him not to get as drunk as he himself intended to do. John's sense of humour had obviously not deserted him.

Tony handed round more glasses of mulled wine as the sound of popular Christmas songs drifted from Katy's private party in the other room. Noddy Holder's gravel voice shouting to all that is was, indeed, Christmas!

"Thank you, Darling." Carol raised her glass. "To the future of Transcon Haulage!"

"And to the good health and prosperity of us all!" Gina added.

Carol snuggled close to Tony. She closed her eyes and wished she could hold this moment forever, it all felt so perfect.

Jeff took a sip then raised his glass once more. "To absent friends," he said quietly.

****